PLEASE RETURN THIS ITEM
BY THE DUE DATE TO ANY
TULSA CITY-COUNTY LIBRARY.

FINES ARE 5¢ PER DAY; A
MAXIMUM OF $1.00 PER ITEM.

DATE DUE			

S Fiction
A gift of joy /

PLEASE LEAVE
CARD IN POCKET

A Gift of Joy

G·K
Hall
&Cº

Also in Large Print:

by Virginia Henley

Desired

by Jo Goodman

Forever in My Heart
Rogue's Mistress

by Fern Michaels

Captive Secrets
For All Their Lives
All She Can Be
Desperate Measures
Serendipity
Tender Warrior

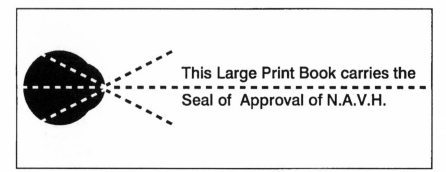

This Large Print Book carries the
Seal of Approval of N.A.V.H.

A Gift of Joy

Virginia Henley
Brenda Joyce
Fern Michaels
Jo Goodman

G.K. Hall & Co.
Thorndike, Maine

Copyright © 1995 by Kensington Publishing Corp.

"Christmas Eve" copyright © 1995 by Virginia Henley
"The Miracle" copyright © 1995 by Brenda Joyce
"A Bright Red Ribbon" copyright © 1995 by Fern Michaels
"My True Love" copyright © 1995 by Joanne Dobrzanski

Published in 1996 by arrangement with Zebra Books,
an imprint of Kensington Publishing Corporation.

G.K. Hall Large Print Romance Collection.

The text of this Large Print edition is unabridged.
Other aspects of the book may vary from the original edition.

Set in 16 pt. Bookman Old Style by Minnie B. Raven.

Printed in the United States on permanent paper.

Library of Congress Cataloging in Publication Data

A gift of joy / Virginia Henley . . . [et al.].
    p.   cm.
    ISBN 0-7838-1872-6 (lg. print : hc)
    1. Large type books. I. Henley, Virginia.
[PS3558.E49634G54   1996]
813'.08508—dc20   96-20715

Contents

Christmas Eve

Virginia Henley

One

*E*ve Barlow was naked.

Her towel had slid to the floor with a whisper and here they stood, finally alone together, staring at each other. She posed provocatively, lifting her long blond hair and letting it waterfall to her shoulders.

"Am I beautiful?" she asked. "Am I sexy?"

The questions proved she was vulnerable, which was the very last thing she wanted to be.

Was that a critical look she detected? Silence filled the bedroom. If the answer to her questions took this long, perhaps the answer was *no!*

She looked straight into the green eyes, saw the humor lurking there, and her exuberant self-confidence came flooding back.

"Yes, you're beautiful; yes, you're sexy! You are also intelligent, successful, and independent," came the answer. The green eyes assessed the full, ripe breasts and watched as the nipples turned to spikes.

"You forgot *crazy,*" she told her reflection as her body shivered with gooseflesh. "Anyone who would stand naked before a mirror

9

when it's below zero outside has got to be crazy!"

Eve knew Trevor Bennett's Christmas present would be a diamond ring. As she drew on her pantyhose, she asked herself if she was ready to be engaged. The answer came back *yes*. She was twenty-six years old — the perfect age for marriage. Everything else in her life was just about perfect, too.

Her career was in high gear, her finances were rock solid, and her fiancé had all the qualities that would make him a perfect husband: sensitivity, kindness, and understanding. Trevor was an English professor at Western Michigan University and often quoted poetry to her.

Eve chose a red wool suit, then pulled on black, high-heeled boots. Even with a power suit she always wore heels. There were no rules that said a career woman couldn't have sexy-looking legs. The minute she picked up her briefcase, the telephone rang.

"Eve? You didn't give me a definite answer about coming home for Christmas, dear."

"Hi, Mom. I sent you an answer on E-mail last night."

"Oh honey, you know I don't understand that computer stuff. Daddy's tried to explain it to me, but I feel so much more comfortable on the phone."

"Of course Trevor and I are coming for

Christmas dinner. It's my turn and I would love to take everyone out to The Plaza — I hate to see you cooking all day. But since you insist on a traditional, home-cooked turkey, I capitulate."

"You know it's fun for me. I just love doing all the things that make Christmas special."

"I know you do, Mom. That's why we all love you so much. I have to run — I have the keys to the office and have to open up today. See you Christmas morning."

"Drive carefully, dear."

Eve sighed. There was absolutely no point in trying to change Susan this late in life. Her mother was a perfectly contented housewife, an angel of domesticity who'd been kept in her place by the men in her life. She had no idea there were worlds to conquer out there.

Susie, as Eve's father insisted on calling her, had made a happy home for her Air Force family, no matter where they'd been stationed. It hadn't mattered much to Susie where she was; Ted was the center of her life and her two children orbited closely around him.

Ted was the macho major who wisecracked about everything, but ruled his family with an iron hand. She had gotten her name from one of her father's wisecracks. He wanted a brother for his first-born, Steven, but when Susie had a girl, he grinned good-naturedly and said, "Now it's Eve 'n' Steven!"

Her brother had followed in his father's footsteps, joining the military and becoming a macho ace before he was twenty. But Eve was determined not to become a clone of her mother. She avoided dominant, controlling men who thought a woman's place was in the kitchen, *unless she was in the bedroom.*

Eve pulled her Mercedes into the parking space that had her name on it, then unlocked the front door of Caldwell Baker Real Estate. Within six months she hoped to be a full partner in the privately owned company.

Before she read all the faxes, the other agents started to arrive. Bob and George arrived together because Bob had cracked up his Caddy on an icy road and it was in the shop awaiting parts. When Eve started working at the agency, they had joked about her aggressive salesmanship, calling her a ball-breaker, but now that her sales topped theirs, they gave her the respect she had earned.

"I'm sorry about your accident, Bob. It must be milder today — the ice was melting when I drove in."

"Warm enough to snow," predicted

George, who tended to look on the dark side.

"Congratulations on breaking into the President's Circle, Eve," Bob said.

She had been in the Multi-Million Dollar Club for the last two years, but now that she was selling commercial as well as residential properties, she had reached new production levels. "I haven't quite made it yet, Bob, but thanks."

"Oh hell, it's only December twenty-third. Still nine days left before the year ends," he said, winking at George.

The sons-of-bitches hope I don't make it, Eve suddenly realized.

Other agents began arriving and the first thing they did was glance toward the coffee urn beside the bank of filing cabinets. When they saw there was nothing brewing, the second thing they did was glance at Eve. Well, they could wait until their Grecian Formula wore off before she would make coffee, she decided, going into her office to go over the listings. She was two hundred thousand dollars short, and determined to reach her goal if it was humanly possible.

When the secretary arrived, the men heaved a collective sigh of relief. They fell over each other helping her off with her coat and boots, then followed her en masse to the coffee urn. *Bo Peep has suddenly found her sheep,* Eve thought sarcastically.

Someone came through the front door. Since all the agents were at the back of the premises, Eve came out of her office to attend to the prospective customer. He was tall with jet black hair, wearing a heavy blue shirt and a leather vest with decorative bullet-holder loops above and below the pockets. This guy apparently didn't know they were decorative; they held real bullets.

"I'm Eve Barlow. May I help you?"

The man's deep blue eyes stared at her mouth, lingered on her breasts, went down to her legs, then climbed back up her body to her blond hair and, finally, to her eyes.

Why don't you take a bloody picture? It'll last longer, she thought silently.

"I don't think so. I'm looking for Maxwell Robin."

He had the deepest voice Eve had ever heard.

"Maxwell has an early appointment; he won't be here until ten. Are you sure I can't be of some service?"

"I can think of a dozen, none of them appropriate for a real estate office." He gave her a lopsided grin.

Eve did not smile back. She turned on her heel and walked back toward her office.

"You could get me a cup of coffee while I'm waiting for Max."

Eve stopped dead in her tracks and

turned to give him a look that would wither a more sensitive male. She bit back the cutting retort that sprang to mind and said coolly, "Feel free to help yourself."

"Don't tempt me." He winked at her.

The sexist son-of-a-bitch actually winked at her! Eve went into her office and slammed the door. She turned on her computer, saw that she had E-mail and accessed it. The message was from Trevor, who stayed many weeknights at the university in Kalamazoo. *No classes Friday, so I'll see you tomorrow night. Would you like to go to Cygnus and dance under the stars?*

Eve answered in the affirmative.

Trevor, I would love to go to Cygnus for dinner, on condition we don't stay too late. I'm probably working Friday.

Within half an hour, Trevor replied. *I understand. It's a date!*

Eve smiled at the words on her computer screen. Trevor Bennett was the most understanding man in the world. He had no problem with her assertiveness, her career, or the fact that she made more money than he. She wondered briefly if she would keep her own name when they married. Eve Barlow Bennett . . . it sounded good to her and Trevor would never object. So why not?

Maxwell's voice came over the intercom, cutting her reverie short.

"Eve, are you free to come into my office?"

15

As she opened her door, she heard the deep voice say, "I don't want a female agent. I want you, Max."

"The property you're interested in is Eve Barlow's listing. It's exclusive."

She gritted her teeth and walked into the owner's office.

"Ms. Barlow, this is Mr. Kelly. He's interested in the lakefront property you have listed up past Ludington. I've just been explaining that's your exclusive."

Eve shook hands with Action Man, as she had already dubbed him, making sure her grip was firm. She knew Max was being generous. The listing *was* hers, given to her by a friend in Detroit who had been left the property by her late parents. However, there was no reason why Maxwell couldn't have sold it — except, of course, he wanted her to qualify for the President's Circle this year.

"I'd like to take a look at it." Kelly turned from Eve to address Maxwell. "Can you go with me?"

"I told you, it's Ms. Barlow's listing. I have appointments all day."

"I'll take you to see it, Mr. Kelly. Are you free to leave now?"

The rugged-looking man drew dark brows together in a frown. "It's a hundred miles."

Eve failed to see his point. "Slightly more. It's a two-hour drive, two-and-a-half in bad

16

weather. Perhaps you don't have time to-day."

"I have all the time in the world."

"Well, that's terrific, Mr. Kelly. Just let me get my briefcase."

In spite of the fact that he resented dealing with a female agent, Kelly helped her on with her camel-hair coat and held the door open for her.

The condescending gestures were politically incorrect in this day and age. Any woman breathing could put on her own coat and open her own doors. Kelly had either been living under a stone, or was being deliberately annoying. She suspected it was the latter.

Eve walked toward her Mercedes, but he did not follow her.

"We'll use my vehicle," he stated.

"It's part of my job to provide the transportation, Mr. Kelly."

"We'll use my vehicle," he repeated.

Eve glanced at the Dodge Ram, four-wheel drive truck and repressed a shudder. They were already in a tug-of-war. "The Mercedes will be more comfortable," she asserted.

"This is a rough terrain vehicle," he pointed out.

"You don't trust my driving?"

"I have nothing against women drivers, but I wouldn't let a woman drive me unless I had two broken arms."

That could be arranged, you sexist swine!

He gave her a meaningful look. "Whatever happened to the idea that the customer is always right?"

Eve decided if she wanted this sale, she had better do things his way. She walked toward the Dodge Ram. It had flames painted across the doors, as if they were coming from the engine.

The first thing she saw when she climbed in was a gun rack, holding a rifle. Action Man was obviously a hunter. She liked him less and less. He drove aggressively. He didn't race, but nothing passed him. Before they got out of the city, it began to snow-flurry.

"So, talk to me, tell me about yourself," he invited. He sounded patronizing.

I'm a feminazi who loathes macho men, she thought, then remembered her six percent commission. "My name is Eve Barlow. I was an air force brat. Lived in Germany, then the Orient. When my dad retired, we moved back to Detroit where he was born, but the crime rate spurred my parents to move to a more wholesome city. They chose Grand Rapids."

"I moved here from Detroit, too, a few years ago. My dad and brothers were police officers, so I know all about the crime rate."

Kelly. Irish cops. Tough as boiled owl, she

thought. *Born with too much testosterone!*

"How did you get into real estate?"

"I chose it very deliberately. It's a field where women can excel. I didn't want to spend years at university, living at home. I wanted to be independent. I'm on my way to breaking the glass ceiling."

"Glass ceiling?" he puzzled.

He's got to be kidding; the man's a Neanderthal!

"Is that some sort of feminist term?"

"Yes. It's a ceiling erected by the men who run the corporate world, to keep women from high earnings and from achieving their potential."

"Bull! If a woman doesn't reach her full potential, she has only herself to blame."

Eve tended to believe that, yet she had an overwhelming urge to oppose him. He had a dark, dangerous quality about him, as if he could erupt. She turned away to look out the window. It was snowing harder now. It seemed to Eve that the harder it snowed, the faster he drove.

"Where's the fire?" she asked.

He began to laugh. His teeth were annoyingly white.

"Let me in on the joke."

"I'm a Fire Captain."

"You're kidding me! You're a fire fighter?"

He nodded. "I'm a captain, studying for my chief's exams."

19

"The flames!" she said, suddenly comprehending.

"My attempt at humor."

Until this moment, Eve had had no idea one had to sit exams to fight fires. The property he was interested in was listed at a quarter of a million dollars. Did Action Man have this kind of money, or was she on a wild goose chase? Eve cleared her throat. "How do you know Maxwell?" she probed.

"I teach scuba. He's in my diving class."

"Really?" Eve was a city girl. Scuba diving was out of her depth of comprehension. It was too physical, too dangerous, too unnatural somehow. Encasing yourself in rubber, sticking a breathing tube in your mouth, then isolating yourself fathoms deep in murky water was not her idea of fun.

"That's one of the reasons I'm interested in the lakefront property. Michigan offers nine underwater preserves. There are miles of bottomland for exploring shipwrecks."

"I see. Wouldn't a summer cottage do just as well? This is a year-round log home." She was trying to hint at the price.

"I need something year-round for ice diving."

"Ice diving?" She said it with abhorrence as if he had said grave-robbing.

"You cut a hole in the ice with an auger.

Of course, you tie yourselves together with a safety rope."

"You do this for pleasure, or as some sort of penance?"

"If that's a jab at my being Catholic, I believe you're being politically incorrect, *Miz* Barlow."

Eve stiffened.

"I'm astounded you even know what political correctness is, Mr. Kelly. You make sexist remarks every time you open your mouth!"

His eyes were like blue ice. His glance lingered on her hair and mouth, dropped to her breasts, then lifted to her eyes. "What a waste; you obviously hate men."

"Your father, the cop, must have shot you in the arse . . . *you* obviously have brain damage!"

"There you go again. He was a police officer, not a cop."

She saw the amusement in his eyes.

"You have a wicked tongue. I could teach you sweeter things to do with it than cutting up men, *Miz* Barlow."

"Don't call me that," she snapped.

"All right. I'll call you Eve. My name's Clint. Clint Kelly."

"Clint? My God, I don't believe it. You've made that up."

His bark of laughter told her that her barbs didn't penetrate his thick hide.

The visibility was deteriorating rapidly. "The weather's closing in. Would you like to turn back?" he asked.

His tone of voice was challenging, almost an insult.

She replied, "If I couldn't handle snow, I wouldn't live in Michigan."

He shrugged. "The decision's yours."

"Good. I like making decisions. And I don't have much use for macho males."

"That's all right, Eve. I don't have any at all for feminists."

Two

*E*ve lit up a cigarette. She was trying to stop smoking, but tended to reach for one when she was annoyed.

Clint frowned. "That's a dangerous habit."

"That's all right — if I set myself on fire, you're obviously qualified to put it out."

He refused to lecture her.

By twelve-thirty they reached Ludington, a thriving tourist port in the summertime but quiet in winter. Two hours was terrific time in adverse weather conditions.

Clint stopped at a service station for gas; Eve used the ladies room.

"How about some lunch before we leave civilization?" he asked.

The town had two good restaurants, but both were closed for Christmas week. "I don't usually eat lunch," Eve said, relieved that she didn't have to sit across a table from Clint Kelly. All she wanted to do was show him the property and get back to Grand Rapids.

There was a fast-food place open as they pulled out of town. Clint stopped the truck. "Can I get you a burger? You should eat something."

"No, thanks. That stuff is incredibly bad for you."

Clint laughed. "And cigarettes aren't?"

She almost asked him to bring her a coffee, but remembered that she had not brought him one earlier.

Clint came back with two hamburgers and a milkshake. He raised his eyebrow, offering her one. When she shook her head, he devoured them both.

Highway 31 turned into an undivided road and Eve recalled that they would have to turn off in just a few miles. She remembered Big Sable River, but couldn't recall if they had to turn off before or after they crossed it.

Clint turned on the radio, but not many stations came in clearly. He found one that was playing country music. "You like country music?"

"Actually, I loathe it." The moment the words were out of her mouth, she suspected she had made an admission she would regret. He made no effort to change the station; in fact, he turned up the volume.

Eve put up with the torture for five minutes, then reached out decisively to shut it off. She cut the announcer off in midsentence as he said, "I have an updated weather —" Then she had to do an about-face and turn it back on.

"— Snow, and lots of it. Blizzard conditions will prevail. Travellers are advised to stay off the roads unless it's an emergency."

"Where is that station?" she asked the air.

"Don't panic. It could be across the lake in Wisconsin, or it could even be Canada."

"I'm not the type to panic," she said coolly.

He gave her a fathomless look. "What type are you, Eve?"

"What type do you think I am, Kelly?"

"You're difficult to read. I can't decide if you're an Ice Queen or simply unawakened."

"You're not difficult to read. You're an arrogant, sexist swine!"

He grinned. "You sure have a short fuse; I was teasing."

"For your information, I'm engaged to be married."

His eyes looked pointedly at her hands.

"I'm getting my ring for Christmas," she explained, then wondered why in hellfire she found it necessary to explain herself to this insufferable devil.

"I take it he's the sensitive type."

"He's an English professor." Why did that sound so wimpy? "An intellectual," she added. "Trevor is the opposite of you. Yes, he's sensitive — and understanding."

"He's passive and I'm aggressive . . . he's a sheep and I'm a wolf."

Eve narrowed her eyes. "He doesn't drive

a truck with flames on it."

"I bet he doesn't drive a Mercedes, either."

His arrow hit its target. "He isn't threatened by the fact that I earn more than he does."

"Then he should be. You intend to wear the pants in the family?"

"No, I intend to be an equal partner. But I admit I'm not domesticated. I don't cook, I don't sew, and I don't cower."

"I bet you even carry your own condoms."

Eve blushed. She had a couple in her shoulder bag. The fact that he could make her blush threw her off balance. "Oh, I think we should have turned off back there."

"You *think?*" He found a place where he could turn around, and showed no impatience. They drove down the snowy road for a couple of miles, but Eve saw nothing that looked familiar. She gave directions, but they were tentative. Finally, she admitted she was hopelessly lost, but only to herself.

"You don't know where this place is, do you?"

"We should be there. You must have passed it."

"Have you actually been to this property?" he asked.

"Of course I have, but it was in the fall. Everything looks different covered with snow. Go back across the river and —"

He held up a commanding hand. "Don't help. I'll find it myself."

By using logic and old-fashioned common sense, he wound his way down a couple of unplowed sideroads until he came to the lake. Then he drove slowly along the lake-shore road until Eve finally recognized the private driveway. It was almost two-thirty. They were no longer making good time.

Eve took the keys from her briefcase and followed Clint Kelly from the truck. The winter winds from Lake Michigan had piled up a huge snowdrift across the front entrance to the house. Clint walked back to his truck, opened the hard box on the back, and pulled out a shovel. "Looks like we'll have to dig our way in," he said without rancor.

"If you had two shovels, I could help."

"Shifting light snow won't exactly prostrate me," he explained.

No, I'd have to hit you over the head with the shovel to do that, she thought.

By the time they got inside the house, it was three o'clock. Eve stamped the snow off her boots and shook it from her shoulders, but she didn't take off her coat because the log house was freezing inside. She walked straight to the telephone to call her boss to tell him they were running late.

"Damn, the phone's been put on holiday

service; no calls can go in or out." She gave him a scathing look. "I have a car phone in my Mercedes."

"That isn't going to help you one bit."

"Exactly!" She threw up her hands.

"Can't you survive without a telephone?"

Eve didn't have to call the office. She lived alone; no one was expecting her. Trevor was in Kalamazoo. "If you don't need to call anyone, I certainly don't."

"If you mean, am I married, the answer is no. Both my brothers are divorced, so I'm wary of women."

"I meant no such thing! I'm not the least bit interested in your personal life."

"Curiosity's written all over your face. You're wondering if I can afford this place."

Damn you, Clint Kelly, you're too smart for your own damn good.

"You turn on the water and I'll check the electrical panel. It'll be dark before we know it."

Eve went downstairs to the basement in search of the water valve. She couldn't find it. She found laundry tubs, a washer and dryer, a water heater that was turned to *off*. She went into the basement washroom. It had a shower, a sink, and a toilet; it even had a shut-off valve, but only for the toilet it was connected to. Without lights, the basement was very dim. She looked under the stairs and finally admitted defeat.

28

"I couldn't find it," she said lamely.

He gave her a pitying glance.

"If you'd turned on the electricity, I might have been able to see down there!"

"The electricity's been cut off," he said shortly. "You start a fire; I'll find the water valve."

Eve stared at the small stack of logs beside the massive stone fireplace. There were no matches. She opened her purse, took out her lighter, and looked about for an old newspaper. Nothing! Paper, where could she get paper? She opened her brief-case and crumpled up some 'Offer to Purchase' forms. Kindling, now she needed kindling. She couldn't start a fire with only paper and logs. Eve spied a basket of pine cones used for decoration and felt quite smug as she carried them to the fireplace. She piled up a pyramid atop the crumpled paper and set her lighter to it. It blazed up merrily, but gradually smoke billowed out at her and she began to cough.

A powerful hand pulled her out of the way, reached up the chimney and pushed an iron lever. "You have to open the damper," he explained.

"Did you locate the water valve?" she challenged.

"Of course."

He had the ability to make her feel use-less. He soon had the logs in the fireplace blazing and crackling. "As soon as you get warm, you can give me the tour."

The log house was truly beautiful. It was a full two storeys. Four bedrooms and two baths opened onto a balcony that looked down on the spacious open-concept living room and kitchen. The bedrooms also opened onto an outside balcony that ran around the entire perimeter of the house.

The views over the lake and forest were breath-stopping. Clint lifted his head and breathed deeply, drawing in the smell of the lake and the woods. She watched, fascinated, as his eyelashes caught the snowflakes.

"Last night was a full moon. It had a ring around it; that always predicts a change in the weather."

"Been reading the *Farmers' Almanac*, have we?"

"I suppose yuppies find folklore exceedingly quaint, but I've learned not to scoff at it."

They went back inside to explore the rooms downstairs. A cobalt blue hot tub had been built into a glass-enclosed room along with a sauna.

How romantic, Eve thought.

"Decadence," Clint said, grinning.

Eve quickly switched her thoughts to the business at hand. "As you know, the asking price is a quarter of a million, but that's

30

furnished. A lot of this furniture is hand-crafted. Isn't it lovely?"

"It is. I make furniture like this. In fact, that sleigh bed upstairs is one of my pieces. Sorry, I digress."

Why was she surprised? The man was an entity unto himself. She began to believe Clint Kelly could very well afford the property.

"I want to look over the acreage before the light goes."

Eve groaned inwardly; it was a blizzard out there.

"Do you have a survey of the property in that briefcase of yours, or is it just for show?"

Eve snapped open the case and rifled through the papers. She pulled out the survey and thrust it at him. "I didn't think you'd be able to read anything so technical," she said sweetly.

Clint ignored the barb. "We'd better hurry. If much more of this comes down, we might not get out of here tonight. I can look around by myself, if the elements are too fierce for you," he goaded.

"Is that more Clint claptrap? You don't have to keep proving what a physical man you are."

"If I intended to prove how physical I can be, I'd have you down to your teddy by now."

Why did her mouth go dry at his provocative words?

Outside, he opened his truck, pulled out a down-filled jacket, and shrugged into it. Then he took a big steel tape from his toolbox. As they set off through the trees, she thought, *Surely he's not going to take measurements in the snow? Please don't let him expect me to hold the other end of the tape. From now on, I'll stick to my own turf: good old city property.*

As if he could read her thoughts, he said, "This is the reason I would have preferred Maxwell to come with me. This isn't a woman's job."

Eve ground her teeth. "There are no such things as *men's* jobs and *women's* jobs."

"Bull! The world has gone nuts. They're even telling us women can be fire fighters!"

"You sound like my father: air force women shouldn't fly combat jets."

"Your father is right. Women are perfectly capable of flying jets, but they shouldn't allow them into combat zones."

Eve had walked out on an argument with her father and brother on this subject, and she was close to walking out on Clint Kelly. *That would be gutless,* she decided. *I'll make this sale if it kills me!*

The barn loomed before them. Clint used his booted feet to kick the drift of snow from the entrance, then they went inside to look around. The first thing Eve noticed was the smell. The scent of hay and straw mingled with the lingering miasma of horses, who had occupied the stalls once upon a time. How was it barns and hay always conjured fantasies of lovemaking, Eve wondered? She'd certainly never had a romantic encounter in a barn . . . yet.

"This place has amazing possibilities."

She turned away quickly so he wouldn't see her blush. She knew perfectly well that his thoughts did not mirror hers; it was simply because of his overt masculinity, and their close proximity in the romantic setting.

All too soon, Clint was again ready for the great outdoors. After they tramped what felt like miles through the deep snow, he selected a spot beside a wire fence and began to dig with his hands.

He had big, strong, capable hands that were well-calloused. Eve reluctantly admitted to herself that she found them strangely attractive.

Clint found what he was looking for — a one-inch square iron surveyor's bar. He didn't ask her to hold one end of the tape, as she expected; instead he began to follow the fence-line, counting his strides.

Eve pulled up her collar and jammed her hands into her pockets. She was freezing.

Clint, hatless, didn't even seem to notice the cold.

"An abundance of wildlife here . . . raccoon, weasel, fox, deer, even elk."

Eve hadn't noticed the animal tracks until he pointed them out. He didn't miss much, she decided. *I bet women fall all over him.* Where the devil had that thought come from? It certainly didn't matter to her what effect he had on women! He had a decidedly abrasive effect on her, yet she didn't think the abrasiveness would affect the sale. He seemed to enjoy sparring with her.

Suddenly, as they came upon a bushy undergrowth, a covey of pheasants flew up into the trees. One bird huddled on the ground.

"It's caught in a snare," Clint said. "Its leg's broken." He immediately wrung the pheasant's neck, then ripped the snare apart in anger and flung it away. "Goddamn snares are as bad as leg-hold traps."

Eve stared at him in horror. "You cruel bastard! Why did you do that?"

"I'm not cruel, nature is. The bird's leg was broken. As soon as it's full dark, a fox would have eaten it."

"We could have taken it with us and nursed it back to health."

"The cold's getting to your brain."

"And you're suffering from necrosis of the cranium! Too bad you didn't have your gun

— you could have shot them all." She turned away furiously and hurried in the direction of the house.

"Eve, get back here." It was an order.

Eve kept on going.

"Don't you dare go off on your own." This time it was more than an order, it was a command. She took great satisfaction in defying it.

Darkness was descending rapidly, but because of the white snow he could see her figure disappearing through the trees. Her black coat soon blended in with her surroundings, however, so that he could no longer see her.

"Bloody women! Can't live with 'em, can't shoot 'em." He tucked the bird inside his jacket and set off after her.

Eve had a soft spot for animals, especially injured ones. She and her mother had once nursed their cat back to health after it had been poisoned. They'd stayed up with it night after night, soothing it, trying one food after another, until they found something its stomach would not reject. The only thing that worked was honey, a dab at a time on its paw. The cat licked it off, again and again, and was able to stay alive.

Looking after injured animals took a great deal of patience and time. Patience she had in abundance — much more for animals than humans — but these days, time was in short supply.

Eve was totally preoccupied with her thoughts and as a consequence, she paid little attention to where she walked. She was going in the general direction of the house and when she saw a clearing where the trees thinned out, she crossed it. Suddenly, a crack like a rifle-shot rent the air and Eve felt the ground give way beneath her.

She cried out in alarm, not knowing what was happening. Then ice-cold water closed over her head. Dear God, she had walked out onto the pond and gone through the ice!

Three

"Help! Help me!" Eve screamed, then the icy water covered her mouth, effectively cutting off her cries. She knew the water was deep. Her feet touched bottom once before she struggled to the surface and grabbed hold of the ice at the edge of the hole she had made. Eve could swim, but her soaked coat and boots felt ten times heavier.

There was no time to pray, no time even to think coherently; sheer panic took control. The more she struggled to grab hold of something, the more ice broke from the edges, until the hole gaped wide. Eve had never experienced cold like this in her entire life. It penetrated her skin, seeped into her blood, froze her very bones to the marrow.

Clint heard her screams — a sound with which he was on intimate terms. He ran through the dusk on the path she had taken, knowing not to run across the open clearing. He saw nothing until she surfaced and cried out again. His eyes went swiftly to the hole in mid-pond — he was alarmed to see Eve was submerged to her neck.

"I see you!" he shouted. "Try not to panic."

"Clint," she wailed. Her voice a mixture of relief and hope.

"Can you stand up?" Clint demanded.

"No!" came the urgent reply.

"Can you swim?" His deep voice carried well.

"My coat is too heavy!"

"Remove it!" he ordered sternly.

Clint's mind flashed about like mercury. He knew if the ice wouldn't support her, it would never hold him. He remembered seeing a long wooden ladder in the garage. He had rope in his truck; he never travelled without it. The danger was two-fold: she could drown or she could die from hypothermia.

He would try to rescue her with rope and ladder. If that failed, he would have to go in after her. Clint preferred to keep his clothing dry. He knew he would need to keep himself warm during the long night that loomed ahead.

He focused all his attention on Eve. "Take off your coat!" he ordered a second time.

Eve's fingers were numb. She fumbled with the buttons. "I can't!" The water closed over her again as she struggled.

"Keep your head up. Concentrate on those buttons. Rip it off!" If she did not get the coat off, she could die, but he hesitated to tell her.

Finally, miraculously, the waterlogged

coat came off and immediately sank from its own weight. Eve felt even colder without the blanket-like coat, but she could move her arms and legs easier.

"I have to get a rope from the truck. Stay afloat, no matter what. Try not to flounder about and break any more ice!"

Clint lunged off toward the house. Inside the garage, he removed his down jacket and threw the dead pheasant on the floor. Then he took the wooden ladder that lay against the wall and carried it outside. He got the long rope from his truck, tied it to the ladder, then raced back to the pond.

When he was halfway there, he began shouting encouragement for her to hang on. His heart started hammering when he got no reply. It was full dark now as he peered across the snow-covered pond to the gaping black hole. He saw nothing!

"Eve! Eve!" he bellowed. Then he heard a whimper and knew she was still alive.

"Hold on, sweetheart, I'm coming. You're so damn brave. I'll have you out in a minute." His voice exuded total confidence, though Clint felt no such thing. It was something he had learned to do over the years. Confidence begot confidence!

Eve could no longer speak. She could only gasp and make small animal sounds every once in awhile. She could no longer feel her arms and legs, and the rest of her body was also slowly becoming numb. She was on the brink of total exhaustion — the icy-cold water had numbed her thought processes as well. She kept her mouth above water by sheer instinct alone, but was dangerously close to the edge of unconsciousness.

Clint Kelly carefully laid the ladder across the ice of the pond, making sure the end of it stopped well back from the black hole. He took the rope firmly in both hands and lay down flat on top of the ladder.

Slowly, inch by inch, he moved his body toward the hole. He was totally focused — there was no room in his mind for failure. He intended to get her out, one way or another. The tricky part was to get her out before it was too late.

When he was halfway along the ladder, he heard a faint cracking noise, but resolutely ignored it and inched forward. He braced himself for the big crack that would sound like a rifle shot. Clint held his breath in dreaded anticipation and forced himself to breath normally.

The crack did not come while his full weight was distributed on the ladder. It came when he slithered his torso across the bare ice, keeping his feet and knees hooked onto the rungs. Clint did not hesitate; he was too close to back off now. With a superhuman effort he lifted her enough to loop the rope around her body, beneath her

40

arms. Only then did he back off, slithering as swiftly as a serpent.

When his whole weight was back on the ladder, he wound the rope around his body, then hauled as he slowly crawled backwards. Sounds of splintering ice filled the darkness, but it didn't matter now. She was anchored firmly to him.

When Clint threw off the rope, then lifted her high against his chest, he saw that Eve was unconscious. He refused to panic, telling himself that this was only to be expected. The falling snow looked like big white goose feathers, blanketing everything it touched. Their tracks were filled in, but by now Clint could have found the house if he'd been blindfolded.

He laid Eve face down on the floor before the dying embers of the fire. Then he straddled her, splayed his large hands across her rib cage, and pressed and released in a rhythm that simulated natural breathing. In less than a minute, Eve coughed up water, gagged up more, then groaned. She opened her eyes briefly, then closed them again, but Clint was satisfied that she was breathing normally.

They needed heat and they needed it now. He immediately piled the remaining wood on the fire and poked it up into a blaze. He gathered half a dozen towels from the linen closet and three large blankets from the bedroom and brought them to the fire. Before Clint went out to his truck, he glanced at Eve to make sure the bluish color was leaving her face.

Clint brought in his tackle box, his rifle and ammunition, and a forty-ounce bottle of whisky he had picked up for a raffle at the firehall. He spread out the towels and began undressing her. He removed her boots first and set them on the hearth. While she was still face-down, he pulled off her suit skirt, then peeled off her panty-hose.

Clint rolled her onto the towels so that she lay face-up. His sure fingers unbuttoned the red jacket, deftly removed it, and tossed the icy wet object beside the fire. A curse dropped from his lips as he noted the logs were already half burned away. He glanced at the girl who lay helplessly before him in a short red slip and bra.

Eve's face and hair had a delicate, unearthly fairness about them that stirred a deep protectiveness within him. Clint tried to crush down the personal feelings she aroused, trying to be detached and totally professional. When he peeled off her wet undergarments, he tried not to stare at her nakedness. He covered her with a towel and began to rub her limbs briskly.

After a couple of minutes, he had her completely dry, but he did not succeed in warming her body. The glowing logs were giving off their last heat, so he knew the fire would be of little use in raising her body temperature. He thanked Providence for providing the whisky and for teaching him emergency techniques. He opened the bottle, poured the amber liquid into his cupped palm, and applied it to her neck and shoulders.

With long, firm strokes he massaged her with the whisky. He had once seen an older firefighter revive a newborn baby with this technique even after oxygen had failed. Clint pulled the towel completely away from her upper body, palmed more whisky and stroked down firmly over her breasts, then between them, across her heart.

Eve opened her eyes and threw him a frightened look. "Don't!"

"Eve, I have to. This is no time for false modesty. I *must* raise your body temperature. You have no food inside you for fuel, you have exhausted all your energy, and we have no wood left."

Eve stiffened.

"No, no, don't be afraid. Relax! Trust me, Eve, trust me. If you can feel what I'm doing to you, that's good. Relax . . . give yourself up to me . . . feel it, feel it."

He poured some of the amber liquid onto her belly, then swept his hands in firm circles, rubbing, massaging, kneading it into her flesh, so that her circulation would improve.

When Clint lifted her thigh and began to stroke it firmly, the word *silken* jumped into his mind. He tried valiantly not to become aroused, but failed miserably! Resolutely, he lifted her other thigh and repeated the ministrations. Clint had never done anything like this before, but it was suddenly brought home to him how pleasurably erotic a body massage could be. If you substituted warm oil, or perhaps champagne, for whisky, you could have one helluva sensual celebration!

He censured himself for his wicked thoughts and gently turned her over. On Eve's back, his strokes became longer, reaching all the way from her shoulders to her buttocks. He bent over her with tender solicitude. "Eve, are you any warmer?"

"Colder." Her voice was a whisper.

As he massaged the backs of her legs he said, "That's because your skin is getting warmer and the alcohol feels cold as it evaporates. It's a good sign that you can feel the surface of your skin."

He sat her up. "I want you to drink some of this. It will warm up your insides."

Eve nodded. She had no energy to protest, no will to object; all she wanted to do was obey him.

There was no time to search for a glass.

44

Etiquette went the way of her modesty as he held the bottle to her lips and she took a great gulp. It snatched her breath away and she began to cough.

"Easy, easy does it." His powerful arm about her shoulders supported her until she could breathe again. Then he gently tipped the bottle against her lips so she could take a tiny mouthful.

By the third or fourth sip she felt a great red rose bloom in her chest; by the eighth, she felt a fireglow inside her belly. Clint moved her from the damp towels onto a blanket and starting again at her neck and shoulders, giving her a second whisky rubdown.

As Eve lay stretched before him, she gradually became euphoric. She thought Clint Kelly's hands were magnificent, and she wanted him to go on stroking her forever. As she watched him beneath lowered lids, a nimbus of light seemed to surround his dark head. She pondered dreamily about what it could be. Was it magic? Was it his aura? Did he emanate goodness and light? Then suddenly it came to her, and the answer was so simple. It was energy! This man exuded pure energy.

When Clint had anointed every inch of her with the warm, tingling whisky, he wrapped her up in the blanket and lifted her to the couch. "Eve, listen to me. I have to leave you for a while. I imagine we're snowed in here for a couple of days and there are things I need to do."

Eve was far too languorous to speak. Instead she smiled at him, giving him permission to do anything he had to. The smile made her face radiant. Clint knew she was intoxicated and would be asleep in minutes.

He retrieved his jacket from the garage and cut a length of green garden hose that was stored inside for the winter. Then he hiked to the barn to get a milk pail he had seen. He carried both to his Dodge Ram and proceeded to siphon the gasoline from the truck. Clint hated the taste of petroleum in his mouth, but he knew of no other way to siphon gas. He spat half a dozen times, then took a handful of fresh snow to his mouth.

He carried the pail of gasoline very carefully to the generator that stood inside a cupboard in the kitchen. Fortunately it had a funnel beside it. *Winter storms in this area must make a generator a necessity,* he concluded.

Clint opened his tackle box and removed a stringer with several large hooks and lures on it, then slipped the box of ammunition into his pocket and picked up his rifle. He shut the front door quietly and went in the direction of the lake. The snow was coming down heavier than ever and the visibility was zero. He stepped cautiously when he sensed he was on the edge of Lake Michigan. He knew it would be frozen, but if the ice on the pond hadn't held Eve, the ice on the great lake couldn't be very thick.

Noting the formation of the trees, he kicked a hole through the ice and set the stringer, then fastened the other end to the closest tree. He turned up the collar of his jacket and set off toward the bush at the back of the property where he had seen a wild apple tree. In the heavy snow, it took him quite some time to locate it, but when he did, he loaded his rifle and hunkered down with his back against a tree trunk to wait.

Eve slept deeply for two hours, then she drifted up through a layer of sleep and began to dream. She was in her parents' house where the air was filled with delicious smells and the atmosphere was warm and inviting. Her mother was cooking, while her father decorated the Christmas tree.

"Susie, can you help me with this?"

When Susan came into the living room wearing oven mitts, Ted grabbed her and held her beneath the mistletoe.

"You devil, Ted Barlow. This is just one of your tricks; you don't need help at all!"

"I couldn't resist, sweetheart; you're so easy to fool."

Eve saw her mother's secret smile and realized she knew all about the mistletoe. Susan went into her husband's arms with joy. The kiss lasted a full two minutes. She looked up at him. "Do you remember our first Christmas?"

"I love you even more than I did then," he whispered huskily, feathering kisses into Susie's hair.

"We had no money, no home; I was pregnant with Steven, and you'd just been posted overseas."

"What the hell did you see in me?" Ted asked, amusement brimming in his deep blue eyes.

"I was so much in love with you, I couldn't think straight, fly boy."

Ted's hands slipped down her back until his hands came to rest on her bottom cheeks. "But why did you love me?" he pressed.

"It was your strength. You were my rock; you made me feel safe. Even though we had almost nothing, I wasn't afraid to go half-way around the world with you."

He kissed her again. "That's the nicest thing anyone ever said to me."

"It's true, Ted. You inspire confidence. Now, it's true confession time for you. What did you see in me?"

"Besides great legs? You were willing to give up everything for me. I made the right choice. We're still lovers, aren't we?"

"Passionate lovers," she agreed.

"Do you think Eve is serious about Trevor Bennett?"

"I think so."

"You don't think she'll marry him, do you?" he asked, untangling a string of lights.

"Don't you like him?"

"Oh sure, I like him well enough, but I don't think he's right for Eve."

"Why not?" Eve demanded, but they couldn't hear her. Eve realized she was invisible. Her parents had no idea she was in the room with them.

"He's one of these sensitive, modern types, always politically correct. He even teaches courses where men get in touch with their feminine side."

Susan laughed at her husband. "And you don't believe you have a feminine side?"

"Christ, if I did, I'd leave it in the closet where it belongs!"

"You worry too much about Eve. She isn't your little girl anymore."

"Oh, I know she does a terrific impression of being able to take care of herself, but she has a vulnerable side."

Am I that transparent? Eve asked.

"And don't kid yourself . . . she'll be my little girl until I give her away — hopefully to a real man."

"What I meant was, don't worry about her making the wrong choice. Eve knows exactly what she needs. And remember, it's her choice, not yours, fly boy!"

Ted grinned at her. "I just want her to have skyrockets, like we do."

Eve was no longer at home. She was somewhere dark and cold, in deep water, and she was desperately searching for a rock.

Four

Clint Kelly held his breath as he saw a shadow move. He had waited two hours because he knew they would come. Deer loved apples. The shadow separated into three when it reached the trees. He selected his target, a young buck, then lifted his rifle and squeezed the trigger. The two does flew past him, sending down an avalanche of snow from the overhanging branches; the buck dropped.

When Clint stood up from his cramped position, he stretched up to fill his pockets with apples; he could hardly feel his feet. He stomped about for a few minutes to restore his circulation before he hoisted both rifle and carcass to his shoulders. Their food worries were over — now he could concentrate on providing fuel.

For the last two hours, thoughts of Eve had filled his head. He knew she would recover from her ordeal, but worried about the pond water she had ingested. Bacteria from the murky water could make her very sick. If luck was with them, however, the germs may have been killed off by the cold.

Clint's thoughts had then drifted along

more personal lines. He couldn't lie to himself; he found Eve Barlow extremely attractive in spite of their differences. Perhaps it was even *because* of their differences. She was a new experience for Clint; independent, assertive, competitive, even combative. A far cry from the clinging types he had dated recently.

Eve was an exciting challenge. Beneath the polished veneer, he might find a real flesh-and-blood, honest-to-God woman! All his thoughts were sexual now. In retrospect, giving Eve the whisky massage had been a very erotic experience. When he had his hands on her body, he had tried to be detached. Now, however, he relived every stroke, every slide of skin on skin. She was ice, he was fire — a combustible combination!

Hers was probably the loveliest female form he had ever seen or touched. She had everything to tempt a man: long blond hair, silky skin, nipples like pink rosebuds, and a high pubic bone covered by pale curls. And long, beautiful legs.

Back in the garage, with axe and hunting knife, Clint skinned the carcass, then dressed and hung the venison. He was considerably warmer by the time he finished. He glanced ruefully along the wall where the woodpile was customarily stacked. All that remained were wood chips, evidence that split logs were usually stored in abundance.

He saw a wooden pallet marked "Evergreen Sod Farm" and speculated that there must be a lawn buried deep beneath the snow. The wood from the pallet wouldn't last an hour, but perhaps he could put it to better use than burning. The beams and column supports in the barn were fashioned from whole trees. If he used the pallet as a sled, perhaps he could drag a tree trunk up here to the garage where he could axe it into logs, then split the logs into firewood. He looked about for his rope, then remembered it was still at the pond with the ladder. *Necrosis of the cranium* — wasn't that what Eve had flung at him? Perhaps she was right, he thought wryly.

Eve stirred in her sleep, then awoke with a start. She felt disoriented for a moment. She knew she had been dreaming, but as she tried to call back the dream, it danced out of her reach. Then she remembered where she was.

The room was silent, dark and very cold. For a moment, panic assailed her. Had he gone off and left her here? Had he abandoned her? Then she laughed at her own foolishness. Clint Kelly wasn't the kind who would desert a damsel in distress. He had rescued her from a watery grave and was probably out gathering wood. He would relish the challenge of being snowbound.

Eve's belly rolled. Lord, she was hungry. She struggled to sit up and realized she had no strength. Her head dropped back to the couch cushion as she drew the blanket closer and closed her eyes. Clint would take care of everything.

The task of dislodging one of the upright tree trunks was more difficult than Clint had anticipated. None of them budged even a fraction, in spite of the stout shoulder he pressed upon them. He selected the one closest to the barn door, wedged the ladder against a beam, then chopped with his axe until he felled it.

He knew the hardwood would have made a fine piece of furniture and under any other circumstances it would be sacrilege to burn it. But it was exactly what they needed. Hardwood burned longer and gave off a fiercer heat than other timber, and even more to the point, it was dry.

Try as he might, Clint could not lift the tree trunk. He decided that expending his energy was foolish. After studying the problem for a moment, once more he put the rope to good use. He tied it to the tree trunk, threw the other end over a barn beam and used it as a pulley to lift the huge log onto the pallet.

With the rope around his chest, he pulled the makeshift sledge through the snow. Fancifully, he realized he was doing what men had done in past centuries: bringing home the Yule Log. The only difference was that he had to do it alone.

Clint needed a rest to catch his breath before he started cutting wood. He slipped quietly into the living room to check on Eve. Though he didn't feel it after his strenuous exertion, he knew the room was far too chilly for someone who needed to keep her body temperature from falling again.

He bent over her with concern. He heard her even breathing and saw the crescent shadows of her lashes as they lay upon her cheeks. Two fingers to her forehead told him that she wasn't fevered. A proprietary feeling stole over him as he stood close to her. Who the devil was this Trevor guy who wanted to marry her? He sure as hell wouldn't be able to give her an engagement ring for Christmas. It was way past midnight; already Christmas Eve.

Clint flexed weary muscles as he thought of all the wood that needed to be chopped, but strangely, he knew he would rather be here tonight than anywhere else on earth.

Clint spent the next three hours alternately sawing the tree into huge rounds and splitting them into logs that would fit in the fireplace. He only stopped working once, and that was to build a roaring fire in the living room.

By the time he was finished, he vowed the first thing he would buy for the new house was a chain saw, and the second, a log-splitter. He lifted the long axe handle behind his head to stretch the kinks out of his shoulder muscles and yawned loudly. Food! His body needed refuelling. Clint carved some thin slices of venison and went in search of a frying pan. He set it on the flames, cut up an apple amongst the meat and sat down on the hearth.

"Mmm, that smells heavenly."

He turned to the couch in time to see Eve stretch and open her eyes. "How do you feel?" he asked, hiding all trace of anxiety.

"Hungry," she replied, eyeing the contents of the pan. "Thanks for cooking my breakfast," she teased, "but what are you going to have?"

He laughed, but warned, "You're going to have to take it easy. If you eat too much or too fast, your stomach will reject it." He searched her face; it didn't look flushed.

"Don't stare! I know I must look a damned fright."

Clint was so relieved she wasn't fevered, he was perfectly happy to let her have the food and cook more for himself. He found her a plate and took the empty pan into the garage with him. When he returned, she said, "This is absolutely wonderful. What is it?"

"Meat," he said evasively, knowing her aversion to guns.

"What kind of meat?"

"Venison."

She went all quiet, but kept on chewing. *He went hunting last night when I fell asleep.* It wasn't a question, it was a deduction. Her gaze moved from Clint to the fireplace. *I woke up about two o'clock. The fire was almost out. He chopped wood after he bagged the deer. He hasn't slept all night!*

Eve was deeply impressed by what he had done for her. From the moment she had gotten herself into such dire peril, all her ideas about this man had been turned upside down. She experienced an overwhelming gratitude. He had saved her life. He had warmed her and sheltered her and fed her. She hadn't had to lift a finger.

Eve felt more than gratitude; she felt respect and admiration. As she searched her emotions, it suddenly hit her like a bolt of lightning. What she felt was desire!

She put her fork down. Damnation, she mustn't let him see how she felt about him.

"Something wrong with the food?"

"It needs salt . . . and you could use a shave," she said.

"Thankless little bitch," he murmured. He

wasn't smiling, but Eve saw that he couldn't hide the amusement in his eyes.

"Why are you always laughing at me?"

"Because you're an impostor."

"What the devil do you mean?"

"You want the world to think you're the competent, self-sufficient, woman-of-the-year type, but it's just a facade. Scratch the surface and you're a little girl who needs someone to take care of her. A little girl from Hell perhaps, but nevertheless —"

"You're wrong!" Eve interjected.

"Am I? Even your clothes give you away."

"My clothes?" She became conscious of the fact that she wasn't wearing any beneath the blanket.

"The briefcase and the power suit present a false image. Once I stripped them away, what did I expose? The most feminine lingerie I've ever seen. It's not just Victoria's Secret, it's also Eve's Secret."

"You're crazy!"

Clint rubbed his backside. "Brain damage from when my father —"

"Shot you," she finished. Suddenly, she began to laugh. Clint joined in.

"I like to see you laugh," he told her. "It really suits you. You should let your hair down and have fun more often."

"*Fun* — what a concept. I haven't had any in so long, I've forgotten how."

"I could teach you."

She lowered her lashes. He was too damned tempting. "Having my eye on advancement and my nose to the grindstone is very demanding."

"It's also a helluva funny position to go through life in. I could teach you other positions."

Her lashes swept up; green eyes met blue.

"I just bet you could, Action Man."

Clint had to call on all his willpower not to kiss her. His need to taste her was so overpowering at that moment, he had to physically remove himself from her space. He could not make love to her right now — it would be taking advantage of her vulnerability. When he made love to Eve, and he fully intended to, he wanted her to be able to give as good as she got. He wanted her energy to be high voltage.

"I need something to wear." She looked at the red heap on the hearth that had once been an Alfred Sung suit. Oh well, perhaps her underwear could be salvaged.

"I'll see what I can find in the bedrooms," Clint offered.

The moment he disappeared upstairs, she struggled into her bra and short satin slip, shoved the mangled pantyhose and briefs beneath the red heap and pulled the blanket back around her.

"Lean pickings, I'm afraid." Clint presented her with his findings, a pair of red longjohns and some ski socks. "Here, take my shirt — it'll cover the longjohns."

He stripped off vest and shirt before she could protest. Eve's eyes slid across the wide expanse of muscled chest, covered by a thick mat of black hair. He put the leather vest back on, leaving his hard biceps exposed.

She simply couldn't help staring at him. "What do you do to keep in shape?" she asked in wonder.

"Nothing. My job and my hobbies do it for me."

There was absolutely no point in her asking him if he would be warm enough. A man like this couldn't possibly feel the cold. He looked like the Marlboro Man!

"I'll bring in more wood while you get dressed," he said tactfully. "There's water, but it's cold. Don't stand under a cold shower long, Eve," he cautioned.

She was devoutly thankful that she had left her shoulder bag with her briefcase when they went out to look over the property yesterday. In the bathroom, she took the shortest shower on record and pulled the longjohns over her satin slip. When she turned to the mirror she was dismayed to see that she looked like a hillbilly from an old "Hee-Haw" rerun.

Eve quickly covered the red longjohns with Clint's blue wool shirt. His male scent enveloped her. She closed her eyes, trying to define its essence. It was a combination of apples and woodsmoke mixed with honest-to-God sweat. It was like an aphrodisiac!

She pulled on the thick socks and ran her comb through her hair. Miraculously, the pond water hadn't done much damage. If anything, her hair was curlier than usual. The only makeup she had with her was a lipstick. She had chosen it to match the Alfred Sung; now it matched the longjohns.

When she came out of the bathroom, he was waiting for her. She said quickly, "Let's go on a scavenger hunt and see if we can turn up anything at all that will be useful."

He grinned at her. "Brilliant as well as beautiful."

When they entered the kitchen, Clint opened a cupboard and showed her its hidden treasure. "This is a generator. I siphoned the gasoline from the truck so we can have electricity. We should ration it, though. Tonight, when it gets dark, we can have lights, use the stove to cook something, and maybe listen to the weather reports on the radio."

Eve grinned at him. "Brilliant as well as handsome."

Inside the numerous kitchen cupboards they found every pot and pan known to man. There was china, silverware, glasses and mugs, but almost nothing edible. There was a rack that contained fifteen different herbs and spices, a box of candles, some tinfoil, a package of napkins from Valentine's Day, and a lone package of Kool Aid that lay forgotten in an empty drawer.

The last cupboard produced a half-jar of instant coffee. To Eve and Clint it was like finding a gold nugget in an abandoned mine.

"Coffee!" they chorused with joy. Clint filled the kettle and set it on the fire. Eve measured a spoonful of the magic brown powder in each of two mugs, then they sat by the fire with bated breath, waiting for the water to boil.

"They say anticipation is the best part," she teased.

"Don't you believe it." His voice was so deep, his double entendre so blatantly clear, a frisson of pleasure ran down her spine.

When he poured the boiling water into her mug, Eve closed her eyes and breathed in its aroma. To Clint, it was a sensual gesture, revealing her passion for everything in life. When he added a drop of whisky to his coffee, Eve held out her mug. When she tasted it, she rolled her eyes. "Now that *is* decadent!" She took two big gulps. "My God, it's better than sex."

Clint laughed. "If that's true, you've had

very inadequate lovers, Eve Barlow."

She wondered if that were true. Until yesterday she would have vehemently denied that, but after spending twenty-four hours with Clint Kelly, her perceptions about a lot of things were changing. She looked him straight in the eye. "I think it's time for your cold shower."

Clint knew it would take more than a cold shower to cure his condition. It would take an ice dive, at least. Then he remembered his fishing line. He picked up his coat.

"Where are you going?"

"To check on my stringer."

When she was alone, she wondered what the devil a stringer was. She also wondered why she had brought up the subject of sex. She must be out of her mind. Then she recalled she had read somewhere that female captives always became enamored of their abductors. It was some sort of syndrome.

Suddenly, Eve began to laugh. Clint Kelly had not abducted her. The captor/captive scenario was a fantasy. *Quit kidding yourself! He's the most desirable man you've ever met in your life, and the attraction is definitely mutual.*

Five

Clint took his axe with him to the lake because the temperature had plummeted and he knew the ice would be thicker now. The snow was still coming down, but it had changed to fine stuff that never seemed to melt.

He followed the line from the tree, taking great care not to walk out onto the lake. When he chopped open the hole, he was gratified to see that he had hooked two walleyes. He carefully removed the lures and set the stringer back in the lake.

Eve's eyes widened when she saw the fish. "You *are* a magic man!"

He held them up by the mouth. "Hocus pocus, fish bones choke us."

She followed him to the kitchen and watched, fascinated, as he skinned and filleted the walleyes. When he was finished, he said, "Now I need that shower."

When Clint came downstairs, she noticed how his black hair curled when it was wet. He hadn't been able to shave and the blue-black shadow on his jaw added to his overt masculinity. With effort, Eve forced herself to stop staring at him.

She busied herself spreading tinfoil to wrap the fish. They selected the herbs together. It seemed a great luxury to have so many choices in the spice rack. They finally decided to sprinkle the fillets with chervil, basil, and dried parsley. Then he sealed the tinfoil and set it amid the smouldering logs.

When the tantalizing aroma of the herbs began to permeate the air, both of them realized how hungry they were.

"I'm drooling," Eve breathed.

Clint's glance flicked over her mouth. "Me, too," he confessed.

The amused look she threw him told him she understood exactly what he meant. She waited most patiently for the fish to cook and then she thought she smelled it burning. They both reached out at the same time. Eve pulled the tinfoil from the fire, but it burned her fingers. With a yelp, she hastily dropped it into Clint's calloused palms.

He set it on the hearth and reached for her hands. His face exuded tenderness as he examined her fingers.

"It's all right, I didn't get burned," she assured him. *Not yet, at least,* she added silently, as she felt heat leap from him into her hands and run up her arms. He gave her back her hands, but not her heart.

When she tasted the walleye, she knew it had been worth waiting for. The delicate flavor was ambrosia to the palate.

"I ate a whole fish, all by myself!"

"Your body needed the nourishment. I'm going to make a spit and roast us a haunch of venison for dinner."

"I'm profoundly grateful to you, Clint Kelly."

"Why do I get the feeling you're going to add a *but* to the end of your sentence?"

"You're a perceptive man. It's time we got down to business."

For one split second his mind went blank. She had the power to make him forget there was anything beyond this moment. Then he realized she wasn't talking about them, she was talking about the house.

"Are you sure you're up to this?"

"I'm positive," she assured him.

"Okay, I make an offer of one hundred and fifty thousand."

"Please be serious, Mr. Kelly."

"I'm deadly serious, Ms. Barlow. My offer is one-fifty."

"You're wasting my time."

That's a moot point, he thought, but kept a wise silence.

"The asking price is *two* hundred and fifty thousand."

"You surely don't expect me to offer the asking price?"

"Well no, but one-fifty is simply unacceptable."

"To whom? You? You aren't the owner,

Ms. Barlow. You merely present the offer."

"I won't present an offer of one-fifty on a property that's worth *two*-fifty!"

"Just a moment. No one said anything about how much this property is worth. We're discussing the asking price. It isn't worth anywhere near two-fifty."

Eve had heard those words before, from her longtime friend, who owned the property. She could hear Judy's voice now. *"It can't be worth more than about one hundred and eighty thousand, Eve. Let's list it for two hundred."*

Eve had replied, *"No way. They aren't making any more lakefront property, you know. If you aren't in a hurry for the money, I'd like to list it at two-fifty and see what happens."*

Actually, nothing had happened. The property had been for sale for nine months without a single offer. Eve knew what she could get for a city property within a few dollars, but country places were not her bailiwick.

"In your exalted opinion, Mr. Kelly, what do you think it is worth?"

He didn't beat about the bush. "It's worth a hundred and eighty thousand."

With all she had learned about him, why had she underestimated his business acumen? "You're wrong, Mr. Kelly. It's worth two hundred and twenty-five. Lakefront property is at a premium and this place is furnished."

"What was the last offer you received, Ms. Barlow?"

"That's privileged information, Mr. Kelly."

Clint grinned. "You've had no offers on this place!"

Eve could have kicked herself for being so transparent.

"How long has it been on the market?" he demanded. "I bet it's been over a year."

"Only nine months!" There was a pregnant pause. "Damn you, Clint Kelly." Eve's resolve hardened. She needed another two hundred thousand to make the President's Circle and she'd get that much if it killed her!

"Write up an offer for one-fifty and I'll sign it."

"No. The asking price is two-fifty and I've already admitted it's only worth two-twenty-five. I've come down, but you haven't budged!"

"I don't have to budge until the seller rejects my offer."

"Mr. Kelly —"

"Clint," he amended.

"Clint, let me explain about real estate. There's a leeway of about five percent. It's like an unwritten law."

"Thanks for the economics lesson. Now let me teach you poker."

"You're laughing at me again."

"Eve, you're required by law to make out an Offer to Purchase. I *have* bought real estate before, you know."

"A cemetery plot?"

"Sarcasm is the lowest form of wit. As a matter of fact, when my dad retired from the force, we became partners in a sports bar."

Eve stared at him. "Not Kelly's?"

"Afraid so," he said, grinning. "Business is my long suit."

"Then you can bloody well afford two hundred."

"I can, but I won't."

"*Why* won't you make me a counter offer?"

Clint's grin widened. "I don't have to; you keep dropping the price."

She covered her ears and screamed in frustration.

"I was afraid you weren't up to this," he said softly.

"Of course I'm up to it . . . well, maybe I'm not." Eve decided to throw herself on his mercy. "Clint, let me be honest with you. If I make a sale of two hundred thousand my earnings for the year will get me into the President's Circle, a very prestigious achievement."

"Now, let me get this straight," he said, trying not to show his amusement. "You want me to up my offer from one-fifty to

69

two hundred because you need the sales figures? Your logic escapes me. We have an impasse. I suggest we take a time-out."

"Do you have to talk to me in sports terms? I know nothing about football."

"We must have something in common. How about hockey?"

"I loathe it!"

Clint brought in firewood and stacked it by the hearth. The fire had to be kept at a constant temperature to roast the venison. The pile of wood that had seemed so large was half gone. Timber on the property was mostly pine that burned too fast, but it was better than nothing. He decided to cut some and bring it into the garage so it could dry a little.

Clint cut a haunch from the deer, found a meat spit in the barbecue, and wedged it in the fireplace, over the glowing logs. "You decide what flavor you'd like."

Eve studied the bottles in the spice rack and came back with fennel and garlic powder. Almost as soon as they were sprinkled on the meat, the air became redolent with a piquant aroma that awoke their taste-buds.

"Call me if the fire burns low."

Eve was restless. She was in a tug-of-war with herself, wanting Clint Kelly to come close, yet keep his distance at the same time. She felt extremely guilty — when Trevor arrived to take her dancing, she wouldn't be there.

To stop her outrageous thoughts about Kelly, Eve went in search of something to read. She was delighted to find a book; when she discovered it was a collection of O. Henry stories, she took the precious volume back to the fire and lost herself in its pages.

Throughout the afternoon, Clint came in and out. He tended the fire and turned the spit, then returned to his woodcutting. The atmosphere between them was cozy and companionable. Eve was palpably aware that they were forging a bond. Strangely, she didn't feel guilty that he was working so hard. He was a man, she a woman; it felt right.

She saved "The Gift of the Magi" for last. It was a Christmas story, a love story so poignant that it evoked tears. When she came to it, however, she found that she could not read it. It was simply too sentimental, too emotional.

Clint removed his jacket and turned the venison, which had crisped to a delicious deep brown. He immediately sensed Eve's melancholy and set about banishing it. He put a couple of apples to roast, then went into the kitchen and flipped the electrical switch to "generator." Light flooded the living room, dispelling all real and imaginary shadows.

Clint brought a carving board to the hearth. When he cut into the venison, succulent juices ran from the pink slices. Eve brought plates, cutlery, and napkins, and filled crystal goblets with water.

As they sat before the fire to dine, Clint lifted his goblet. "Happy Christmas, Eve."

She touched her glass to his. "Happy Christmas, Clint."

They ate in companionable silence, paying tribute to the food. When they were almost done, Clint set about amusing her. "We must have something in common, let's find out what it is." He deliberately suggested something he knew she would hate. "How about camping?"

She grimaced. "How about shopping?"

He shuddered. "Darts?"

She shook her head. "Chess."

"Read the comics?"

"Poetry," she said softly.

"Phil Collins?" he suggested.

"Barbra Streisand," she countered.

Clint chuckled and turned on the radio. Between Christmas carols, the only topic of conversation was the weather. They described how many inches had fallen and how many more were expected. They warned drivers to stay off the roads and told of flight cancellations. They reported power failures, downed lines, and over-loaded telephone circuits. They asked every-one to exercise patience. They announced that the snow plows would be working all night.

Clint tried every station. The reports were identical. He switched it off just as Nat King Cole's beautiful voice sang, *Unforgettable, that's what you are.* He and Eve looked at each other, knowing they were exactly where they wanted to be.

"Coconut cream pie?" he suggested.

She shook her head. "Lemon."

"Baseball?"

Eve got to her feet. "Yes!"

"Detroit Tigers!" Clint shouted.

"Yes! Yes!" Eve's face was radiant. "Blame it on my father — it's in my genes."

"Cecil Fielder," he said with reverence.

"Mickey Tettleton," she enthused.

Clint took hold of her hands. "One hun-dred and seventy-five thousand."

"You devil, you know I need two hundred!"

"I know what you need," he said huskily, drawing her into his arms and covering her mouth with his.

The way he kissed made her weak at the knees. There was nothing tentative about it. He kissed the same way he did every-thing else; he simply took charge. His mouth was firm and demanding and pos-sessive. His mouth was . . . perfect. He kissed her the way a man should kiss a woman, but seldom did.

Clint did not try to part her lips with his tongue. He was in no hurry. Even kissing had its foreplay. Her mouth was soft and yielding and told him without words that she loved what he was doing.

Clearly, he enjoyed kissing; probably because he was so good at it. His hands cupped her face and he lifted it for another kiss. He did it reverently as if he held something delicate and priceless. Clint's hands were just as sensual as his mouth. They were calloused, capable, and downright carnal as they caressed her skin. His fingertips explored her features, and the backs of his fingers stroked across her cheekbones.

"Sweet, sweet," he murmured, seeing how her lashes were tipped with gold, seeing the fine down upon her brow, seeing her cheeks tint shell-pink, seeing everything.

Her breath came out on a sigh. How beautiful he made her feel, how utterly lovely. He conveyed with a look, with a touch, how special he found her. He kissed her eyelids and the corners of her mouth, delighting when they turned up with pure pleasure. And then his whole focus centered on her mouth, and she opened to him as a flower being worshipped by the sun.

He outlined her lips with the tip of his

tongue. When the tip of her tongue touched his, a tremor of need made her throat and breasts quiver. His fingers slid into her hair, holding her, then his tongue mastered hers. This was only the first part of his body to enter hers, but she moaned low with the deeply erotic sensations it evoked.

Her hands moved from his leather vest to grip his bare arms where his biceps bulged so boldly. She clung to him, relishing his strength, loving his hardness, both above and below. She longed for more. It was her first experience with raw lust. She was already love-drunk, and all he had done was kiss her!

His lips were against her throat. "Evie," he murmured. How the diminutive pleased her; she never wanted to be called Eve again. How feminine it made her feel. He was teaching her the nuances of domination and submission, the sheer bliss that transforms a female who yields all to the male.

She stood obediently while his powerful hands removed the shirt and stripped the long red undergarment from her slim body and long legs. She was impatient for him to remove his own clothes, but she didn't paw at him; she waited, knowing it would be worthwhile.

With the lights blazing, they stood and looked at each other. Really looked. His body tapered down to slim hips. His flanks were long and hard. The dark pelt on his chest narrowed to a line of black hair that ran down his flat belly, then bloomed like a blackthorn bush. His manroot stood up, thick and powerful — a testament to her breathstopping beauty.

Clint's eyes licked over her like a candle flame. "Have you any idea how lovely you are?"

Truly, she could not answer his question. He took hold of her hand and traced her own fingertips from her temple to her lips. "Your eyes are Irish green, your mouth tastes like honeyed wine." He drew her fingertips slowly down the curve of her throat, then down to her breast, where a golden tress lay curled. "Your hair is the color of moonlight."

His voice, so low, so deep and masculine, did glorious things to her. He drew her fingers across the swell of her breast to the nipple. He drew her fingers down her body. "Your body is like silk." He touched one fingertip to her navel. "It has hidden depths."

Eve caught her breath. Surely he wouldn't make her touch herself? But he did. He held their hands so that their fingers threaded through the curls of her mons. Then he traced one of her fingertips along the folds of her pink cleft, then slipped it inside to touch the center of her womanhood. "A rosebud drenched with dew." He brought her fingers to his mouth and tasted them.

Eve was adrift on a sea of sensuality. His powerful hands cupped her shoulders to steady her. "I'm going to turn out the lights now to conserve our fuel. Don't move; I want to see you by fireglow. Then I'm going to pull down the couch. It has a bed inside."

Nothing escapes him, she thought dreamily. She knew she didn't have to worry about protection; Clint was the kind of man who took care of everything.

Six

Clint set lighted candles on the hearth before he came back to her. After he kissed her, he placed her in front of him so that she faced the fire. She leaned back, revelling in the solid feel of him. His hands were free to seek out all her secret places. He warmed her at the fire before he lifted her to their bed.

But Eve was already on fire. His arousal made her feel as if she were smouldering, longing for the moment she would burst into white hot flame. When the firestorm came, and she knew it would, it might consume her. But she was ready, nay eager, to go up in smoke.

He never left her mouth for long. In the first hour, they shared what seemed like ten thousand kisses. One powerful arm enfolded her as his calloused palms cupped her breasts, and then he began to focus all his attention upon her nipples.

Clint knew that when he licked, some sensation would be lost as it moved back and forth under his tongue. To prevent this, he placed his fingers on either side of her nipple and pressed down, not hard, but firmly. Then he spread his fingers apart, holding it totally immobile, and lowered his lips to her.

Her nipple swelled up into his mouth like a ripe fruit. When he began to slowly lick her, Eve went wild! She covered his breast-bone with tiny love bites, then took his other hand to her mouth, drew one of his fingers inside, and began to suck, hard. His love-play made her drown in need. She writhed against him. The friction of sleek skin on skin made her flesh feel like hot silk.

He knew she needed immediate release. Then he would be able to start again, build-ing her passion slowly, so they could make love for hours. He moved her up in the bed until his cheek lay against her silken thigh. Then she felt a wet slide of tongue, followed by a deep thrust. His tongue curled about her bud exactly as it had her nipple, and she was undone. She cried out into the flickering shadows that hid their secret rites, and arched herself into his masterful mouth.

Clint moved up in the bed so that he could catch her last soft cry with his mouth. Eve tasted herself on his lips and felt delicious as original sin. Most of the sensations she experienced were new to her, and Clint's earlier words drifted through her con-sciousness: "I can't decide if you're an Ice Queen or if you're simply unawakened."

Obviously, I was both!

She couldn't believe how highly aroused he had made her or how she had peaked so beautifully, and they hadn't even completed coitus. That adventure still lay ahead. She wanted to scream from excitement.

Now he began to whisper love words, each phrase more erotic than the last. She would never have guessed he could be poetic. But had she not underestimated everything about him?

Clint expected her second arousal to be slow, but it was not. She became wildly inquisitive about his body — the feel of it, the man-scent of it, the salt taste of it. The masculine roughness of his beard sent thrills spiralling through her consciousness, driving her to touch his male center, to stroke, squeeze, play and tease. His testes were big and heavy, more than a handful for her. How she loved the feel of this big, hard man.

Clint slipped a finger into her sugared sheath. This was the second part of his body he'd put inside her, and it was every bit as exciting as the first. He withdrew it slowly, and she gasped as he slid two fingers into her. Her sheath pulsated and clung to him tightly. When she became slippery, he knew she was ready.

He positioned the swollen head of his

shaft at the opening of her cleft, then pushed up gently, inch by inch, until he was fully seated. Then all semblance of gentleness fell away. His lovemaking became fierce and savage. She adored every rough, elemental stroke as he anchored deep in her scalding body, then pulled all the way out so he could repeat the deep penetration over and over until her nails raked him. He took her to the edge of sanity. She became aware of every pulse-point on her body.

The moans in his throat were raw and it came as a blinding revelation that he was receiving as much pleasure as he gave. Then suddenly the night exploded for both of them. They keened and arched as they spent, and she mourned that she could not fully feel his white-hot seed spurt up inside her.

Eve thrashed her head from side to side with the intensity of her release, and Clint's hand came up to cup her cheek and hold her still. Then his mouth joined hers in a deep kiss.

When he rolled from her, he brought her against his side possessively. Eve had never felt more alive in her life. Her eyes sought his, but they were closed and she realized he was asleep. Her face softened as she gazed at him. He hadn't slept in over forty hours.

Eve lay entranced for a long time, savouring the feel of her body, watching the play of firelight make strange shadows on the ceiling. Their lovemaking had been a ballet of domination and submission, yet the strange thing was, they had each given and taken in equal measure. Male and female were only halves of one magnificent whole. *Equal* halves! She had not been diminished in any way; she had been exalted.

Inevitably, reality stole into her consciousness. She pushed away all thought of Trevor. She would deal with it later. In this isolated haven, where the pristine snow lay all about them, she wanted no footprints of others to mar the beauty that enfolded them. At least for tonight, the world must be held at bay.

Eve, a million miles from sleep, brought book and candle back to the bed. She propped herself up quietly and turned to "The Gift of the Magi." She was transported back in time to another Christmas Eve. The couple in the story were so real, she was in the room with them.

O. Henry's words brought her deep pleasure. When she finished the story, her eyes were liquid with unshed tears. The young man had pawned his watch to buy combs for his wife's beautiful hair; she had sold her hair to buy him a watch chain. The objects in the story were symbols. What they had really given each other were gifts of love.

More than anything, she wanted to give Clint Kelly a gift of love, and she knew exactly what it would be. She slipped from the bed, opened her briefcase, and removed an Offer to Purchase form. Then she made out the offer in the amount of one hundred and seventy-five thousand dollars. She knew Judy would accept it and the knowledge filled her with joy. He belonged here; this house and property were already a part of him.

That she would not qualify for the President's Circle seemed unimportant when she compared it to making him happy. She blew out the candles and curled up beside him. This Christmas Eve had been pure magic.

The first sound Eve heard on Christmas morning was a groan. She sat up quickly and looked down at Clint stretched beside her. He looked flushed. "Are you all right?"

"I'm fine," he croaked.

His beautiful, deep voice had been replaced by a rasp. "You're not fine at all! You have laryngitis at the very least." She touched his brow. "You're warm; you have a fever."

"I never get sick," Clint protested in a hoarse whisper.

"You mean, you never admit you get sick."

"Same thing." He gave her a lopsided grin

and threw back the covers.

"Oh, no, you don't," Eve said, pushing him back down and covering him with the blankets. "You're sick because you over-taxed yourself, hunting and cutting wood and going without sleep."

He laughed at her. His throat sounded like he'd been gargling with gravel. "It was child's play compared to a twelve-hour night shift, fighting a fire in below-zero temperatures."

Eve glared at him, daring him to make a move from the warm bed. "Wasn't it another Clint who said, *A man should know his limitations?* It's my turn to take care of you."

She took a one-minute cold shower, pulled on her satin slip, then stepped into the red longjohns and blue wool shirt. She felt Clint's amused eyes on her as she built up the fire. In the kitchen she turned on the generator just long enough to boil the kettle for coffee. She mixed up the orange Kool-Aid, sliced some cold venison from the haunch, and carried a tray to the bed.

His dark eyebrow lifted at the glass of Kool-Aid.

"It's pretend orange juice. Didn't you ever play pretend?"

"I played house, too," he croaked.

She made sure he ate everything, then poured the last of the whisky into his coffee. "I want you to go back to sleep."

"It's Christmas Day — there's stuff that needs doing," he protested.

"And I'm the one who's going to do it," she said flatly.

As Clint sipped his coffee, he took delight in looking at her. He didn't know what had brought about this transformation to domesticity. Perhaps his slight ailment brought out a need to nurture him. It felt strange to be pampered. He handed her his empty mug, pulled up the covers, and turned over.

By the time she finished her breakfast, she heard his even breathing and knew he was asleep. Eve's mind overflowed with plans for their Christmas Day. She pulled on her boots, ignoring the fact that the insides had hardened as they had dried by the fire. She slipped into Clint's down jacket and went to the garage for his axe.

When she went outside, she saw that it had stopped snowing and the sun was turning the landscape into a glittering fairy-land. She didn't have to venture far to find a small pine tree. The one she selected was literally buried beneath the snow, with only its growing point sticking up. It took her quite a while to scoop away the snow so that she could reach its trunk with the axe. Her hands were freezing by the time she chopped it free and dragged it up to the house.

Eve warmed her hands at the fire, glancing at Clint's unmoving form in the bed. When he awoke, he would be surprised. It was fun trying to make their Christmas special. Eve needed something that would act as a tree stand. She went into the garage and looked about carefully, knowing she had to use her ingenuity. There was a cement block, probably used as a door prop, and she decided that would do the trick.

When her eyes fell on the pheasant, she felt a pang of regret that the poor creature had been caught in a snare. That thought drifted away as she realized, here was their Christmas bird! Eve had not lived years in the Orient without learning how to pluck and clean fowl.

She hummed to herself as she boiled the water and performed the odorous chore. A flash of remembrance came to her. Hadn't she seen a few onions hanging in the basement when she'd been searching for the water valve? She went downstairs to retrieve them, wondering how she'd overlooked such a treasure.

Eve sprinkled the bird with sage and thyme, set it in a shallow roasting pan with a square of tinfoil over it, and put the pan on the logs. Then she carried in the cement block and stuck the tree upright in it. She certainly didn't have much in the way of decorations, but again she used her ingenuity. She took the red Valentine napkins and fashioned paper flowers of a sort.

She had seen some old dried corncobs in the barn. She wondered if she could pop the kernels and string some popcorn. It wouldn't be edible, but it would be okay for decorating the tree. Nothing seemed too much trouble. Once more she slipped on the boots and coat and plodded off to the barn.

Stable smells assailed her as she entered, and it was suddenly brought home to her that this day was celebrated because of the Christ Child born in a manger. She thought of Mary giving birth in such a place, and then she thought of her own mother. How worried Susan must be because Eve hadn't shown up this morning. They would be searching for her, and it would very likely ruin their Christmas.

She felt guilty. She loved them very much and regretted causing them worry. It was so frustrating when she could do nothing about it, but Eve had learned to accept things that couldn't be altered.

Back in the kitchen, she cut the kernels from the old corncobs and turned on the generator long enough to pop the corn on the stove. She carried the big bowl to the living room and opened Clint's tackle box, thinking to thread the popcorn on fishing line. Some of his lures were so colorful that she hung them on the tree.

Before she sat down to thread the popcorn, she basted the pheasant, leaving the tin foil off so it would brown. The onions in the roasting pan gave off a tantalizing aroma. Eve offered up a prayer of thanks.

In Grand Rapids, Susan Barlow was also praying. She had called her daughter to wish her a happy Christmas, but there had been no answer. She assumed Eve was already on her way, but when half an hour elapsed and she didn't arrive, a vague uneasiness touched her. After a whole hour, she voiced her worry to her husband, who had just finished shovelling the driveway.

"Ted, I called Eve over an hour ago. When she didn't answer, I assumed she was on her way, but she should be here by now."

"The main streets are all plowed, so she shouldn't have had any trouble. Maybe she and Trevor are stopping somewhere before they come here."

Susan pulled back the sheers. "Oh, here's Trevor's car now. Thank heavens!"

Still wearing his boots, Ted went outside to greet them. Trevor was alone. "Where's Eve?"

"I couldn't get her on the phone and when I got to her apartment, the Mercedes was gone. I assumed she was here."

"No," Ted said, shaking his head. "We're worried about her."

"Oh, I wouldn't worry too much, Mr. Barlow. Eve can take care of herself."

Ted frowned at Trevor, but bit back a retort. When they went inside, Ted got on the computer. *Eve, if you're there, please answer. If you're sick, let us know. If you can't start your car and are waiting for the Motor League, send a message.*

Susan brought them coffee and hot muffins with homemade jam. Trevor had just taken his first bite when Ted said, "I'm going over there. Come on." He touched his wife's cheek to reassure her. "Don't worry, sweetheart, we'll find her."

When Ted saw that Trevor was right and his daughter's Mercedes was not in the parking lot of her apartment building, he went upstairs and banged on her door. Then he banged on the superintendent's door and insisted he open up Eve's apartment. At first the man said he couldn't do that, but he hadn't reckoned with Ted Barlow. Reluctantly, he finally agreed to use his master key.

Trevor demurred. "I don't really think this is wise . . . you're violating Eve's privacy."

"Bullshit!" Ted replied shortly.

Inside the apartment, everything was in its place but her winter coat, her purse, and briefcase were missing. As they looked about, Trevor said, "See how efficient and organized she is? By the time we get back to your house, she'll be there."

Her father decided to drive to Eve's office; she was a voracious worker. A lone car sat in the parking lot. When he brushed off the foot of snow, he saw it was Eve's Mercedes. Ted was really worried now and even Trevor was beginning to feel uneasy. "There has to be a logical explanation for this," he assured her father.

Ted drove back home and got on the phone to Maxwell Robin. "Max, Eve's missing! Her car is parked at the office. Do you know where she is? Have you spoken with her?"

"No, Ted. The last time I saw her was the day before yesterday. She drove a client up to that country property she has listed for that friend of hers. Well, actually, now that I think of it, the client did the driving."

"Damn, they must have got caught in the storm. It's been a real blizzard north of here. Who is the client? Do you know anything about him?"

"Yes, I know him personally. Name's Clint Kelly. He's a diving instructor and also a Fire Captain. In an emergency situation she couldn't be in better hands."

"Thank God for that. Where exactly is the property?"

"I don't know off the top of my head, but it has to be in the files at the office. I'll meet you there."

"I'll call her friend Judy and get it from the horse's mouth. Your kids probably haven't opened their presents yet," Ted said.

"You've got to be kidding; they were up at six o'clock! Listen, Ted, call me if you need me."

Ted Barlow telephoned Eve's friend in Detroit and got directions to the log house, while Susan silently prayed that her daughter was safe. When Ted got off the phone he announced, "I'm on my way!"

"I think we should call the police," Trevor advised.

"The police won't even file a missing persons' report until after seventy-two hours."

"The State Troopers then. They'll search the highways. They'll have any accident reports and can check out the hospitals."

"That's a great idea, but I'm still going," Ted insisted.

"Leave it to the professionals. It's too risky in blizzard conditions. You could get stuck or lost and that would just compound the problem."

Susan looked at Trevor bleakly. He might as well save his breath to cool his soup. If Eve needed rescuing, Ted Barlow would be in the vanguard!

Seven

*W*hen Clint awoke, he felt miraculously restored. He threw off the blanket and stretched. Before he could lower his arms, the mouthwatering aroma of roasting game assaulted his senses. He sat up and blinked his eyes. Where the devil had the Christmas tree come from, or its decorations?

"Evie," he bellowed. His throat was much improved, sounding only slightly husky.

She had been waiting for him to awake, anticipating his reaction to her surprise. She pulled off his blue shirt and stood in front of the bathroom mirror in the red longjohns. She stuffed the cushion down the front and fastened the buttons over the bulge. She had taped her blond curls across her face as a makeshift beard and mustache, and knew she looked ridiculous. But Eve didn't care; inside, her silly juices were bubbling.

She took a deep breath and bounded into the living room. "Ho! Ho! Ho! Merry Christmas!"

Clint began to laugh. If he hadn't, Eve would have been devastated. She joined in the laughter, holding her cushion belly with both hands.

"I see you're feeling better."

His eyes glittered with amusement. "You were so much woman, you almost finished me off."

Eve's blush competed with her longjohns, but she needed the acknowledgment that he remembered last night's glow — that she lingered in his consciousness, as he did in hers.

"You went out and cut a tree all by yourself, then thought up these ingenious decorations."

"I'm not just a hairy face," she beamed.

"And the pheasant! I thought you told me you couldn't cook."

"No, I told you I *didn't* cook, not that I couldn't. My mother was Susie Homemaker — I had to learn how to cook."

"Santa Claus, you're full of surprises."

She handed him an envelope.

Clint opened it and read the Offer to Purchase. "What's this?" he asked softly.

Eve smiled into his eyes. "I know the seller will accept a hundred and seventy-five."

"What about your President's Circle?"

"My gift to you means more than the President's Circle." She bent down to kiss him.

"Germs," he warned huskily.

"Santa is immune," she whispered.

He took her in his arms and brushed her curls away from her mouth. Then he claimed it, kissing her thoroughly.

In the same husky voice he had used last night, she repeated his words: "I know what you need."

"What?" he murmured, wanting her to say it.

"A sauna."

Clint groaned with anticipation.

"I've already stacked the wood into it. After we eat our pheasant, all we have to do is light that fire."

"All these gifts for me. What can I give you, Evie?"

She almost melted with desire. "I'll think of something, Action Man," she whispered.

"I was going to give you scuba lessons, but it pales in comparison to your generosity."

Suddenly, she began to laugh. Her pillow belly bobbed up and down. She pulled it from her longjohns and threw it at him. "Only an insensitive male could offer diving lessons to a woman who almost drowned in murky pond water!"

He gave her a lopsided grin, his teeth showing white against his dark, unshaven jaw.

Eve realized that with Clint Kelly beside her, she wouldn't even be afraid of being submerged underwater. She set the table as elegantly as she could for their Christmas dinner, with crystal goblets of water and lighted candles.

Clint donned his leather vest and held out her chair with a flourish. The flesh of the pheasant, seasoned with the sage and thyme, tasted better than any turkey she could ever remember. The roasted onions were elevated from common vegetables to savory delicacies.

Clint was beguiled by Eve's transformation from career woman to chatelaine. The role suited her to perfection in his eyes. He speculated on what had brought it about. Was it the Christmas season, being snowed in, or a direct result of what had happened between them last night? He had known from the moment he undressed her that she was a real flesh and blood woman.

Eve watched the man sitting across the table from her. What was it about him that brought out her domesticity? She believed his masculinity called out to her femininity. She had no desire to compete with him; she had only the desire to nurture him and make him happy.

Her thoughts drifted to her mother and father, and she realized that was the kind of relationship they had. Susan was fulfilled as a woman and her contentment and happiness was visible to everyone. It was a heady sensation to have the power to make a man completely happy. She was revelling in that new-found power at the moment.

Their time together here would be so short.

When they finished dinner, Eve picked up an apple and held it out to him. The picture she made entranced him. In the Bible, Adam said, *The woman tempted me.* Well, if Adam's Eve was anything like his Eve, no wonder he had succumbed.

"We can have dessert in the sauna," he said, rising and taking her hand. She knew he had something more exotic than apples in mind. "I'll light the fire so the logs will have a chance to glow, while we undress."

Eve wrapped her nakedness in a towel; Clint was less modest. He opened the sauna door and peered into its dark interior. "We'll need a candle." There was no way he was going to make love to her without being able to see her.

When Eve stepped inside, the aromatic cedar wood of the walls and seats gave off a heady scent that filled her senses. It was already deliciously warm and inviting, like a cocoon that enveloped them in a small, private world. Along two of the walls, the bench seats were normal height, while the third wall had a very low one, so you could stretch out your legs across the floor. The remaining wall had just the opposite, a bench seat set high so it could be used as a ledge to set things on, or to perch upon for maximum heat.

Clint set the candle on the ledge and lifted

off her towel. Eve had no objections. When Clint lifted her against him, she cried out with excitement; she wrapped her arms around his neck, clinging to him as he took total possession of her mouth.

"Wrap your legs around me," he demanded. Eve obeyed willingly, loving the feel of his big calloused hands beneath her bottom. When beads of moisture formed along his collarbone, she licked them off playfully at first, then sensually, as she became more highly aroused.

The feel of her rough pink tongue gave Clint desires of his own. He lifted her high until she was perched on the shelf, opened her thighs and stepped between. His mouth was on a level with her belly. He trailed kisses down it, taking the drops of moisture onto his tongue. Then with his fingers, he opened the delicate pink folds between her legs and gazed at her woman's center. He worshipped her with his eyes, then dipped his head and made love to her with his mouth. With his lips against her cleft, he murmured, "God, you're so hot inside."

She was hot because she was on fire. Eve knew it had very little to do with the sauna. She writhed and arched, threading her fingers into his black hair and holding him to her center, faint with the ravishing. He swung up to perch beside her, gathering her close to watch her green eyes glitter with passion.

Eve needed to vent that passion in an abandoned act of worship. She slid down from the high seat. Her head was on the level of his knees. She parted them and stepped close. Standing on tiptoe, she delicately licked the tiny opening at the tip of his phallus, then drew its swollen head into her hot mouth. She swirled her tongue, spiralling it around and beneath the ridge of his cock.

"Enough, Evie, or I'll spill." It was all new to her. She was receiving as much pleasure as she was giving. Clint slid from his high perch. "No, sweet, I don't want it that way."

Dimly, she realized that though Clint had loved what she was doing, he could not spend in such a passive manner.

He stood her on the low seat, pressed her against the wall and thrust up inside her. The savage force of his entrance lifted her, and he took her hips in powerful hands to anchor her in place for his plundering. Their bodies, drenched with moisture, slid against each other like wet silk, driving them wild. He slowed his thrusts deliberately to draw out the loving. Then he told her in that dangerous, deep voice all the things he was going to do to her that night, when they went to bed.

Ted Barlow decided to take his snowmobile with him on his drive north. Pulling a trailer would slow him down and even add to the hazard of driving, but he had a gut feeling it would come in very handy if the roads to the property had not been plowed out.

Trevor was on the telephone to his mother. He was about to tell her that Eve was missing, but he detected such a plaintive note in her voice, that he hesitated. "Are you all right?" he asked anxiously.

"Oh, I'll be all right, Trevor. Don't worry about me being here alone — I'm used to it. Just so long as you're enjoying your Christmas; that's all that matters to me, dear."

Trevor was covered with guilt. He was torn between conflicting duties, as usual. Being in the middle was so unfair. He had given up his date with Eve last night to stay at his mother's. Thank heavens her illness had turned out to be merely indigestion. In retrospect, things had worked out for the best, because Eve apparently wasn't here anyway.

She had a tendency to be willful and impulsive and as a result had gone dashing off to show a property a hundred miles away. She certainly wouldn't appreciate his rushing after her. Eve Barlow had a mind

99

of her own. That's what attracted him, however. His mother was so clinging, he only sought out independent females.

Trevor glanced through the window and saw Ted Barlow hook up his trailer and snowmobile. God, the man was so gung-ho! He'd flown rescue missions during the Korean War and had obviously bought into the hero syndrome. Now he was off on a wild goose chase that would physically exhaust a much younger man. Into the phone he said, "You sound like you need my company, Mother. I'll be there in about an hour."

Trevor went outside and stood beside Susan Barlow. "My mother's not very well."

"Oh, Trevor, I'm so sorry."

Ted rolled down the van window and said to Trevor, "Are you coming?"

Susan spoke up quickly. "His mother is ill. He has to go to Kalamazoo, honey."

"Oh, sorry. Susie, I'll call the minute I have news. Try not to worry, love."

She waved until he was out of sight. "I'll call you right away, if there's any news, Trevor."

He took her small hand in his. "Thanks, Mrs. Barlow. I'm so sorry about all the food you cooked."

"Don't give it a second thought. The people we love come first."

For the most part the highways had been

plowed up as far as Ludington. It took Ted Barlow over three hours to cover the hundred miles. Everything was closed for Christmas Day, even the gas stations; it was a good thing he carried extra cans in the van.

The highway ended north of Ludington where the forests began. Ted located a State Troopers' Headquarters and explained the situation. They told him they had been in constant communication with the Department of Highways, who'd had their plows out since the blizzard began, as well as Michigan Power who had their linemen on overtime.

Ted Barlow showed them a sketch he'd made of Judy's property.

"Back on the twenty-third, traffic was still going in and out of that particular area until late afternoon. After that, anything that went in didn't come out."

They put in a call to the Department of Highways to see when the lakeshore road leading to this property would be plowed out, and then sipped coffee and waited for the information to be relayed to them.

It occurred to Ted Barlow that he should take advantage of a telephone while there was one available. He asked the clerk for a phone directory and began calling hospitals. None of them had admitted a young woman by the name of Eve Barlow. That

101

was good, he told himself, that was very good news indeed.

The State Troopers' office checked over all the accident reports filed in the area since the twenty-third of December. Ted cursed himself for not finding out what Clint Kelly was driving, but at least neither the name Kelly nor the name Barlow showed up in any of the reports. Ted was an optimist and honestly believed his daughter and her client were holed up at the property, safe and sound. They had simply been snowed in and knew they wouldn't get out until the roads were cleared. The alternative was unthinkable.

Finally a report came in from the Department of Highways. Though they would be working all night, they wouldn't get to isolated roads until morning. It was strictly a matter of priorities. Ted Barlow was faced with two choices. He could stay at the troopers' headquarters tonight and follow the first plow in the morning, or he could head out on his snowmobile.

It was one of the easiest decisions he'd ever made. He took an extra gas can from the van and put it under the seat of the snowmobile in the storage compartment. A State Trooper tried to talk him out of it, but realized if his own daughter were missing, he'd do exactly the same thing.

Ted changed into his snowmobile suit,

then put on his goggles and heavy leather gauntlets. The visibility was good, but his progress was slower than usual. A snowmobile was at its peak performance on fresh powder or when a crust of ice had formed on top of the snow. Today, the sun had produced a partial thaw and as a result, the snow was wet and heavy.

He kept his goal foremost in his mind, telling himself over and over that it was less than twenty miles. When his snowmobile hit a particularly slushy patch and bogged down, he got off the machine and dug it out with his hands.

He shook his head and chuckled at the irony. His son couldn't come home this Christmas. Steven was halfway around the world in a new posting at Camp Page in South Korea. Although there was no war, he flew jets very close to the border of the unpredictable North Koreans. Up until today, Ted's thoughts had been preoccupied with the danger his son might be in this Christmas season, so far away from his family and his country. Then, wouldn't you know it? It was Eve, who lived in little old Grand Rapids, a place renowned for its safety and security, who was missing!

Ted offered up a prayer for both of his children as he restarted the stalled machine and set off again with renewed determination.

Eve yawned as she sat before the fire. She was so relaxed after the sauna and Clint's lovemaking, she couldn't lift a finger, and what was more, she didn't wish to. *It should be against the law to feel this content,* she thought. Eve had never been cut off from the world before; it certainly had its advantages.

Although she hadn't been too keenly aware of it before, now she realized she'd been on edge lately. The stress of city living and constantly competing in a man's world had made her uptight. Now she felt at peace with herself; she felt happy.

Clint stood gazing out the window. He realized their idyll would soon be over. It hadn't snowed all day, and by tomorrow at the latest, the roads would likely be plowed out and they would be connected with civilization again.

His gaze travelled possessively over the landscape. He felt elated that it would soon be his. No matter the asking price, he had decided this property would belong to him. He had discovered something precious here — a peace and quiet that had a healing quality about it. He loved his job and would have no other, but it was said that the constant flow of adrenaline brought on by danger was addictive.

After fighting a great conflagration, when

he had beaten it and knew his men were safe, he felt totally drained. This house, this land not only cleansed him, it renewed his vitality and filled him with strength and power. The woman in the room with him had a similar effect. She filled him with a glorious feeling of omnipotence.

Clint wondered why he was so pensive. He had just found his dream home — why wasn't he dancing an Irish jig? The answer was simple; his heart was sinking because there was a piece missing from his happy picture. At the moment everything was perfect, but once Eve departed and took up her life where it had left off, there would be a hole in his future existence.

He didn't want their time together to end.

He didn't want to let her go!

Clint turned from the window. His face softened as he watched her sitting curled up, dreaming and drowsing before the fire.

"I love this place . . . share it with me, Evie."

Eight

*E*ve's lashes flew up. The magic spell was broken. Their idyll was over. He'd said the words that rang the death knell to their intimate interlude. Reality suddenly raised its unwelcome head and rushed in upon her.

She leapt off the couch and took two steps toward him. By that time, Clint had reached her. She raised her fingers to his lips as if to stay his words, but of course it was too late. They had been uttered and could not be recalled.

Eve agonized over her reply. The last thing on earth she wanted to do was hurt this man who had saved her life, fed her, warmed her, and loved her. She had to find the right words. Guilt assailed her from all sides. Not guilt over what they had done — she would never feel even the smallest pang for that, nor one tiny shred of regret. But guilt because she had somehow conveyed the possibility that what they had shared could go beyond this time, beyond this place.

And terrible guilt toward Trevor. She had betrayed his trust and in doing so had discovered another man who eclipsed him

106

in her eyes. What made it worse, unforgivable almost, was the undeniable fact that the things she found irresistible were Kelly's dominance, macho attitude, and strength. Poor Trevor with his gentleness, kindness, and understanding came off a poor second.

Clint watched the play of emotions cross her lovely features, one after another. He had known from the outset that this woman was committed to another, yet he had deliberately set out to seduce her. To him she had been fair game. He was a man, she was a woman; they were alone together. To a male predator, that was all that counted.

She had been a great challenge to him, with her feminist attitudes. Then Providence had tipped the scales in his favor. By almost drowning, she had become completely vulnerable. Then he was able to shine at all the things he did best. But, underneath her polished veneer, he had found trust, generosity, and an innocence that captured his heart.

At first, he had thought, if he couldn't steal this female from a passive professor of English who spouted poetry, he wasn't worth his salt as a red-blooded American male. But the seduction had backfired. Once he stole her, he wanted to keep her.

Eve took a tremulous breath. "Clint . . . I can't," she said softly.

His face seemed to harden.

"You have such formidable attributes, Clint. I'm attracted to everything about you. I'm racked with guilt, but I could never leave Trevor."

Clint's bright blue eyes took on the cold gray of Lake Michigan.

"Trevor is such a fine person, so completely understanding and sensitive. I can't just leave him and come to you. I couldn't be that cruel!"

"You don't think you're capable of cruelty?" he asked drily.

She tried desperately to make him understand. "We have an understanding, a commitment. God help me, Clint, I can't walk out on him. I have too much compassion for that."

Clint was acutely aware that she made no protestations of love.

Eve avoided speaking of love; did not dare even think of love. It would open a door she wished to keep firmly closed. Her gaze slipped from his hard mouth to his powerful shoulders, then down to his big, calloused hands. *He's so tough, I bet he's never cried in his life.*

"Clint, you do understand?" she agonized.

"No." Silence filled the room and stretched to the breaking point. "I've asked you once. I won't beg," he said quietly.

Both their heads turned at the same time

as they heard a noise.

"That's some sort of machine. Is it a plow?" she asked.

Clint went to look out the window. "I don't think so. The sound of the motor is too high-pitched." He went to the door and opened it. "It's a snowmobile," he said over his shoulder. "We have company."

Eve peeped out from behind Clint, not wanting anyone to get a clear view of her in the red longjohns. "It's my father!" she cried.

Removing his boots and snowmobile suit, Ted Barlow began to joke. "Since you didn't show up for Christmas, the mountain decided to come to Mohammed."

"Oh, Dad!" She threw her arms around him, knowing how worried he must have been, and how he must have struggled for hours to get to her. His wisecracks camouflaged his enormous relief.

Still holding her hands in his, he held her away from him and looked askance at her red suit. "Did you mug Santa?"

"Dad, this is Clint Kelly, who intends to buy the house; Clint, this is Ted Barlow."

The men shook hands, assessing each other in the first thirty seconds. Both liked what they saw. Ted realized Clint had given the shirt off his back to his daughter and he wondered what had happened to her clothes.

"We wouldn't have been snowed in if it hadn't been for my stupidity. We were out on the property Thursday afternoon, just before it got dark, when I walked straight onto the pond and went through the ice."

"Is the pond deep?" Ted asked.

"About fifteen feet. I almost drowned, but Clint saved my life!"

Ted looked from one to the other. "How did you manage to rescue her?"

"With a rope and a ladder. I'm a fire-fighter; I know rescue techniques."

"Thank God you were with her."

"He didn't just rescue me from the pond. I was unconscious from the cold water. He revived me and spent the rest of the night chopping wood for the fire."

Ted's eyes showed his admiration. They all moved to the fireplace and sat down to recount the rest of what happened.

"Was there stuff here to eat?" Ted inquired.

"No. Clint hunted for food. I've dined like a queen on venison and pheasant — oh, and walleye . . . he fished, too!"

"Walleye? Lord, I haven't had a feed of walleye in a donkey's age. My mouth is watering."

"There's probably some out there on my stringer now. I'll go take a look." Clint knew father and daughter might want a private conversation. He put on his jacket and disappeared through the door.

When they were alone, Eve's father asked, "Are you okay, honey? You weren't afraid of this guy, were you?"

"No, I wasn't afraid of him. At first we rubbed each other the wrong way. He wanted Maxwell to show him the property, hated like hell having a woman agent. I didn't like him any better. He was so damn macho, I called him Action Man. But Dad, when I got into trouble, he really came through for me. I stopped laughing at his muscles when he used them to save us."

Ted observed her closely, wondering what had gone on between them. A man and woman isolated together for days was tempting, intimate, even romantic. He didn't ask; it was none of his business, and he wouldn't be upset if Eve did form a romantic attachment to someone like Clint Kelly.

"I'm sorry I couldn't call you. The telephone service has been temporarily discontinued. Even the electricity is off. Clint siphoned gas from his truck to run the generator, but we've had to ration it." She asked the question uppermost in her mind. "Did I really upset Mom?"

"She was worried, but she hides it real well. She's had a lot of practice with some of my hare-brained adventures, and Steven's."

111

"How did you find me?"

"Well, Trevor arrived without you this morning, so we drove back to your place and when your car wasn't there, I went to your office. Then I called Max and told him your Mercedes was still at work. He told me the last time he saw you, you were driving up here to show this guy the property. I phoned Judy to get directions, and here I am!"

"I ruined your Christmas."

"Like hell you did! Instead of sitting around eating my head off and being a couch potato in front of the television set, I had a great snowmobile adventure! And the best part is, it had a happy ending . . . I found you safe and sound."

Eve grinned at her father. "Actually, it was a great adventure for me, too. Don't breathe it to a soul, especially Trevor, but I wouldn't have missed it for the world. I learned so many survival techniques." Eve blushed because of the other techniques she'd learned.

"Trevor didn't come because his mother was ill. But he was reluctant anyway. Some bull about you not appreciating him running after you. Is he afraid of you, Eve?"

She smiled. "Aren't most men afraid of women when it comes right down to it?"

"Most," he acknowledged, "but not all." He winked at her. "Action Man doesn't look like he'd intimidate easily."

Clint returned with five beautiful wall-eyes. Ted couldn't believe their size.

"It won't take me long to clean them and we can cook them on the fire," Clint offered. "You probably haven't eaten since breakfast."

"That's too tempting to refuse," Ted admitted.

Eve wondered why everything her father said made her want to blush. "We had pheasant for our Christmas dinner, but I made such a pig of myself, there's none left."

Clint glanced at Ted. "She was entitled; she not only cooked it, she plucked and cleaned it first."

"You must have taken Trevor's course in how to get in touch with your feminine side," Ted wisecracked.

Clint was amused; Eve was not.

Her father relished the fresh-caught fish. Clint sat down with him and devoured a whole one himself. Eve was amazed at Clint's hearty appetite. She wouldn't be able to manage another mouthful of food until tomorrow.

"How close did you get with your car?" Clint asked.

"Less than twenty miles. Only took me about an hour. I stopped at the State Troopers Headquarters and they checked on all the accident reports for this area and the Department of Highways to see what had been cleared out. The plows won't be on this road until tomorrow. There aren't many residents at the lake this time of year, so it's a matter of priorities."

"The first thing I'd better get is a plow blade for the front of my truck," Clint decided.

"Well, I hate to eat and run, but we'd better get started. It'll take us an hour to get to the van and three hours from Ludington to Grand Rapids."

"I have no clothes! My winter coat is at the bottom of the pond, and my wool suit is shrunk beyond recognition."

"Take my jacket; I'm not going anywhere until tomorrow. I have no gasoline anyway."

"I have an idea. We'll leave your jacket at the troopers' office. I'll even give you enough gas to get there in the morning," Ted offered.

A worried frown creased Clint's brow as he handed Eve his coat. "On a snowmobile your legs will freeze!"

"I'll wrap towels around them and I'll take one of the blankets, too," Eve decided.

Ted donned his snowmobile suit and pulled on his boots.

"Don't forget my briefcase."

"Your case will fit in the storage under the seat, after I remove the extra gas tank.

I'll just fill up, and you can have what's left, Clint." He held out his hand. "I don't know how to thank you for what you did. Everyone thinks Eve can take care of herself, but her old dad knows better."

Alone, she and Clint faced each other. Eve Barlow's sophistication had gone the way of the Alfred Sung suit. She gave him back his blue shirt in exchange for the down jacket. She looked a fright wrapped in the blanket and towels.

Clint reached for his belt. "Why don't you wear my jeans —"

She held up her hand. "Keep your pants on, Action Man." She tried not to let the sound of tears show in her voice.

"It's a bit late for that, Evie."

She burst into laughter. It kept the tears at bay. She wanted him to hold her. *If only things were different,* she thought. "I'll put in your offer first thing in the morning and be in touch as soon as I have something."

He nodded and watched her go out the door. Once she was a safe distance away, she turned to wave. "It was the best Christmas Eve I ever had," she called impulsively.

She watched him cup his hands around his mouth to call back, but the noise of the snowmobile drowned it out.

"Hang on tight — this is going to be a bumpy ride!"

Eve smiled as she put her arms around her dad. The old Bette Davis line dated him. She suddenly realized he must be close to fifty, yet his vigour belied his age. She pressed her cheek against his back. Not only did it shelter her from the cold wind, it made her realize how safe she felt with this man in control. She tried not to think of Clint Kelly. It was no good longing for what could not be. She had lived the fantasy, but now it was time to leave it behind.

Ted was making much better time on the trip back. The sun had disappeared early, as the afternoon advanced. Because the temperature had dropped, the snow was no longer mushy, and had a fine coat of ice on its surface.

In less than an hour they reached the State Troopers' Headquarters. Eve refused to go inside. "It's Christmas, not Halloween," she protested.

"Okay, I'll turn on the heater in the van. You can give me Clint's jacket and put on my snowmobile suit. It'll be too warm to keep it on while I'm driving. I'll call your mom. Are you sure you won't come in and talk to her? These guys probably haven't had a good laugh all Christmas!"

"Just tell her I love her, and ask her to call Trevor for me." Designer clothes were no longer quite as important to Eve, but she'd be damned if she'd let a bunch of macho officers see her in red longjohns!

When she removed Clint's jacket, she experienced a sense of loss — not just the warmth, but a loss of security. And something else, harder to define: an invisible link that connected them. Eve was brought out of her pensive mood when Ted opened the van door and climbed in. "Your mom was so relieved about both of us. Imagine worrying about me!" But Eve could tell he was delighted with his wife's response.

"I promised her I'd drive slowly and told her not to expect us until after nine. She's going to call Trevor and tell him we'll celebrate our Christmas tomorrow."

On the drive home they sang carols and Eve was amazed that her father knew all the words to the parodies of Christmas songs that were currently popular. They were also extremely irreverent, but men get a kick out of being irreverent in these times of political correctness.

When they finally turned down their street, Susan had all the Christmas lights blazing. "Poor Mom — she's had such a lonely day."

Ted looked up at the lights as he turned off the engine. "She's always been my beacon."

Eve's memory stirred faintly as she remembered them kissing beneath the mistletoe. It was a shining strand, a thread, ephemeral as a dream. "You're still in love, after all these years."

"Passionately," Ted said, watching his beautiful wife fling open the front door and run down the steps to welcome them home.

The first thing Eve did was telephone Trevor. "Hi! I'm so sorry about all this. I guess my mother explained I was snowed in at a country property I was trying to sell."

"Eve, you know there's no need to apologize to me. These things happen. I understand, just as you would have understood when I couldn't take you dancing the other night."

When Eve realized he hadn't shown up either, she suddenly felt a little less guilty. But only a little!

"I knew there was a logical explanation for your absence, and I knew you would be perfectly all right."

But I wasn't all right, Eve thought. *Aren't you even going to ask me about the man I spent the last three days with?*

"Things usually have a way of working themselves out for the best. My mother needed company over the holiday. It's lonely being a widow. We'll celebrate our Christmas tomorrow."

"That'll be lovely, Trevor. I hope we don't get any more snow. Drive carefully from Kalamazoo. I'll see you around noon."

"Good night Eve. I can't wait until you

open your present!"

After she hung up, she stood with her hand on the phone. Surely he was the most understanding man in the whole world. Apparently she wasn't going to get the third degree. Trevor would never display childish jealousy. He was a mature adult.

Susan made them turkey sandwiches and hot chocolate. Eve nibbled on homemade shortbread and Christmas cake soaked in rum while she told her mother about the incredible things that had happened over the last three days. "Can I stay here tonight?"

"As if you need to ask! It'll be fun to have you sleep over," her mother said, delighted to have her baby under her roof again.

"I need a warm bath, and I really need to wash my hair."

"Didn't you have water to bathe?"

"We had water, but it wasn't warm. We had to take cold showers."

"I'll get you a warm robe and some slippers," Susan said, running upstairs. Eve followed her, but she was too tired to run.

When Susan came downstairs, she put her arms around Ted. "Thanks for going all that way and bringing her home."

"You should have seen this Clint Kelly she spent the last three days with. Muscles, shoulders, a real lady-killer. She calls him Action Man. Well, you heard what she said."

"What?" Susan asked.

"They had to take cold showers!"

"Oh, you!" Susan gave him a punch.

Nine

*E*ve slipped down in the warm water and sighed with pure pleasure. How good the simple things of life feel when you've been deprived of them!

She tried not to analyze the conversation she'd had with Trevor, or her reaction to his attitude. They had been dating steadily for over a year and she had spent a lot of that time asserting her independence, so that they didn't live in each other's pocket. Now, she felt neglected. What a perverse creature she was!

It would be simply awful if the man she was about to become engaged to flew into a jealous rage and demanded she tell him everything. And the truth was, he had lots to be jealous about! Eve blushed, and slid further down in the warm, scented water.

Though she was tired, her body felt good. A bath was a sensual experience when you relaxed. Her thoughts drifted inexorably toward Clint Kelly. Fancifully, she decided a bathroom was the most private place in a house. You always locked the door so that no one could intrude, then you removed your clothes and were free to indulge in your most intimate thoughts.

Eve leaned her head back, closed her eyes, and allowed herself to re-live every moment she'd spent with Kelly. Every look, every word, every smile, every touch, every kiss, every act . . . every climax!

As the water grew cold, thoughts of Trevor intruded. His last words repeated themselves in her mind: *I can't wait until you open your present!* Resolutely, she pushed those words away and climbed from the tub. She'd feel differently tomorrow. A new chapter of her life would begin. She would close the door on her past and open up another to the future. She knew she should count her blessings.

Sunday dawned dull and overcast. The temperature rose, and by the time the Barlows finished breakfast, all the white snow had turned to gray slush.

Still in robe and slippers, Eve opened her briefcase and took out the Offer to Purchase, then she telephoned Judy.

"Hello, Eve? How dare you get yourself into a scrape without me?"

"You don't know the half of it. I'll fill you in on the details someday when you have a few hours to kill."

"How in the world did you manage up there without food, heat, electricity, or telephone? I suppose getting snowed in put an end to any hope of selling the white elephant?"

"Judy, it's not a white elephant. It's a valuable piece of real estate. I'd buy it myself, if I could afford it."

"Come on, Eve, you're a city girl, like me. Watching trees grow can't be your idea of fun."

Judy was in the marketing department at one of Detroit's largest auto makers, and Eve knew she hadn't visited her late parents' property in about two years.

"Judy, I have an offer for you."

"You're kidding! What the hell did you have to do to get it?"

Eve blushed. "Mr. Kelly is offering a hundred and seventy-five thousand. I'll fax it to you in about an hour." A slight pause on the other end of the phone prompted Eve to be scrupulously honest. "Kelly is a stubborn negotiator, but I really believe he'll go to two hundred thousand if you turn down this offer."

"Turn it down? Eve, bite your tongue. I accept the offer. Fax it to me right away so I can sign it before he changes his mind."

"He won't change his mind, Judy. He genuinely loves the place, and the house and property seem to have accepted him. He's a real outdoorsman; scuba dives and all that."

"He sounds like a hunk."

"He is, but he's also a male chauvinist."

Judy sighed. "In my experience you can't have it both ways. If they're hunks, they're chauvinistic; if they accept you as an equal, they're either wimps or they're gay!"

"Fax me a closing date. I have a check here for you. If it's a done deal and the weather cooperates, I could drive to Detroit Tuesday or Wednesday."

"Why don't I meet you halfway and we could have lunch together?"

"Wonderful idea. There's this terrific restaurant I know in Lansing. Mountain Jacks-Okemos on Grand River Avenue; they specialize in seafood or prime rib. I remember that used to be your favorite."

"Still is, to which my hips will grandly attest!"

"Well, this is great. I can't wait to see you. I'll call and let you know which day."

"Okay. Thanks a million, Eve. I appreciate it."

"Hey, it's my job, for which I am well paid."

Eve went into the kitchen where her mother was already working on their Christmas feast. "Mom, will you lend me a pair of slacks? I have to drive to my place to pick up your Christmas presents and put on something glamorous for Trevor."

Ted took out his keys. "Do you want to take the van, or do you just want me to drive you to your car?"

"If you don't mind going out, I'd rather you took me to my car. Leaving a Mercedes just sitting there is asking for it to be stolen."

Eve faxed Judy the Offer to Purchase before she changed her clothes. Back in her own bedroom, she found herself before the mirror exactly as she had been the last time she was in this room. "Not exactly," she said to her reflection. She no longer needed to ask if she was beautiful or sexy. She knew she was both. Clint Kelly had convinced her of that.

She went to her closet and moved aside a red dress. After the red suit, followed by the red longjohns, she was ready for a change. She looked at the lavender; her favorite color, both because it enhanced her pale hair and because she thought it lucky. However, it wasn't exactly a Christmas color, so she decided on the avocado green silk with matching suede belt and shoes.

Eve unlocked the top drawer of her desk and took out the envelope that held her Christmas gift to her mother and father. Trevor's gift wouldn't be so easy to carry. She got out her luggage carrier and loaded the carton onto it. It wasn't really all that large, just heavy.

Eve heard her fax machine and was surprised at the speed Judy had returned the signed Offer to Purchase. The closing date she suggested was thirty days, or sooner, if it suited the client. Eve knew Clint Kelly would be thrilled. How she would love to hand him the acceptance and watch the grin spread across his face. But that was out of the question. She mustn't see him again, if it was at all possible. They had made a clean break, and that's the way she had to keep it.

She would send all the papers by courier, then his lawyer could collect the check and the signed documents. She glanced at her watch. Kelly couldn't possibly be back yet. This was a good time to call and leave a message. She dialed the number. Her stomach lurched as she heard his deep voice.

"You've got my machine, so talk at it."

"It's Eve Barlow, calling Sunday the twenty-sixth. Your offer has been accepted with a thirty-day closing date, or sooner, if you can arrange the money. I'll send the documents over by courier. Congratulations!"

When she hung up, her hands were shaking and her mouth had gone dry. What the devil was the matter with her? She was behaving like an adolescent with her first crush. She admonished herself sternly to pull herself together. Today would probably be one of the most significant days of her life. It was a special day for Trevor as well, and she had to be very careful not to spoil it in any way. Trevor was a sensitive man who could pick up on her vibrations, so she had to make sure they were happy ones.

Eve threw on her coat, picked up her briefcase, and pulling the luggage carrier behind her, took the apartment elevator to the ground floor. She was relieved that she arrived back at her parents' house before Trevor got there. Her mother warned her, "Don't go in the family room. Your dad's setting up your Christmas present."

Eve was mystified about what it could be.

"That's a beautiful dress, dear."

"Thank you," Eve said, rubbing her hands over her hips. "I love the way it feels."

The doorbell chimed.

"Oh Lord, he's here," Eve murmured. "Don't tell me it's already noon."

Trevor came in bearing gifts. He gave Susan a huge poinsettia and when Ted slipped in from the family room to greet him, Trevor handed him a bottle of imported sake.

"Thanks! I haven't tasted this stuff in years."

Eve smiled at Trevor. He'd put a lot of thought in the bottle he'd selected for her dad. "How's your mother?" she asked, taking his coat.

"Much better. She'll be just fine."

"Shoo," Susan said. "If everyone stays out

of the kitchen, I'll have dinner ready in an hour."

Eve and Trevor moved toward the living room and Ted began to follow them.

"Not you, dear," Susan called after him. "I need your help."

Trevor caught Eve's hand and pulled her beneath the mistletoe. He kissed her gently and, after a brief hesitation, she kissed him back. "You look lovely," he told her. "Would you look at this tree — it must have cost a fortune." He sounded as if he didn't quite approve of spending so much money on something that was simply for decoration. When they sat down on the couch, he asked, "How did you make out up north?"

For a moment, Eve stared at him, not knowing exactly what he was asking. She colored slightly, before the penny dropped into the slot. "Oh, I sold it."

"Good for you," he said, patting her knee with his smooth white hand. "You have to forgive your dad. He's from a generation that doesn't realize a woman can do any-thing a man can do."

But a woman can't do all the things a man can do, Eve protested, silently. She had been prepared to tell him about the fright-ening pond episode, but suddenly decided against it. If she admitted to fear and help-lessness, it would negate her equality, and she would seem diminished in his eyes. At least she suspected she would. It was all very well to claim equality on an intellectual level, she thought, but the reality was that on a physical level, comparing strength and endurance, a man was superior to a woman, or he should be.

Eve changed the subject so that the conversation focused on Trevor. A few months back he had been passed over at the university for Head of Department. It had been a bitter pill, but with Eve's support, he had gotten over the disappointment.

He told her there were rumors flying all over the campus that the professor who had been promoted over him was proving unsatisfactory. Everyone in the English Department was grumbling over one thing or another.

Eve gave him all her attention and sympathy, but she couldn't help wondering if this was what the rest of her life would be like — politely listening while Trevor catalogued his grievances. *Stop being a bitch!* she told herself. Trevor had been devastated when he was passed over. He was a sensitive man who craved approval and affirmation, and up until now she had been happy to oblige.

Eve was relieved when dinner was ready and they joined her parents for the festive meal. The table was a work of art. Her mother was an accomplished hostess and a gourmet cook. There was turkey with chestnut dressing and giblet gravy, as well as a whole glazed ham patterned with cherries and cloves. The vegetable dishes were culinary delights. Mushrooms with almonds and shallots sat beside cinnamon yams, tender steamed leeks, and balsamic-glazed pearl onions. Baby brussels sprouts sat on a bed of wild rice, and a whole squash had been stuffed with gingered pork.

Susan's homemade pickles included walnuts, olives, and dills, and she had combined cranberries with orange peel for a sauce that was piquant in taste and aroma. Ted opened both red and white wine so they could have their choice. They drank to Steven's health, toasting him across the world.

When the dinner was over, none of them had room for dessert, so they decided to have it later, after they had opened their gifts. They moved into the family room and Eve saw her Christmas present immediately.

"Oh my gosh!" she exclaimed with genuine surprise. "When I mentioned I needed a treadmill to keep in shape, I never expected you would actually buy me one! Thank you both, so much."

Ted showed her the different speeds and

how to preset a program with the multi-window electronics. He also demonstrated it, then Eve tried it out and so did Trevor, who seemed as pleased with the useful gift as she was.

Eve opened her purse and handed her mother the envelope. Susan opened it and cried out with delight. "Oh, honey, you shouldn't have. Ted, it's cruise tickets! We fly to Tampa, then sail ten days in the Caribbean. We visit Martinique, Barbados, Antigua, St. Maarten, St. Thomas, and San Juan. I can't believe it!"

"Well, I'm ready for a second honeymoon; when can we leave?" Ted teased.

Eve was filled with so much warmth, her heart overflowed. Her parents usually went to Florida or Arizona for a month in the wintertime, but they'd never been on a cruise.

Susan made Ted dig out the Atlas so they could see the route the cruise ship would take. Trevor presented each of them with an identically wrapped gift and sat back to watch as they were opened. He hadn't really approved of Eve spending so much money on her parents, but what could he say? She earned the money and was free to spend it any way she chose. He had not protested because he avoided confrontations at all costs.

Susan and Ted unwrapped them at the

same time. They were monogrammed passport holders. "Thank you so much, Trevor. I guess you knew about the cruise tickets."

Ted handed Trevor the present Susan had picked out for him, with their daughter's advice. Trevor was delighted with the pair of brass book ends, declaring they were exactly what he needed. When he opened Eve's gift, a great lump came into his throat. It was a leather-bound collection of the complete works of Shakespeare. He'd coveted books like this since he was a boy.

Eve watched Trevor's hand caress the volumes with reverence. She preferred Dickens, but Trevor lusted for Shakespeare, and when she saw how he treasured the books, she was glad she had ordered them all those months ago.

The afternoon light was gone from the sky; it looked as if they were in for another snowstorm. Ted turned on all the lights in keeping with the cheery holiday atmosphere. "Let's have that dessert now, Susie," Ted suggested.

Trevor was just as happy to wait a little while longer before he gave Eve her present. A little suspense was good before a dramatic moment. Rather like a play, he thought fancifully. Trevor winked at Eve and whispered, "They say anticipation is the best part."

Don't you believe it. Clint Kelly's words

slipped into her mind with amazing facility. Eve forced her memories away from Kelly to focus on her mother's delicious desserts — rum pecan pie, lemon cheesecake, and traditional mince pie.

As Eve forked the last mouthful of lemon cheesecake, she sighed, "I'm surely going to need that treadmill after today."

Trevor helped himself to another piece of mince pie. "These are even better than my mother's."

Ted could not resist trying everything Susan had baked. "The woman is a temptress."

"Well, the way to your heart is certainly through your stomach. Help me load these in the dishwasher. Trevor would probably like to give Eve her gift in private."

Ted's eyes met Eve's. She wanted to cry, *Don't leave me!* Ted looked mutinous, as if he didn't want to leave his daughter with this man, but he rose reluctantly and carried out the plates.

As Eve watched Trevor take a small wrapped gift from his pocket, his movements seemed to distort into slow motion. Eve experienced a moment of sheer panic. She jumped up quickly and babbled, "I'll be right back. I have to go to the powder room. I don't want to spoil this moment for you."

Eve locked the bathroom door and leaned

back against it. She had had to get out of the room; she had felt it closing in on her. She was so tense, her stomach muscles were in knots. *Dear Lord in Heaven, what am I going to do?*

The answer came back clearly, *Pull yourself together and get back out there. You cannot spoil this man's precious moment for him.* She did not dare look at herself in the mirror. She turned on the tap and let cold water run over her wrists, then she splashed her flushed cheeks until they felt cooler. She had let this thing go too far to draw back now. She straightened her shoulders. She would not allow a brief infatuation ruin her future plans. She took a deep breath and unlocked the bathroom door.

As Trevor handed her the gift, she gave him a tremulous smile. She removed the silver ribbon and wrapping paper with steady hands, but when they held the velvet jeweler's box, they began to tremble. With an iron resolve she pushed away a feeling of dread. She opened the box and stared down at a pair of diamond earrings!

Ten

*E*ve looked up at Trevor in disbelief, then her gaze dropped to the small velvet box to make sure her imagination wasn't playing a trick on her.

"You look so stunned, Eve. I thought you guessed I was buying you diamonds."

"Diamonds did cross my mind," she admitted in a faraway voice. A small ripple of relief began inside her that spread through her veins. By the time it reached her brain, it was a tidal wave! Trevor was not giving her an engagement ring. This man was not asking her to marry him!

"Trevor, I don't think I can accept these."

He looked a little sheepish. "They are sort of a bribe, or I suppose a more correct word might be *incentive*. I think it's time we started living together, Eve. If we can do that successfully, then I would have no hesitation about getting married down the road."

"Down the road?" she repeated vaguely.

"Perhaps next Christmas. It's time we started thinking about a permanent commitment."

"Next Christmas?" She felt like a parrot.

"It's economically unwise for us to pay rent on two apartments when we could share one. The only thing is, I've been considering living in Kalamazoo, where I work, and where my mother lives. Of course, I understand this will be a big decision for you, and want to give you plenty of time to think about it."

Eve's eyes made direct contact with Trevor's. She took a deep breath. "You're right. This is a big decision. I don't know if I can accept what you're offering me, Trevor, though it's an honor to be asked." She smiled feebly. *At least you believe you're honoring me, you poor deluded man,* she added silently.

Ted Barlow walked in on them. "Sorry to intrude, but there's a weather advisory on TV. We're in for a severe ice storm. Perhaps you'd better get cracking, unless you're going to stay put for the night."

"Oh, no, I have to get home — I have work to do," Eve said quickly. "I'll leave my car, though; Trevor will drive me." She showed her parents the diamond earrings, which they admired thoroughly. At the same time Ted and Susan exchanged glances and raised their eyebrows. Both of them had expected Trevor to present Eve with an engagement ring. Ted was relieved; Susan only wanted what Eve wanted.

They all said their goodbyes and thanked

each other again for the Christmas gifts and Susan's marvelous dinner.

"Mom, I want all your recipes. Do you have one for coconut cream pie?"

"You're going to start cooking?" her father asked with a frown. Perhaps these two were going to move in together after all.

"A New Year's resolution," Eve replied.

On the drive to her apartment, Eve was strangely silent. The rain, which was rapidly turning to ice, was coming down pretty heavily and Trevor had to keep his mind on his driving. She knew when they got to her place, he would take it for granted that he could spend the night. Eve knew she had to speak up before he parked and turned off the engine.

She turned to look at him. "Trevor, I don't want you to spend the night at my place." It was brutally blunt. She softened it a little. "You've given me a lot to think about and I have some decisions to make. I need to be alone."

Trevor's mouth turned sulky, but after a minute he said, "I understand. Take all the time you need."

"Thank you. Good night, Trevor." The kiss she gave him was a generous one. It was probably the last kiss they would ever share.

"I'll call you tomorrow," he said.

"I'm going to the office, so call me tomorrow night."

Once Eve was safely inside her own apartment, she pushed the deadlock bolt on the door and let the second wave of relief wash over her. She felt free, like a bird escaped from its cage. Perhaps the cage had been safe and sensible, but it had come to her in a flash that she hated safe and sensible!

She threw off her coat and shoes and danced about the room. She had no plans for the future, but she was very sure of one thing: that future did not include Trevor Bennett. She sat down at her desk and began preparing the papers that Clint Kelly would need to sign, about a dozen in all. There would be more later, on closing. She then prepared a list of costs and adjustments regarding paid-up taxes, settlement and transfer charges, and brokerage fees.

Eve then called the courier service and was surprised when they arrived for the pick-up within thirty minutes. She gave the young man a generous tip because it was Boxing Day, because the weather was appalling, and because she felt benevolent toward everyone on earth tonight!

As she climbed into bed, she realized it had been an emotional day — emotionally exhausting, then emotionally exhilarating. Her mind flitted about like a butterfly, momentarily touching one thing, then off to another. But always, it came back to Clint Kelly. Thoughts of him clung to her; he was completely unforgettable.

As she drifted off to sleep, she heard a far-off fire siren and she knew she would never hear that sound for the rest of her life without thinking of him.

The following morning, Eve took a cab to the office. The streets were extremely icy, but the sky looked clear. Only a couple of agents showed up and it was quiet enough that she got caught up on all her paper-work. Eve felt restless, so at lunchtime, she took a cab to her parents' place so she could pick up her car.

Her mother insisted she stay for lunch, and her dad turned off the one o'clock news on television so he could join them in the kitchen. "Fire last night," he informed them.

"I heard the siren. What was it?" Eve asked.

"Industrial warehouse across the city."

"Eve, your dad and I were convinced Trevor was going to give you a ring for Christmas."

Eve shook out a napkin and sat down at the counter. "To be honest, so did I. When I opened that velvet box and saw diamond earrings instead of a diamond ring, I couldn't believe my eyes!"

"Were you terribly disappointed, dear?" her mother asked gently.

"No! It sounds awful, but I was relieved. Trevor isn't right for me, and what's more, I'm not right for him either. I feel wretched that it took me this long to realize it."

"I've always known he wasn't right for you," Ted insisted.

Eve gave her dad a curious look. "You never said anything."

"Your mother wouldn't let me!"

Eve gave him a skeptical look. "Right. As if that would stop you."

"It's true. She insisted I trust you to make the right decision."

"Why, thank you . . . both of you. I had no idea you didn't like Trevor."

"Honey, we have nothing against him. He's a fine man, but we want you to have skyrockets!"

Eve looked from one to the other. "You have skyrockets, don't you? It's funny, but I've only realized that lately."

"Did you end it last night?" her mother probed.

"No. It took me by surprise. I was all psyched up to get engaged and resign myself to being a professor's wife — I couldn't think on my feet when he threw me a curve."

"When will you tell him?" Susan asked.

"Tonight. I'll tell him tonight. The last

thing in the world I want to do is hurt him, but a quick, clean break is best for everyone."

Her parents didn't pursue the subject any further. Ted suspected her weekend with Clint Kelly had put an end to Trevor Bennett's hopes. But he knew Eve would confide in them in her own good time.

"If you're going home now, why don't I bring over your treadmill and set it up for you?"

Eve almost told him he was too old to be carrying heavy stuff like that. She bit her tongue. He was only fifty, and he was the best judge of his ability. She had to trust him to make his own decisions, as he had trusted her.

As he was adjusting the digital settings on her treadmill, her father talked about the International Fly-in that Oshkosh, Wisconsin, held every summer. Because of his experience with planes, he'd been invited to be a judge of the "homebuilt" flying machines entered in the week-long event.

As Eve listened to him, she finally understood why her mother was still in love. He took a vital interest in everything and he kept himself in great shape. Eve had always known that her father was a man's man; now she saw that he was also a woman's man.

"Thanks, Dad. I could never have figured

it all out on my own." It was only a slight exaggeration; she couldn't have learned how to set it half so quickly.

When she was alone, she began walking on the new treadmill. She decided it was a wonderful invention. It gave the body a workout, while allowing the mind total freedom. She spent the next couple of hours rehearsing what she would say to Trevor when he called. When the phone rang at exactly five o'clock, she said to herself, *God, he's so regimented!*

The moment Trevor spoke, she could hear the vulnerability in his voice. He was expecting her to reject his offer and she was going to fulfill his expectations. Eve felt like a monster. She knew the kindest thing to do was get straight to the heart of the matter. She would not indulge in a cat and mouse game. It was at this point that she became absolutely convinced she was doing the right thing. When she was cast in the role of cat and he was reduced to a mouse, it was all over.

"Trevor, I've thought about us all day and it isn't going to work. We're wrong for each other. You need someone I'll never be. I take the blame for the failure of our relationship. You've been gentle, kind, and understanding from the beginning and none of this is your fault."

"Eve, please don't be so hasty. Give us

another chance. I won't pressure you into living together; I'll forget about marriage."

"It's best to make a clean break, Trevor. I don't want to give you pain, but I think we should end it."

There was a long silence, then in a resigned voice, he said the thing he always said: "I understand."

Eve sat down to write him a kind letter. He understood and appreciated the written word. She used a philosophical tone, implying "What will be, will be." She knew he read Omar Khayyam. She told him she had been enriched by their relationship, and that with all her heart she wished him well. Then Eve wrapped up the diamond earrings and called the courier.

It was the same young man she had generously tipped the night before. He returned the package of papers addressed to Clint Kelly.

"I'm sorry, Ms. Barlow, there was no one home at this address. I tried to deliver it last night and again today."

"Hang on a minute — I'll telephone him." Eve dialed Kelly's number and heard his deep voice, but only on the answering machine. "It's Eve Barlow, six o'clock, Monday the twenty-seventh. Would you give me a call as soon as you can?"

She told the courier, "Leave the package

and take this one instead." She gave him another generous tip.

Eve made herself dinner, then hesitated to go down to the laundry room in case she missed Kelly's call. She rinsed out a few things in the bathroom sink. She was in such a reflective mood, feeling guilty over Trevor, justifying ending their relationship. Eve desperately needed an escape from her introspection. She felt like running five miles or climbing a mountain, but the weather was so foul, she couldn't even go for a drive.

She almost turned on the television set, then she happened to remember she bought a Christina Skye novel just before Christmas and hadn't had a chance to read it. Eve curled up on the couch and began to read *Hour of the Rose*. Skye was a superb writer. From the first haunting sentence, Eve was swept away to another time and place.

It was after midnight when she glanced at her watch. She was torn between reading 'til dawn and putting the book down so she could savor it and make it last longer. She decided on the latter; she just might be spending a lot of her evenings home alone for awhile.

When she got to the office the next day, Eve was inundated with people who were looking for new office space. It seemed as if every lease in Grand Rapids expired in January. She tried phoning Kelly a couple of times, and when she was unsuccessful, called Judy to tell her their lunch would have to be postponed.

"Do you think there might be a problem?" Judy asked.

"No, no," Eve assured her. "Mr. Kelly is a Fire Chief who works shifts. It's just taking a while to get together with his lawyer. It will probably be after New Year's before I have everything for you."

"That would be better for me too, Eve. By the way, I had the phone taken off holiday service and also had the power put back on. I don't want anyone else getting into difficulties up there."

"That was a good idea. I'll put the costs in the adjustments," Eve assured her.

She worked late at the office, then on impulse on the way home, took a detour to Clint Kelly's apartment. There was no answer to her knock. She pulled out a business card, wrote on it, "Call me!" and shoved it under his door.

She waited for his call all evening. When it didn't come, she convinced herself that he had taken such offense over her rejection that he was deliberately avoiding her. *To bloody hellfire with all men!* Eve picked up *Hour of the Rose* and took it to bed with her.

When dawn arrived, Eve found herself lying awake, reflecting on all that had happened over the holidays. She recalled reading somewhere that more romantic relationships ended at this time of the year than any other. It was like an adage; if it wasn't rock solid, it wouldn't survive Christmas!

Men seemed to fall into two categories. They were either mothers' boys or macho chauvinists. Where were all the men in between? Where were the men who could be strong and take control when it was necessary, yet show ineffable tenderness or be moved to tears at life's poignant, touching moments?

Eve laughed at herself and threw back the covers. The ideal man was a myth. And if there was such a paragon, he was seeking the ideal woman!

When she opened her closet, she knew she needed to choose something that would lift her spirits. She decided to wear her lucky color. Eve pulled on a pair of lavender slacks and a lambswool sweater to match. They were the antithesis of a power suit, making her look soft and feminine. She even put on her amethyst earrings that were strictly evening wear, deciding she would never be regimented again.

Eve's car seemed to have a mind of its own this morning, heading in the direction of Kelly's apartment building rather than her office. Upstairs, she knocked politely on his door and waited. Perhaps he was sleeping. If he'd worked all night, he could be dead to the world by now. Eve lifted her fists and pounded. Absolute silence met her ears. She should have saved herself the trouble by phoning!

Eve was annoyed. This was no way to conduct business. She was his broker, representing his purchase of a house. He should at least have the common courtesy to touch base with her. She drove to the office, fuming all the way. When Maxwell arrived, she followed him into his office.

"Did you have a scuba lesson last night?"

"No. There was no lesson scheduled for the week between Christmas and New Year's. We pick up again after the holidays. Thinking of joining the class?" he asked casually.

"No," she said sweetly, "I'm thinking of drowning someone."

By noon, her patience snapped. She decided to track Action Man down. Eve was hungry and knew exactly where she was going to eat lunch.

Kelly's Sports Bar and Grill was crowded. She searched the room looking for a six-footer with black hair and dark blue eyes. She ordered a corned beef sandwich and a draft beer. The dill pickle was so good it made her tastebuds stand at attention. It must have been pickled in a barrel.

At one o'clock the crowd thinned out dramatically, and Eve carried her empty mug to the bar. The resemblance was so marked she had no difficulty realizing this was Kelly's father. The retired policeman was heavier, of course, and his handsome face lay in ruins, but he was hard-edged and cocksure; still master of his domain.

"Hello, Mr. Kelly. I'm Eve Barlow and I'm looking for your son, Clint."

"Call me Clancy," he said, giving her an appreciative look that swept from breasts to thighs.

Clancy? I don't believe it. He's more Irish than Paddy's Pig!

"You're not a reporter, are you?" he demanded.

"No. I'm his real estate agent."

Clancy whistled with disbelief. "Well, I'll be damned. He sure knows how to pick 'em!"

"Mr. Kelly —"

"Clancy."

"Clancy. Do you know where I can find your son?"

"Nope."

"You have no idea where he might be reached?"

"Nope."

"It's imperative I get in touch with him.

Doesn't he come here to the bar?"

Clancy rubbed his nose thoughtfully, then seemed to come to a decision. He reached beneath the bar and pulled out a newspaper. It was two days old.

Eve's eyes ran down the page, then stared hard at the picture. It portrayed a firefighter carrying a child in his arms. His helmet was decorated by a row of icicles. His face was grim, his eyes stark. Quickly she read the headline, then the article.

Two boys had been playing with matches on the third floor of a furniture warehouse. The ten-year-old had been rescued and taken to a hospital. The nine-year-old had not survived.

"Fire Chief Kelly said the floor collapsed before he could reach the second boy. He performed cardiopulmonary resuscitation for over an hour, but it was hopeless. Kelly's crew fought the fire for twelve hours in below-zero temperatures."

Eve looked up from the newspaper to find Clancy's eyes on her.

"When something like this happens, we don't see him for a few days. He likes to be alone."

Eve nodded. She looked at the eyes in the picture again, and felt his pain. She handed back the paper. "Thank you," she whispered.

Eve Barlow threw jeans, sweaters, and underclothes into an overnight bag, then grabbed makeup and shampoo. Her instincts had taken over and she had a gut feeling about where she would find Clint Kelly.

On the drive north to the property she made one stop at a store to purchase a present and put it in the trunk with her overnight bag. Eve drove carefully, but as fast as road conditions allowed.

She could not get the picture of Kelly holding the dead child out of her mind. Why in the name of heaven had she thought Clint incapable of tears? His job did not merely deal with danger, it encompassed anguish, fear, and tragedy. It involved the loss of life, as well as property. On a daily basis Clint Kelly was expected to perform heroically, and to deal with death when heroics weren't enough. No wonder he had taken over so completely when her life was in danger. He had been trained to cope with emergencies and disasters. Treating hypothermia was probably second nature to him; he and his team must have experienced it firsthand fighting fires, soaked to the skin, in below-zero temperatures.

Clint was a born leader; a take-charge kind of man who made instant decisions and issued orders, expecting them to be obeyed. The time she spent with him had taught her so much about him, certainly enough to make her fall head-over-heels in love! But she now realized she had barely scratched the surface. There were still volumes to learn, depths to plumb.

Clint saw her Mercedes as it pulled into the long drive. He started running. He reached the car in time to open the door for her.

She watched him run toward her. He was carrying something black in his hand. She smiled when she saw it was a camera.

"Eve!"

"Hello, Clint. I've been trying to get hold of you for days. I didn't know about the fire until I went to your dad's bar."

"He didn't know where I was."

"No, but I did," she said quietly, getting out of the car and standing close, looking up at him. *Thank God the pain has left his eyes. This place is good for him!* She would be good for him, too. She'd start by making him laugh. "Remember that engagement ring I was getting for Christmas? It turned out to be diamond earrings."

He didn't laugh; his eyes burned into hers. "Marry me, Eve!"

It wasn't a question, it was more like a command. His arms went around her. "Evie, if that's what it takes to win you, I'll even quote poetry."

151

She laughed into his eyes and called his bluff. "Let's hear you."

Clint's dark brows drew together for a minute. Then he said:

"I'm only a man,
We'll get along fine,
Just so long as you remember
I'm not yours; YOU'RE MINE!"

Eve melted into his arms and lifted her lips for his kiss, knowing that was an effective way to stop his dreadful doggerel.

"I take it your answer is yes?"

"Clint Kelly, it's no such thing! You're going way too fast for me."

"When I see what I want, I walk a direct path to it."

"We have nothing in common. You would turn my life upside down."

"We can work things out. Come inside and we'll negotiate. If we talk, we can find common ground."

"We have so little in common, it would be a disaster."

"You think I can't handle disaster?" He raised one black eyebrow.

"I know you can," she said softly. She knew if he began to touch her, her objections would dissolve along with her bones.

In front of a blazing fire, with Clint Kelly sitting across from her, Eve's resistance began to thaw. He was such a persuasive man — she knew she had to negotiate while she still had her wits about her.

"I want a fifty-fifty partnership. I don't want a marriage where the man is the boss and the woman is the little housewife."

Clint grabbed a piece of paper and began making a contract. "Agreed; fifty-fifty," he promised.

"I intend to work, whether you like it or not. I won't stay home baking coconut cream pies."

"Agreed," he said, scribbling furiously. She was independent, assertive, competitive, and combative, but every once in a while he knew she would lean on him.

"And I don't want to have to break your arms every time I want to drive."

His face was sober, but his eyes danced with amusement. "You missed your calling. You should have been a comedian."

"This isn't meant to be funny — I'm serious! These are definitely not jokes."

"Then why am I laughing?"

"Because you're a sexist swine, of course."

"Evie, I'm so much in love with you, I'll agree to anything."

Eve stopped talking and looked at him. This man was everything she'd ever wanted. It was time to face the truth. She tore the paper into small pieces and threw it into the air. It came down like confetti. "Clint, I wouldn't want you any other way!"

He threw back his head and yowled like a wolf. It was a cry of victory. "Now that we've got business out of the way, can we indulge in a little pleasure?"

She took his hand. "Come with me. I have a present for you." Eve unlocked the trunk and handed him her overnight bag. Then she gave him his present. When Clint opened the brown bag and saw the bottle of whisky, a wicked grin spread across his face.

"I'll let you be the judge of that, Action Man. You're going to have to reel out more hose, or get closer to the fire. Just don't rub me the wrong way!"

"After experiencing Christmas Eve," he said, making a word-play of her name, "I can't wait for New Year's Eve!"

The Miracle

Brenda Joyce

One

Newport Beach, 1902

*I*t was Christmas Eve, and Lisa had never been as miserable or frightened in her entire short life.

She was hiding from her fiancé, the Marquis of Connaught. She had run away from him two months ago, on the night of their engagement party. But now she was desperate. She did not know how much longer she could continue to hide like this, alone and cold and hungry — and so terribly unhappy and afraid.

Lisa shivered. She was wrapped in a mohair throw, for she was only wearing a white poplin summer dress. When she had fled her engagement ball, she had fled without any clothes except for the evening gown she was wearing. That had been discarded immediately. And it was frigidly cold outside, the sky dark and threatening, and as freezing inside her parents' huge summer home. But she did not dare make a fire for fear of alerting a local resident or a passerby to her presence. For fear of alerting Julian St. Clare to her presence.

How she hated him.

Tears did not come to Lisa's eyes, however. On the night of her engagement party she had cried so hard and so thoroughly that she doubted she would ever cry again. Julian's betrayal had been a fatal blow to her young heart. How naive she had been then, to think that such a man had come courting her out of love and not more sanguine reasons. He had only been interested in her because she was an heiress. He did not want her, had never wanted her; he only wanted her money.

A loose shutter began banging wildly against the side of the house. Lisa was huddled on the floor in a corner of her bedroom. The shutters there were open, as were the blue and white drapes, so that the faded winter light could filter into the room. The house was low on supplies. Although there were gaslights, Lisa dared not use them, using only candles. The candles were all but gone. She was almost out of food, too, as there were but a few canned items left in the pantry. Yesterday she had begun using the last bar of soap.

Dear God, what was she going to do?

Lisa wiggled her toes, which were numb from the cold. She stared out the window. It had begun to flurry.

Even though the window was closed and made of double-paned glass, Lisa could hear the thundering of the surf on the shore not far from the back of the house.

It was Christmas Eve. Lisa imagined the cozy family parlor of her Fifth Avenue home. Right now her father was undoubtedly poking the logs in the fire, watching the flames crackle, clad in his favorite paisley smoking jacket. Suzanne, her stepmother, would be descending the wide sweeping stairs, dressed formally for supper. And Sofie, who had returned from Paris with her beautiful baby daughter, was she there, too? Lisa's heart twisted. She missed her father and stepmother and stepsister terribly. A sense of loss swept through her, so acute it made her breathless and dizzy.

Or was she faint from hunger and lack of sleep?

Lisa slept fitfully at night, her dreams deeply disturbing. As if she were a child, she dreamed of being pursued by monsters and beasts. She was always running in terror, afraid for her life, for she knew if the beast caught her, he would coldly, cruelly destroy her. He was a shaggy, wild creature, horrific and not human at all. Until she saw his face.

The beast always had a face. He was blond and gray-eyed and coldly patrician. He was devastatingly handsome. His face was Julian St. Clare's.

Lisa listened to the banging shutter and

the pounding surf. His face had fooled her. His face and his kisses. How stupid she had been. Lisa knew now from overhearing the gossips at her engagement party that his reputation was vast and well known — he was impoverished, reclusive, and he disliked women. He was only marrying Lisa because she was an heiress. And Julian had not denied it when Lisa flung the accusation in his face.

Lisa shivered again. This time the cold was far more than bone-chilling — it wrapped icy fingers around her heart. According to Sofie, St. Clare was more coldly furious with her each and every passing day. And more determined to find her. He had hired detectives to aid him in his quest.

Would he never grow weary of this game? Lisa prayed daily that he would give up, find himself another American heiress, and return to his ancestral home in Ireland.

The banging of the shutter was louder now, more forceful and rhythmic.

Sofie knew where she was. If St. Clare left, Lisa was certain that Sofie would reveal that fact to her immediately so Lisa could go home.

Bang. Bang. Bang.

Lisa's brief reverie of returning home and being swept into her father's arms was rudely interrupted. Something was not right. She strained to hear.

Bang. Bang.

Lisa sat up straighter. The shutter was still banging wildly in the wind, but something was banging downstairs, too. A new noise, a different noise. It was rhythmic, forceful.

Lisa was on her feet. Panic washed over her. Was someone knocking on the front door?

No! Of course not! But she dropped the throw and ran down the hall to the second-floor landing. Hanging onto the smooth teak banister, she peered down into the foyer. This time there was no mistaking the sound of someone banging on the front door. Every drop of blood drained from her face.

Bam. Bam.

And then the brass doorknob rattled.

Lisa was frozen. It crossed her stunned mind that St. Clare had found her.

Suddenly the glass window beside the front door shattered. Lisa started to scream, but her mouth was so dry with terror that she could not utter a single sound.

A heavy broken branch poked through, sweeping glass shards from the frame. And then St. Clare's head appeared in the opening.

Their gazes met.

His gray eyes glittered with anger.

Lisa's teeth chattered and her knees buckled.

"Open this door," the Marquis commanded above the howling wind.

Lisa whirled and began to run back down the hall.

"Lisa!" he shouted.

She did not know what to do, where to go. As she raced towards her bedroom she realized she would be trapped if she returned there. She ran past it, panting, her heart pounding. Lisa skidded down the back stairs. She realized that he would find her if she attempted to hide in the house. As she flew across the back foyer, she could hear him running down the corridor upstairs.

She had to escape.

Lisa threw the bolt on the back door. As she flung it open, a gust of freezing wind and snow blasted her. Lisa did not notice as she raced outside.

She was stumbling down the stone steps which led to the back lawns and tennis courts and ultimately the beach when she heard him shouting her name. Lisa flung a glance over her shoulder as she ran across the snow-dusted lawn. St. Clare was just barreling out of the house.

Lisa screamed as she slipped and fell. She pushed herself up from her knees, but got caught on the frothy lace hem of her skirts. Stumbling, she wrenched at her skirts and took another step forward. And then a hand clamped down hard on her shoulder.

Lisa's slipper-shod feet continued to move, but her body was hauled backwards. A pair of muscular arms wrapped around her. Lisa did not hesitate — she sank her teeth into one of those arms.

But all she got was a mouthful of his overcoat, while he did not appear to notice anything. A moment later St. Clare had thrown her over his shoulder and was hurrying back to the house.

He was tall and muscular and Lisa was petite, so her eyes were level with the small of his back. She did not give up. "No!" she shouted, beating his back with her fists, her cheek rubbing against his wool coat. If he noticed her wild resistance, he gave no sign. Lisa pummeled him harder as sobs choked their way out of her throat.

St. Clare strode into the back hall, kicking the door closed. To Lisa, the kick seemed brutal and violent. Her fists uncurled, stilled. Abject fear seized her again.

He did not pause. He strode purposefully through the house, kicking open both doors to a front parlor. Without breaking stride he entered the dark room and deposited Lisa on the sofa. Their gazes met.

Some of the cold fury dimmed in his eyes.

His gaze swept her from head to toe and widened.

Lisa realized her teeth were chattering. She was shivering uncontrollably, not just from fear. From the freezing cold.

"Good God," he said grimly, his jaw flexing. He shrugged out of his overcoat and flung the coat on top of Lisa. Before Lisa could protest, he tucked it firmly about her. "You little fool," he said.

Lisa burrowed into his coat, which was wonderfully warm, trying not to notice the musky male scent that clung to it. She never removed her eyes from his. Her teeth chattered more loudly than before, and her shivering continued unabated.

His mouth tightened. St. Clare immediately turned on a gaslamp. The room was flooded with light. He went to the hearth, knelt, and began to make a fire. Within moments flames began to dance, but he wasn't through. Soon the hearth was blazing.

Lisa remained on the couch, staring at his broad back, filled with dread and too stunned to think coherently. She could not believe that she had been caught.

Finished with the fire, he turned and strode to her.

Lisa could not help but flinch, pressing herself against the back of the sofa.

His gaze darkened. "You're blue," he said

flatly. "Has it not crossed your mind that you might catch pneumonia and die wearing a summer dress like that in this weather?"

Lisa's reply was instantaneous. "Then you would have to find another heiress, wouldn't you?"

He started, eyes wide.

Lisa wished she had kept silent.

His expression hardened. "Yes, I would."

Lisa inhaled. "I hate you."

"You have made that very clear." Suddenly he reached for her.

Lisa cried out.

He lifted her into his arms. "I am not going to hurt you," he said coldly, moving back to the fire. "You may have a suicide wish, but I do not share it." A shadow Lisa did not comprehend clouded his expression.

Lisa was tense, acutely aware of being cradled against his broad, hard chest. His masculine scent assailed her. Lisa squirmed. She despised him, and she was not going to marry him, but he was a devastatingly attractive man, and she could not forget the few times he had kissed her when he was courting her — before she had learned the truth about him. Lisa had had many beaux before St. Clare, even though she was just eighteen. Young men had always flocked about her, vying for her attention. But only one young man had dared to kiss her before St. Clare, a friend who had confessed at the time that he was miserably in love with her. His kiss had been chaste and totally unremarkable. Julian's kisses had seared not just her body, but her soul. And they hadn't been chaste at all.

Lisa realized that he had halted in front of the fire with her in his arms. He was staring at her almost fixedly.

Lisa prayed her thoughts did not show. Flushing, wetting her lips, she said hoarsely, "Put me down."

His temples throbbed visibly as he tore his gaze away and laid her on the rug in front of the hearth.

Terribly relieved to be out of his arms, Lisa resolved to forget the past and the dreams she had once had for them, no matter how difficult it might be. She would never allow him to kiss her again, and she certainly wasn't going to marry him, no matter what he and her father had planned.

But she was acutely aware of him standing beside her just as she was acutely aware of the tension simmering between them.

Lisa was determined to ignore him, and in spite of the roaring fire, she had never been colder in her life. She refused to think that he was being kind. Clearly he was not a kind man. He was only concerned about her because he wanted her fortune.

"You may ignore me if it pleases you," he said from beside her, staring at her again. "I had planned to return to the city tonight, but will wait until the morning. I will send my driver into town to bring us a hot supper and anything we might need. And some suitable clothing for you."

Lisa sat up, facing him. A momentary feeling of light-headedness afflicted her, but she ignored it. "You may certainly return to New York City tonight. Don't linger on my account."

His eyes darkened. "Lisa, you are returning with me."

"Then you will have to act forcibly, sir."

"You are a stubborn bit of baggage," he said coolly. "And I suggest that you cease trying to antagonize me in this childish manner."

"Oh, so now I am a mere child?" Lisa felt hurt, bitterly so. "You did not treat me like a child, St. Clare, when you were courting me — and kissing me!"

His fists found his hips. His stare found her mouth.

Lisa wished she had not brought up the subject. "Just go away and leave me alone," she said, staring at the floor.

"I cannot do that, Lisa."

Her head flung up. "I am not marrying you," Lisa said vehemently. "Were you the

167

last man on this earth, I would not marry you!"

He folded his arms and looked down at her. "Ahh, so now we get to the gist of the matter."

"Yes. The gist. The gist is that you are a cold, uncaring man. You are a fraud, St. Clare." Unfortunately, Lisa's tone was tremulous. She hoped all the hurt she was feeling was not showing in her eyes. She had never been a good actress.

His expression was impossible to read. "Let us finish this once and for all. I am sorry. I apologize to you for not being forthright from the start. Perhaps if I had been honest and explained to you the reasons I sought your hand in matrimony, we would not be at this impasse now."

Lisa was incredulous. She got to her feet abruptly, leaving his coat on the floor. But instantly she was assailed with a wave of dizziness and she could not respond as she wished to do.

St. Clare gripped her arms. "You are ill."

Lisa allowed him to steady her. "No, I am fine. I am just hungry," she said, as her vision cleared. Then, realizing that his warm palms gripped her bare wrists, she shrugged free of him. "Stop touching me," she snapped.

Shadows crossed his eyes, but he dropped his hands. "You are ill," he repeated, staring closely at her.

"I am fine. I am tired, that is all. And I do not accept your apology, St. Clare."

He eyed her. "I see. You intend to fight me to the bitter end?"

"Yes. Nor do you see. I doubt you see anything at all except your own selfish wishes. You are a cold, ugly man. Your face might be beautiful, but you have no heart — and you toyed with mine, which is unforgivable!" To Lisa's dismay, hot tears suddenly filled her gaze.

He was silent. "You are so very young," he finally said. "I also apologize for hurting you, Lisa. That was not my intention."

"What was your intention?" she cried. "Other than to marry an unsuspecting heiress."

His jaw flexed. "I am tired of your accusations. It is very common for an heiress to seek a title, just as it is common for a nobleman like myself to seek an heiress. You are acting like this is a crime akin to murder. We are not the first to find such an accommodation, Lisa."

"No!" Lisa shook her head. Her long, dark hair, which had long since come loose of its coil, fell like black silk across her shoulders.

"This marriage can be a success if we reach an understanding, you and I."

"No," Lisa said fiercely. "No. When I marry,

I am marrying for love."

Something flickered in his eyes. "I am afraid that is not possible."

Lisa did not like his tone. "I shall beg my father to break this off. Surely now that he knows how resistant I am, he will not force me to wed you. My father loves me."

"It is too late," Julian said quietly.

"Of course it's not too late!"

He hesitated, staring. "Lisa, we were married by proxy last week."

Lisa could not move. Surely she had misheard?

His mouth was a thin, tight line. "We are already man and wife."

Two

Lisa had maintained a stoic silence ever since Julian had informed her of the fact of their marriage. He did not want to feel guilty, and he certainly did not want to feel sympathetic toward her, but it was very hard for him to maintain his distance whenever he looked into her expressive amber eyes. She could not hide her feelings of hurt and bitterness and despair. She was only eighteen — so very young.

He almost cursed himself for what he had done, but he had not had any choice. He was only a man, he could not change God's will, and he had been desperate.

Julian could not eat. He sat at the dining table with his bride at a long, oval table that could accommodate a dozen diners with ease. Lisa had chosen to sit opposite him at the table's far end, a foolishly defiant gesture, and she refused to look at him or speak with him. But then, she appeared to be starving, and she had not stopped eating since his manservant had laid out the repast.

He watched her help herself to another serving of roasted chicken and boiled pota-

171

toes. He could not believe how thin she had become in these past two months. He kept remembering how, when he had lifted her in his arms, she had been as light as a feather. Dark circles were etched beneath her eyes. He could not ignore his responsibility in this affair, or the guilt which filled him as he faced it.

He knew he should have chosen a different bride.

Lisa was too young, too vulnerable, and if he dared be honest, far too pretty as well.

She did not suit him, and she would hate his home, Castleclare, when he took her there.

He shut off his thoughts. They were becoming distinctly painful. He knew he shouldn't think about faults, especially not his own, for then his thoughts would take him backwards in time, to a place he dared not go. Not ever again.

Lisa suddenly sighed.

Julian knew he was staring at her, and now that she was finally finished eating, she lifted her head and their gazes collided. He felt unbearably tense. He suddenly knew he could not take her with him to Castleclare. His every instinct warned him against it. She was trouble.

Suddenly she was slapping her napkin down and rising to her feet, a clear breach of etiquette. Coolly she said, "I am retiring

172

to my room." Her gaze flickered with hostility.

He chose to stand politely. "Good night, madam," he said, inclining his head.

Giving him half a glare, for the effect was ruined by the hurt in her eyes, she shoved back her chair as noisily as possible and marched from the room.

Julian sighed and collapsed in his seat. He was well aware that she was trying her damnedest to provoke him. He was, perhaps, relieved that she had gone.

O'Hara appeared magically in the room. Short and round and old enough to be Julian's father, he was Julian's single manservant, acting as butler, valet, footman, and coachman as need be. He had insisted on accompanying Julian to America.

"That poor lass be starvin', m'lord," O'Hara said accusingly.

Julian leveled him with a cool stare. "I am well aware of Her Ladyship's condition."

Without asking, O'Hara filled Julian's wineglass. "Ain't right, m'lord. Her bein' so unhappy an' —"

"O'Hara," Julian said calmly, "you are going too far."

O'Hara ignored the unveiled warning. "Mebbe y' should court the lass just a tiny bit."

Julian stood up abruptly, scowled, and left the dining room, taking his red wine with him. In the library he stared out the window, for no one had thought to draw the brocade draperies. It had begun to snow heavily and the sky was opaque, the front lawns already covered with several inches of snow. He hardly cared. His bride was upstairs, hurt and unhappy, all because of him. Why did he keep thinking about her?

Ever since he met her, he'd had no peace, none at all.

Julian set the wineglass down. Unwelcome images invaded his mind — images of Lisa curled up in her four-poster, her mouth full and red and inviting, her small nose tilted upward, eyes closed as she slept, her black lashes fanning on her pale cheeks. Her dark hair would be rippling across her shoulders, her naked shoulders . . .

Julian swallowed and turned away from the window. His groin was suddenly, shockingly, full.

He had no right to such thoughts.

But it had been so goddamn long.

Lisa woke with a cry of fright.

Morning sunlight was streaming into her bedroom and a fire blazed in the hearth, warming it. But she was not alone.

Julian St. Clare, the monster of her dreams, stood beside her bed, staring down at her, his face impossibly handsome —

and impossible to read.

Complete comprehension struck Lisa immediately. She recalled all of the events leading up to that moment in the space of a single heartbeat. With that realization came dread and despair. Sitting up, brushing loose strands of hair from her face, she realized she was wearing nothing but a thin, sleeveless summer nightgown.

Lisa yanked the covers up to her chin, her face flaming. Julian had seen her breasts. Her heart raced alarmingly. "What are you doing in my room?!"

A flush also colored his cheeks. "I knocked several times but you failed to awaken. I came in to tend to the fire," he said stiffly.

"Well, now you can get out."

Julian's eyes flashed. "I suggest that you moderate your tone, madam."

Lisa hugged the covers to her breasts, wondering how long he had been staring at her while she slept in such a state of immodesty. "My rudeness only matches yours," she managed, more meekly. "No gentleman would invade a lady's bedroom, sir, for any reason."

He sighed, clearly annoyed. "It is freezing cold, Lisa, and you have suffered greatly in the past two months. Do you wish to ruin your health?"

"What do you care?" Lisa shrugged. And

received an angry look which somehow pleased her immensely.

He began to leave, then halted, facing her again. "We are snowed in."

"What?!"

"It snowed all night. The driveway is impassable, and the roads can be no better. We are snowed in."

Lisa stared at him in growing horror.

"I will see you in the dining salon," Julian said. "O'Hara has prepared breakfast." His smile was cool. "I am afraid we will have to remain here for several days, Lisa, you and I, together."

When he was gone, Lisa sagged against her pillows. "No," she whispered miserably. "Oh, no!"

There was only one way for Lisa to survive the next few days until Julian took her home and that was to remain inside her bedroom, avoiding his presence and company completely. Except, however, for meals.

Lisa had no intention of starving herself now that there was food in the house, not after these past two very lean months. She arrived at the breakfast table at a quarter to ten. Julian was reading a day-old newspaper he had brought from New York. As she entered the room wearing a pale pink day dress, he rose to his feet. In spite of herself, Lisa had to admit that his manners were impeccable.

And that, even though he was wearing very old riding boots, breeches which fit him like a glove, and an equally old houndstooth riding jacket, he exuded an intensely masculine appeal. Lisa was careful to pretend to be oblivious of him as she took her seat at the other end of the table. Of course, it was impossible — she felt him looking at her with frightening intensity.

Surely he was wrong, she thought in sudden despair. They could not be married by proxy. It was an intolerable thought.

O'Hara came bustling into the room carrying a platter of sausages and eggs and freshly toasted muffins. "Good morning, m'lord, m'lady," he said jovially with his thick lilting Irish brogue. He beamed. "Merry Christmas!"

Lisa froze. She had forgotten what day this was.

Julian also remained immobile at the other end of the table. Their gazes clashed instantly.

Lisa quickly looked away, murmuring "Merry Christmas" to the servant but not to Julian, a man who might be her husband, feeling awful about being so petty. Christmas was a special day, a day of love and joy and celebration. Yet this day was a day of sorrow and despair. Lisa yearned to be at home with her family. How she needed her father and stepsister now.

And although Lisa had been famished, she suddenly lost her appetite. She lurched to her feet. "Excuse me. I . . ." She could not continue. Vaguely aware of Julian's riveted gaze — and the fact that he was also standing — she turned and rushed from the room.

"Wait, Lisa," Julian said, hurrying after her.

She whirled in the corridor. "Please, just leave me alone," she begged.

He froze. "Lisa, it is time for us to talk."

"No," she cried and shook her head fiercely. Her thick braid swung like a rope against her back.

He gripped her elbow. "Come with me." His tone was soft but firm; it was a command.

Hating him intensely, Lisa realized she had no choice and allowed him to lead her into the library. He released her but did not bother to shut the doors. He turned his back to her and stared out at the snow as it was blown into an odd assortment of puffy shapes on the lawn.

Lisa hugged herself. This was the worst Christmas she could imagine. Her heart felt broken all over again. How alone she felt.

Slowly Julian faced her. "You deserve some explanation."

Lisa said nothing. There was nothing to say.

"It was not my choice to remarry, Lisa. In truth, had I a choice, I would never have married again."

Lisa swallowed, feeling quite ill. "You are definitely making me feel better, St. Clare."

"Please. Take off the gauntlets for a moment, Lisa."

She blinked and finally, reluctantly, nodded. Even though she despised him for his deception and treachery, she wanted to know what he was thinking, wanted to hear what he would say.

He coughed to clear his throat. "Circumstance forced me to wed."

"An heiress like myself?"

"Yes." His gaze found hers. He appeared regretful.

"This hardly exonerates you, St. Clare," Lisa snapped. "Another woman might be happy with this kind of arrangement, but not I."

"My brother is ill."

Lisa stiffened, all ears now.

Julian's jaw was tight. He avoided her eyes. "Robert is my younger brother, my only brother. Our parents died years ago. He is the only family I have, and his welfare is my complete responsibility."

Lisa did not move. But Julian's anguish was a vivid thing, shimmering in his eyes, consuming him. She wished she were unaware of it.

"He has been diagnosed with consumption," Julian said.

Lisa stared. Consumption was fatal. His brother would, sooner or later, succumb to the disease and die. "I am sorry."

His head swiveled, his stare pierced her. His expression was stoic, except for his burning gray eyes. "Are you?"

"Of course."

He coughed again before speaking. The tip of his nose had grown pink. "He is at a spa in Switzerland and he must remain there for the rest . . . for the rest of his life. The treatment is very costly."

"I see," Lisa said, beginning to understand.

Julian abruptly turned his back to her. "I cannot pay the bills. But the Irish climate does not suit him. Robert, of course, prefers London, but that is as bad. He must remain in Switzerland. Yet I have no funds."

"So you came to America to marry an heiress."

He did not face her. Lisa thought he shuddered very slightly. "Yes. I had no choice. My brother's health is at issue."

His health, his life. Lisa did not want to feel Julian's pain, but it was so palpable that she did. She took a deep breath, wanting to flee the room, wanting to flee him. "I am sorry, St. Clare, about your brother. But your explanation changes nothing."

Slowly he faced her. "I see."

She took a step backwards, away from him. "I still don't want to be your wife."

"It's too late, Lisa," Julian told her. "It has been done. We are married." For a single moment, before he lowered his gaze, Lisa saw the burning intensity in his gray eyes.

Her heart was hammering madly. What had that look meant? It was not the first time she had glimpsed it. And should she really care to decipher his innermost feelings? She wanted nothing to do with him.

Lisa clenched her fists. "Take my money and return to Ireland and pay your brother's bills. But leave me here."

He stared at her dispassionately. Yet behind his stoic expression, she felt a fresh wave of anger building.

Lisa did not wait for him to respond. She ran from the room.

Lisa found solace in her bedroom. She flung herself facedown on the bed. She was acutely aware of the man downstairs, a stranger she despised, a stranger who was her husband — a man who was hurting because his brother was dying. Lisa told herself that it was not her affair, that she must not feel sympathy for him. She did not care. She must not care.

And surely he would agree with her final suggestion? Surely he would leave her in New York with her family and take her money instead? After all, he had not wanted to remarry in the first place. How hurtful that statement had been.

But St. Clare was full of surprises. What if he felt it his duty to import her to Ireland and his rundown ancestral estate?

What could she do? Defy both her father and St. Clare yet again? Lisa was exhausted from the past two months of hiding. She did not fool herself. Her strength — and bravery — were sapped. She could not run away again.

Which meant she must accept her fate. And if her fate was to go with Julian to Ireland . . .

St. Clare's image swam before her mind. When he had first come calling, she had been overwhelmed with his masculine beauty, his formal bearing, and his utterly aristocratic demeanor. Lisa was no longer deluded. He was only pleasing on the surface; he was a cold, heartless man.

He was not the knight in shining armor she had dreamed of and yearned for ever since she was a young girl.

Lisa felt like weeping. If only he were as ugly on the surface as he was on the inside.

A light rap sounded on her door. Lisa jerked, knowing who it was. She sat up, flinging her braid over her shoulder, but said not a word. Maybe he would think that she had fallen asleep.

"Lisa, it is I. Julian. There is more which we must discuss."

Her heart beat at a gallop. "There is *nothing* more to discuss," Lisa cried at the closed door. "Go away, St. Clare."

He opened the door and stepped inside. Lisa regretted not locking it, too late. He eyed her. Lisa realized her skirts were billowing about her legs in utter disarray. And that she probably looked quite indecent, lounging about the bed. She slipped to the floor.

His jaw flexing, he said, "We must finish this once and for all. You cannot hope to avoid me."

To hide her roiling emotions, she cried, "I can do my best to avoid you, St. Clare. And I intend to avoid you as much as possible from now until death do us part!"

He stared at her, first at her defiant face, then at her mouth, and finally his gaze slid down her bodice and skirts to her toes. "You are a contradiction, Lisa, for you are far tougher than you appear — and you appear a delicate beauty, fragile and ephemeral. I would never have dreamed you capable of running away and hiding from me for two full months. Your determination and courage are astounding."

"I do not think you are complimenting me," Lisa said.

"I am not complimenting you." His gaze was piercing. "You *are* far stronger than you appear, yet I sense you are not really as tough as you try to seem. I think that defiance runs against your true nature."

"So now you are an expert on my true nature?" Lisa scoffed, but she was alarmed. This man was also astute. Defiance was not characteristic of her. She had never been defiant before in her life. Lisa's temperament was basically even and pleasant. She was not strong. Her stepsister, Sofie, was strong. These past two months had taken every ounce of courage she possessed and then even more, a resolve which she had not even known herself capable of.

Lisa moved to a plush red chair and sank down, clasping her hands tightly in order to hide their trembling. She did not want St. Clare to guess how unnerved she really was. What did he want now? And why did he have to seek her out in the intimate confines of her bedroom?

He turned and slowly closed her door, worrying Lisa even more. Then he faced her, leaning one broad shoulder against it. His stare was unyielding.

And Lisa wanted him out of her room. She leapt to her feet. "What is it that you want?"

His gaze narrowed. "Why are you distraught, Lisa? You have no reason to fear me. I will never hurt you. I am a civilized man."

She lifted her chin. "I am not afraid of you."

"You are quaking."

"Hardly," Lisa lied. "I am . . . cold."

His mouth seemed to ease into a smile. Briefly it transformed his face, making him far more stunning than should be possible. "I only wish to discuss the future with you."

Lisa's eyes flashed. "We have no future!"

"You are being childish again. We are married and that is not going to change. However, I think you will be happy to learn that I am leaving for Europe the moment we return to New York City."

Lisa stood up. She wanted him gone, she did, but that meant that he would be leaving in a few days. She was too stunned to speak.

"Sorry to see me go?" he mocked.

"I am glad to see you go!" she cried, but her words felt like a contradiction, like a lie. Then she jerked, stricken with another inkling. "Wait — you are taking me with you?"

He shook his head. "No. I did not say that *we* were leaving. I am leaving. I have matters to attend to that cannot wait. I will send for you in the spring."

It took Lisa a full moment to grasp what

he was saying, and even then, she did not comprehend his words completely. He was going to do as she had suggested. He was going to leave her in New York, taking only her money with him. Lisa knew she should be elated. Instead, she was strangely dismayed.

Clearly he had told her the truth earlier, that, given a choice, he would never have remarried; clearly he did not care for her at all.

It should not hurt. Her heart was already broken. Then why did she feel so bruised and battered now?

He returned her shocked gaze. "This is what you want, isn't it, Lisa? For me to take your money and leave you behind?"

Lisa's bosom began to heave. "Yes," she managed, without any conviction.

"I *will* send for you in the spring," he said firmly.

Lisa shook her head. "B-but I won't come."

His stare remained on her face. "Do not think to defy me another time, Lisa. Do not force me to return to America to fetch you." His words were soft and filled with warning.

Lisa was trying to imagine the next six months, being married to him, yet residing worlds apart. Why wasn't she thrilled? "I will not obey your summons like some well-trained and docile lackey, St. Clare, when it comes next spring. Do not bother sending for me."

He stared at her tightly folded arms. "Then I shall come to fetch you."

"Why?" Lisa cried. "Y-you don't want me — so why?" And even she heard the hurt in her tone.

He had turned toward the door, but now he froze. Her words seemed to hang in the air . . . *you don't want me.*

"I shall send for you in the spring because, madam, you are my wife, for better or for worse."

"Oh, God," Lisa whispered. "I am doomed."

He hesitated, suddenly appearing uncertain and far younger than his thirty years. "Lisa, perhaps in six months time you will grow up and realize that your lot could be much worse."

She waved a hand at him, unable to speak, hot tears burning her eyes, wanting him to go. When she found her voice, her tone was both bitter and hoarse. "I want to be alone."

He finally nodded and walked to the door. But he did not pass through it after he opened it and Lisa could not resist having the last word. "Julian."

He started at the sound of his given name.

Her smile flashed, tearful and bitter, in her pale face. "Merry Christmas, St. Clare."

He blanched, staring. And left without another word.

Three

Castleclare, Clare Island, 1903

Clare Island formed a buffer between the roiling Atlantic Ocean and the wild western Irish coast. Its windward side was impassable, a jumble of soaring cliffs and jagged hills that were mostly bare, constantly buffeted by the wind and the sea. But the island's leeward side was lushly green and fertile; the high, sloping hills were dotted with sheep capable of nimbly maneuvering amongst the stony slopes and twisting paths that dissected the countryside. On a good day, the shepherds could just make out the sandy beaches of Connaught County on the far side of Clew Bay.

Castleclare was perched on the northernmost side of the island, facing Achill Island. Built in the thirteenth century by the first Earl of Connaught, the original keep had been added onto many times since. Pale stone walls enclosed numerous rambling structures, but the turreted towers of the castle itself rose above it all. Julian had not been home in over six months. But he was hardly soothed by the sight of the ancient barbican and the central tower looming beyond it. He had been all over Europe on a wild goose chase.

Julian stared grimly ahead as his carriage rolled down the dirt road towards the castle. He intended to wring his brother's neck if he found him at Castleclare, and as he had looked everywhere else, he expected to locate him there.

The old, rusted iron portcullis was open, as always. Julian's coach rumbled through. O'Hara braked far too abruptly, the two bays squealed, and Julian was thrown off his seat. Sighing, he flung open the door, its hinges protesting noisily. His coach was as old as his manservant. He wouldn't mind purchasing a new conveyance, but he was loath to let the old family retainer go, no matter how annoyed he might occasionally be.

"M'lord, beg yorr pardon," O'Hara wheezed, panting and out of breath.

Julian gave him an impatient look and did not wait for him to dislodge himself from the upper driving seat. Stepping from the coach, he strode across the dirt and gravel drive and pushed open the heavy and scarred front door. He paused inside the cavernous central hall.

It was a part of the original, thirteenth century keep. As such, it was entirely composed of stone, thus cold, and being windowless, dark. Pennants hung from the rafters. Swords, maces, and a crossbow hung on the walls, all weapons from another, earlier era. Julian glanced around. The centuries-old trestle table, heavily scarred, was coated with dust. The oversized hearth, set against the far wall, was devoid of a welcoming fire. The stone floors were bare and frigid. Julian could feel the cold seeping up through the worn soles of his riding boots. Last week he had discovered the beginnings of another hole on his left sole.

"Robert," he barked.

There was no answer, nothing except the echo of his own voice, but he had not expected one. His home was far too large. He passed through the hall, seeing not a soul. He had cut his staff down long ago to the all-purpose O'Hara, two equally generic maids, and a cook. Because his staff could hardly keep up with his immense home, he ignored the dust motes hanging in the air and the cobwebs in the corners. He could not help thinking about the bride he had not wanted to begin with. She would hardly find his home pleasant after the pomp and splendor of New York City's highest society. His pulse raced disturbingly at the thought.

Julian traversed another dark, unlit corridor, leaving behind the keep. The wing the family inhabited had been built in the sixteenth century. The floors were parquet, the windows wide. Numerous works of art lined the walls, including a Botticelli, a Velasquez, and a Courbet. Julian had never been able to part with the art his family had accumulated and admired for centuries.

At the door to his brother's chamber he paused, just long enough to hear a feminine giggle. Julian's eyes widened and he shoved open the door.

Robert sat on his four-poster bed, which showed signs of recent activity. He was dressed only in a pair of fine gray wool trousers. His arm was around a local girl Julian vaguely recognized. Julian's stare hardened.

The girl was also half-clad. She squealed, pulling her dress up to cover her abundant breasts. Robert took one look at Julian and turned a ghastly shade of white. He jumped up from the bed while the girl fled. "Julian! You're home!"

"How clever of you, Robert," Julian ground out. He stared. "You are supposed to be at the spa."

Robert ran a hand through his thick chestnut hair. "Julian, can you blame me for wanting to have fun? Before it's too late for me to enjoy myself?"

Julian felt a stabbing all the way to his soul. "No, I do not blame you, but your hedonistic tendencies must be modified,

Robert." His gaze had already found the empty bottle of port on the bedside table. "Dammit, the doctors told you to drink less, and not to exert yourself."

Robert smiled slightly. "A little bedsport, brother, is hardly an exertion." Suddenly Robert's expression changed. Julian tensed as he began to cough, uncontrollably, for several moments. Very grim, Julian waited until the fit had passed before speaking. Walking to the bedside table, he poured his brother a glass of water and handed it to him.

"How often have I told you to stay away from the local girls?" he asked quietly.

"She's a widow," Robert said mildly. "I'm hardly as noble or as clever as you, but I'm not stupid."

Julian studied his brother. They were very different men, and not just because Robert was seven years younger and gravely ill, and not because Robert was fair and auburn-haired. Robert had always been a charming, reckless rake. He had left a trail of broken hearts from Clare Island to Dublin and then to London as well. Julian's eyes narrowed. Although Robert's cheeks were flushed, he had not lost any more weight. The last time Julian had seen his brother he had dark circles under his eyes, his skin had been pasty white, and he had looked terrible. He appeared to have improved. "You look very well."

Robert smiled, his gray eyes guileless. "I have had a very good week, Julian. I think the doctors are wrong. I think this climate is less damaging than they say."

"I want you to return to the spa," Julian said flatly. "No ifs, ands, or buts about it."

Robert was dismayed. "Julian, I know you have an open mind. We must speak of this at length. I do not want to spend my final days in the goddamned spa!"

Julian's chest heaved. "You are hardly at Death's door!" he snapped furiously. "Do not talk that way!"

Robert's expression was mulish. "I want to enjoy the last years of my life."

Julian stared. Aching.

Robert smiled and walked over to his brother and slipped his arm around him. "I am feeling so much better ever since I came home. My spirits are as important as my health."

Julian felt himself relenting. "They say you only stayed at the spa for a month. The moment I sailed for America you left."

Robert shrugged guiltily. "I took advantage of your absence." He hesitated. "Have you come home alone?"

An emotion Julian had no wish to identify swept through him. His entire body stiffened. "Yes. But have no fear. I have done my familial duty. I merely left my rich little bride in New York until the spring."

"You are married!" Robert was elated. His eyes danced. "Julian, that is wonderful — tell me about her!"

"There is nothing to tell." Julian looked away as Lisa's lovely image filled his mind.

But Robert was not about to be put off. He flung his arm around Julian, still grinning. "Is she pretty?"

"Yes."

Robert waited, and when no elaboration was forthcoming, he shook Julian lightly. "Well? Is she fair or dark? Plump or slender? What is her name?"

Julian felt his temples throbbing. "Her name is Lisa. She is Benjamin Ralston's only daughter, and she has the kind of fortune we need to provide your medical treatment and keep up this estate."

Robert stared at him searchingly. "Why don't you send for her now?"

Julian shrugged free of his grasp and paced to the window — only to realize his mistake. From Robert's room there was a perfect view of the shimmering lake. Immediately he turned away. "I have no wish to send for her."

Robert stared; their gazes locked. The silence was tense and laden with unspoken denial. "You need her here, Julian. Don't deny it."

"That's absurd."

"It's been ten years!" Robert cried.

Suddenly Julian was enraged. "Don't tell me how long it has been!" he shouted, his face a dark, furious red.

Robert's eyes widened and he stepped back, as if fearing Julian would strike him.

Julian wanted to hit him. He realized that his fists were clenched, painfully so.

"Julian," Robert said, braced for a blow.

Julian became aware of the rage that threatened to consume him, body and soul. He began to shake. He was terrified of his feelings. But he was a man of iron will, and that will had been honed and strengthened for ten long years. He forced the rage down, forced the fury back to the place where it had been born. When he had gained control, he was drenched with sweat and gasping for breath.

All the while, Robert watched him, tears in his eyes. "Let go," the younger man finally whispered. "Let go. *They're dead.*"

Julian refused to look at him. He left the room.

Robert felt a tear trickle down his cheek. "Goddamn it," he said to himself. "I want my brother back."

It was a prayer.

London

Lisa felt that she was traveling to her

doom. She stood motionless at the steamer's railing, staring blindly as London's jagged skyline emerged into view. She had traveled abroad numerous times as a child and as an adolescent with her parents. Once she had loved the sight of St. Paul's needlelike cathedral soaring above the city. Now she did not even notice it.

Lisa gripped the railing with both gloved hands, her pale blue parasol forgotten at her feet. Oh, God. In a few moments she would finally come face-to-face with St. Clare again.

Lisa closed her eyes, feeling quite dizzy and very ill. In the past six months, she had tried very hard to pretend to herself and the world at large that she was still Lisa Ralston, and not St. Clare's wife. But it had quickly proved impossible. At every social occasion, she was introduced as Lady St. Clare, the Marchioness of Connaught, Julian St. Clare's wife. At every tea and soirée the ladies flocked to her, oohing and aahing over her successful marriage to the blue-blooded and oh-so-noble Marquis. "How could you let him leave without you?!" she was asked again and again. The ladies thought Lisa so terribly lucky. Not only had she married a title, but her husband was also astoundingly handsome.

She had not wanted to obey his summons when it had come, just as he had promised.

But her father was adamant. He had betrayed her with the proxy marriage, and now he had betrayed her yet again, insisting that she join her husband.

How she despised St. Clare.

Yet he haunted her thoughts constantly. Not an hour went by that Lisa did not recall one of their hostile exchanges and his too-handsome face. At night, he frequented her dreams. Too often, then, Lisa was swept back to an earlier time, when he was courting her and she was falling in love, blithely unaware of his motives. She would awaken strangely elated until reality claimed her, leaving her ill and shaken by her comprehension of the truth.

Glumly, Lisa stared over the railing of the steamer. She finally noticed the rowboats floating by the river banks, where parasoled ladies flirted with gentlemen in their derbies and shirtsleeves. The steamer was just passing the London Tower. Two swans drifted by the wharf, and redcoated soldiers guarded the riverside entrance. Lisa stared at the thick, dark walls. Today, the Tower reminded her of a prison. And that was where she was going — to a prison of her own, a prison with no escape. Her spirits had never been lower.

Yet she was trembling, too, her heart racing uncontrollably. In a few more minutes her ship would find its berth. St. Clare

198

would be waiting. Not for the first time, Lisa thought about leaving the ship and fleeing into London's midst. Yet she had failed to escape Julian in New York; she was convinced he would find her if she dared to run away again. His will was far stronger than hers.

The ship was guided to its dock by belching tugboats. Lisa scanned the waiting throngs as the anchors were lowered, the vessel secured, and the gangplanks thrown down. She gripped her parasol so tightly that her gloved hands ached. She did not remark a tall, golden-haired man standing a head above the rest of the cheering crowd.

The passengers began to disembark. Lisa had traveled with her maid, a plump and pretty blond girl Lisa's own age. Betsy loved to chatter, but she was silent now, her blue eyes as large as saucers as she stared at the city of London. Lisa was relieved. Betsy had talked ceaselessly for the entire trip, and Lisa was not in the mood now for her inane conversation. Betsy following, they walked down the gangplank.

There was pandemonium all around them on the wharf. Passengers were embraced and greeted by relatives and friends. Ladies wept. Children jumped up and down. Gentlemen grinned from ear to ear, and Lisa espied a couple passionately entwined. She recognized the gentleman as a fellow passenger, and suddenly she was envious.

If only . . .

She shoved aside her thoughts.

"Lisa?"

The man's voice was unfamiliar, but unmistakably Irish. Lisa turned to see a tall, handsome gentleman. "Lady St. Clare?" he asked, his gaze sweeping over her so thoroughly that she became aware of being hot and disheveled and probably quite untidy as well.

"I am Lisa *Ralston* St. Clare."

Suddenly he smiled. "And I am your brother-in-law." He gripped her gloved hands tightly, giving Lisa the distinct impression that he wanted to embrace her. "Robert St. Clare, in fact. It is wonderful to finally make your acquaintance."

Lisa managed a wan reply. So this then was the brother with consumption. She had expected a pale invalid, not this charming and flamboyant rake.

Robert did not give her a chance to gather up her thoughts, other than to wonder where St. Clare was. "Good God, how beautiful you are. Julian never said a word!"

Lisa turned red. Her heart banged painfully against her breast. Of course St. Clare hardly thought her beautiful; in fact, he probably described her as a hag.

"I am sorry." Robert tucked her arm in

his. "Forgive me. But you know Julian." He laughed uneasily.

Lisa could not hold her tongue. "No. I do not know your brother, not at all." Her tone was acerbic.

Robert stared at her searchingly.

Lisa flushed again and glanced away, reminding herself that she was a lady and she must not allow her ill will towards her husband make her act in any other manner.

"Perhaps, in time, you will understand Julian better," Robert said at last.

Lisa glanced around carefully. "He is not here." She refused to be disappointed. He had not even come to greet her after her week-long journey and their six-month separation.

"No," Robert protested, "Julian went to make certain that all of our arrangements at the hotel were satisfactory. He should be here at any moment."

Lisa did not comment upon the fact that Robert could have checked upon the arrangements, allowing Julian to greet her. How eager he was to see her again.

But Julian suddenly pushed through the crowd, materializing before her very eyes.

Lisa froze at the sight of him.

His strides faltered as well.

Lisa was momentarily stricken. She had forgotten how stunning he was, how patrician and how elegant — how incredibly masculine. Her heart skipped a beat as their gazes caught and held.

He too appeared stunned by her presence, yet he was the first to look away.

It was then that Lisa noticed the woman he was with. Tall, willowy, and blond, she was as patrician as he. In fact, she might have even been his sister. She was only a few years older than Lisa. Did Julian have a sister?

St. Clare moved forward, taking one of her hands and bowing over it, avoiding her eyes. "I hope your journey was not too tiring," he said, his tone formal. And then he glanced up.

Lisa could not look away. For one moment she felt that she was drowning in a sea of gray. The very same magnetism which had captivated her so thoroughly when they first met pulled at her now — the same magnetism and the same soul. Something stirred deep inside her. But Lisa had been determined to avoid this pull ever since his deception. She would avoid it now by re-minding herself of the short history they had shared.

Lisa extracted her hand from his. His palm was hard and warm, even through her white cotton gloves. "The voyage was fine."

"Good." His glance wandered to hers again. And raked over the bodice of her short, fitted jacket and the length of her narrow skirt, both the palest blue muslin and the latest fashion, to the very tips of her white patent shoes. He turned abruptly, leaving Lisa shaken, and the blond woman stepped forward.

"May I introduce my neighbor, Lady Edith Tarrington," Julian said. "Edith is also staying at the Carleton. When she learned that I was meeting you at the wharf, she expressed her desire to join me. Edith, my . . . bride, Lady St. Clare."

Edith Tarrington smiled at Lisa. "I am so pleased to meet you," she said. "The whole county has been in quite a state since Julian returned home and declared that he had wed. We have all been eagerly awaiting your arrival, Lady St. Clare."

Lisa managed a faint smile. She did not know what to think. Who was this neighbor of Julian's? She was far too beautiful for Lisa to be at ease. Then Lisa realized that Julian was regarding her intently again.

His gaze quickly lowered. "A hansom is waiting. We will spend the night in London, then take another steamer to Castleclare."

At first Lisa failed to reply. She glanced from Julian to Edith Tarrington and back again. Surely Julian would not introduce her to a woman who was significant to him. Surely not. "That is fine."

They stared at one another, almost help-lessly.

Robert coughed, grinned, and slapped Julian's shoulder. "To the Carleton then, my friends. Your beautiful bride is surely tired and eager for the finer comforts of life!" His smile faded slightly. "Of course, you will join us, Edith, if you have no other plans?"

Her expression cooled. "How kind of you, Robert. In fact, I am free this evening, and I will gladly join your group."

Lisa felt dismayed, but she told herself that she was being foolish.

Then Edith touched Julian's arm. It was a brief gesture, yet it bespoke years of familiarity. "If it is all right with you, Jul-ian." Her tone was low, intimate.

But Julian was looking at Lisa. "Of course," he said. Then he stepped aside, gesturing for Lisa to precede him. "After you, ladies," he said formally.

And as Lisa walked forward with Edith Tarrington towards the line of waiting car-riages, she felt his eyes on her back, burn-ing with the intensity she had somehow forgotten.

Four

Supper was at eight. St. Clare had re-
served a private room for the four of them
that was just off the Palm Court, an exalted,
palm-filled atrium which replicated the fa-
mous interior of the Paris Ritz almost exactly. The Carleton Hotel had been opened
by Cesar Ritz three years earlier, and he
had done his best to bring France in all of
its glory to London.

Lisa was in a state of nervous tension as
she exited her rooms. The last person she
wished to see was Edith Tarrington, but
the other woman was just departing her
suite across the hall as Lisa shut her door.
The two women paused, looking uncer-
tainly at one another. Lisa forced a smile.
"How lovely you look, Lady Tarrington." It
was hardly a fabrication. Edith was one of
those rare women who looked superb in pale
pink, and her evening gown revealed far more
of her willowy figure than it concealed.

Edith smiled slightly. "Thank you. Your
gown is stunning. I am sure Julian will be
impressed."

Lisa had found it almost impossible to
decide what to wear. She was loath to dress

for the husband she did not want, but she had chosen a silvery chiffon gown that she knew was superb, far more low-cut and provocative than she was used to wearing. Yet she muttered, "Julian will not notice this dress, I assure you of that," before she could think better of it.

Edith started.

Lisa wished she had reined in her unruly tongue. She felt her cheeks burning, yet could not come up with a comment to distract Edith Tarrington. Fortunately, Edith resumed her usual genteel expression, and gestured for Lisa to precede her. Lisa was glad to do so.

A moment later she came to the head of the stairs, which looked down on the Palm Court. She tripped.

Edith steadied her with a gloved hand under her elbow. "Careful —" she began, then instantly followed Lisa's gaze to the two gentlemen standing on the landing below.

Julian and his brother were a magnificent sight in their tuxedos, apparently waiting to escort the ladies through the atrium to the private dining room. Robert had been speaking, while Julian had seemed restless. Now they were both motionless, staring up at the women.

Lisa had seen Julian in evening clothes before, of course, but the impact was still shattering and physical. Her heart skidded to a stop. Her mouth became unbearably dry. In his black tailcoat and trousers and snowy white shirt, Julian St. Clare was utterly devastating.

Lisa wished, she desperately wished, that he were an ugly, old man. She could not continue to fool herself. She despised him, oh yes, she did, but whenever she looked at him her heart stopped and her body tightened. She remembered every single one of his soul-shattering kisses. Oh, God. How had she come to this impasse? To be married to a man she despised — one so terribly beautiful — a man who did not care for her at all?

Then Lisa thought about the beautiful blonde beside her, and she peeked at her. Edith appeared as mesmerized by Julian as Lisa was, and Lisa's heart sank. Were her suspicions correct?

Yet Julian was staring at Lisa — she was certain of it. And when their gazes connected, there was no more doubt.

She had become utterly motionless, poised on the stairs with one hand on the smooth wooden banister. She could not seem to direct her slippered feet to move. His eyes had drained her of the ability to function.

Julian finally looked at Edith with a small smile. His jaw was flexed and he had jammed his hands in the pockets of his tuxedo.

Then Robert came forward. "Ladies, you are a sight for sore eyes. How lovely you are!" He smiled at Lisa, ignoring Edith.

Lisa came down the last three steps. "Thank you."

Julian faced her, extending his arm somewhat stiffly. His glance included Edith. "My brother is correct. You are both lovely. Shall we? Our room is ready."

Lisa's heart sank even further, dismay welling deep inside her. She had wanted some small sign from him that he found her attractive. Clearly he was unimpressed. Or equally impressed with Edith. She forced a smile, giving him her arm. She reminded herself that she did not care. If she should care now about what he thought of her she was forever doomed.

But she noticed that Robert shot his brother a dark look. And in that moment Lisa knew that they would be friends.

Julian escorted her through the hotel lobby. Lisa was aware of the guests, the men in their tailcoats, the ladies in their brilliantly hued evening gowns, turning to stare at them as they passed. What a couple they must make, Lisa thought, suddenly saddened. So clearly at odds with one another. So clearly miserable together.

Julian held out a chair for her, putting

Lisa on his right. As she sat, one of his hands accidentally brushed her shoulder blade. She stiffened, shocked by the feeling of his palm on her bare back.

She glanced up at him. His eyes were wide and riveted upon her as well, as if he were as surprised and shaken as she.

Abruptly he turned away.

Robert seated Edith across from Lisa. The men sat down between the ladies, facing one another. Robert leaned toward Lisa. When he spoke, his tone was low, so no one could overhear him. "You make a striking couple. Everyone in the lobby is whispering about the two of you. They want to know who you are."

Lisa could only stare at him; then she realized that Julian was frowning at them both — and that Robert's hand was covering hers.

Julian fingered his glass of wine, unable to ignore Robert as he leaned close to Lisa, regaling her with story after story about his university days. He had been amusing her all evening. Lisa was smiling, as she had been most of the night. Smiling at Robert.

But then, his brother was a charming rakehell with a reputation half as big as London. Of course Lisa was charmed and amused. Robert was an expert when it came to seducing women.

Julian was relieved, of course, that his brother was being his normal amiable self. Robert, of course, had no interest in Lisa other than a familial one. His gallantry allowed Julian to be a silent observer — it also allowed him to brood.

He had forgotten just how pretty Lisa was.

No, not pretty, breathtaking. So tiny, so dark, and so lovely.

So entirely different from Melanie.

Julian slammed his gaze to the table, lifted his glass, and drained it. He reminded himself that he had no right to any feelings other than formal ones, that she was his wife in name only, and he intended to keep it that way.

"Julian?" Edith's voice was soft with concern. Her gloved fingertips rested briefly on his arm. She had also spent most of the evening silently watching Robert flirt with Lisa. Although most of the county thought that Edith hankered after Julian and was heartbroken over his marriage to another woman, Julian did not believe it — he never had. "Are you all right?" she asked quietly.

Julian surprised them both by answering Melanie's younger sister honestly. "Given the circumstances, I am faring as well as possible." He turned his gaze directly toward her. "And you?"

Edith held his eyes, her own shadowed

with unhappiness. "I suppose my answer is precisely the same." She turned her head and glanced at Lisa and Robert again.

Julian thought that his suspicions about Edith were correct. Having known what it was to love and lose, he pitied her. And Robert, the fool, did not even guess.

His glance strayed yet again across the table to his bride. To his lovely bride, whom he did not want. Not in any way.

Then Julian's grip tightened on his wine-glass. Whom was he fooling? The French burgundy he was drinking, and had been drinking steadily all night, had caused a gentle unfurling of warmth in his gut. But it had also caused another reaction, one he was determined to ignore: an incipient full-ness in his loins. He had ignored it for some time now, and intended to do so forever if need be.

Then Julian realized that Lisa was not listening to Robert, who was talking about the opera. She was staring at him, her expression frozen. Julian realized that Edith's fingertips still rested upon his arm.

He flushed, realizing what Lisa must be thinking.

Edith must have realized at the same time, because she paled, dropping her hands to her lap.

Lisa turned to Robert abruptly, her face stricken with hurt although her lips formed a stiff smile. Robert said, "Of course, the very next day I woke up on the sofa and couldn't remember where I was. It was downright embarrassing."

Lisa laughed, but this time the sound was shrill and hollow. Her eyes turned to Julian.

Julian could not look away. Her gaze was filled with silent accusation and profound hurt.

He wanted to tell her again that he was sorry. Not for the misunderstanding about Edith, which was ridiculous, but for marrying her against her will, for spoiling all of her girlish dreams. He wasn't an expressive man. He wondered if he could find the right words. Suddenly he knew he had to reassure her. He shoved his chair back abruptly, surprising everyone, even though they had long since finished dessert. "Lisa, would you care to join me for a breath of air?"

The color drained from Lisa's face.

Lisa was surprised by Julian's invitation, surprised and anxious. He did not hold her arm as they wandered into the hotel's gaslit garden which fronted on Haymarket Street. High brick walls enclosed the garden from the public's view. Lisa was immediately assaulted by the fragrance of lilies, which were on display everywhere. Julian paused by a marble water fountain. Goldfish swam there, catching the light of the tall gaslamps and a beaming full moon.

Lisa stepped away from him, her heart pounding. What did he want?

She had tried not to look at him all evening, to concentrate on Robert, whom she already liked, but it had been impossible. Not when he was seated directly across the table from her, not when his presence was so virile and commanding. And not when Edith and he seemed to share a deep and sincere friendship. But surely they were not lovers. Surely not.

Lisa flushed, because if Julian were in love with Edith Tarrington it would explain so much. It would certainly explain his disinterest in Lisa herself. The possibility had distressed her all night, yet she knew she shouldn't care. Why was she torn this way? She didn't want St. Clare. Yet she was jealous of another woman.

And what did he want now? Lisa could not imagine why he had asked her outside. Certainly not to talk, and certainly not for any other intimacy.

Her thoughts quickly became fixated. He was her husband, and if he was not involved with Edith, he might very well intend to kiss her now, or even later, in her rooms.

Lisa's pulse raced.

And what might happen later? They were man and wife, but they had never consum-

213

mated their marriage. Did he think to come to her room tonight — to come to her bed? Surely he must do so eventually.

Lisa felt faint at the thought. She had no real desire to let him into her bed — not under these circumstances, dear God. But she was not immune to his virility. A part of her yearned for his caress, his kiss. Oh, damn her secretly passionate, unladylike soul!

"Lisa?"

She was so lost in her thoughts that she jumped at the sound of Julian's deep voice. She looked up at him, wide-eyed and breathless. "Y-yes?"

He folded his arms across his chest. "I wish . . . I hope you enjoyed supper to-night."

She nodded, unable to look away. "Everything was fine."

He continued to stare at her face. Or was he staring at her mouth? Lisa began to tremble. She could not think of a thing to say. His relentless stare was causing her heart to ricochet inside her chest.

Lisa wrung her hands, certain he was thinking about kissing her. She tried to get a grip on reality by reminding herself that he had married her for her money, regardless of her will. But the night was warm, the moon benevolent, enticing. The scent of freesia and orange blossoms mingled with that of lilies. Lisa was a captive of her husband's charisma, and she could not look away. She wet her lips desperately. "Wh-what is it th-that you wish to say, Julian?"

His jaw was tense. His eyes seemed smoky, warmer than before. He cleared his throat. "There are several matters we must discuss."

Lisa was paralyzed by the increasingly husky sound of his voice.

Julian shoved his hands into his pockets. "I asked you to join me outside because I wished to apologize yet again."

Lisa started. "Apologize?"

"We have gotten off to an exceedingly bad start, you and I. We must rectify this."

"Y-yes," Lisa whispered, hope burgeoning in her breast. Perhaps they might start anew. Perhaps they might even fall in love.

He inhaled. "I have already explained to you about Robert's health and his medical bills." He hesitated. "What is done is done, Lisa. We are married, and surely we can be civilized about this."

Lisa was stiff. She did not like his use of the word "civilized." Nor did she like being reminded of his motives in marrying her in the first place. She waited, hoping he would tell her he cared for her in spite of his need for her money, that he found her pretty, that he wanted to make their marriage a real one . . . a happy one.

Julian swallowed. "Many couples find themselves in a situation similar to the one we are in. Surely you realize that."

Lisa managed a nod, her heart banging like a drum.

"I am not the beast you think me to be — not completely, anyway. For instance, I am prepared to accept the fact that you will not like Castleclare. This evening it occurred to me that if you wish, I will not mind if you reside half the year in New York."

Lisa managed, "I . . . I see." But she was dismayed. How could they build their future if she was away half of the time?

"No, I don't think that you do see." Julian was flushing now, high up on his cheekbones. "What I really want to say is that we must make this marriage a civil one, an amicable one. I shall try to understand you. Thus, if you wish to spend half the year in New York, I shall not prevent you from doing so."

Lisa did not know what to think. What did he mean by an amicable marriage? "I . . . I also wish for this marriage to be amicable, Julian," she said tremulously. "I wish for us to be friends." She could not smile. Her entire future seemed to be hanging in the balance of their conversation.

He stared at her. "I do not think you understand. What I am trying to say is that

I will not make any bestial demands upon you."

Lisa could not move. "You are right — I do not quite understand," she whispered finally, but she was lying. Her temples began to throb as the realization of what he was trying to tell her began to sink in.

"God," he cried, raking his short blond hair with one hand. "You are so naive, so innocent. You cannot hide a single one of your feelings!" He faced her squarely, his legs braced wide apart, as if prepared to do battle. "I am not trying to hurt you again."

"You are not hurting me," Lisa lied, praying she would not cry. Something warm and wet trickled down one cheek.

"You don't understand, do you?" He was suddenly bitter. "You are young and you have a full life ahead of you. My life is over. I do not want you to suffer on my account. In fact, if you wish, you can return to New York tomorrow."

Tears filled Lisa's eyes. She heard herself say, "I want to try to make this marriage a successful one. Even you suggested that in New York. We are man and wife — there is no other choice."

"If you mean what I think you mean then the answer is *no*. It is impossible."

Lisa was desperate. "Nothing is impossible. Surely we can become friends."

He spoke thickly. "We cannot become

friends. Not in your sense of the word."

"But one day I will have your children!" Lisa cried.

He turned white. "You don't understand!"

"No, I don't. I don't understand *you* at all."

His chest heaved. "Lisa, I think I failed to make myself clear in New York. Our marriage will be successful if we respect one another and treat one another with decency." He paused. *"There will not be any children."*

Lisa had already sensed that this was coming, already dreaded it. She shook her head helplessly.

"This will be a marriage in name only."

"No," Lisa cried, aghast.

"There is no other alternative," Julian said flatly. But his gaze was agonized. "Lisa, you must try to understand."

"No! I do not understand!" Lisa sobbed and fled the garden.

Julian almost called her back. Instead, he sank down on the edge of the marble fountain, covering his face with his hands. He had the distinct feeling that he had just destroyed the last of her innocence without even laying a hand upon her.

Five

Castleclare, Clare Island

"These are your rooms, my lady," O'Hara said happily.

Lisa stared. From the moment they had arrived on Clare Island, she felt as if she were entering an ancient world. The small village where the ferry docked had mesmerized her — thatched-roof cottages of stone and timber appeared to have survived for centuries. There were no gaslines or telephone poles, no motor cars or even horse-drawn trolleys. Smoke puffed out from each and every stone chimney, even on this cool but pleasant May day. A man guided a donkey laden with wooden faggots down one street, a carter drove a shaggy pony down another. A woman stood on one unpaved corner, her plaid apron full of fresh, warm eggs. Barefoot women washed their laundry in a lazy river. And St. Clare's coach had to meander through a flock of sheep crossing the town's largest thoroughfare, an unnamed main street.

But perhaps the most shocking element of all was the silence. Except for the occasional bark of a sheepdog, a baby's cry, and the song of treetop birds, the world of Clare Island was stunningly quiet.

Castleclare belonged to the era of knights in shining armor and their damsels in distress. When St. Clare's coach had finally topped the highest hill, Lisa first glimpsed the castle. Her heart skipped a beat. This was St. Clare's home?

Beige stone walls guarded the castle, a half dozen square watchtowers rising from them at intermittent intervals. The entrance to the castle consisted of a real barbican — even if it was half in ruin — and an ancient portcullis remained dubiously aloft. Behind those walls a single round tower soared above all the steeply pitched thatch and slate interior rooftops.

Lisa only had to blink to see mailed knights riding through the barbican and archers in their jerkins. With another blink she could see the lady of the castle standing on the imposing front steps of the keep, waiting for her warrior husband to return.

"My lady?" O'Hara intoned.

Lisa did not hear the beaming old man. Eyes wide, she glanced around the huge bedchamber which was now hers. A fire blazed in a huge hearth below an exquisite green marble mantel — one in need of polishing. A beautiful antique gold clock graced it, two standing Grecian statuettes guarding the timepiece. The clock needed a good cleaning. A faded Aubusson rug covered the parquet floor. Lisa noticed several holes. The walls were covered in yellow silk, worn and stained in places, and even torn. The moldings on the ceiling were the most intricate Lisa had ever seen, and above her head, in a trompe l'oeil window, cherubs floated in a blue sky blowing gold trumpets. Tired gold damask draperies adorned the oversized windows. Through them, Lisa had a stunning view of the rolling countryside of Clare Island.

She stared at her canopied bed. It appeared to be a bed of state. It was huge, the coverings mostly gold and purple, the velvet curtains tied back with tasseled cords. Lisa could not imagine sleeping in such a bed. She wondered who had slept there before her, which statesmen, which royalty.

The rest of the room's furniture was as tired and as old, but every faded chair and scratched table reeked of history. Lisa was used to wealth — her father's house was one of the finest in New York — but this was entirely different. She felt as if she had been swept back in time. She could hardly believe that Castleclare was her home, that this was her room.

Yet she liked the room. Very much, in fact.

She liked Castleclare.

For the first time in two days, for the first time since Julian had shocked her with his announcement that he intended no real marriage between them, Lisa felt a rush of excitement. She would spend hours and hours exploring the island and the castle. She could hardly wait to begin.

"M'lady, I am sending up one of your maids with a spot of tea and muffins. Will you be needin' anythin' else? A hot bath, mayhap?"

Lisa started. She had forgotten the butler was there. Then her quick smile faded, because the very bane of her existence stood in the open doorway behind O'Hara.

Her gaze on Julian, Lisa heard herself say, "That will be fine. Thank you, Mr. O'Hara."

He bowed, beaming, patting his worn jacket as he exited.

Lisa's eyes narrowed. O'Hara needed a new suit. His clothing was a disgrace.

Lisa realized now that she was alone in her room with St. Clare. She did not like the intimacy. Not at all. Her gaze lifted to his.

Julian stared at her. "I realize that this hardly meets with your satisfaction," he said impassively. "But you have carte blanche. Please feel free to redecorate this and any other room that you think needs such care — with the exception of my private apartments, of course. Relay your instructions to myself or O'Hara, and they will be carried out."

Lisa lifted her chin, her eyes flashing. "I don't want to redecorate this room."

"Sulking will not improve things," Julian said, his eyes far too probing for comfort.

Lisa did not like looking into his turbulent gray eyes, but could not glance away. The silence grew between them. Stunned, she realized that, in spite of what Julian wished, there was a bond between them — a bond of tension and heat. Ducking her head and angry with herself for wanting him as a man, she said, "I like this room just the way it is."

He started.

"Now, if you will excuse me?" Lisa knew she was being unforgivably rude, but she marched to the door and held it, making it clear that she wished him to leave. His proximity unnerved her. That and her own treacherous thoughts.

Julian looked at her one last time, a sweeping glance that began at her eyes and finished at her toes, then he bowed and strode away. For some reason, Lisa thought that he seemed angry. That pleased her to no end.

Lisa was lost, but she did not mind. She

was deep within the castle in yet another, newer wing, a long gallery lined with dozens of portraits of St. Clares. How handsome the men tended to be, handsome and commanding, she mused, and how pretty and elegant the women. But not a single ancestor could compete with Julian's patrician looks.

She wondered where his portrait was, and if it was even in the gallery. She strolled down the length of narrow room until she found it. She faltered. If the gilded label on the frame had not read "Julian St. Clare, thirteenth Earl of Connaught," she would not have recognized him.

He was smiling.

Her heart hammering wildly, Lisa moved closer to the portrait, her eyes wide. It had probably been painted ten or eleven years ago. Clearly Julian had been a much younger man. But God, he had been so different! His smile was genuine. It reached his eyes, it came from his soul. It was the smile of a happy man.

Lisa wondered what had happened in the past ten years to turn him into such a cold, aloof man. She could not help being disturbed. She would have liked to know the man in the portrait. She sensed that she never would — that he was gone forever. Inexplicably, she was sad.

Lisa decided to leave the gallery, too disturbed to remain. But as she turned her eye caught a glimpse of the portrait besides Julian's, that of an extraordinarily pretty blond woman.

Suddenly filled with dread, Lisa came closer, already certain of what she would find, certain of who that woman was.

"Lady Melanie St. Clare, the thirteenth Marchioness of Connaught," Lisa read aloud.

She stared grimly at the young woman. Lisa could not help noticing how utterly different Julian's first wife was from herself. Not only was she blond, she had a fragility about her, an ethereal quality that made her beauty astounding. Upon closer inspection Lisa saw that her eyes were a robin's egg blue, her complexion perfectly porcelain. And the way that the portraits were placed, it appeared that she and St. Clare were smiling at one another — for all eternity.

Oddly enough, Lisa's heart sank.

What had happened to her? Lisa only knew that she had died. Had Julian loved her? That thought was distinctly upsetting. Worse, Lisa remarked now that Melanie St. Clare bore a distinct resemblance to Edith, although Edith was a much stronger version of the dead woman. She did not like the fact of their resembling one another, not at all. Lisa turned and left the gallery, her stride swift. She had little doubt that Julian had loved his first wife completely.

Was Edith related to her? A cousin or a sister, perhaps? Did Julian see his first wife in the other woman every time he looked at her? Did he yearn for Edith now because of her resemblance to Melanie?

In the corridor outside, Lisa paused, trying to shake both her thoughts and her distress. To make matters worse, she was uncertain about which way to go. Finally she bore left, passing numerous closed doors as she did so. The castle was completely silent except for the harsh echo of her own footsteps.

The corridors were dark. She began to grow uneasy when she did not find the stairwell. She started to feel that she was not alone, which was ridiculous. She began to start at her own shadow. It occurred to her that a castle like this might very well be haunted. Lisa had never faced a ghost before, but she now knew that she believed in their existence.

She finally knocked on a door, not expecting a response. When she dared to open it, she found a dark, dusty bedroom, the furniture covered in tattered sheets. How many apartments, she wondered, did Castleclare contain?

A movement made her screech. Lisa gasped in relief when she spotted a mouse scurrying across the floor.

Waiting for her pounding heart to still, Lisa realized that she would like to renovate Castleclare. Not redo it, but open and air all the rooms, refinish the furniture, clean the rugs and drapes. Restore the castle to all of its original magnificence and ancient glory.

Lisa hurried on. Relieved, she finally spied a staircase, quickly following it down. She was certain now that she was on the castle's second floor, the floor where her own apartment was.

She could not help wondering, not for the first time, if Julian's rooms were on this floor as well.

Lisa tried another door. It opened with a noisy protest and she barged in on Robert.

He was reclining in bed, fully dressed, but his shirt was open halfway down his chest. He wore his socks but no shoes. He was reading.

He started when he saw her, exactly as Lisa did. She blushed. "I am so sorry!" she cried. "I am lost."

"Please, don't be sorry," Robert smiled, closing the book and standing. "I am glad to see you. Come in."

It wasn't proper, not at all, and Lisa hesitated.

Robert's eyes widened. "I thought we were friends."

"We are," Lisa said firmly. Still blushing, she entered the room, wondering if she dared ask Robert about Julian's first wife. She hovered close to the door.

"Were you exploring your new home?" Robert asked, sauntering over to her.

"Yes. This castle is vast. How many rooms does it contain?"

"I forget whether it's fifty-six or fifty-seven," Robert said lightly. "A hundred years ago the St. Clares were very wealthy and powerful. We had numerous estates, here in western Ireland and in southern England. But my father and grandfather were both gamesters, and between the two of them, they gambled away everything except Castleclare."

"Oh," Lisa said. "That is terrible."

"I believe my brother could turn our fortunes around if he wished to." Robert smiled. "He is a clever man. Many years ago he made some successful investments. But these past ten years, he has lost all interest in the estate."

Lisa wondered if Julian's loss of interest had to do with the obvious change in his character. She hesitated, wetting her lips. "I found the portrait gallery."

"Ah, yes. Did you have a nice visit with all the St. Clare ghosts?"

"It was very interesting." Lisa fidgeted, dying to ask him what was really on her mind while dreading his answer. Then she blurted, "I found Julian's portrait."

Robert had ceased smiling. His gray gaze was curious. "Yes. That was done a dozen years ago. Julian was eighteen and newly wed."

Her heart was hammering. "He was a happy man then."

"Yes. He was. And he was my hero." Robert smiled pensively. "He was seven years older and could do no wrong. I worshipped him. I followed him everywhere. He did not mind. Until . . ." He paused, his glance fastening to hers.

"Until?" Lisa prodded.

"Until he met Melanie."

"His first wife."

"Yes."

Lisa paced across the room and stared out of the thick, grayish window at a small, shimmering lake. She realized she was hugging herself. She turned. "What happened?"

"She was Anglo-Irish. Although her father had an estate here, just across the channel, Melanie was raised in Sussex. The summer she was sixteen she came here with her parents, and she and Julian met and immediately fell in love. She refused to leave her father's Irish estate, and Julian began courting her in earnest. They were wed the following year."

"So he really loved her," Lisa said, feeling

miserable. "She was very pretty."

"She was very weak," Robert said, his tone harsh and accusing.

Lisa jerked.

"Yes, Julian loved her, but she was as fragile as handblown glass." Robert's stare was chilling. "You don't know what happened, do you? How she died? He hasn't told you, has he, about the accident?"

Lisa shook her head. She was perspiring in spite of the castle's ever-present chill.

"But he wouldn't. He won't speak about it. He's never spoken about it, not to anyone. It happened ten years ago, and Julian has never been the same. When they died, I lost my brother." Robert's voice had become thick.

Lisa trembled. *"They?"*

"They had a child. A little boy. Eddie. He was two years old, blond and beautiful, a little angel. He drowned in the lake."

"Oh, my God," Lisa whispered, turning to look at the jewel-like lake. In spite of the leaded glass, it was the color of emeralds, sparkling in the spring sun. A place of peace — a place of death.

Robert's eyes were filled with tears. "Julian was bereft. Hysterical. As was Melanie. Instead of comforting one another, they retreated from one another. Melanie locked herself up in her rooms, Julian in his. And there was anger. So much anger with the grief. I begged Julian to come out. I was so frightened. Although Melanie had taken Eddie to the lake that day, Julian blamed himself for the tragedy."

Lisa was breathless with dread. *"What happened?"*

"Two days after Eddie died, Melanie left her rooms. No one knew — it was at sunrise. She went down to the lake clad only in her nightclothes." He stopped and brushed his eyes with his fist.

"No," Lisa said, already understanding, horrified.

"Yes," Robert said softly. "She drowned herself."

Six

Lisa had to sit down. She was vaguely aware of Robert guiding her to a chair. She covered her face with her hands. She ached for Julian with every fiber of her being. And now she understood.

Oh, God, how she understood.

"He has never recovered," Robert said, kneeling on the floor beside her. He took her two hands in his. "I know you are angry with my brother for marrying you without love, against your will. He told me how you ran away. You are a brave, strong woman, Lisa, and a beautiful woman — exactly the kind of woman my brother needs."

Lisa wiped her eyes, unable to put the tragic double death out of her mind. She stared at Robert. "I am not sure what you mean. Julian doesn't need me. He did not marry me out of choice. I thought he was falling in love with me, fool that I was. I had no idea that he had come to America to wed an heiress." She was careful not to mention that she knew about Robert's consumption. She wasn't sure if he would be pleased that she was aware of his ill health.

"That is the past. What is done is done.

232

He does need you, Lisa," Robert said in an urgent tone.

Their eyes met. For an instant, Lisa was unable to move. "What are you saying?" Her pulse was racing. Surely Robert did not mean what she thought he meant.

He gripped her hands more tightly. "I have no doubt that you will thaw his icy heart. And bring back the man we have all lost."

Lisa laughed in disbelief. "Me?" She was strangely out of breath. "How on earth could I thaw his heart?"

"The way all women thaw all men, Lisa, sweet. By making him fall in love with you."

Lisa was so stunned that she could not make a sound. She did not even blink.

Robert chuckled. "Surely you are up to the task?"

"T-task?!" she squeaked. She found her tongue. "He doesn't even think I'm pretty!"

Robert snorted. "You are beautiful. No man could think otherwise, and that includes my brother."

"I . . . other men have found me attractive," Lisa said hesitantly. "Robert, this is absurd! Julian truly does not know I exist!"

"He knows."

Lisa trembled. She was frightened — exhilarated. "What about Edith?"

"Edith?" Robert's tone was strange. "She is Melanie's youngest sister, you know. But she is nothing like Melanie. Julian never considered marrying her. I know that for a fact."

"Are they . . . close?"

Robert hesitated. "They are friends. Forget about Edith. Julian is an honorable man. He is not dallying with her, Lisa. I am certain of it."

Lisa studied her hands. Robert's proposal had left her breathless.

"The alternative is to give up on him, to let your relationship flounder, to remain perfect strangers," Robert pointed out.

Lisa was afraid. The stakes were so high — if she dared attempt what Robert suggested, if she dared to try to tame the beast and set Julian free. "Just what is it that you expect me to do?" she whispered. "How would I even start to make him . . . fall in love with me?"

Robert's grin was reckless. "That's easy, sweetheart. Seduce him."

Lisa opened her mouth to protest, but no sound came out. Her eyes were as round as saucers.

"You could do it, Lisa," Robert said fiercely, his gray eyes flashing. "And I would help you. I know all there is to know about seduction."

Seduce Julian. Seduce him — win his heart — make him fall in love with her. Lisa was in shock.

It was a monumental task. She did not

know the first thing about seduction — she was no temptress. She would make a fool of herself, she was certain, if she dared to try what Robert was so firmly suggesting. "Perhaps," she said huskily, "I might befriend him first?"

Robert's wide grin flashed. "Seduction is the way to a man's heart — especially in my brother's case."

Lisa was frozen. Her mind raced. Panic warred with excitement, despair with hope. And her anger was gone. It had drained away, leaving in its place a deep, abiding compassion. He had loved once and lost everything. How could she turn her back on him now, ignoring what she knew, no matter how afraid she was of his rejection?

"Well?"

Lisa was suddenly quite faint with the prospect. "You are mad," she managed in a rough whisper. "We are both mad."

"Is that a yes? Do you agree?" Robert asked exultantly.

Lisa nodded.

They stared at one another, the first bonds of conspiracy forming between them.

"I will tell you exactly what to do, even what to wear," Robert told her in a low, confidential tone.

But Lisa did not hear him. Images danced in her head of herself, clad in one of her lacy peignoirs, sauntering over to Julian, who was reading in front of the fire. She would sashay just a bit, the way the hussies did on stage in theatrical productions, and suddenly he would realize that she was there. He would be stunned. His gaze would slide over her. Lisa would smile seductively, and as she turned to face him, her silk jacket would open . . .

Lisa sighed. Who was she fooling? Not once in her life had she sashayed around in her peignoir, and she knew nothing about seduction, nothing at all. Even with Robert's help, she would probably make a fool of herself. "I am going to need a lot of help."

"Have no fear," Robert said with absolute assurance.

Lisa was not soothed. And her trepidation increased when Robert's door swung open and Julian entered. She stiffened as her cheeks turned red.

"Robert," Julian said irascibly, not having seen Lisa yet, "do you know where my little bride . . ." He stopped in mid-sentence, his eyes widening as they found her.

Robert dropped his hand from Lisa's shoulder and rose to his full height. "Yes?"

Julian looked from Robert to Lisa, his expression one of utter surprise — and then one of stern displeasure. "I see," he said slowly.

Lisa got to her feet. Her nerves were

rioting, her face burning. Surely Julian did not think that she and Robert were carrying on in any illicit manner? Her gaze met his. His was cold and dark and seemed angry. Lisa regretted being closeted with Robert in his bedroom.

"Hello, Julian," she said unsteadily. "I was lost and I had no idea that I was outside of Robert's room."

Julian's expression was set in stone. "You are hardly outside of my brother's room." He looked again at Robert. "What were the two of you discussing with your heads so close together?"

Lisa could not think of a suitable reply.

"Your bride was exploring. She has been in the portrait gallery. We were talking about the family, of course." Robert smiled and walked over to his brother, then smacked his shoulder. "What's wrong? Are you jealous, Julian? Am I not allowed to converse with your bride?"

Julian flushed. "Do not be absurd," he snapped. He directed his cool stare at Lisa. "The cook wishes to discuss the evening's menu with you, Lisa."

"Of course," she managed, fingering the fabric of her skirt. She could not force a smile, not even a small one. She desperately wanted to tell Julian that she understood, that she was sorry. She also wanted to explain that there was nothing improper between her and Robert, and that there never would be. Suddenly feelings she had thought dead and buried were welling up inside of her — feelings of wild, aching love. Lisa was shocked to recognize them.

Robert seemed amused. "I am not feeling very well. I think I will take a nap. Why don't you show Lisa to the kitchens, Julian? She won't be able to find the way herself."

Julian nodded curtly. He gestured, and Lisa preceded him from the room. She was acutely aware of him directly behind her.

They traversed the corridor and went downstairs in silence. Lisa had to hurry to keep pace with Julian. As they crossed the cavernous central hall, she drew abreast of him and dared to peek at his face. Was he angry? Or had she imagined it? Was he jealous?

Could it be possible?

A man had to have strong feelings in order to be jealous. Julian had never given her any indication that he had any feeling towards her at all.

Lisa could stand it no more. She plucked on his sleeve. When he failed to halt, she gripped it more firmly. "Julian, stop!"

He paused, his hands on his hips. It was an intimidating posture. "You have something to say to me?"

Lisa dared not think. "Yes. Julian, Robert

and I were only talking, and surely you don't —"

"Of course I don't," he said coldly.

Lisa flushed. "I have displeased you."

"No. To the contrary, I am glad that you and my brother are such good friends." His tone did not soften.

Lisa was afraid to bring up the subject of his first wife and son. But she stared up at him, hurting for him, feeling for him, consumed with the love she had thought lost forever. "Julian?"

He waited, his gaze upon her upturned face.

Her heart pounded explosively. "Julian, I saw your portrait in the gallery," she began.

Julian's head shot up, his entire body stiffening. "I am sure that you had an amusing afternoon," he said, cutting her off, "but the cook is waiting." He turned abruptly, crossing the hall with long, hard strides, not even waiting for her.

Lisa was frozen. Had he guessed what she wanted to discuss? Had his rudeness been intentional — and meant to prevent her from raising the subject she so desperately wished to explore? Lisa could not help but think so.

Slowly, she followed him to the kitchens. Now that she understood what the shadows in his gray eyes meant, she could not stop thinking about him and his tragic loss. Her mind was made up.

Lisa paced her bedroom, still in her purple evening gown, an immodest iridescent affair which Robert had chosen. She was trying to decide what to do. Supper had been tense. Julian had not noticed her gown; in fact, Lisa thought that he had hardly noticed her. Julian had spent the evening studying his wine and pushing his food around. His mood had never been darker. Thank God for Robert, who had chatted with Lisa for most of the night.

She had not been able to take her eyes from Julian, who was so incredibly handsome even while so taciturn. Whenever she had thought about what she must do later that night, she had shivered with an odd combination of terror and excitement.

There was a soft rapping on her bedroom door. Lisa quickly opened it and Robert slipped into her room.

"What are you waiting for?" he asked, but he was not smiling. "Julian has gone to his rooms."

"Oh, God," Lisa whispered, suddenly so terrified she was ready to give up their plan before even starting.

Robert gripped her arm. "You have to do this."

She looked into his intense gray eyes and slowly nodded. "Tell me how to — start."

He smiled briefly. "Tell him that you wish to discuss the castle's condition. Choose a chair and sit down. Lean forward a bit. Do not worry if he looks down your dress."

Lisa felt her cheeks turning red.

"Talk about hiring more staff and spring cleaning. Look up at him with wide eyes. You have wonderful eyes, Lisa, so very expressive. Don't be afraid to use them."

Lisa nodded fearfully.

"At some point go up to him and place your hand on his arm and ask him in a soft voice if he truly minds what you intend to do. Be as soft and feminine as possible."

"I don't know about this, Robert," Lisa said. "How do I get him to kiss me?"

"Tonight is not a night to entice him into kissing you," Robert said. "Don't even worry about it, unless he kisses you. If he does, be receptive. Respond naturally. I am sure I don't have to tell you what to do." Suddenly he appeared anxious. "Has Julian ever kissed you, Lisa?"

She blushed. "When he was courting me."

His gaze was direct. "Did you like his kisses?"

"Robert!" Lisa protested.

He smiled briefly. "Well, that is a relief."

"He hasn't kissed me since I ran away from him the night of our engagement party," she said somewhat miserably.

"He will." Robert sounded confident. "Forget about kissing tonight. I just want you there in his room, looking so beautiful and innocent. You will stir his heart and soul, Lisa, as well as his body. I am sure of it."

Lisa gnawed on her lip. "I seem innocent?"

"Very."

Feeling as if she were about to face the hangman, Lisa turned towards the door. Robert halted her. "One more thing," he said, his hand on her shoulder, "don't talk about the accident."

Lisa started, about to protest, as Robert opened the door and gave her a gentle push. She found herself in the dimly lit corridor.

Her heart thundering in her ears, she refused to deliberate. She had already learned that Julian's suite was at the other end of the floor. Quickly she traversed the hall. Suddenly quaking with fear, Lisa knocked on his door.

It was opened instantly.

Seven

*J*ulian stood on the threshold of his suite in his shirtsleeves, which were rolled up to his elbows to reveal muscular forearms dusted with golden hair. His shirt was unbuttoned to his waist. Lisa almost gasped at the breadth of his chest and the tense lines of his abdomen. He was still wearing his black wool trousers, but his feet were bare. She had never seen a man in such deshabille before. She could hardly tear her gaze upwards to his face.

But she did. And when their eyes met, time stood still. Lisa could actually hear her own racing heartbeat.

Julian's expression shut down. He took a step backwards, his lean, broad-shouldered body blocking his doorway as effectively as any physical barrier. "You wish to speak with me?"

It was very hard to formulate the single word, "Yes." Lisa's voice was a shaky whisper.

His gaze darted to hers again, searchingly. As he stared at her, Lisa thought he would refuse her request. Instead, his expression hard and somehow stoic, he stepped aside. Lisa entered the sitting room of his suite.

She did not notice its appointments other than the hearth containing a blazing fire and a pale, worn rug that covered the wooden floors. Her senses were rioting and focused only on the tall, golden-haired man standing beside her. Lisa was trying to remember Robert's instructions but her mind remained a solid blank. Only one word was engraved there — seduction.

"Lisa," he said harshly. "You wish to speak to me?"

Lisa jerked. Panic filled her. What was she supposed to say? Oh, yes, the castle! "The castle," she whispered hoarsely, beginning to feel flushed.

"The castle?" he echoed, his gray gaze riveted on her.

Lisa tried to unscramble her brain. "Castleclare."

"I know the name of my home," he snapped.

Lisa flinched.

He turned away, his shoulders squared. He ran a hand through his short, golden hair, then faced her grimly. "You wish to speak to me about Castleclare. What is on your mind?"

Lisa had been staring at his mouth. His mobile, surprisingly full mouth. Flushing hotly, she nodded, still attempting to gather her wits. She was supposed to sit down and lean forward. Relieved, she suddenly darted across the room, aware that Julian was watching her like a hawk, and perched stiffly on a faded red velvet settee with gold trim and tassels. Julian stared at her, his brow furrowed.

"We need staff," Lisa blurted. And then she remembered to lean forward.

His stare did not waver. "Yes, we do," he said slowly. Suddenly his gaze slipped below her throat.

Lisa could not believe that Robert's plan was working. Julian was actually looking at her decolletage. Her heart skidded to a stop.

His eyes rose abruptly, and for a split second, their gazes locked. His gray eyes were distinctly bright. A scant instant later he wheeled and was pacing the room. Lisa took a deep, fortifying breath. She could not tear her own gaze from him. The muscles in his thighs and buttocks kept pulling the fabric of his wool trousers taut.

But she was less afraid now, even growing elated. Robert's plan was working, for she was almost positive that Julian's expression meant he did desire her.

He faced one of the triple-sized windows, speaking without turning to face her. "You may hire more staff. Draw up a list of the servants you require. I shall glance over it tomorrow."

Lisa did not move. But she recalled the rest of Robert's instructions now and knew that she was supposed to get up, sashay over to him, and place her hand on his arm. She was so nervous she felt frozen.

Julian whirled. "Is there something else?" His tone was like the lash of a whip. His gaze remained riveted on her face — as if he were afraid of looking anywhere else.

Slowly, Lisa stood up.

Julian's expression turned slightly comical — as if he knew what was about to happen but just could not believe it.

Lisa began to walk towards him, feeling as if she were in a trance. Then she remembered she was supposed to sashay. She swung her hips. Julian's eyes widened. Feeling rewarded, she put more effort into each pelvic tilt. Forward and back, then side to side. Julian stared at her, wide-eyed and motionless.

Lisa reached him, panting from her efforts. She looked up at him, recalling what Robert had said about using her eyes. She batted her lashes, something she had never done before. Julian stared down at her, a flush high upon his cheekbones.

Lisa placed her small, soft palm on his hard, bare forearm. Touching him caused a quick thrill to sweep over her; it left her breathless, even giddy. "Julian?" Lisa whispered, batting her lashes again.

His chest rose and fell. His nostrils flared. His eyes blazed. *"What the hell do you think you're doing?"* he muttered furiously.

Lisa felt as if she had been socked. In the abdomen. For a moment, as their gazes locked, she thought she had misheard him. But there was no mistaking his anger.

"Lisa?" he demanded. Suddenly his hand closed on her wrist, yanking her palm from his arm. He flung her hand aside. *"Just what the hell is going on?"*

Lisa jerked, realizing with horror that she had not enthralled him, only enraged him.

He towered over her, his hands on his hips. "I think you should return to your room," he said tersely.

Lisa's eyes filled with tears. Oh, God! She had made a fool of herself — as she had known she would! Lisa turned to flee. Instead, she tripped on the flounced hem of her gown and crashed to the floor, landing on her hands and knees.

"Lisa!" Julian cried, the anger gone from his tone.

She was intent on running away to the sanctuary of her room. She should have never listened to Robert. She tried to get up, but her skirts made it an impossible task, and she was also hampered because she couldn't see clearly, her vision blurred by tears. She was still on her hands and knees when she felt Julian kneel beside her. She froze.

Suddenly he gripped her waist, his hands hard and strong and large. Their effect was like a red-hot iron brand.

Julian had frozen as well.

Stunned by the suddenly explosive feeling pervading her, Lisa shifted slightly so she could look into his eyes. His were glittering and hot.

For the space of a single heartbeat neither of them moved. Julian's hands still held Lisa's waist, but his gaze was fastened on her mouth.

Lisa wanted his kiss. She had never wanted anything more. His name was on the tip of her tongue. It rode her soft, trembling breath. *"Julian."*

He tore his eyes away. "Let me help you up," he said thickly.

Lisa found herself on her feet a moment later, Julian having put a safe distance between them. She could not seem to slow her rioting heart, or calm her rampaging senses.

Julian's fists slammed into the pockets of his trousers. Lisa's eyes widened and she couldn't help but stare. There was a long, thick protrusion behind his button-front fly.

"Lisa, it is time for you to leave."

Lisa dared not look at him again. She walked to the door, her knees weak and buckling. She paused, her hand on the knob, feeling his eyes burning holes in her back. She jerked around. "Julian . . ."

She could not continue. In truth, she did not even know what she wanted to say. His eyes ensnared her again, their ferocity frightening her, thrilling her.

"I am asking you to leave now," he said very forcefully.

She met his stormy eyes. "Why won't you kiss me?"

He inhaled, the sound sharp and ripe.

"Julian?" Lisa said desperately.

His temples pounded visibly. "I thought I made myself clear," he ground out, "that this marriage is one in name only."

"Why?" Lisa implored. "Julian, why?"

"Because," he said, perspiring, "it is what I wish."

Tears filled Lisa's eyes again. "So you shall be loyal to a dead woman for the rest of your life?"

He stiffened abruptly.

Lisa could not stop. "I am sure that you loved her, and that she was wonderful as a woman and a wife. I do not think to compete with her — I would not dare — but can't you give me a chance?"

One word, rasped. "No."

Lisa recoiled.

"No!" Julian shouted.

Lisa was frightened, for Julian was furious. She fought with a bravery she had never known she possessed. "She is dead, Julian. Melanie and Eddie are dead. Your loyalty won't bring either of them back. It accomplishes nothing. Please think about what I have said."

"Do not say another word," Julian cried in a dangerous voice.

But Lisa was compelled. She had to finish what she had begun. "Julian, do not misunderstand. If I could change the past and make things right for you, I would. I would give her back to you if I could, her and your son. I don't know why I have this desire, I don't know why I care at all when we are perfect strangers and I have been so hurt and betrayed by you. But I do care, I do. About you. It is time to let them go. I am so sorry, Julian. So sorry."

Julian stared at her, incredulity and rage suffusing his face. "Get out," he said, bracing himself on one of the bed's posters, his body shaking.

He was in pain. Terrible, terrible pain. Lisa saw it, sensed it — felt it. She wanted, desperately, to gather him to her breast as one would a hurt, frightened child. She moved across the room. She did not think. She wrapped her arms around him from behind and laid her cheek against his trembling back.

He whirled violently, the movement throwing her across the room. Lisa almost fell again, but managed to regain her balance.

"Do not interfere! Get out! Leave me alone!" he roared.

Lisa jumped backwards, cringing against the bureau.

He suddenly moved forward, towards her. Lisa pressed her spine into the wood, suddenly regretting everything, realizing the jeopardy she was in. He towered over her. "Never dare to speak to me about them!" he shouted. "You have no right!"

Lisa wanted to tell him that she had every right. She was his wife now, his flesh-and-blood wife, not the ghostly Melanie. But she did not dare. Tears streaked her cheeks, tears of despair, of fear. She quite expected him to strike her.

But he suddenly turned away with a soft, ragged moan. Covering his face with his hands, he whispered, "Get out, Lisa."

She was immobilized, wondering if he was crying.

"Please," he said, his back to her, his shoulders sagging.

Lisa's heart broke. She slipped past him and fled.

Eight

No matter what, he was going to stay away from her.

At all costs.

Julian's room was immersed in darkness, lit only by the glow of the dying fire in the pale, marble-manteled hearth. He was not in the stately canopied bed. He stood motionless by one of the windows, staring out into the moonless night. From his bedroom window, he could just make out the flash of whitecaps on the pitch-black bay.

If only he could stop thinking about her.

Her. Lisa. He refused to think of her as his wife.

Yet her image haunted him. What had she intended? To seduce him? The idea was almost laughable. Instead, a wave of grief rose up in him, so intense that it almost choked him.

He covered his face briefly with his hands. A tremor swept through his lean body. He realized, too late, his mistake. He had married a girl who was charmingly innocent, naturally good-natured, and far too beautiful. How could he have been such a fool?

He should have attached himself to a

skinny, older woman like Carmine Vander-
bilt, who had been in the market for a titled
husband for more years than anyone could
count. Then, he would not have been so
terribly tempted.

Julian cursed his body for its betrayal.

He paced. Lisa knew nothing about seduction, and her efforts might have been
comical if they had not been so utterly
original and somehow so damn enticing in
spite of her bumbling. Dammit. He couldn't
laugh, and he couldn't cry, not when he
was filled with such lust.

It had been so goddamn long.

He paced, cursing himself for being a
mere man.

The real problem was that Lisa was not
just innocent and beautiful, but compas-
sionate and kind. He had chosen her thinking her nothing but a hothouse flower, a
spoiled and spineless debutante. How
wrong he had been. She possessed nerves
of steel, iron-willed determination, and the
courage of an entire pride of lions. Yet she
was naive, innocent and, except for her
amateur attempt at seduction, incapable of
manipulation. Her every emotion was expressed on her face and in her golden-
brown eyes. Tonight Julian had hurt her
yet again, as unintentionally as all the other
times.

How he hated hurting her.

But she had felt far more than hurt, and far more than compassion. Julian recalled a single shared look, after Lisa had tripped and fallen, when he was helping her to her feet. God, she had wanted him then, too.

Julian's hand slipped, once, and he touched himself. In his mind he pretended it was Lisa touching him and he could not stand it.

How could he survive like this?

He had to stay away from his bride. Dear God, he had to.

But a tiny voice taunted him, saying, so what? So what if you take her to your bed? *So damn what?*

The rage came so quickly that Julian did not recognize it until it was too late. His hand flew out, striking the vase of flowers from the corner table. Blue and white porcelain hit the floor, shattering loudly. Wildflowers lay strewn on the old Arabian rug amidst the broken shards and the puddle of water.

Julian groaned. Regret seized him, body and soul. Not just regret for breaking the vase his mother had cherished, a gift from Julian's grandmother, but a vast, deep, bitter regret.

He regretted the past, he regretted the present — and he feared the future.

Breathing harshly, ignoring his sex, Julian walked to the sideboard and poured himself a shot of Irish whiskey. It was a poor substitute for what his body needed.

But he had no choice.

Passion was to be denied at all costs. Forever. Just as he must forever deny himself his heart.

Lisa had not seen Julian in days. The morning after her humiliating effort at seduction, he had left Castleclare, leaving her only a brief note. *Matters of business require my attention in London immediately. Regretfully, Julian St. Clare.*

Lisa did not believe him for a moment.

He was running away from her and their problems.

She sat on a red plaid blanket with Robert, a picnic of roasted chicken, vegetable salads, and hot buns laid out beside them. She could not stop thinking about Julian, wishing desperately that there had been a different ending to that other night.

Lisa knew now that Robert was wrong. She was not going to seduce Julian and make him fall in love with her. He was a man stricken with dark demons, and she was only a young, sheltered woman hardly capable of exorcising them.

How she ached though, wishing that she could.

A part of her still yearned to try.

Robert tugged playfully on her hair. "A

penny for your thoughts, sister-in-law?"

Lisa smiled wanly. "I am not sure that they are worth that."

Robert was stretched out on his side, his jacket was open, hatless, as the May sun beat down on his pale face. Had he not been so pasty, with dark circles under his eyes, Lisa would never have thought him a man soon fated to die.

"Then I'll guess," he said, grinning. His smile faded. "You are thinking about my pigheaded brother."

Lisa hugged her knees to her chest, her blue and white skirt belled out around her. "Yes."

"He is afraid of you, Lisa. Afraid of his own feelings. That is why he has run away."

"It would be nice if you were right, but after the other night, he probably cannot stand the sight of me," Lisa replied. She had told Robert almost everything.

"After much reflection, I have decided that the other night actually went well."

"How can you say that?" Lisa gasped. "It was so horrible — you have no idea!"

"Surely you are not ready to give up?"

Lisa stared at Robert's cheerful face. How *could* she give up? After a few days respite, she felt far less humiliated than she had, but she could not shake Julian's image from her mind. Sometimes she even imagined him looking at her with his hot eyes.

At other times she saw him with his hands covering his face, his body wracked with a pain that was not physical.

"Why did he love her so much?"

Robert was somber. "Lisa, when she took her own life, they were still newlyweds. She was beautiful but very simple. She was sweet and uncomplicated. Yet he is a very complicated man. I am not sure Julian would fall in love with Melanie if he met her today, but they truly suited each other then."

"That hardly matters," Lisa said morosely. "Julian is in love with a ghost."

Robert sat up with a wry smile. "Do you really think he is still in love with her, Lisa?"

Lisa sat up straighter, her heart pounding. She thought about what Robert had said. "There are probably many feelings locked up inside Julian. Love may very well be one of them."

"I think there is a single feeling inside my brother, and it is not love. It is rage."

Lisa stared, her fists curled by her sides. "Yes," she said slowly, "Julian is certainly angry. But I am not sure that your plan will work. In fact, I doubt it. I do not think I am woman enough to mend his soul and steal his heart."

"I think," Robert said lazily, picking up a handful of cherries, "that you are precisely the woman for the task."

Julian had stayed in London for a fortnight. He had taken care of several affairs, most of which involved paying off debts acquired over the past ten years and re-establishing his and his brother's personal credit. A gentleman survived with credit, and Julian had been tardy in rectifying matters since his marriage to Lisa.

But the closer he came to Castleclare, the more tense he became. Lisa's image had stayed with him during the entire trip. He had not been successful in forcing it to the back of his mind. Now, as he strode through his home, he could think of little else. Inexplicably, he wanted a glimpse of her. Or had she left him while he was gone? Julian would not be surprised. He would be relieved — he would be dismayed.

O'Hara met him in the library. "Her Ladyship is out with your brother, m'lord," he said blandly. "Cook made them a hearty picnic."

Julian felt a stab of jealousy, but was rational enough to realize that it was misplaced. Robert had only brotherly feelings for Lisa. In the next instant, the jealousy returned with a vengeance. But what if Lisa fell in love with Robert?

Many women had succumbed to his gallantry and charm.

Tersely, Julian asked, "Are they alone?"

"Yes, m'lord." O'Hara smiled. "Y' know yer brother. Robert said he had no need of grooms. Guess he wants the lass all t' himself."

Julian was well aware of O'Hara's prompting. He tamped down a scowl. "Where are they?"

"They took the small gig and drove out towards the lake."

Julian halted in mid-stride, a feeling of nausea rising in him. He ignored it and it subsided. A moment later he was hurrying outside and ordering his favorite mount brought around. While he was waiting for the seventeen-hand sorrel, he saw a rider enter Castleclare through the barbican. It was Edith Tarrington.

Julian mounted as she rode up to him at a canter. Edith was a superb horsewoman who often hunted with the hounds. "Hello, Edith."

"Julian, have you just returned?" She reined in besides him.

"Yes."

"Where are you off to in such a rush?" she asked, studying his face. She was wearing a pale green riding habit that set off her porcelain complexion perfectly.

"Robert has taken my bride on a picnic," Julian stated, aware of how frequently he now thought of and referred to Lisa as his bride. He refused to wonder why.

"I see," Edith said somberly.

Julian looked her in the eye. "Why don't we join them?"

Edith nodded, her face reflecting a tension that was hardly characteristic of her. In unison, they wheeled their mounts and cantered down the drive and through the raised portcullis. Julian could not enjoy the fast ride. He kept thinking about Robert and Lisa sharing the picnic, imagining Robert's amusing quips and Lisa's honest laughter. He kept imagining her smile, her dimples, and her shining eyes.

A moment later he and Edith topped a rise. Julian's reaction was immediate. He halted his cantering horse far too abruptly, causing the animal to rear. Below, he saw the shimmering, emerald green lake where Eddie had drowned and Melanie had taken her life.

"Julian?"

It was a moment before he could speak. The nausea seized him again; he ignored it. "I am fine," he lied. He had not been to the lake since their deaths.

He spurred his sorrel forward, having spied Robert and Lisa as small figures beneath several trees. Edith followed.

He cantered down the slope. Robert and Lisa heard him approaching and turned to watch. Julian halted his gelding but did not dismount. He barely glanced at Robert, who rose to his feet, grinning amiably. Julian could not take his eyes from Lisa.

As she returned his stare, a warm pink crept up her cheeks.

Julian could not ignore it. Desire stabbed him harshly, directly in the loins, and with it, a soul-felt yearning far more potent.

Lisa remained motionless.

The devil inside him taunted, *Why not? Why not let go of the past?*

Then Edith came cantering up behind Julian. Reining in, her gaze swept everyone. "Hello, Lisa, Robert."

As Robert replied, Julian slid to his feet, his jaw set with the resolve he had lived with for a decade. He left his horse drop-reined and moved slowly towards her. Lisa began to rise as Julian extended his hand. Their palms clasped. As he pulled her to her feet he felt his pulse racing uncontrollably. He had not planned to approach her this way.

And he knew, *he knew*, that he should release her hand, turn around, and go — but he was incapable of behaving rationally.

She wet her lips. "Hello, Julian. Did you have a pleasant trip?"

He knew he was staring, but he could not tear his gaze away. She was so perfect and so lovely, and her lips were full and ripe and meant for kissing. If only he could forget those few times he had plundered there when he was courting her in New York City. "Yes."

Lisa looked at her toes, fidgeting.

Suddenly Julian heard himself say, tersely, "Walk with me."

She started, her eyes wide and wary. Wincing, he remembered his previous rejection of her. Julian tried to force a smile and failed. He held out his arm.

Slowly, Lisa placed her palm in the crook of his elbow.

They walked away from Robert and Edith in a strained silence. Julian's heart was drumming. He knew he should speak, any trivial subject would do, but instead, he was consumed with the idea of kissing her, just once. Dammit. He wanted to kiss her, badly, so badly, but knew he did not dare.

He would never be able to stop with a single kiss.

"Julian?" Lisa asked in a nervous tone. "Are you all right?"

Julian paused beside a pile of boulders which blocked his view of the lake. He raked a hand through his hair. It was trembling. "Why do you ask?"

"You keep staring," Lisa said tersely.

Julian's jaw ground down. It was on the tip of his tongue to tell her that he kept staring because she was impossibly lovely, but that kind of talk did not come easily to a man like himself — and he had not flattered any woman since Melanie. "I am sorry. I am just . . . tired."

Lisa licked her lips again. "Perhaps we should all go back to Castleclare."

"Yes," he said, when he really wanted to say no. Lisa turned to walk back to the picnic area. Julian had to clench his fists to stop himself from seizing her — and pressing her body tightly against his.

Reluctantly, torn as never before and acutely aware of it, Julian followed her. Over Lisa's shoulder, he saw Robert and Edith standing in awkward silence. Then he looked at Lisa's rigid back.

Oh, God, he thought with an inward groan. He should have stayed in London. Returning to Castleclare was a mistake. He wanted her so fiercely — he could not remember ever wanting a woman this much before. But surely that was because of the physical state he was in. Surely that was because he hadn't had a woman in ten achingly long, lonely years.

Not in ten goddamn years.

Nine

Although Julian had returned home, Lisa did not see hide nor hair of him in the next few days, except at suppertime. He remained locked in his library or he rode out across the island. After the fiasco Lisa had caused with her miserable attempt at seduction, she did not dare intrude when he was closeted with his business affairs, or ask to join him when he galloped through the castle gates.

But she would watch him ride away through her bedroom window, a magnificent figure astride his sorrel, and her heart would twist, hard. His misery had affected her greatly — she could not bear to witness it. If only he would extend his hand even halfway towards her, Lisa would meet him the rest of the way.

She could not stop thinking about him. Could not stop imagining how it might be if only he would bend just a little. Lisa could imagine passion bursting between them — and the following blossoming of love. If only . . .

To soothe her injured soul, to heal the ever-present hurt in her heart, and to distract herself from what was fast becoming an obsession, Lisa focused her efforts on restoring Castleclare. Through O'Hara, Julian had approved her plans, although Lisa was not certain he had really paid any attention to them. She and Robert hired a dozen carpenters and twice as many maids, several gardeners and groundskeepers, and eight new permanent staff, including a housekeeper. Lisa now awoke every morning not to cheerful birdsong and the quiet country silence of Clare Island, but to the sound of banging hammers and rasping saws.

Lisa hugged her arms to her breasts and watched the men working in the ballroom. Julian had agreed that, when Castleclare was ready, they would have a ball. One entire wall was being repaneled, as a centuries-old leak had destroyed the original woodwork. Maids were waxing the parquet floors. Tapestries had been taken outside to be beaten and aired and when needed, repaired. Two young men stood on ladders and were painstakingly cleaning every crystal on the Louis Quatorze chandelier.

"You should be proud of yourself, little sister-in-law," Robert said, entering the room. The windows were open and the fresh, mid-May air was filtering into the huge, bright room. He sniffed appreciatively and sighed. "Castleclare has needed a woman's loving touch for a long time," he declared.

But Lisa hardly heard him. She was wondering where Julian was. She had seen him riding away very early that morning at a near-gallop. Did he despise her so much that he could not remain in his own home with her? Or was he, possibly, tempted by her presence, and thus seeking to avoid her almost desperately?

"You should be pleased with yourself," Robert repeated softly.

Lisa faced him, forcing a smile. "I love Castleclare. I am happy to see the beauty of this place restored."

He studied her and said softly, "Julian will come around."

She bit her lip. "He hasn't paid me any attention since the day he returned — not since the picnic." She could not hide her wounded feelings from Robert. "He hasn't even noticed the changes in his own home — or bothered to thank me for my efforts."

"I am certain that he notices everything," Robert said with a smile. "It is time for you to make another move, Lisa."

She stiffened. "I hope you are not suggesting what I think you are suggesting," she said huskily, her cheeks flaming.

"This time when you go to his room, wear a peignoir. I happen to have the perfect garment for you, something made in Paris."

Lisa was frozen; then her color increased. "I can't."

"Yes, you can," Robert said, laughing.

"You can and you will and this time, my beauty, I daresay you might succeed in taming the beast."

Lisa was filled with dread. She knew she was a miserable excuse for a temptress.

But she could not stand the status quo. She had never been more unhappy. She could not continue living with him and being so thoroughly neglected, so ignored. She had to do something to get Julian's attention.

A movement caused them to glance up. Lisa stiffened. Edith Tarrington stood on the threshold of the ballroom, regarding the two of them, her brows knitted together. In her pale gray riding habit she was impossibly beautiful.

Robert did not greet her, so Lisa went towards her. She had already overheard three new maids talking about Edith's unrequited love for the Marquis. Apparently she had comforted Julian after Melanie's death when she was a blossoming young woman of fifteen.

"Hello, Edith. How nice of you to call," Lisa managed with a smile.

Edith nodded, glancing around the room, but not at Robert, who still did not move or make any effort to greet her. "You are doing a wonderful job here, Lisa," she said softly. Her gaze finally fastened on Robert. "Hello, Robert."

His jaw flexed. "Edith. I am afraid that Julian has already ridden out. You have missed him." His gray eyes flashed.

Edith twisted her riding crop in her gloved hands. "I . . . I had heard there was renovation here, and I was curious to take a look," she said. She appeared to be lying. She was not good at deceit.

Robert made a harsh sound, like a snort.

Although more dismayed than before, Lisa said gamely, "I would be happy to give you a tour, Edith."

Suddenly Robert moved forward, his stride aggressive. He inserted himself between Lisa and Edith. "Aren't you needed in the kitchens, Lisa? I need some air myself. Why don't I escort you back to Tarrington Hall, Edith?" His tone was hostile.

Edith paled.

Robert gripped her elbow firmly. "Come." Without waiting for her answer, he began propelling her from the room.

When they had left, Lisa thanked her stars for Robert, a real friend and ally, and walked slowly after them. Her heart was drumming wildly. Did she dare do as Robert suggested?

But what if Julian rejected her yet again?

Lisa did not think she could stand it.

On the other hand, the romantic fool within her wondered what would happen if he did not reject her this time.

"You are hurting me," Edith cried, yanking her arm from Robert's grasp. They stood outside the stables in the bright morning sun, Edith's mount tied at the post rail a few yards away.

"I do apologize," Robert said coldly.

Edith's mouth trembled but her eyes flashed. "You are a boor, Robert. I do not know why the ladies find you so attractive when you are so rude!"

Robert's eyes narrowed. "I hardly care what you think of me, Edith."

"That has been made very clear," she said as she turned her back on him.

He whipped her around so that she faced him again. Her face paled as his head ducked close to hers. "But I am very tired of your chasing after my brother," Robert said through clenched teeth.

Edith was frozen for a single instant, then her gloved hand shot out. In spite of the soft deerskin, the slap to Robert's face cracked loudly. His head jerked back and his eyes widened. So did Edith's.

The sound still reverberating between them, they stared at one another in shock.

Edith took a step backwards and cried breathlessly, "Oh, God! I am sorry! I —" But she never had the chance to finish.

Cursing, his face tight with tension,

Robert seized her by her shoulders, pulled her up against him, and ground his mouth down on hers. Edith was so stunned she could not move. Robert clamped one arm around her waist and deepened the kiss, forcing Edith's lips open.

Edith's hands slowly gripped his shoulders, not pushing him away but not clinging either.

Robert tore his mouth from hers. He was panting. Angry. "Maybe now you will stop chasing after my brother."

Edith stared at him, touching her swollen mouth with her gloved fingertips.

Some of Robert's anger faded as he stared into her blue eyes. Suddenly he realized what he had done. "Edith . . . God," he murmured softly. "I am sorry."

Edith squared her shoulders, her eyes glistening with tears. She turned her back on him abruptly, hesitated — then she whirled. Very distinctly, she said, "I am not chasing Julian." Then she about-faced and rushed to her horse.

Robert watched her mount, making no move to help her. He stared as she urged her dappled mare into a canter and then galloped across the ward and through the barbican.

He cursed.

When Julian returned to Castleclare, the

sun was just beginning its descent. He reined in his sorrel outside of the gates, briefly admiring the orange-red sun as it hung over the crenelated roof of the central tower, the bay glistening darkly blue just behind it. Then, tension he could not escape mounting inside him, he spurred his sorrel forward.

A few moments later he had entered his home. The hall was empty and silent, but a cheery fire blazed in the hearth. He looked around, almost grimly. The ancient trestle table had been polished until it gleamed. The stone floors had been waxed; they glistened like silver. Even the coat of mail in one corner had been tended to, and he saw no dust motes in the air nor any cobwebs in the corners. His mouth tight, Julian crossed the hall.

He turned down the corridor and entered that part of the castle which had been begun in the sixteenth century and completed at the turn of the seventeenth. His footsteps slowed as he approached the ballroom.

He paused on the threshold, taking a deep breath. God, it looked the way it had when he was a small boy of six or seven, before his father had gone so deeply into debt when his mother had had the resources to keep the place up. Julian's heart twisted as Lisa's image filled his mind.

All because of the little bride he did not want — yet wanted far too badly.

Julian stared at his reflection in the Venetian mirror above a small Chippendale table on the opposite side of the room. He glimpsed himself standing in his oldest riding jacket and threadbare boots in the magnificent room. Overhead, the chandelier sparkled, even in the fading twilight. How alone and forlorn he appeared. His face was a mask devoid of emotion, stern and patrician.

This was not going to work.

Lisa was no vain, shallow society heiress. She was sweet and lovely and she loved his home and dear God, she was willing to give him another chance. He knew it. Every time he dared to look at her he saw her every emotion shimmering in her amber eyes.

"Julian?"

He whirled, steeling himself against her. He nodded without speaking, but could no more stop himself from glancing at her thoroughly, from the top of her head to the tip of her toes, than he could stop the sun from setting.

Her gaze was fastened upon his face. "I . . . saw you ride in," she said hesitantly.

Had she been watching for him? His pulse raced; his heart tightened; his loins filled. He clenched his fists tightly so he would not reach out, grab her, and do the unthinkable — so that he would not kiss her.

"Do you . . . like it?" she asked.

His jaw flexing, he forced himself to respond. "Everything is fine."

Lisa's gaze searched his, as if trying to read past his words to delve into his heart and his soul.

Abruptly Julian strode past her, his face a harsh mask. It was either that or succumb to temptation.

Lisa wrung her hands, trying again and again to decide what she had done to anger Julian so. Why wasn't he pleased with her efforts to restore Castleclare? Had she somehow offended him? She covered her racing heart with her hand. It hurt her so much. How could she go on this way, loving him, aching for him, wanting to be with him — while he avoided her so completely?

She walked over to the Victorian mirror to survey herself in the peignoir Robert had left for her.

It was white silk trimmed in white lace. Breathtakingly beautiful, it was also scandalous. Lisa's nude body was almost visible through the fabric. When the jacket opened, she could see her nipples through the thin silk.

He will not be able to resist you. So Robert had said. And what did she have to lose? She wanted him so much. She was so desperate, she would welcome the briefest of embraces, the shortest of conversations, a single touch.

Screwing up her courage, terrified of failure, Lisa walked to the door. Supper had been over hours ago; the household was asleep.

But not Julian. Robert had assured her that his brother stayed up late, reading.

Barefoot, Lisa walked silently down the hall to his apartments, her heart banging like a drum. She could hardly breathe.

She poised herself to knock, then she decided against it. If he saw her like this, he would never let her into his rooms. He would guess her intentions immediately.

Flushed and breathless, Lisa tried the knob. The door opened and Lisa glided inside.

The sitting room was lost in darkness, except for the fire dying in the hearth. A quick look assured Lisa that Julian was not within. Did she really dare enter his bedroom?

Wetting her dry lips, Lisa crossed the small salon. She peeked into his bedroom.

Julian sat in bed, wearing nothing but the gray trousers he had worn to supper that night. His chest formed thick slabs of muscle, his stomach was concave and flat. Lisa could not tear her eyes from him.

He was not reading. A book lay by his hip,

but it was closed. He was staring at the fire.

Suddenly his head jerked around and he saw her. His eyes shot open, traveling up and down her nightgown.

Lisa could not move.

Julian remained staring, wide-eyed and frozen.

Lisa forced her legs to function and entered his room. "Julian," she said hoarsely.

He swung his strong legs over the side of the bed, his thighs straining the fabric of his trousers, and rose to his feet. He was still staring at her, stunned.

Lisa hugged herself. Her mind was failing her, and she could not think of what to say or do.

Julian's gaze dropped to her breasts, pushed into prominence by her folded arms. He immediately looked at her face, jamming his hands into the pockets of his trousers. His erection was impossible to miss. "What do you want?" he snapped.

Lisa felt a moment of pure panic. She cried, "Julian, don't send me away! At least let us talk! I cannot continue this way! Please!" she heard herself beg.

His gaze again slammed down her breasts and thighs, lingering on the place where they joined. He jerked his eyes to hers. A tremor passed visibly through his body. "No."

One single word, filled with steely resolve,

and Lisa felt as if it were the first nail in her coffin. *"Please."*

"No!" he shouted, his eyes blazing.

Lisa choked on a sob. She was frightened of his anger and knew she must flee. But instead her feet carried her forward, to him. Incredulity changed his expression.

Ignoring his disbelief, Lisa gripped his bare arms. "Julian, why are you doing this? Why?" she asked, begging hysterically. And as she gripped him she felt his heat and his power, both utterly male. A searing sensation filled her loins — never before had she been overcome with such physical desire.

Lisa wanted him. She wanted to take his face in her hands, devour his mouth, then open her thighs and accept his big body inside of hers.

Suddenly his hands closed on her shoulders. Lisa saw the savagery in his eyes and felt a flash of fear, thinking he intended to push her away. Instead, his palms tightened. Lisa cried out. Their gazes locked, and the sound of their harsh breathing filled the room.

"Damn you!" Julian said, and then Lisa was crushed against his hard, hot body, while his mouth seized and opened hers. His tongue swept deep. His hands slid down her back, then up, and down again, finally gripping and spreading her buttocks. Unthinkingly, instinctively, Lisa pressed her pelvis against the massive ridge of his erection.

Julian froze, holding her up against him, his mouth still fastened on hers, their tongues entwined.

And Lisa knew that he would leave her.

She locked her hands around his neck, pressing shamelessly against him, kissing him frantically, trying to express all of her love.

Then Julian ripped his body from hers.

Lisa stumbled, falling against the bed. She caught herself before she fell to the floor, lifting her head just in time to see Julian striding from the room, his face stark with lust, with anger, with denial.

Ten

*H*er room was bathed in moonlight.

He stood on the threshold, the corridor behind him dimly lit, staring at her sleeping form. She appeared, in that moment, to be an angel.

An angel sent from heaven to aid him, to heal him.

Julian closed his eyes. He was trembling. He dared not move, afraid to leave, so afraid, and worse, terrified to go closer. He did not trust himself. He was losing control.

He reminded himself that she was no heavenly angel, but a flesh and blood woman who had somehow managed to turn his carefully constructed life upside down.

Lisa. How had she managed to break the steel bonds surrounding him? He wanted to send her back to New York City. God, he did. But if he did, the small spark she had stirred inside his breast would die, and suddenly he did not want to be a dead man again.

God, no.

But he was also afraid to live.

What would happen if he allowed himself to respond to her? What if he allowed himself to love her? Julian choked. He did not dare. Once upon a time he had loved so much and lost everything, even himself. He could not withstand such tragedy and grief again.

Julian turned and left Lisa's room.

"Why aren't you smiling when you are so lovely tonight?" A soft male voice said in Lisa's ear.

Lisa shifted in order to see Robert. It was the evening of the ball, but Lisa felt no excitement. Instead, the hurt of rejection filled her breast, and she ached with it. "How can I smile when he has avoided me like the plague these past few weeks?"

Robert sighed, putting his arm around her. The guests were just beginning to arrive, one grand covered coach after another rolling up the drive and pausing by the open front doors to allow their passengers to alight. Lisa stood with Robert in the great hall, acutely aware of Julian standing by the doorway in his elegant black tuxedo. His back was to her, his shoulders squared.

"He did not even say hello to me when I came downstairs," Lisa said, her mouth trembling. "The tension has worsened between us. I do not know how I can go on."

Robert hugged her to his side. "He is fighting himself, Lisa. When you enter the room, he cannot keep his eyes off you."

"I don't think so," Lisa said in a tight voice.

"When you look at him he turns away, but when you are oblivious, his eyes devour you," Robert said. "I know you will break down his resolve."

Lisa no longer believed Robert, even though she knew his intentions were good. "I have to join Julian to greet the guests," she said sadly, pulling away from her brother-in-law. "And somehow pretend that our marriage is not a miserable sham that is destroying me."

Before Robert could reply, Lisa spied Edith Tarrington and her father entering the hall. Edith had never looked lovelier than she did in her silver chiffon gown. Lord Tarrington and Julian shook hands. Lisa watched Julian lean towards Edith, kissing her cheek while she gripped his palms. Lisa's heart sank. Robert was also regarding them, and he muttered something that sounded suspiciously ill-mannered under his breath.

Lisa lifted her chin and sailed forward. This was her home, her ball, these were her guests. As she came abreast of Julian he finally looked at her; their gazes collided, held, locked. Hurt and anger vied for predominance in Lisa's heart and soul. It was very hard to tear her gaze away.

But she did and said gamely, "Hello,

Edith, Lord Tarrington. It is so wonderful that you could join us for Castleclare's first ball in so many years." Smiling in a manner which she desperately hoped was gracious, her back to Julian, Lisa extended her hand.

She did not have to look at Julian now to know that he stared unblinkingly at her.

"The first dance is ours," Julian said in her ear.

Lisa jerked. His warm breath sent unwanted heat unfurling throughout her body. All the guests had arrived and were mingling in the newly renovated ballroom. The ladies were ravishing in their rainbow-hued gowns and glittering jewelry, even if some of it was glass and paste, the men resplendent if not always elegant in their black tailcoats and white shirtwaists. Two buffets had been set up at the far end of the room, and waiters were passing flutes of champagne. The orchestra awaited orders to begin.

Lisa stared up at Julian's handsome but grim face. Her heart was pounding madly. He stood so close to her that their bodies almost touched. "I beg your pardon?"

"The first dance is ours." Not waiting for her acceptance, he took her gloved hands in his. Lisa stiffened in shock, not so much at his presumption after these past miserable weeks, but at the sensation engendered by his touch. Her mouth turned dry.

His jaw flexed. "It is traditional, Lisa, nothing more."

She felt like wrenching her hands free of him, in spite of all their guests, and slapping him silly. Slapping him until he told her why he refused to look at her, why he was determined to avoid her, why he was such a coward. Until he told her why they could not have a wonderful life together. Instead, Lisa plastered a smile on her face and moved into Julian's arms. He nodded to the orchestra which immediately began a waltz.

As he began to sweep her effortlessly around the floor, she closed her eyes, acutely aware of every powerful inch of him, and of the extraordinary tension filling them both.

If only she could stop loving him.

If only her heart could be as cold as his.

The crowd applauded them.

Tears stinging her eyes, Lisa met Julian's gaze. Seeing his expression she stumbled, but he caught her. His eyes were twin mirrors of warmth and concern. His next words startled her. "Don't cry," he whispered.

His unexpected sympathy and sudden tenderness undid Lisa. Tears spilled down her face. Julian halted in mid-stride. Trying to break free of his embrace, Lisa began to weep. She realized that Julian was watching her, apparently horrified. The crowd was utterly silent.

Lisa lifted her gown and whirled and ran from the room.

She could take it no more.

"This is all your fault," Robert said harshly.

Edith stiffened. "That is unfair. What's more, it is untrue!"

They stood shoulder to shoulder near the entrance of the ballroom, and Lisa had just run past them, sobbing. Julian stood alone in the center of the dance floor, his face white. Glaring at Edith, Robert jerked his head at the orchestra, and followed that unqualified gesture with an upward slash of his hand. The conductor could not misunderstand and immediately the band began the same sedate waltz again. None of the guests moved as an astonished silence filled the ballroom.

Suddenly Robert seized Edith by the elbow and led her onto the dance floor. She cried out as he put one hand on her waist, gripped her other palm, and began to whirl her about. "Relax," he snapped, his gray eyes blazing.

"You are hurting me," she gritted, her blue eyes heated.

Robert eased his hold fractionally. "Someone ought to turn you over his knee," he said grimly.

She jerked as he spun her around. "How dare you suggest such a thing."

"Perhaps I'll be the unfortunate soul to administer such a painful lesson?" Robert's smile dripped vinegar.

"I need no lesson, especially from a rogue like you!" Edith cried. But then Julian strode through the ballroom, his face flushed, and he disappeared across the threshold. Other couples began to filter out onto the floor.

"Poor Julian," Edith said softly, her gaze still on the open doors through which he had vanished.

"I have had it!" Robert shouted, causing a couple to falter and gawk at them. But Robert did not care. He had halted in mid-stride; he held Edith hard against his chest. "Leave my brother alone. He is falling in love with his wife! Do not interfere."

Tears filled Edith's eyes and she nearly spat, "I don't want your brother! I never have! How many times must I deny it?" She wrenched free of Robert, very much as Lisa had moments ago, and hurried from the ballroom.

Robert stared after her, uttering a string of curses no well-bred gentleman should ever express in polite society.

Lisa lay weeping in a heap on her huge canopied bed, her gold satin ballgown crushed beneath her. Julian stood in the doorway, overwhelmed by her pain, acutely aware that he was the cause of it. "Forgive me," he said harshly.

Lisa stopped crying. Slowly she sat up, staring at him. Julian met her glistening amber eyes and felt the blow all the way to his stomach. Despite his bitter regret, he was thoroughly aware of how gorgeous she was, even disheveled and teary-eyed, her ebony hair rioting about her bare shoulders. How gorgeous and good, how vulnerable and young. "Lisa . . ." He did not know what to say.

"Get out," she said tremulously.

"Not until you forgive me," Julian said firmly, his gaze fastened upon her. "Lisa . . . please. I never meant for any of this to happen."

"But it has!" She lifted both hands as if to ward him off. "I want to go home. I give up. I concede defeat. Take my money. Just let me go."

Julian was aware of his heart slamming to an unpleasant stop. Her words had caused another blow, one even more physical in sensation than the previous time. He could not respond. An image of Lisa leaving Castleclare pervaded his mind.

"I am going home. You cannot stop me."

Julian was overcome with tension, immobilized by it. Grief welled up out of nowhere. "I will not try to stop you," he said hoarsely. But his mind screamed at him — *Don't let her go!*

Lisa stared at him, a beseeching look suddenly in her eyes.

Julian wanted to speak, but did not dare, afraid he would voice his traitorous thoughts. Afraid he would beg her to reconsider, to stay. She was right — she should go. But . . . Oh, God. Could he survive her leaving him? Suddenly he wiped his eyes with the back of his hand. He was shocked to realize that he was crying.

"Julian?" Lisa whispered, poised as if she intended to rise and rush to him.

"You are right. This has been a disaster. It is best that you leave," he said unsteadily. His heart was hammering, each blow so painful that he could hardly think. He was almost ready to refute what he knew was best, and call her back.

Somehow he bowed. Somehow he kept his face devoid of all emotion. "I apologize, madam, for all the inconvenience." He turned and left the room.

"Julian!"

In the hall, his strides faltered.

"Julian!"

He began to run.

Eleven

*T*he ball continued, the sounds of the orchestra and the laughing, conversing guests filling the castle, but Julian did not care. He felt as if he were in some kind of living nightmare, and he was both horrified and shocked.

He shoved open the front doors, ignored the footmen, and left Castleclare.

His strides long and hard, he walked rapidly past the coaches and broughams double- and triple-parked around the circular drive, across the ward and through the barbican. He did not know where he was going; he did not care. One thought drummed in his mind: Lisa was leaving and he had to let her go.

His strides lengthened. The night was starry and bright and in a few more days there would be a full moon, so Julian had no trouble seeing the rough ground. Lisa's tearful image remained stamped upon his mind. Of course she wanted to leave him. And he, of course, wanted her to.

Didn't he?

Yes, he did — he wanted nothing more!

Suddenly Melanie's face swam before his

eyes, and as always, Julian forced her image away. But this time he realized that her face was blurred and indistinct, as if he could not quite recall precisely what she had looked like. And then, Lisa's fine features were transposed upon Melanie's.

Julian's strides quickened until he was running. He welcomed the exertion. He pumped his arms and legs, gulping in the cool, early June air. Sweat streamed down his face and body. Still, he could not seem to outrun Lisa's crystal-clear image or Melanie's faded one.

He had destroyed his marriage. But he had not wanted another marriage in the first place. The first one had ended in tragedy, which haunted him to this day. Why did it seem as if this second one was ending in another tragedy?

Julian halted, out of breath and panting. He had topped a painfully familiar rise. Below him, the lake shimmered in the starlight, wet and shiny and black, streaked with silver, the landscape around it dark and shadowy and vague. Julian's heart lurched.

The words came up, without thought, erupting before he even understood them. *"Damn you, Melanie."*

He froze, stunned by the sentiment. Worse, he was aware of a seething hatred welling up inside of him, a hatred directed at his first wife.

Julian could not move. This was all wrong. He *loved* Melanie. He had loved her from the moment he had first laid eyes upon her. And he still loved her, even now, ten years after her death.

Julian's blood was pumping violently now, and he did not feel any love inside of himself; no, he felt a furious hatred — oh, God.

Everything, dammit, was *her* fault.

Eddie's death, her suicide, the endless torment of his life, and now Lisa's desertion.

Lisa. Julian covered his face with his hands. His shoulders shook. He felt torn — torn between a dead woman who had betrayed him by taking her own life and a live woman whom he had hurt again and again when she only wanted to love him.

He turned his back on the lake abruptly, the lake where Melanie's body lay with that of his only son. He had a vicious urge to destroy everything in his path. He wanted to rant and rave at the moon. He wanted to exhume her body from the bottom of the lake and wring her neck.

Julian gasped, then shut his eyes in dismay. How could he feel this way towards Melanie? What was happening to him?

It wasn't her fault. She had been weak, frail. He had known from the beginning she was as fragile as glass. He hadn't cared. He had loved her completely. It was his fault, wasn't it, his and his alone?

He should have prevented her death!

Julian shuddered, rage and guilt twisting up inside him, seething and confusing and overwhelming him until he could hardly remain upright. And from where he stood, Julian could see his magnificent home, splendidly alight because of the ball Lisa had insisted on having, a ball he had not given a damn about. His home, which she had restored to its former magnificence because she loved Castleclare even though she was an outsider — because she loved him. And he could just faintly hear the band, the pretty, happy strains of the piano and violins on the Irish sea breeze, sounds as pretty and happy as his second wife. Suddenly he began to choke, because his home was alive now, alive the way it had been in the first years of his marriage and in all the time prior to that, when it had been nothing but a haunted tomb for so very long.

For a moment Julian remained motionless. The lake which held all the secrets and tragedy of the past rooted him in place, yet Castleclare beckoned him in a way he felt almost incapable of resisting.

Julian found himself walking back towards Castleclare.

But he was acutely aware of the lake

behind him where Melanie was entombed, and as acutely, he stared at the castle ahead of him where Lisa wept in grief.

Lisa had dried her red, swollen eyes, but she had no intention of returning to her guests. How could she? Julian had destroyed her. Never had she loved this way before, never would she love this way again. It was hopeless. To love such a complex man, a man so determined to cling to the past, yet filled with such anguish, was impossible. Lisa wanted to comfort and hold and cherish Julian until death parted them naturally fifty years hence. Yet he would not even speak to her, was determined to ignore her. God, it wasn't worth the pain.

Tomorrow she would go home.

Lisa had made up her mind.

Her bedroom door suddenly swung open. Lisa stiffened in utter surprise. Julian stood on the threshold, his eyes hot and wet, his trousers streaked with dirt and mud, his shirt open to the waist. He stared at her. Lisa's mouth became completely dry, because she saw something in his eyes that she had never seen before — the whole man, complete with his soul.

"Julian?" she whispered, her insides fluttering with hope.

His body began to shake. "I came . . ." he

began, and could not continue. He licked his lips. "I came," his voice was harsh and low, "to say goodbye."

Tears filled Lisa's eyes. She gripped the bedding so tightly she was sure she was shredding it. She must try to reach him one last time — something had changed. "Julian, perhaps I don't have to leave," she whispered, her gaze locked with his.

He was trembling, and he almost appeared to be crying. He shook his head. "You must go. I . . . understand."

Her heart exploded with his pain. Lisa was almost certain that he did not want her to leave him. She was on her feet before she could think otherwise, rushing to him. But Julian raised both hands, halting her in the center of the room. "Don't!" he shouted. "Can't you see? I am trying so very hard . . ." Tears suddenly spilled onto his cheeks, "So very goddamn hard to let you go!"

Lisa froze as she recognized the extent of his conflict. He wanted her, she knew he did, and she was joyous. But the fury she saw in his eyes terrified her. Instinct made her whisper, "Let me help you, Julian."

"You cannot," he shouted, his eyes blazing. He raised his fist and shook it at Lisa. "You cannot help me, Lisa — no one can."

She pursed her lips, choking on a sob.

Then Julian shouted, "Dammit! Damn

her! Damn Melanie!"

Lisa inhaled hard, wanting to go to him but afraid to. Julian covered his face with his hands, his body shaking.

Lisa said softly, "Curse her again Julian, if you must. She left you, Julian. She was weak — she left you."

Julian dropped his hands from his face and stared at her almost blindly. "I hate her." Abruptly he turned and struck out, his fist hitting a pitcher on the bureau and sending it crashing to the floor.

Lisa jumped away from him.

Then he faced her, shaking with rage. "I hate her," he said, each word distinct. "I hate her!"

"Julian . . ."

"Dammit!" he cried, and with the sweep of his arm he sent everything on the bureau crashing to the floor. "She let Eddie drown! And then she took her own life! She left me — damn her!"

"Julian!" Lisa cried, frozen in the center of the room.

But if he heard her, he gave no sign. He went berserk. With the strength of several men, he upended the huge oak bureau. Lisa watched, mesmerized and terrified, as it crashed over in the center of the room. But Julian did not stop. His expression twisted with rage and madness, he pulled out the top drawer and flung it clear across the chamber. Lisa fled to the other side of the bed as the four other drawers were also heaved at the far wall.

Julian ripped the hangings from her bed, tearing them apart with his bare hands, while Lisa cringed, unable to look away or even flee and hide. He tore the draperies from the window on that side of the bed and kicked over the bedstand, surely damaging his foot. The gaslamp spilled as he sent books flying in every direction. A man possessed, he finally lifted the beautiful standing Victorian mirror and sent that thudding against the opposite wall where it broke apart, glass shattering all over the floor.

Lisa watched and wept as he expelled a decade of pentup rage. She was very afraid, for she could hardly trust him now, but she also knew that he had to finish this, until the rage was gone, or she would never have a chance to love him and be loved by him.

When Julian was finished — and it could not have been more than five or six minutes — her room was destroyed. He stood gasping in its center amidst the jumble of broken chairs, drawers, the upended bureau and bedstand, the ripped bedding and draperies, the broken vases and lamps and cosmetics. His face was red with exertion; his tuxedo jacket was torn between the shoulders and arms. An unnatural silence filled Lisa's room, broken only by the sound of Julian's harsh breathing.

Lisa swallowed. She was as rigid as a board, unable to react or speak.

Julian remained unmoving, his head hanging. Suddenly he said, "It's my fault, too."

Lisa jerked.

Julian whispered, *"My fault."*

Lisa cried out, "No. It's not your fault. God took Eddie, Julian, and I cannot explain why. No one can, but Melanie was a grown woman — her suicide was *not* your fault!"

"She was a child," Julian moaned.

Slowly, Lisa began to weave her way across the room, through the chaos, toward him.

Julian covered his face with his hands. Tears streaked through his fingers.

Lisa did not hesitate. When she was close enough to touch him, she wrapped her arms around him. "Oh, Julian, dear, it is not your fault. Melanie was old enough to know better. Don't blame yourself."

For one moment, his body stiffened in resistance against hers. But Lisa held him hard, stroking his back, his hair, murmuring endearments, telling him that it was not his fault, that if anyone was at fault, other than Melanie, it was God. And suddenly his body melted against hers and he was crushing her against him and murmuring her name. The tears fell yet again from Lisa's eyes; his hard palms stroked down her back and up and down again. They clung to each other.

For a very long time.

Lisa knew that she had found ecstasy at last.

But then Julian finally moved, shifting her in his arms. "Lisa," he whispered roughly.

She lifted her face upwards. His gray gaze was shining. When their eyes finally met, so did their souls.

Very tenderly, he cupped her face with his palms, his hands strong and filled with barely controlled intensity. Then, slowly, he leaned over her. Lisa's heart soared as his mouth touched hers gently. For a brief moment, their mouths brushed. And then Julian claimed her.

Hungrily, without control, his mouth seized hers while he locked her against his rigid body; Lisa did not protest. She strained against him so that her softest parts met his hardest ones, while their mouths fused. His tongue sought hers and she opened wider, accepting all of him. As desire coursed through every inch of her body, joy infused her entire soul.

Suddenly Julian lifted her in his arms, stepping over the drawers and bureau. He carried her to the bed and laid her down, his hot eyes meeting hers, a question there. Lisa held her arms out to him. "Yes," she whispered, beaming. "Oh, yes!"

He came down on top of her, wrenching off his torn tailcoat, never taking his eyes from hers. Lisa reached up and laced her hands behind his head, smiling at him happily.

His eyes brightened and a beautiful smile transformed his handsome features, until his head dipped and he took her mouth again.

Lisa sighed.

Tenderly, his lips moved over her face, cherishing each eyelid, her cheekbones, and her nose. Lisa did not move. Her body had become boneless, melting into the bed, while wet heat flared deep inside of her. Julian began nuzzling her neck, her shoulders, and the bare skin of her upper chest, then lower, where her bodice ended. His breathing filled the room, harsh and male and impatient.

Lisa moaned softly, recognizing his need because it matched her own. He rubbed his cheek against her breasts and he was moaning, too.

His head moved lower. One of his arms became an iron band beneath her, lifting her slightly. "Lisa, how I want you," he said, kissing her stomach through her satin ballgown. "I have wanted you for a very long time, from the moment we first met."

Lisa's pulse quickened, joy racing in her veins. "Oh, Julian —"

"Lisa, I need you." He lifted his head and stared into her eyes. "God, how I need you. In every way."

She understood what he was trying to tell her and her vision blurred as she reached up to cup his cheek. "I need you, too, Julian." She paused, their gazes locked, and Lisa felt herself drowning in his shimmering gray eyes. "Julian, I love you."

He froze. His expression was stunned and joyous at once. He appeared to be very near tears.

"I love you," Lisa repeated vehemently. "I always have, I always will."

He laughed roughly, and Lisa smiled, equally moved, and then his hand fluttered over her face. "I love you, too," he said suddenly, his tone thick.

Lisa began to weep. The kiss which followed was long and deep. Time stopped for them.

Julian's mouth began an unerring descent. Lisa began to squirm as he kissed and nibbled her throat and chest. She did not protest as his hand went underneath her, unbuttoning her gown. Her heart was pounding so hard with excitement and anticipation that she felt faint. Except for the astounding torment building between her legs.

Shifting restlessly, Lisa allowed him to remove her dress between kisses, her body deeply flushed. She was vaguely aware of the impropriety of making love like this, with the room utterly alight and herself immodestly naked and a houseful of guests on the floor below. Yet she did not protest. Breathless, her eyes transfixed, she watched Julian's hands cupping and molding her firm breasts through her sheer silk chemise. Lisa's nipples were erect and when Julian lowered the edge of the chemise, prominently displayed. "You are the most beautiful woman I have ever met," he whispered.

Lisa was about to refute him, then thought the better of it, for Julian's tongue was flicking out to tease each erect tip. She gasped. And as his mouth finally claimed one nipple, his hand moved over her silk-draped thighs, roving there gently, finally brushing her pubis. She began to breathe in earnest. She could not believe the torrent of sensation coiling inside of her. *"Julian."*

Julian made a harsh, ragged sound. Before Lisa was completely aware that she was utterly naked — and that he was still fully dressed — he was nuzzling her thighs and the hot juncture between them. Lisa *was* shocked, but even more, she was fascinated, especially because he was kissing her there, kissing her as if she had a second mouth, oh God . . .

Lisa began to pant, her mind shutting down. Her hips began a fierce undulation of their own. His tongue played havoc with her swollen lips and the painfully aroused protrusion between them, while his fingers combed through her hair. He spread her wider. Lisa sagged against the pillows as he kissed her fully again and again. Suddenly she was arching up off the bed, crying his name, lights sparking inside of her head, blinding her, dazzling her . . .

"Yes, Lisa, darling," Julian whispered, and then he continued his exquisitely thorough torturing of her.

Lisa had been returning to this world, but her body tightened and tensed and her pulse picked up its beat all over again. She was shamelessly gripping Julian's head. Shamelessly moaning his name.

Julian loomed over her now, his thighs pushing hers as far apart as possible, something huge and hard and warm and wet prodding her. Lisa managed to focus just enough to realize that his eyes blazed with lust, just enough to understand what he intended. She looked down at his manhood as he rubbed languidly against her. Oh, God, she thought, because he was beautiful and magnificent and so power-

300

fully male. "Julian, come to me," she whispered.

His eyes flared hotter and he obeyed, thrusting just enough to insert his swollen head inside of her. Lisa tensed, her eyes widening.

"Don't be afraid," he murmured. "It will hurt, but only for one brief moment."

Lisa wet her lips, staring downwards at their partially joined bodies. "I am not afraid," she managed.

He laughed — a harsh, male sound, bent and kissed her mouth, her ear, and then tongued her nipple. All the while pushing gently against her, into her. As Lisa relaxed he invaded inch by hard, vibrating inch, until he had sheathed himself inside of her as far as he could go without doing the necessary damage. Lisa wrapped her arms around his broad back and clung to him.

"Now," he told her, and he thrust deep.

The pain was brief and inconsequential, because Lisa now possessed all of him, body and heart and soul, and as he moved inside of her, his rhythm increasing, she found herself beginning that otherworldly ascent again. "Julian," she cried as their mouths mated.

"Lisa," he cried in response and then he was above her, straining, and when Lisa could stand it no more she shouted his name wildly, exploding, and he bucked in response, convulsing inside of her. And there, while inside her, he began to weep, as they found ecstasy together, and love.

Twelve

*J*ulian lay back, his eyes closed, one arm flung outwards, towards Lisa. She was floating slowly back to reality. Her body felt delicious, soft and nearly boneless, still quivering with delicious sensations. *Julian.* Lisa's eyes opened and she turned to him, her heart bursting with joy and hope and love. And for the first time since she had met him, she saw his face devoid of tension, his expression utterly relaxed and at peace. Lisa waited for him to return to reality, too.

His eyes fluttered open and he turned his head and looked directly at her. For a single moment they stared at one another, unsmiling. Lisa was suddenly stiff with anxiety — and then Julian smiled.

It was a smile filled with warmth and tenderness and it came from the heart.

Lisa smiled back, overwhelmed with relief.

He reached out and pulled her into his arms and up against his body. Lisa snuggled against him, thinking, *thank you, God, thank you.*

"Lisa," Julian whispered, stroking her dark hair.

Lisa shifted to meet his gray eyes. She

was stunned to see tears there. "Yes?"

"I am not good with words," he said ruefully. "Somehow, I want to apologize — and thank you."

Lisa laid her palm on his chest and leaned upwards to kiss his mouth lightly. "You need not apologize, Julian, not for anything. I understand completely."

"You are an angel," he murmured, his tone low and seductive, his eyes far warmer than before. His hand slid down her spine, sending hot little shivers up Lisa's back.

"Don't be silly," she retorted, although she was secretly very pleased. If he wanted to insist that she was an angel, who was she to protest? "Julian, there is no need for you to thank me, either."

His smile was tender, in stark contrast to the smoldering heat of his eyes. "My life has been miserable, Lisa. I did not really realize how unhappy I was until you entered it. Of course, then I was even more miserable, wanting to touch you, to love you, yet unable to do either." His lips feathered hers. "Thank you, Lisa, for being a *determined* angel of mercy."

Lisa laughed, filled with pleasure.

"It is one of the things I like best about you," Julian said, smiling at her.

"That I am an angel?" Lisa quipped.

"That you are determined, and strong, and brave."

Lisa's smile faded. "Oh, Julian," she whispered, unbearably moved. "That is the nicest thing you could possibly say to me."

He did not hesitate, and pulling her close, he said, "That is why I fell in love with you."

Lisa blinked back tears, and managed to say, "You mean, it wasn't my ravishing face or exquisite body or feminine ways which did you in?"

He laughed. "I admit to being enticed on other, more mundane, levels." His hand slipped over her breast.

Lisa knew she should be shocked, but she was too interested in her body's nearly magical response. "How can such a big man be so gentle?" she murmured huskily as he began to caress her. "Perhaps I shall have to explore this contradiction further."

"Explore as you will." Julian laughed, pulling her down onto the bed, claiming her lips with his.

And Lisa kissed him back fiercely, the sounds of his warm laughter lingering in her mind.

Three days later, Robert paced the dining room, brooding. Clearly Julian and Lisa were reconciled. No one had seen hide nor hair of them since the night of the ball, as they remained locked in Julian's suite. No one, that is, except for O'Hara, who had faithfully brought refreshments upstairs.

And every time he had returned, he had been beaming.

Robert was thrilled, of course. But now he had a serious dilemma to face. The truth would have to come out. Julian was going to be furious, absolutely furious, when Robert told him all that he had done.

Robert sighed. Perhaps he would put off his confession just a little while longer. He was not pleased at the prospect of sporting one or two black eyes.

O'Hara paused on the threshold. "Lord Robert, sir, Lady Tarrington is here."

Robert had already spotted her standing behind the butler, her cheeks pink, no doubt from her habit of riding like the wind. He felt tension coiling within him. "How come this is no surprise?" he said rudely.

Edith had already entered the dining room, but his tone caused her to halt abruptly.

"As you can see, we are alone," Robert continued in the same harsh voice, gesturing around the room.

She was flushed. "Good morning, Robert. The ball was a success. The entire county is talking about little else."

"Come, Edith, let's forego the small talk, shall we? We both know why you are here."

Edith's small smile vanished. Her eyes were hurt, not angry. "Why must you be this way with me?"

Robert ignored the question. "Julian is upstairs, abed. In fact, he has been upstairs, abed, for the past three days. And he is not alone."

Edith turned a fiery shade of red.

He strode over to her until he towered above her, his expression furious. "He is with his bride, my dear."

Edith's hand shot out. Robert was prepared this time and he seized her wrist before she could strike him. "Once was enough," he growled. "Never try to slap me again!"

"You are disgusting," Edith hissed. But her eyes were suspiciously moist. "No gentleman would ever refer to what you have referred to in the presence of a lady."

"A true lady would not be chasing a married man, darling," Robert said with contempt.

"I am not chasing Julian," Edith cried, still trying to yank her wrist free of his grasp and failing. "What do I have to do to convince you of that?"

"Edith, all of Connaught County has known for years that you yearn for my brother."

"All of Connaught County is *wrong*," Edith snapped, her gaze openly furious.

They stared at one another coldly.

"I do not believe you," Robert finally said. His grip on her wrist had eased.

"That is because you are a fool."

"Hardly."

Edith wet her lips. "Tell me something, Robert. Tell me why you despise me so much?"

His head jerked. He did not reply immediately.

"You are gallant with all the ladies, even with your London trollops, but with me, you are cold and cruel. Why?" Edith cried.

He hesitated. "Because of Julian."

"But it is not Julian I am in love with," Edith said fiercely.

Robert's gaze turned sharp.

Edith hesitated, then did the unthinkable. She stepped forward, gripped his lapels, and, eyes closed, she planted a solid kiss on his mouth. Robert did not move.

For a moment Edith remained on her tiptoes, her mouth pressed to his, her heart pounding wildly. Robert did not respond. Choked with bitter defeat, she released him and stepped away. Edith began to tremble, appalled with her own behavior.

Robert stared at her in amazement.

Edith turned abruptly, intending to flee.

As she raced for the door, Robert overtook her with three long strides. Edith cried out as he caught her from behind, whirling her around. Their eyes met, hers frightened, his dark and wide. And then his arms went around her as he crushed her to his chest, and his mouth was on hers, hot, hard, impatient and demanding. Edith gasped.

And Robert kissed her with a decade's worth of longing, again and again.

When Lisa and Julian finally came down for a late breakfast the third day after the ball, they were holding hands and smiling. O'Hara beamed at them as they approached him in the corridor. "Good day, m'lord; good day, m'lady."

Julian smiled at his manservant. "Good morning, O'Hara. It's a beautiful day, is it not?"

Tears welled in the butler's eyes. So that His Lordship would not see, the old man turned away, blowing into a handkerchief. He had not seen the Marquis smile quite like that since the tragedy, and he was undone.

"It is a good day, isn't it, O'Hara?" Lisa sang sweetly. Her face somehow glowed. She flashed him a wide smile; she had never been lovelier.

O'Hara finally regained control just as they passed him. " 'Tis the best o' days," he murmured happily.

Lisa and Julian halted abruptly on the threshold of the dining room. "Oh, dear," Lisa said softly, as she and Julian caught Robert and Edith in a passionate embrace. "Oh, my," she added.

Julian laughed. "I cannot say that I am surprised," he said. "I have waited for this day for a very long time."

"Oh, really?" Lisa cocked her head.

At the sound of their voices Robert and Edith leapt apart, both of them flushing brightly. Edith's long, platinum hair had come loose from its coil and was streaming down her back.

"Good morning," Julian said heartily.

Robert appeared dazed. He blinked at Lisa and Julian. "Hello." He hesitated, then glanced at Edith, who was frozen with embarrassment and indecision. Their eyes held.

Robert put a comforting hand upon her waist, her eyes instantly softened. "Why don't you tidy up and join us . . . me . . . for breakfast?"

Her mouth opened, but she made no sound.

Robert smiled at her. "I shall not take no for an answer," he said softly.

"Then my answer is yes," Edith whispered, smiling.

"But you might want to wait a moment," Robert said suddenly, flushing. He coughed several times.

Julian had begun to pull out a chair for Lisa, but he paused at the sound of Robert's cough. His brow furrowed with concern.

Robert forced a smile. "I am only clearing

my throat, Julian. There is something I wish to say to everyone."

Julian's relief was visible. Lisa reached for his hand and gripped it, her newfound happiness pierced with the dark shadow of dread. How could she be so happy when Robert was ill with consumption? When he would one day die? Julian had already suffered so much — Lisa wished that she could spare him yet another tragedy. But at least she would be there when the time came to comfort him.

Robert coughed again. Everyone faced him expectantly.

Robert wet his lips. "First I would like to say that my greatest dream has come true." He smiled, looking at Lisa and Julian. "And that dream was to see my brother happy and whole again." His gaze warm, he regarded Lisa. "Thank you, Lisa. I knew you were up to the task of winning my brother's heart."

Lisa beamed. "Thank you, Robert, for your advice and help."

Julian put his arm around her. "I never had a chance," he said, serious and teasing at once.

Lisa laughed.

Robert glanced at each and every one in turn. "But there is something I must confess." He was grim and pale. "Julian, promise me that you shall hold your terrible temper in check."

Julian cocked his head. "Have you done something I should be angry about?"

"I'm afraid so," Robert said uneasily. "Remember, I am your only brother and you adore me."

"I can hardly forget who you are, Robert. Out with it, then, so we may eat breakfast and enjoy the day."

Robert glanced at Edith as if she might help him with his confession, but she was openly perplexed.

"What is it?" Edith asked softly. "What could be so terrible? Julian will not be angry with you, Robert, I am certain."

"I am afraid that you are very wrong." Robert sighed, glancing heavenwards just once. "Julian, everything I did, I did for you."

Julian eyed him suspiciously.

"I knew that you had to start living again. At the very least, to manage the estate responsibly. We needed money, of course. Clearly you had to be motivated to go out and wed an heiress. I decided to provide the proper motivation."

"The proper motivation," Julian repeated. His eyes narrowed. "Go on." It was a soft command.

"But my motivations were even grander than wanting you to have the means to provide for us and manage Castleclare and our holdings. I was sure you needed a woman — a wife — to make you happy again. And I was certain you would not wed a woman you were not secretly fond of. And I was right, was I not?" Robert's face brightened hopefully.

"You were very right," Julian said, sharing a warm glance with Lisa. "What is it you are trying to tell me, Robert?"

"Well, here is the good news," Robert said as he laughed nervously. "I am not dying."

Everyone stared.

"The bad news is that I deceived you so that you would be forced to wed," he added in a rush.

"Oh, my God," Lisa whispered, shocked.

Edith stared at Robert and began to weep.

Immediately Robert reached for her. "Edith, there's no need to cry," he began.

She wept harder.

Lisa was beginning to cry, too. This was the most wonderful news possible! She reached for and clung to Julian's hand. But he did not notice.

Julian gawked at Robert. "You are not dying?" he said roughly.

Robert faced him squarely, nodding.

"You pretended to be ill?" Julian said.

Robert nodded again. "Julian, remember, you do love me!"

"I think I might kill you myself," Julian cried, rushing forward.

"Julian, no! This is wonderful," Lisa cried, trying to grab him and missing.

Robert tensed.

"The agony you have put me through!" Julian shouted, and then he embraced Robert, hugging him so hard that he lifted him off of his feet. "Damn you," Julian whispered against his brother's cheek. Then, setting him back down, he said, "Thank you, God!" He released his brother, tears spilling down his cheeks.

"You will not kill me?" Robert said in his usual roguish manner.

"I will wait until tomorrow to kill you," Julian promised hoarsely. He put his arm around Lisa. "Today I am too gloriously happy. You are well — you little bastard — and I am in love." He turned and Lisa moved into his arms. He held her there, the two of them absolutely motionless and content just to hold one another.

"I think we must forgive him, Julian," Lisa whispered, deliriously happy. "Do not forget, Robert's deception brought us together. We owe him, darling."

"Yes, we will have to forgive him, won't we?" Julian murmured, stroking her hair. "But I will forgive him only after I throttle him, hmm?"

Lisa laughed and strained upwards as Julian bent to kiss her. Their mouths touched, fused. The kiss deepened and deepened and did not appear to have any inclination to end.

Robert smiled and held out his arm as Edith moved against him. Silently, so as not to disturb the newlyweds, they left the room.

Lisa and Julian did not notice.

Epilogue

Castleclare, 1904

*L*isa could not stand it.

Stealing a glance at Julian, who remained soundly asleep in their bed, she slipped to the floor, quickly donning a quilted wrapper. As she stole across their bedchamber, shivering, she peeked at him again. But he remained unmoving, breathing deeply, eyes closed. The barest of smiles graced his handsome face. Lisa could not help but marvel at the magnificent sight. She still could not believe that she was his and he was hers and that they were deliriously in love.

Lisa fled their room.

The castle was eerily silent. It was Christmas Day, 1904. And Lisa could not wait another moment to find out what Julian had given her as a present on their first real Christmas together.

She grinned as she hurried downstairs. Her gift to Julian was going to be a big and, she hoped, happy surprise.

Lisa paused in the ballroom. They had had a Christmas ball a few days ago for most of the county, and a huge Christmas tree stood in the center of the far wall, heavy with tinsel and candy canes, a pretty angel gracing its peak. The angel was symbolic and Lisa knew it.

Lisa rushed to the tree and began pawing through the many gifts. She found presents for everyone, including herself, but nothing from Julian. She checked again. Robert and Edith, who had married in the fall and were already expecting a child, had left gifts for Lisa, as had O'Hara and her maid, Betsy. But there was not a single package from Julian.

Lisa was in shock. She sat down hard on the wood floor in her nightclothes and bare feet. Had he forgotten? Was it possible?

"Is something amiss, darling?" Julian said teasingly from the threshold of the ballroom.

Lisa knew he had forgotten. She forced a smile. "No, of course not! Good morning, Julian. Merry Christmas." She stood up.

His gray eyes were twinkling mischievously. "Merry Christmas, angel."

And Lisa realized from his low, sexy tone that he was up to something. She regarded him suspiciously, perplexed.

"Merry Christmas!" shouted a group of voices in unison, and suddenly three people came barging into the room.

Lisa cried out as her father, Benjamin Ralston, reached her first. He lifted her off her feet and swung her around. "Lisa, Merry Christmas!"

"Papa!" she gasped. Over his shoulder she spied her beloved stepsister, Sofie, and Sofie's dashing husband, Edward Delanza. When Benjamin released her, Lisa flew across the room. Sofie met her halfway. Both women were crying as they embraced.

"Don't I get a turn?" Edward asked roguishly.

"Of course you do," Lisa cried, and was instantly swallowed up in his arms.

Finally the tearful greetings were over. Lisa moved to Julian's side, looking around at everyone. "I am in a state of disbelief," she confessed.

He laughed, putting his arm around her. "That is obvious."

Lisa glanced at her father and stepsister. "I have missed you so — I am so glad you are here!" Then she turned to her husband. "Julian, this is the most wonderful Christmas I have ever had."

His smile faded, his gaze intense. "This is only our very first one, angel. There will be many, many more."

Tears filled Lisa's eyes. As she moved into his embrace, the rest of the room ceased to exist; there was only Julian and herself. "How I love you," she whispered.

"You are my life," he said, and his eyes were shining and moist.

Lisa smiled shakily, then said, "I have a surprise for you, too, Julian."

His glance did not stray to the gifts beneath the tree. "Really? Last night I failed to find a present from you, darling, when I sneaked downstairs myself."

Lisa laughed, realizing that Julian had also checked the gifts beneath the tree surreptitiously. "You won't find my present gift-wrapped and in a box," Lisa said huskily.

His brow lifted. His hands were still clasped behind her back. "What will I find, then?"

"I do hope you will not be disappointed," Lisa said, then added, "five months from now."

He froze.

Lisa wet her lips. "I am having our child, Julian. In May."

His expression was transformed. Joy lit up his face. Lisa found herself in his arms, her feet no longer touching the floor, as Julian crushed her to him.

Lisa began to laugh. "I am having Julian's baby!" she shouted to the interested onlookers.

Edward and Benjamin cheered. Sofie laughed, crying, "That is wonderful, Lisa!"

Then Julian slid her to the ground, inch

by interesting inch. Lisa found her thoughts quite distracted by the time her feet reached the floor. "Julian . . ."

"I have never been happier," he whispered huskily. "Nor have I ever loved anyone the way I love you. Thank you, Lisa, thank you."

"I have done nothing," she said.

"You have wrought a miracle," he replied unevenly. "And you know it."

Lisa did know it. She lifted her hand and cupped his cheek.

"Let's have our own private celebration, angel," Julian whispered.

Lisa was about to agree, but they were suddenly besieged by her family. "Forget it," Edward said jovially. "This is a family day and we have traveled the Atlantic to share it with you."

"That's right," Benjamin said, clapping Julian on the shoulder. "C'mon, son, all that hiding has given me an appetite. Lead the way to your dining room."

Sofie shared a warm look with Lisa, smiling. "I want to know *everything,*" she said.

Lisa sighed happily and looked at Julian, who was being propelled across the ballroom by her father. She shrugged helplessly. "It *is* a family day," she cried.

Pausing, he gave her an intimate look and said, "Later, angel."

Her heart flipped hard. Julian smiled as Lisa decided that she could, indeed, wait.

Their gazes locked soulfully.

"Merry Christmas, darling," she whispered.

"Merry Christmas, angel," he said.

A Bright Red Ribbon

Fern Michaels

*E*ven in her dream, Morgan Ames knew she was dreaming, knew she was going to wake with tears on her pillow and reality slapping her in the face. She cried out, the way she always did, just at the moment Keith was about to slip the ring on her finger. That's how she knew it was a dream. She never got beyond this point. She woke now, and looked at the bedside clock; it was 4:10. She wiped at the tears on her cheeks, but this time she smiled. Today was the day. Today was Christmas Eve, the day Keith was going to slip the ring on her finger and they would finally set the wedding date. The big event, in her mind, was scheduled to take place in front of her parents' Christmas tree. She and Keith would stand in exactly the same position they stood in two years ago today, at the very same hour. Romance was alive and well.

She dropped her legs over the side of the bed, slid into a daffodil-colored robe that was snugly warm, and pulled on thick wool socks. She padded out to the miniature kitchen to make coffee.

Christmas Eve. To her, Christmas Eve was the most wonderful day of the year.

Years ago, when she'd turned into a teenager, her parents had switched the big dinner and gift opening to Christmas Eve so they could sleep late on Christmas morning. The dinner was huge; friends dropped by before evening services, and then they opened their presents, sang carols, and drank spiked eggnog afterward.

Mo knew a watched kettle never boiled so she made herself some toast while the kettle hummed on the stove. She was so excited her hands shook as she spread butter and jam on the toast. The kettle whistled. The water sputtered over the counter as she poured it into the cup with the black rum tea bag.

In about sixteen hours, she was going to see Keith. At last. Two years ago he had led her by the hand over to the twelve-foot Christmas tree and said he wanted to talk to her about something. He'd been so nervous, but she'd been more nervous, certain the something he wanted to talk about was the engagement ring he was going to give her. She'd been expecting it, her parents had been expecting it, all her friends had been expecting it. Instead, Keith had taken both her hands in his and said, "Mo, I need to talk to you about something. I need you to understand. This is my problem. You didn't do anything to make me . . . what I'm trying to say is, I need more time. I'm

326

not ready to commit. I think we both need to experience a little more of life's challenges. We both have good jobs, and I just got a promotion that will take effect the first of the year. I'll be working in the New York office. It's a great opportunity, but the hours are long. I'm going to get an apartment in the city. What I would like is for us to . . . to take a hiatus from each other. I think two years will be good. I'll be thirty and you'll be twenty-nine. We'll be more mature, more ready for that momentous step."

The hot tea scalded her tongue. She yelped. She'd yelped that night, too. She'd wanted to be sophisticated, blasé, to say, okay, sure, no big deal. She hadn't said any of those things. Instead she'd cried, hanging on to his arm, begging to know if what he was proposing meant he was going to date others. His answer had crushed her and she'd sobbed then. He'd said things like, "Ssshhh, it's going to be all right. Two years isn't all that long. Maybe we aren't meant to be with each other for the rest of our lives. We'll find out. Yes, it's going to be hard on me, too. Look, I know this is a surprise . . . I didn't want . . . I was going to call . . . This is what I propose. Two years from tonight, I'll meet you right here, in front of the tree. Do we have a date, Mo?" She nodded miserably. Then he'd added,

"Look, I have to leave, Mo. My boss is having a party in his townhouse in Princeton. It won't look good if I'm late. Christmas parties are a good way to network. Here, I got you a little something for Christmas." Before she could dry her eyes, blow her nose, or tell him she had a ton of presents for him under the tree, he was gone.

It had been the worst Christmas of her life. The worst New Year's, too. The next Christmas and New Year's had been just as bad because her parents had looked at her with pity and then anger. Just last week they had called and said, "Get on with your life, Morgan. You've already wasted two years. In that whole time, Keith hasn't called you once or even dropped you a post card." She'd been stubborn, though, because she loved Keith. Sharp words had ensued, and she'd broken the connection and cried.

Tonight she had a date.

Life was going to be so wonderful. The strain between her and her parents would ease when they saw how happy she was.

Mo looked at the clock. Five-thirty. Time to shower, dress, pack up the Cherokee for her two-week vacation. Oh, life was good. She had it all planned. They'd go skiing, but first she'd go to Keith's apartment in New York, stay over, make him breakfast. They'd make slow, lazy love and if the mood called for it, they'd make wild, animal love.

Two years was a long time to be celibate — and she'd been celibate. She winced when she thought about Keith in bed with other women. He loved sex more than she did. There was no way he'd been faithful to her. She felt it in her heart. Every chance her mother got, she drove home her point. Her parents didn't like Keith. Her father was fond of saying, "I know his type — he's no good. Get a life, Morgan."

Tonight her new life would begin. Unless . . . unless Keith was a no show. Unless Keith decided the single life was better than a married life and responsibilities. God in heaven, what would she do if that happened? Well, it wasn't going to happen. She'd always been a positive person and she saw no reason to change now.

It wasn't going to happen because when Keith saw her he was going to go out of his mind. She'd changed in the two years. She'd dropped twelve pounds in all the right places. She was fit and toned because she worked out daily at a gym and ran for five miles every evening after work. She'd gotten a new hair style in New York. And, while she was there she'd gone to a color specialist who helped her with her hair and makeup. She was every bit as professional looking as some of the ad executives she saw walking up and down Madison Avenue.

She'd shed her scrubbed girl-next-door image. S.K., which stood for Since Keith, she'd learned to shop in the outlet stores for designer fashions at half the cost. She looked down now at her sporty Calvin Klein outfit, at the Ferragamo boots and the Chanel handbag she'd picked up at a flea market. Inside her French luggage were other outfits by Donna Karan and Carolyn Roehm.

Like Keith, she had gotten a promotion with a hefty salary increase. If things worked out, she was going to think about opening her own architectural office by early summer. She'd hire people, oversee them. Clients she worked with told her she should open her own office, go it alone. One in particular had offered to back her after he'd seen the plans she'd drawn up for his beach house in Cape May. Her father, himself an architect, had offered to help out and had gone so far as to get all the paperwork from the Small Business Administration. She could do it now if she wanted to. But, did she want to make that kind of commitment? What would Keith think?

What she wanted, really wanted, was to get married and have a baby. She could always do consulting work, take on a few private clients to keep her hand in. All she needed was a husband to make it perfect.

Keith.

The phone rang. Mo frowned. No one ever called her this early in the morning. Her heart skipped a beat as she picked up the phone. "Hello," she said warily.

"Morgan?" Her mother. She always made her name sound like a question.

"What's wrong, Mom?"

"When are you leaving, Morgan? I wish you'd left last night like Dad and I asked you to do. You should have listened to us, Morgan."

"Why? What's wrong? I told you why I couldn't leave. I'm about ready to go out the door as we speak."

"Have you looked outside?"

"No. It's still dark, Mom."

"Open your blinds, Morgan, and look at the parking lot lights. It's snowing!"

"Mom, it snows every year. So what? It's only a two-hour drive, maybe three if there's a lot of snow. I have the Cherokee. Four-wheel drive, Mom." She pulled up the blind in the bedroom to stare out at the parking lot. She swallowed hard. So, it would be a challenge. The world was white as far as the eye could see. She raised her eyes to the parking lights. The bright light that usually greeted her early in the morning was dim as the sodium vapor fought with the early light of dawn and the swirling snow. "It's snowing, Mom."

"That's what I'm trying to tell you. It

started here around midnight, I guess. It was just flurries when Dad and I went to bed but now we have about four inches. Since this storm seems to be coming from the south where you are, you probably have more. Dad and I have been talking and we won't be upset if you wait till the storm is over. Christmas morning is just as good as Christmas Eve. Just how much snow do you have, Morgan?"

"It looks like a lot, but it's drifting in the parking lot. I can't see the front, Mom. Look, don't worry about me. I have to be home this evening. I've waited two long years for this. Please, Mom, you understand, don't you?"

"What I understand, Morgan, is that you're being foolhardy. I saw Keith's mother the other day and she said he hasn't been home in ten months. He just lives across the river, for heaven's sake. She also said she didn't expect him for Christmas, so what does that tell you? I don't want you risking your life for some foolish promise."

Mo's physical being trembled. The words she dreaded, the words she didn't ever want to hear, had just been uttered: Keith wasn't coming home for Christmas. She perked up almost immediately. Keith loved surprises. It would be just like him to tell his mother he wasn't coming home and then show up and yell, 'Surprise!' If he had no intention of honoring the promise they made to each other, he would have sent a note or called her. Keith wasn't that callous. Or was he? She didn't know anything anymore.

She thought about the awful feelings that attacked her over the past two years, feelings she pushed away. Had she buried her head in the sand? Was it possible that Keith had used the two-year hiatus to soften the blow of parting, thinking that she'd transfer her feelings to someone else and let him off the hook? Instead she'd trenched in and convinced herself that by being faithful to her feelings, tonight would be her reward. Was she a fool? According to her mother she was. Tonight would tell the tale.

What she did know for certain was, nothing was going to stop her from going home. Not her mother's dire words, and certainly not a snowstorm. If she was a fool, she deserved to have her snoot rubbed in it.

Just a few short hours ago she'd stacked up her shopping bags by the front door, colorful Christmas bags loaded with presents for everyone. Five oversize bags for Keith. She wondered what happened to the presents she'd bought two years ago. Did her mother take them over to Keith's mother's house or were they in the downstairs closet? She'd never asked.

She'd spent a sinful amount of money on him this year. She'd even knitted a stocking for him and filled it with all kinds of goodies and gadgets. She'd stitched his name on the cuff of the bright red stocking in bright green thread. Was she a fool?

Mo pulled on her fleece-lined parka. Bundled up, she carried as many of the bags downstairs to the lobby as she could handle. She made three trips before she braved the outdoors. She needed to shovel and heat the car up.

She was exhausted when she tossed the fold-up shovel into the back of the Jeep. The heater and defroster worked furiously, but she still had to scrape the ice from the windshield and driver's side window. She checked the flashlight in the glove compartment. She rummaged inside the small opening, certain she had extra batteries, but couldn't find any. She glanced at the gas gauge. Three-quarters full, enough to get her home. She'd meant to top off last night on her way home from work, but she'd been in a hurry to get home to finish wrapping Keith's presents. God, she'd spent hours making intricate, one-of-a-kind bows and decorations for the gold-wrapped packages. A three-quarter tank would get her home for sure. The Cherokee gave her good mileage. If memory served her right, the trip never took more than a quarter of a tank. Well, she couldn't worry about that now. If road conditions permitted, she could stop on 95 or when she got onto the Jersey Turnpike.

Mo was numb with cold when she shrugged out of her parka and boots. She debated having a cup of tea to warm her up. Maybe she should wait for rush hour traffic to be over. Maybe a lot of things.

Maybe she should call Keith and ask him point blank if he was going to meet her in front of the Christmas tree. If she did that, she might spoil things. Still, why take her life in her hands and drive through what looked like a terrible storm, for nothing. She'd just as soon avoid her parents' pitying gaze and make the trip tomorrow morning and return in the evening to lick her wounds. If he was really going to be a no show, that would be the way to go. Since there were no guarantees, she didn't see any choice but to brave the storm.

She wished she had a dog or a cat to nuzzle, a warm body that loved unconditionally. She'd wanted to get an animal at least a hundred times these past two years, but she couldn't bring herself to admit that she needed someone. What did it matter if that someone had four legs and a furry body?

Her address book was in her hand, but she knew Keith's New York phone number by heart. It was unlisted, but she'd managed to get it from the brokerage house

Keith worked for. So she'd used trickery. So what? She hadn't broken the rules and called the number. It was just comforting to know she could call if she absolutely had to. She squared her shoulders as she reached for the portable phone on the kitchen counter. She looked at the range-top clock. Seven forty-five. He should still be home. She punched out the area code and number, her shoulders still stiff. The phone rang five times before the answering machine came on. Maybe he was still in the shower. He always did cut it close to the edge, leaving in the morning with his hair still damp from the shower.

"C'mon, now, you know what to do if I don't answer. I'm either catching some z's or I'm out and about. Leave me a message, but be careful not to give away any secrets. Wait for the beep." Z's? It must be fast track New York talk. The deep, husky chuckle coming over the wire made Mo's face burn with shame. She broke the connection.

A moment later she was zipping up her parka and pulling on thin leather gloves. She turned down the heat in her cozy apartment, stared at her small Christmas tree on the coffee table, and made a silly wish.

The moment she stepped outside, grainy snow assaulted her as the wind tried to drive her backward. She made it to the

Cherokee, climbed inside, and slammed the door. She shifted into four-wheel drive, then turned on the front and back wipers. The Cherokee inched forward, its wheels finding the traction to get her to the access road to I-95. It took her all of forty minutes to steer the Jeep to the ramp that led onto the Interstate. At that precise moment she knew she was making a mistake, but it was too late and there was no way now to get off and head back to the apartment. As far as she could see, it was bumper-to-bumper traffic. Visibility was almost zero. She knew there was a huge green directional sign overhead, but she couldn't see it.

"Oh, shit!"

Mo's hands gripped the wheel as the car in front of her slid to the right, going off the road completely. She muttered her favorite expletive again. God, what would she do if the wipers iced up? From the sound they were making on the windshield, she didn't think she'd have to wait long to find out.

The radio crackled with static, making it impossible to hear what was being said. Winter advisory. She already knew that. Not only did she know it, she was participating in it. She turned it off. The dashboard clock said she'd been on the road for well over an hour and she was nowhere near the Jersey Turnpike. At least she didn't think so. It was impossible to read the signs with the snow sticking to everything.

A white Christmas. The most wonderful time of the year. That thought alone had sustained her these past two years. Nothing bad ever happened on Christmas. Liar! Keith dumped you on Christmas Eve, right there in front of the tree. Don't lie to yourself!

"Okay, okay," she muttered. "But this Christmas will be different, this Christmas it will work out." Keith will make it up to you, she thought. Believe. Sure, and Santa is going to slip down the chimney one minute after midnight.

Mo risked a glance at the gas gauge. Half. She turned the heater down. Heaters added to the fuel consumption, didn't they? She thought about the Ferragamo boots she was wearing. Damn, she'd set her rubber boots by the front door so she wouldn't forget to bring them. They were still sitting by the front door. She wished now for her warm ski suit and wool cap, but she'd left them at her mother's last year when she went skiing for the last time.

She tried the radio again. The static was worse than before. So was the snow and ice caking her windshield. She had to stop and clean the blades or she was going to have an accident. With the faint glow of the taillights in front of her, Mo steered the Cherokee to the right. She pressed her flasher button, then waited to see if a car would pass her on the left and how much room she had to exit the car. The parka hood flew backward, exposing her head and face to the snowy onslaught. She fumbled with the wipers and the scraper. The swath they cleared was almost minuscule. God, what was she to do? Get off the damn road at the very next exit and see if she could find shelter? There was always a gas station or truck stop. The problem was, how would she know when she came to an exit?

Panic rivered through her when she got back into the Jeep. Her leather gloves were soaking wet. She peeled them off, then tossed them onto the back seat. She longed for her padded ski gloves and a cup of hot tea.

Mo drove for another forty minutes, stopping again to scrape her wipers and windshield. She was fighting a losing battle and she knew it. The wind was razor sharp, the snow coming down harder. This wasn't just a winter storm, it was a blizzard. People died in blizzards. Some fool had even made a movie about people eating other people when a plane crashed during a blizzard. She let the panic engulf her again. What was going to happen to her? Would she run out of gas and freeze to death? Who would find her? When would they find her? On Christmas Day? She imagined her parents' tears, their recriminations.

All of a sudden she realized there were no lights in front of her. She'd been so careful to stay a car length and a half behind the car in front. She pressed the accelerator, hoping desperately to keep up. God in heaven, was she off the road? Had she crossed the Delaware Bridge? Was she on the Jersey side? She simply didn't know. She tried the radio again and was rewarded with squawking static. She turned it off quickly. She risked a glance in her rear view mirror. There were no faint lights. There was nothing behind her. She moaned in fear. Time to stop, get out and see what she could see.

Before she climbed from the car, she unzipped her duffel bag sitting on the passenger side. She groped for a tee shirt and wrapped it around her head. Maybe the parka hood would stay on with something besides her silky hair to cling to. Her hands touched a pair of rolled-up sleep sox. She pulled them on. Almost as good as mittens. Did she have two pairs? She found a second pair and pulled them on. She flexed her fingers. No thumb holes. Damn. She remembered the manicure scissors she kept in her purse. A minute later she had thumb holes and was able to hold the steering wheel tightly. Get out, see what you can see. Clean the wipers, use that flashlight.

Try your high beams.

Mo did all of the above. Uncharted snow. No one had gone before her. The snow was almost up to her knees. If she walked around, the snow would go down between her boots and stirrup pants. Knee highs. Oh, God! Her feet would freeze in minutes. They might not find her until the spring thaw. Where was she? A field? The only thing she knew for certain was, she wasn't on any kind of a road.

"I hate you, Keith Mitchell. I mean, I really hate you. This is all your fault! No, it isn't," she sobbed. "It's my fault for being so damn stupid. If you loved me, you'd wait for me. Tonight was just a time. My mother would tell you I was delayed because of the storm. You could stay at my mother's or go to your mother's. If you loved me. I'm sitting here now, my life in danger, because . . . I wanted to believe you loved me. The way I love you. Christmas miracles, my ass!"

Mo shifted gears, inching the Cherokee forward.

How was it possible, Mo wondered, to be so cold and yet be sweating? She swiped at the perspiration on her forehead with the sleeve of her parka. In her whole life she'd never been this scared. If only she knew where she was. For all she knew, she could be driving into a pond or a lake. She shivered. Maybe she should get out and walk.

Take her chances in the snow. She was in a no-win situation and she knew it. Stupid, stupid, stupid.

Maybe the snow wasn't as deep as she thought it was. Maybe it was just drifting in places. She was saved from further speculation when the Cherokee bucked, sputtered, slugged forward, and then came to a coughing stop. Mo cut the engine, fear choking off her breathing. She waited a second before she turned the ignition key. She still had a gas reserve. The engine refused to catch and turn over. She turned off the heater and the wipers, then tried again with the same results. The decision to get out of the car and walk was made for her.

Mo scrambled over the back seat to the cargo area. With cold, shaking fingers she worked the zippers on her suitcases. She pulled thin, sequined sweaters — that would probably give her absolutely no warmth — out of the bag. She shrugged from the parka and pulled on as many of the decorative designer sweaters as she could. Back in her parka, she pulled knee-hi stockings and her last two pairs of socks over her hands. It was better than nothing. As if she had choices. The keys to the jeep went into her pocket. The strap of her purse was looped around her neck. She was ready. Her sigh was as mighty as the wind howling about her as she climbed out of the Cherokee.

The wind was sharper than a butcher knife. Eight steps in the mid-thigh snow and she was exhausted. The silk scarf she'd tied around her mouth was frozen to her face in the time it took to take those eight steps. Her eyelashes were caked with ice as were her eyebrows. She wanted to close her eyes, to sleep. How in the hell did Eskimos do it? A gurgle of hysterical laughter erupted in her throat.

The laughter died in her throat when she found herself facedown in a deep pile of snow. She crawled forward. It seemed like the wise thing to do. Getting to her feet was the equivalent of climbing Mt. Rushmore. She crab-walked until her arms gave out on her, then she struggled to her feet and tried to walk again. She repeated the process over and over until she was so exhausted she simply couldn't move. "Help me, someone. Please, God, don't let me die out here like this. I'll be a better person, I promise. I'll go to church more often. I'll practice my faith more diligently. I'll try to do more good deeds. I won't be selfish. I swear to You, I will. I'm not just saying this, either. I mean every word." She didn't know if she was saying the words or thinking them.

A violent gust of wind rocked her backward. Her back thumped into a tree, knocking the breath out of her. She cried then, her tears melting the crystals on her lashes.

"Help!" she bellowed. She shouted until she was hoarse.

Time lost all meaning as she crawled along. There were longer pauses now between the time she crawled on all fours and the time she struggled to her feet. She tried shouting again, her cries feeble at best. The only person who could hear her was God, and He seemed to be otherwise occupied.

Mo stumbled and went down. She struggled to get up, but her legs wouldn't move. In her life she'd never felt the pain that was tearing away at her joints. She lifted her head and for one brief second she thought she saw a feeble light. In the time it took her heart to beat once, the light was gone. She was probably hallucinating. Move! her mind shrieked. Get up! They won't find you till the daffodils come up. They'll bury you when the lilacs bloom. That's how they'll remember you. They might even print that on your tombstone. "Help me. Please, somebody help me!"

She needed to sleep. More than anything in the world she wanted sleep. She was so groggy. And her heart seemed to be beating as fast as a racehorse's at the finish line. How was that possible? Her heart should barely be beating. Get the hell up, Morgan.

Now! Move, damn you!

She was up. She was so cold. She knew her body heat was leaving her. Her clothes were frozen to her body. She couldn't see at all. Move, damn you! You can do it. You were never a quitter, Morgan. Well, maybe where Keith was concerned. You always managed, somehow, to see things through to a satisfactory conclusion. She stumbled and fell, picked herself up with all the willpower left in her numb body, fell again. This time she couldn't get up.

A vision of her parents standing over her closed coffin, the room filled with lilacs, appeared behind her closed lids. Her stomach rumbled fiercely and then she was on her feet, her lungs about to burst with her effort.

The snow and wind lashed at her like a tidal wave. It slammed her backward and beat at her face and body. Move! Don't stop now! Go, go, go, go.

"Help!" she cried. She was down again, on all fours. She shook her head to clear it.

She sensed movement. "Please," she whimpered, "help me." She felt warm breath, something touched her cheek. God. He was getting ready to take her. She cried.

"Woof!"

A dog! Man's best friend. *Her* best friend now. "You aren't better than God, but you'll damn well do," Mo gasped. "Do you understand? I need help. Can you fetch help?" Mo's hands reached out to the dog, but he backed away, woofing softly. Maybe he was barking louder and she couldn't hear it over the sound of the storm. "I'll try and follow you, but I don't think I'll make it." The dog barked again and as suddenly as he appeared, he was gone.

Mo howled her despair. She knew she had to move. The dog must live close by. Maybe the light she'd seen earlier was a house and this dog lived there. Again, she lost track of time as she crawled forward.

"Woof, woof, woof."

"You came back!" She felt her face being licked, nudged. There was something in the dog's mouth. Maybe something he killed. He'd licked her. He put something down, picked it up and was trying to give it to her. "What?"

The dog barked, louder, backing up, then lunging at her, thrusting whatever he had in his mouth at her. She reached for it. A ribbon. And then she understood. She did her best to loop it around her wrist, crawling on her hands and knees after the huge dog.

Time passed — she didn't know how much. Once, twice, three times, the dog had to get down on all fours and nudge her, the frozen ribbon tickling her face. At one point when she was down and didn't think she would ever get up, the dog nipped her nose, barking in her ear. She obeyed and moved.

And then she saw the windows full of bright yellow light. She thought she saw a Christmas tree through the window. The dog was barking, urging her to follow him. She snaked after him on her belly, praying, thanking God, as she went along.

A doggie door. A large doggie door. The dog went through it, barking on the other side. Maybe no one was home to open the door to her. Obviously, the dog intended her to follow. When in Rome . . . She pushed her way through.

The heat from the huge, blazing fire in the kitchen slammed into her. Nothing in the world ever felt this good. Her entire body started to tingle. She rolled over, closer to the fire. It smelled of pine and something else, maybe cinnamon. The dog barked furiously as he circled the rolling girl. He wanted something, but she didn't know what. She saw it out of the corner of her eye — a large, yellow towel. But she couldn't reach it. "Push it here," she said hoarsely. The dog obliged.

"Well, Merry Christmas," a voice said behind her. "I'm sorry I wasn't here to welcome you, but I was showering and dressing at the back end of the house. I just assumed Murphy was barking at some wild animal. Do you always make this kind of entrance? Mind you, I'm not complaining. Actually, I'm delighted that I'll have someone to share Christmas Eve with. I'm sorry I can't help you, but I think you should get up. Murphy will show you the way to the bedroom and bath. You'll find a warm robe. Just rummage for whatever you want. I'll have some warm food for you when you get back. You are okay, aren't you? You need to move, get your circulation going again. Frostbite can be serious."

"I got lost and your dog found me," Mo whispered.

"I pretty much figured that out," the voice chuckled.

"You have a nice voice," Mo said sleepily. "I really need to sleep. Can't I just sleep here in front of this fire?"

"No, you cannot." The voice was sharp, authoritative. Mo's eyes snapped open. "You need to get out of those wet clothes. Now!"

"Yes, sir!" Mo said smartly. "I don't think much of your hospitality. You could help me, you know. I'm almost half-dead. I might still die. Right here on your kitchen floor. How's that going to look?" She rolled over, struggling to a sitting position. Murphy got behind her so she wouldn't topple over.

She saw her host, saw the wheelchair, then the anger and frustration in his face. "I've never been known for my tact. I apologize. I appreciate your help and you're right, I need to get out of these wet clothes. I can make it. I got this far. I would appreciate some food though if it isn't too much trouble . . . Or, I can make it myself if you . . ."

"I'm very self-sufficient. I think I can rustle up something that doesn't come in a bag. You know, real food. It's time for Murphy's supper, too."

His voice was cool and impersonal. He was handsome, probably well over six feet if he'd been standing. Muscular. "It can't be suppertime already. What time is it?"

"A little after three. Murphy eats early. I don't know why that is, he just does."

She was standing — a feat in itself. She did her best to marshal her dignity as Murphy started out of the kitchen. "I'm sorry I didn't bring a present. It was rude of me to show up like this with nothing in hand. My mother taught me better, but circumstances . . ."

"Go!"

Murphy bounded down the hall. Mo lurched against the wall again and again, until she made it to the bathroom. It was a pretty room for a bathroom, all powdery blue and white with matching towels and carpet. And it was toasty warm. The shower was obviously for the handicapped with a special seat and grab bars. She shed her clothes, layer by layer, until she was naked. She turned on the shower and was rewarded with instant steaming water. Nothing in the world had ever looked this good. Or felt this good, she thought as she stepped into the spray. She let the water pelt her and made a mental note to ask her host where he got the shower head that massaged her aching body. The soap was Ivory, clean and sweet-smelling. The shampoo was something in a black bottle, something manly. She didn't care. She lathered up her dark, wet curls and then rinsed off. She decided she liked the smell and made another mental note to look closely at the bottle for the name.

When the water cooled, she stepped out and would have laughed if she hadn't been so tired. Murphy was holding a towel. A large one, the mate to the yellow one in the kitchen. He trotted over to the linen closet, inched it open. She watched him as he made his selection, a smaller towel obviously for her hair. "You're one smart dog, I can say that for you. I owe you my life, big guy. Let's see, I'd wager you're a golden retriever. My hair should be half as silky as yours. I'm going to send you a dozen porterhouse steaks when I get home. Now, let's see, he said there was a robe in here. Ah, here it is. Now, why did I know it was going to be dark green?" She slipped into it, the smaller towel still wrapped around her head. The robe smelled like the shampoo. Maybe the stuff came in a set.

He said to rummage for what she wanted. She did, for socks and a pair of long underwear. She pulled on both, the waistband going all the way up to her underarms. As if she cared. All she wanted was the welcome warmth.

She looked around his bedroom. His. Him. God, she didn't even know his name, but she knew his dog's name. How strange. She wanted to do something. The thought had come to her in the shower, but now it eluded her. She saw the phone and the fireplace at the same time. She knew there would be no dial tone, and she was right. She sat down by the fire in the nest of cushions, motioning wearily for the dog to come closer. "I wish you were mine, I really do. Thank you for saving me. Now, one last favor — find that Christmas ribbon and save it for me. I want to have something to remember you by. Not now, the next time you go outside. Will you do that for . . . ?" A moment later she was asleep in the mound of pillows.

Murphy sat back on his haunches to stare at the sleeping girl in his master's room. He walked around her several times, sniffing as he did so. When he was satisfied that all was well, he trotted over to the bed and tugged at the comforter until he had it on the floor. Then he dragged it over to the sleeping girl. He pulled, dragged, and tugged until he had it snugly up around her chin. The moment he was finished, he beelined down the hall, through the living room, past his master, out to the kitchen where he slowed just enough to go through his door. He was back in ten minutes with the red ribbon.

"So that's where it is. Hand it over, Murphy. It's supposed to go on the tree." The golden dog stopped in his tracks, woofed, backed up several steps, but he didn't drop the ribbon. Instead, he raced down the hall to the bedroom, his master behind him, his chair whirring softly. He watched as the dog placed the ribbon on the coverlet next to Mo's face. He continued to watch as the huge dog gently tugged the small yellow towel from her wet head. With his snout, he nudged the dark ringlets, then he gently pawed at them.

"I see," Marcus Bishop said sadly. "She does look a little like Marcey with that dark hair. Now that you have the situation under control, I guess it's time for your dinner. She wanted the ribbon, is that it? That's how you got her here? Good boy, Murphy. Let's let our guest sleep. Maybe she'll wake up in time to sing some carols with us. You did good, Murph. Real good. Marcey would be so proud of you. Hell, I'm proud of you and if we don't watch it, I have a feeling this girl is going to try and snatch you away from me."

Marcus could feel his eyes start to burn when Murphy bent over the sleeping girl to lick her cheek. He swore then that the big dog cried, but he couldn't be certain because his own eyes were full of tears.

Back in the kitchen, Marcus threw Mo's clothes in the dryer. He spooned out wet dog food and kibble into Murphy's bowl. The dog looked at it and walked away. "Yeah, I know. So, it's a little setback. We'll recover and get on with it. If we can just get through this first Christmas, we'll be on the road to recovery, but you gotta help me out here. I can't do it alone." The dog buried his head in his paws, but made no sign that he either cared or understood what his master was saying. Marcus felt his shoulders slump.

It was exactly one year ago to the day that the fatal accident had happened. Marsha, his twin sister, had been driving when the head-on collision occurred. He'd been wearing his seat belt; she wasn't wearing hers. It took the wrecking crew four hours to get him out of the car. He'd had six operations and one more loomed on the horizon. This one, the orthopedic specialists said, was almost guaranteed to make him walk again.

This little cottage had been Marcey's. She'd moved down here after her husband died of leukemia, just five short years after her marriage. Murphy had been her only companion during those tragic years. He'd done all he could for her, but she'd kept him at a distance. She painted, wrote an art column for the *Philadelphia Democrat*, took long walks, and watched a lot of television. To say she withdrew from life was putting it mildly. After the accident, it was simpler to convert this space to his needs than the main house. A ramp and an oversized bathroom were all he needed. Murphy was happier here, too.

Murphy belonged to both of them, but he'd been partial to Marcey because she always kept licorice squares in her pocket for him.

He and Murphy had grieved together, going to Marcey's gravesite weekly with fresh flowers. At those times, he always made sure he had licorice in his pocket. More often than not, though, Murphy wouldn't touch the little black squares. It was something to do, a memory he tried to keep intact.

It was going to be nice to have someone to share Christmas with. A time of miracles, the Good Book said. Murphy finding this girl in all that snow had to constitute a miracle of some kind. He didn't even know her name. He felt cheated. Time enough for that later. Time. That was all he had of late.

Marcus checked the turkey in the oven. Maybe he should just make a sandwich and save the turkey until tomorrow when the girl would be up to a full sit-down dinner.

He stared at the Christmas tree in the center of the room and wondered if anyone else ever put their tree there. It was the only way he could string the lights. He knew he could have asked one of the servants from the main house to come down and do it just the way he could have asked them to cook him a holiday dinner. He needed to do these things, needed the responsibility of taking care of himself. In case this next operation didn't work.

He prided himself on being a realist. If he didn't, he'd be sitting in this chair sucking his thumb and watching the boob tube. Life was just too goddamn precious to waste even one minute. He finished decorating the tree, plugged in the lights, and whistled at his marvelous creation. He felt his eyes mist up when he looked at the one-of-a-kind ornaments that had belonged to Marcey and John. He wished for children, a house-ful. More puppies. He wished for love, for sound, for music, for sunshine and laugh-ter. Someday.

Damn, he wished he was married with little ones calling him Daddy. Daddy, fix this; Daddy, help me. And some pretty woman standing in the kitchen smiling, the smile just for him. Marcey said he was a fusspot and that's why no girl would marry him. She said he needed to be more outgoing, needed to smile more. Stop taking yourself so seriously, she would say. Who said you have to be a better engineer than Dad? And then she'd said, *If you can't whistle when you work you don't belong in that job.* He'd become a whistling fool after that little talk because he loved what he did, loved managing the family firm, the largest engineering outfit in the state of New Jersey. Hell, he'd been called to Kuwait after the Gulf War. That had to mean something in terms of prestige. As if he cared about that.

His chair whirred to life. Within seconds he was sitting in the doorway, watching the sleeping girl. He felt drawn to her for some reason. He snapped his fingers for Murphy. The dog nuzzled his leg. "Check on her, Murph — make sure she's breathing. She should be okay, but do it anyway. Good thing that fireplace is gas — she'll stay warm if she sleeps through the night. Guess I get the couch. He watched as the retriever circled the sleeping girl, nudging the quilt that had slipped from her shoulders. As before, he sniffed her dark hair, stopping long enough to lick her cheek and check on the red ribbon. Marcus motioned for him. Together, they made their way down the hall to the living room and the festive Christmas tree.

It was only six o'clock. The evening loomed ahead of him. He fixed two large, ham sandwiches, one cut into four neat squares, then arranged them on two plates along with pickles and potato chips. A beer for him and grape soda for Murphy. He placed them on the fold-up tray attached to his chair. He whirred into the room, then lifted himself out of the chair and onto the couch. He pressed a button and the wide screen television in the corner came to life. He flipped channels until he came to the Weather Channel. "Pay attention, Murph, this is what you saved our guest from. They're calling it The Blizzard. Hell, I could have told them that at ten o'clock this morning. You know what I never figured out, Murph? How Santa is supposed to come down the chimney on Christmas Eve with a fire going. Everyone lights their fireplaces on Christmas Eve. Do you think I'm the only one who's ever asked this question?" He continued to talk to the dog at his feet, feeding him potato chips. For a year now, Murphy was the only one he talked to, with the exception of his doctors and the household help. The business ran itself with capable people standing in for

357

him. He was more than fortunate in that respect. "Did you hear that, Murph? Fourteen inches of snow. We're marooned. They won't even be able to get down here from the big house to check on us. We might have our guest for a few days. Company." He grinned from ear to ear and wasn't sure why. Eventually he dozed, as did Murphy.

Mo opened one eye, instantly aware of where she was and what had happened to her. She tried to stretch her arms and legs. She bit down on her lower lip so she wouldn't cry out in pain. A hot shower, four or five aspirin, and some liniment might make things bearable. She closed her eyes, wondering what time it was. She offered up a prayer, thanking God that she was alive and as well as could be expected under the circumstances.

Where was her host? Her savior? She supposed she would have to get up to find out. She tried again to boost herself to a sitting position. With the quilt wrapped around her, she stared at the furnishings. It seemed feminine to her with the priscilla curtains, the pretty pale blue carpet, and satin-striped chaise longue. There was also a faint powdery scent to the room. A leftover scent as though the occupant no longer lived here. She stared at the large louvered closet that took up one entire wall. Maybe that's where the powdery smell was coming from. Closets tended to hold scents. She looked down at the purple and white flowers adorning the quilt. It matched the drapes. Did men use fluffy yellow towels? If they were leftovers, they did. Her host seemed like the green, brown, and beige type to her.

She saw the clock, directly in her line of vision, sitting next to the phone that was dead.

The time was 3:15. Good Lord, she'd slept the clock around. It was Christmas Day. Her parents must be worried sick. Where was Keith? She played with the fantasy that he was out with the state troopers looking for her, but only for a minute. Keith didn't like the cold. He only pretended to like skiing because it was the trendy thing to do.

She got up, tightened the belt on the oversize robe, and hobbled around the room, searching for the scent that was so familiar. One side of the closet held women's clothes, the other side, men's. So, there was a Mrs. Host. On the dresser, next to the chaise longue, was a picture of a pretty, dark-haired woman and her host. Both were smiling, the man's arm around the woman's shoulders. They were staring directly at the camera. A beautiful couple.

A friend must have taken the picture. She didn't have any pictures like this of her and Keith. She felt cheated.

Mo parted the curtains and gasped. In her life she'd never seen this much snow. She knew in her gut the Jeep was buried. How would she ever find it? Maybe the dog would know where it was.

Mo shed her clothes in the bathroom and showered again. She turned the nozzle a little at a time, trying to get the water as hot as she could stand it. She moved, jiggled, and danced under the spray as it pelted her sore, aching muscles. She put the same long underwear and socks back on and rolled up the sleeves of the robe four times. She was warm, that was all that mattered. Her skin was chafed and wind-burned. She needed cream of some kind, lanolin. Did her host keep things like that here in the bathroom? She looked under the sink. In two shoeboxes she found everything she needed. Expensive cosmetics, pricey perfume. Mrs. Host must have left in a hurry or a huff. Women simply didn't leave a fortune in cosmetics behind.

She was ready now to introduce herself to her host and sit down to food. She realized she was ravenous.

He was in the kitchen mashing potatoes. The table was set for two and one more plate was on the floor. A large turkey sat in the middle of the table.

"Can I do anything?" Her voice was raspy, throaty.

The chair moved and he was facing her.

"You can sit down. I waited to mash the potatoes until I heard the shower going. I'm Marcus Bishop. Merry Christmas."

"I'm Morgan Ames. Merry Christmas to you and Murphy. I can't thank you enough for taking me in. I looked outside and there's a lot of snow out there. I don't think I've ever seen this much snow. Even in Colorado. Everything looks wonderful. It smells wonderful, and I know it's going to taste wonderful, too." She was babbling like a schoolgirl. She clamped her lips shut and folded her hands in her lap.

He seemed amused. "I try. Most of the time I just grill something out on the deck. This was my first try at a big meal. I don't guarantee anything. Would you like to say grace?"

Would she? Absolutely she would. She had much to be thankful for. She said so, in great detail, head bowed. A smile tugged at the corners of Bishop's mouth. Murphy panted, shifting position twice, as much as to say, let's get on with it.

Mo flushed. "I'm sorry, I did go on there a bit, didn't I? You see, I promised . . . I said . . ."

"You made a bargain with God," Marcus said.

"How did you know?" God, he was handsome. The picture in the bedroom didn't do him justice at all.

"When it's down to the wire and there's no one else, we all depend on that Supreme Being to help us out. Most times we forget about Him. The hard part is going to be living up to all those promises."

"I never did that before. Even when things were bad, I didn't ask. This was different. I stared at my mortality. Are you saying you think I was wrong?"

"Not at all. It's as natural as breathing. Life is precious. No one wants to lose it." His voice faltered, then grew stronger.

Mo stared across the table at her host. She'd caught a glimpse of the pain in his eyes before he lowered his head. Maybe Mrs. Bishop was . . . not of this earth. She felt flustered, sought to change the subject. "Where is this place, Mr. Bishop? Am I in a town or is this the country? I only saw one house up on the hill when I looked out the window."

"The outskirts of Cherry Hill."

She was gobbling her food, then stopped chewing long enough to say, "This is absolutely delicious. I didn't realize I had driven this far. There was absolutely no visibility. I didn't know if I'd gone over the Delaware

Bridge or not. I followed the car's lights in front of me and then suddenly the lights were gone and I was on my own. The car just gave out even though I still had some gas left."

"Where were you going? Where did you leave from?"

"I live in Delaware. My parents live in Woodbridge, New Jersey. I was going home for Christmas like thousands of other people. My mother called and told me how bad the snow was. Because I have a four-wheel drive Cherokee, I felt confident I could make it. There was one moment there before I started out when I almost went back. I wish now I had listened to my instincts. It's probably the second most stupid thing I've ever done. Again, I'm very grateful. I could have died out there and all because I had to get home. I just had to get home. I tried the telephone in the bedroom but the line was dead. How long do you think it will take before it comes back on?" How anxious her voice sounded. She cleared her throat.

"A day or so. It stopped snowing about an hour ago. I heard a bulletin that said all the work crews are out. Power is the first thing that has to be restored. I'm fortunate in the sense that I have gas heat and a backup generator in case power goes out. When you live in the country these things are mandatory."

"Do you think the phone is out in the big house on the hill?"

"If mine is out, so is theirs," Marcus said quietly. "This is Christmas, you know."

"I know," Mo said, her eyes misting over.

"Eat!" Marcus said in the same authoritative tone he'd used the day before.

"My mother always puts marshmallow in her sweet potatoes. You might want to try that sometime. She sprinkles sesame seeds in her chopped broccoli. It gives it a whole different taste." She held out her plate for a second helping of turkey.

"I like the taste as it is, but I'll keep it in mind and give it a try someday."

"No, you won't. You shouldn't say things unless you mean them. You strike me as a person who does things one way and is not open to anything but your own way. That's okay, too, but you shouldn't humor me. I happen to like marshmallows in my sweet potatoes and sesame seeds in my broccoli."

"You don't know me at all so why would you make such an assumption?"

"I know that you're bossy. You're used to getting things done your way. You ordered me to take a shower and get out of my wet clothes. You just now, a minute ago, ordered me to eat."

"That was for your own good. You are opinionated, aren't you?"

"Yep. I feel this need to tell you your long

underwear scratches. You should use fabric softener in the final rinse water."

Marcus banged his fist on the table. "Aha!" he roared. "That just goes to show how much you really know. Fabric softener does something to the fibers and when you sweat the material won't absorb it. So there!"

"Makes sense. I merely said it would help the scratching. If you plan on climbing a mountain . . . I'm sorry. I talk too much sometimes. What do you have for dessert? Are we having coffee? Can I get it or would you rather I just sit here and eat."

"You're my guest. You sit and eat. We're having plum pudding, and of course we're having coffee. What kind of Christmas dinner do you think this is?" His voice was so huffy that Murphy got up, meandered over to Mo, and sat down by her chair.

"The kind of dinner where the vegetables come in frozen boil bags, the sweet potatoes in boxes, and the turkey stuffing in cellophane bags. I know for a fact that plum pudding can be bought frozen. I'm sure dessert will be just as delicious as the main course. Actually, I don't know when anything tasted half as good. Most men can't cook at all. At least the men I know." She was babbling again. "You can call me Mo. Everyone else does, even my dad."

"Don't get sweet on my dog, either," Marcus said, slopping the plum pudding onto a plate.

"I think your dog is sweet on me, Mr. Bishop. You should put that pudding in a little dessert dish. See, it spilled on the floor. I'll clean it up for you." She was half out of her chair when the iron command knifed through the air.

"Sit!" Mo lowered herself into her chair. Her eyes started to burn.

"I'm not a dog, Mr. Bishop. I only wanted to help. I'm sorry if my offer offended you. I don't think I care for dessert or coffee." Her voice was stiff, her shoulders stiff, too. She had to leave the table or she was going to burst into tears. What was wrong with her?

"I'm the one who should be apologizing. I've had to learn to do for myself. Spills were a problem for a while. I have it down pat now. I just wet a cloth and use the broom handle to move it around. It took me a while to figure it out. You're right about the frozen stuff. I haven't had many guests lately to impress. And you can call me Marcus."

"Were you trying to impress me? How sweet, Marcus. I accept your apology and please accept mine. Let's pretend I stopped by to wish you a Merry Christmas and got caught in the snowstorm. Because you're a nice man you offered me your hospitality. See, we've established that you're a nice

366

man and I want you to take my word for it that I'm a nice person. Your dog likes me. That has to count."

Marcus chuckled. "Well said."

Mo cupped her chin in her hands. "This is a charming little house. I bet you get the sun all day long. Sun's important. When the sun's out you just naturally feel better, don't you think? Do you have flowers in the spring and summer?"

"You name it, I've got it. Murphy digs up the bulbs sometimes. You should see the tulips in the spring. I spent a lot of time outdoors last spring after my accident. I didn't want to come in the house because that meant I was cooped up. I'm an engineer by profession so I came up with some long-handled tools that allowed me to garden. We pretty much look like a rainbow around April and May. If you're driving this way around that time, stop and see for yourself."

"I'd like that. I'm almost afraid to ask this, but I'm going to ask anyway. Will it offend you if I clean up and do the dishes?"

"Hell, no! I hate doing dishes. I use paper plates whenever possible. Murphy eats off paper plates, too."

Mo burst out laughing. Murphy's tail thumped on the floor.

Mo filled the sink with hot, soapy water. Marcus handed her the plates. They were finished in twenty minutes.

"How about a Christmas drink? I have some really good wine. Christmas will be over before you know it."

"This is good wine," Mo said.

"I don't believe it. You mean you can't find anything wrong with it?" There was a chuckle in Marcus's voice so Mo didn't take offense. "What do you do for a living, Morgan Ames?"

"I'm an architect. I design shopping malls — big ones, small ones, strip malls. My biggest ambition is to have someone hire me to design a bridge. I don't know what it is, but I have this . . . this thing about bridges. I work for a firm, but I'm thinking about going out on my own next year. It's a scary thought, but if I'm going to do it, now is the time. I don't know why I feel that way, I just do. Do you work here at home or at an office?"

"Ninety percent at home, ten percent at the office. I have a specially equipped van. I can't get up on girders, obviously. I have several employees who are my legs. It's another way of saying I manage very well."

"It occurs to me to wonder, Marcus, where you slept last night. I didn't realize until a short while ago that there's only one bedroom."

"Here on the couch. It wasn't a problem. As you can see, it's quite wide and deep —

the cushions are extra thick.

"So, what do you think of my tree?" he asked proudly.

"I love the bottom half. I even like the top half. The scent is so heady. I've always loved Christmas. It must be the kid in me. My mother said I used to make myself sick on Christmas Eve because I couldn't wait for Santa." She wanted to stand by the tree and pretend she was home waiting for Keith to show up and put the ring on her finger, wanted it so bad she could feel the prick of tears. It wasn't going to happen. Still, she felt driven to stand in front of the tree and . . . pretend. She fought the burning behind her eyelids by rubbing them and pretending it was the wood smoke from the fireplace that was causing the stinging. Then she remembered the fireplace held gas logs.

"Me, too. I was always so sure he was going to miss our chimney or his sleigh would break down. I was so damn good during the month of December my dad called me a saint. I have some very nice childhood memories. Are you okay? Is something wrong? You look like you lost your last friend suddenly. I'm a good listener if you want to talk."

Did she? She looked around at the peaceful cottage, the man in the wheelchair, and the dog sitting at his feet. She belonged in a scene like this one. The only problem was, the occupants were all wrong. She was never going to see this man again, so why not talk to him? Maybe he'd give her some male input where Keith was concerned. If he offered advice, she could take it or ignore it. She nodded, and held out her wineglass for a refill.

It wasn't until she was finished with her sad tale that she realized she was still standing in front of the Christmas tree. She sat down with a thump, knowing full well she'd had too much wine. She wanted to cry again when she saw the helpless look on Marcus's face. "So, everyone is entitled to make a fool of themselves at least once in their life. This is . . . was my time." She held out her glass again, but had to wait while Marcus uncorked a fresh bottle of wine. She thought his movements sluggish. Maybe he wasn't used to so much wine. "I don't think I'd make a very good drunk. I never had this much wine in my whole life."

"Me either." The wine sloshed over the side of the glass. Murphy licked it up.

"I don't want to get sick. Keith used to drink too much and get sick. It made me sick just watching him. That's sad, isn't it?"

"I never could stand a man who couldn't hold his liquor," Marcus said.

"You sound funny," Mo said as she realized her voice was taking on a sing-song quality.

"You sound like you're getting ready to sing. Are you? I hope you aren't one of those off-key singers." He leered down at her from the chair.

"So what if I am? Isn't singing good for the soul or something? It's the feeling, the thought. You said we were going to sing carols for Murphy. Why aren't we doing that?"

"Because you aren't ready," Marcus said smartly. He lowered the footrests and slid out of the chair. "We need to sit together in front of the tree. Sitting is as good as standing . . . I think. C'mere, Murphy, you belong to this group."

"Sitting is good." Mo hiccupped. Marcus thumped her on the back and then kept his arm around her shoulder. Murphy wiggled around until he was on both their laps.

"Just what exactly is wrong with you? Or is that impolite of me to . . . ask?" She swigged from the bottle Marcus handed her. "This is good — who needs a glass?"

"I hate doing dishes. The bottle is good. What was the question?"

"Huh?"

"What was the question?"

"The question is . . . was . . . do all your parts . . . work?"

"That wasn't the question. I'd remember if that was the question. Why do you want to know if my . . . parts work? Do you find

371

yourself attracted to me? Or is this a sneaky way to try and get my dog? Get your own damn dog. And my parts work just fine."

"You sound defensive. When was the last time you tried them out . . . what I mean is . . . how do you know?" Mo asked craftily.

"I know! Are you planning on taking advantage of me? I might allow it. Then again, I might not."

"You're drunk," Mo said.

"Yep, and it's all your fault. You're drunk, too."

"What'd you expect? You keep filling my glass. You know what, I don't care. Do you care, Marcus?"

"Nope. So, what are you going to do about that jerk who's waiting by your Christmas tree? Christmas is almost over. D'ya think he's still waiting?"

Mo started to cry. Murphy wiggled around and licked at her tears. She shook her head.

"Don't cry. That jerk isn't worth your little finger. Murphy wouldn't like him. Dogs are keen judges of character."

"Keith doesn't like dogs."

Marcus threw his hands in the air. "There you go! I rest my case." His voice sounded so dramatic, Mo started to giggle.

It wasn't much in the way of a kiss because she was giggling, Murphy was in the way, and Marcus's position and clumsy hands couldn't seem to coordinate with her.

"That was sweet," Mo said.

"Sweet! Sweet!" Marcus bellowed in mock outrage.

"Nice?"

"*Nice* is better than *sweet.* No one ever said that to me before."

"How many were there . . . before?"

"None of your business."

"That's true, it isn't any of my business. Let's sing. 'Jingle Bells.' We're both too snookered to know the words to anything else. How many hours till Christmas is over?"

Marcus peered at his watch. "A few." He kissed her again, his hands less clumsy. Murphy cooperated by wiggling off both their laps.

"I liked that!"

"And well you should. You're very pretty, Mo. That's an awful name for a girl. I like Morgan, though. I'll call you Morgan."

"My father wanted a boy. He got me. It's sad. Do you know how many times I used that phrase in the past few hours? A lot." Her head bobbed up and down for no good reason. "Jingle Bells . . ." Marcus joined in, his voice as off-key as hers. They collapsed against each other, laughing like lunatics.

"Tell me about you. Do you have any more wine?"

Marcus pointed to the wine rack in the kitchen. Mo struggled to her feet, tottered to the kitchen, uncorked the bottle, and carried it back to the living room "I didn't see any munchies in the kitchen so I brought us each a turkey leg."

"I like a woman who thinks ahead." He gnawed on the leg, his eyes assessing the girl next to him. He wasn't the least bit drunk, but he was pretending he was. Why? She was pretty, and she was nice. So what if she had a few hangups. She liked him, too, he could tell. The chair didn't intimidate her the way it did other women. She was feisty, with a mind of her own. She'd been willing to share her private agonies with him, a stranger. Murphy liked her. He liked her, too. Hell, he'd given up his room to her. Now, she was staring at him expectantly, waiting for him to talk about himself. What to tell her? What to gloss over? Why couldn't he be as open as she was?

"I'm thirty-five. I own and manage the family engineering firm. I have good job security and a great pension plan. I own this little house outright. No mortgages. I love dogs and horses. I even like cats. I've almost grown accustomed to this chair. I am self-sufficient. I treat my elders with respect. I was a hell of a Boy Scout, got lots of medals to prove it. I used to ski. I go to church, not a lot, but I do go. I believe in God. I don't have any . . . sisters or brothers. I try not to think too far ahead and I do my best not to look back. That's not to say I don't think and plan for the future, but in my position, I take it one day at a time. That pretty much sums it up as far as my life goes."

"It sounds like a good life. I think you'll manage just fine. We all have to make concessions . . . the chair . . . it's not the end of the world. I can tell you don't like talking about it, so, let's talk about something else."

"How would you feel if you went home this Christmas Eve and there in your living room was Keith in a wheelchair? What if he told you the reason he hadn't been in touch was because he didn't want to see pity in your eyes. How would you feel if he told you he wasn't going to walk again? What if he said you might eventually be the sole support?" He waited for her to digest the questions, aware that her intoxicated state might interfere with her answers.

"You shouldn't ask me something like that in my . . . condition. I'm not thinking real clear. I want to sing some more. I didn't sing last year because I was too sad. Are you asking about this year or last year?"

"What difference does it make?" Marcus asked coolly.

"It makes a difference. Last year I would have . . . would have . . . said it didn't matter because I loved him . . . Do all his parts . . . work?"

"I don't know. This is hypothetical." Marcus turned to hide his smile.

"I wouldn't pity him. Maybe I would at first. Keith is very active. I could handle it, but Keith couldn't. He'd get depressed and give up. What was that other part?"

"Supporting him."

"Oh, yeah. I could do that. I have a profession, good health insurance. I might start up my own business. I'll probably make more money than he ever did. Knowing Keith, I think he would resent me after awhile. Maybe he wouldn't. I'd try harder and harder to make it all work because that's the way I am. I'm not a quitter. I never was. Why do you want to know all this?"

Marcus shrugged. "Insight, maybe. In case I ever find myself attracted to a woman, it would be good to know how she'd react. You surprised me — you didn't react to the chair."

"I'm not in love with you," Mo said sourly.

"What's wrong with me?"

"There's nothing wrong with you. I'm not that drunk that I don't know what you're saying. I'm in love with someone else. I don't care about that chair. That chair wouldn't bother me at all if I loved you. You said your parts work. Or, was that a lie? I like sex. Sex is wonderful when two people . . . you know . . . I like it!"

"Guess what? I do, too."

"You see, it's not a problem at all," Mo said happily. "Maybe I should just lie down on the couch and go to sleep."

"You didn't answer the second part of my question."

"Which was?"

"What if you had made it home this Christmas and the same scenario happened. After two long years. What would be your feeling?"

"I don't know. Keith whines. Did I tell you that? It's not manly at all."

"Really."

"Yep. I have to go to the bathroom. Do you want me to get you anything on my way back? I'll be on my feet. I take these feet for granted. They get me places. I love shoes. Well, what's your answer? Remember, you don't have any munchies. Why is that?"

"I have Orville Redenbacher popcorn. The colored kind. Very festive."

"No! You're turning into a barrel of fun, Marcus Bishop. You were a bossy, domineering person when I arrived through your doggie door. Look at you now! You're skunked, you ate a turkey leg, and now you tell me you have colored popcorn. I'll be right back unless I get sick. Maybe we should have coffee with our popcorn. God, I can't wait for this day to be over."

"Follow her, Murph. If she gets sick, come and get me," Marcus said. "You know," he said, making a gagging sound. The retriever sprinted down the hall.

A few minutes later, Mo was back in the living room. She dusted her hands together as she swayed back and forth. "Let's do the popcorn in the fireplace! I'll bring your coffeepot in here and plug it in. That way we won't have to get up and down."

"Commendable idea. It's ten-thirty."

"An hour and a half to go. I'm going to kiss you at twelve o'clock. Well, maybe one minute afterward. Your socks will come right off when I get done kissing you! So there!"

"I don't like to be used."

"Me either. I'll be kissing you because I want to kiss you. So there yourself!"

"What will Keith think?"

"Keith who?" Mo laughed so hard she slapped her thighs before she toppled over onto the couch. Murphy howled. Marcus laughed outright.

On her feet again, Mo said, "I like you, you're nice. You have a nice laugh. I haven't had this much fun in a long time. Life is such a serious business. Sometimes you need to stand back and get . . . what's that word . . . perspective? I like amusement parks. I like acting like a kid sometimes. There's this water park I like to go to and I love Great Adventure. Keith would never go so I went with my friends. It wasn't the same as sharing it with your lover. Would you like to go and . . . and . . . watch the other people? I'd take you if you would."

"Maybe."

"I hate that word. Keith always said that. That's just another way of saying no. You men are all alike."

"You're wrong, Morgan. No two people are alike. If you judge other men by Keith you're going to miss out on a lot. I told you, he's a jerk."

"Okayyyy. Popcorn and coffee, right?"

"Right."

Marcus fondled Murphy's ears as he listened to his guest bang pots and pans in his neat kitchen. Cabinet doors opened and shut, then opened and shut again. More pots and pans rattled. He smelled coffee and wondered if she'd spilled it. He looked at his watch. In a few short hours she'd be leaving him. How was it possible to feel so close to someone he'd just met? He didn't want her to leave. He hated, with a passion, the faceless Keith.

"I think you need to swing around so we can watch the popcorn pop. I thought everyone in the world had a popcorn popper. I'm improvising with this pot. It's going to turn black, but I'll clean it in the morning. You might have to throw it out. I like strong black coffee. How about you?"

"Bootblack for me."

"Oh, me, too. Really gives you a kick in the morning."

"I don't think that's the right lid for that pot," Marcus said.

"It'll do — I told you I had to improvise."

"Tell me how you're going to improvise this!" Marcus said as the popping corn blew the lid off the pot. Popcorn flew in every direction. Murphy leaped up to catch the kernels, nailing the fallen ones with his paws. Marcus rolled on the floor as Mo wailed her dismay. The corn continued to pop and sail about the room. "I'm not cleaning this up."

"Don't worry, Murphy will eat it all. He loves popcorn. How much did you put in the pot?" Marcus gasped. "Coffee's done."

"A cup full. Too much, huh? I thought it would pop colored. I'm disappointed. There were a lot of fluffies — you know, the ones that pop first."

"I can't tell you how disappointed I am," Marcus said, his expression solemn.

Mo poured the coffee into two mugs.

"It looks kind of . . . syrupy."

"It does, doesn't it? Drink up! What'ya think?"

"I can truthfully say I've never had coffee

like this," Marcus responded.

Mo settled herself next to Marcus. "What time is it?"

"It's late. I'm sure by tomorrow the roads will be cleared. The phones will be working and you can call home. I'll try and find someone to drive you. I have a good mechanic I'll call to work on your Jeep. How long were you planning on staying with your parents?"

"It was . . . vague . . . depending . . . I don't know. What will you do?"

"Work. The office has a lot of projects going on. I'm going to be pretty busy."

"Me, too. I like the way you smell," Mo blurted. "Where'd you get that shampoo in the black bottle?"

"Someone gave it to me in a set for my birthday."

"When's your birthday?" Mo asked.

"April tenth. When's yours?"

"April ninth. How about that? We're both Aries."

"Imagine that," Marcus said as he wrapped his arm around her shoulder.

"This is nice," Mo sighed. "I'm a home and hearth person. I like things cozy and warm with lots and lots of green plants. I have little treasures I've picked up over the years that I try to put in just the right place. It tells anyone who comes into my apartment who I am. I guess that's why I like this cottage. It's cozy, warm, and comfortable. A big house can be like that, too, but a big house needs kids, dogs, gerbils, rabbits, and lots of junk."

He should tell her now about the big house on the hill being his. He should tell her about Marcey and about his upcoming operation. He bit down on his lip. Not now — he didn't want to spoil the moment. He liked what they were doing. He liked sitting here with her, liked the feel of her. He risked a glance at his watch. A quarter to twelve. He felt like his eyeballs were standing at attention from the coffee he'd just finished. He announced the time in a quiet voice.

"Do you think he showed up, Marcus?"

He didn't think any such thing, but he couldn't say that. "He's a fool if he didn't."

"His mother told my mother he wasn't coming home for the holidays."

"Ah. Well, maybe he was going to surprise her. Maybe his plans changed. Anything is possible, Morgan."

"No, it isn't. You're playing devil's advocate. It's all right. Really it is. I'll just switch to Plan B and get on with my life."

He wanted that life to include him. He almost said so, but she interrupted him by poking his arm and pointing to his watch.

"Get ready. Remember, I said I was going to kiss you and blow your socks off."

"You did say that. I'm ready."

"That's it, you're ready. It would be nice if you showed some enthusiasm."

"I don't want my blood pressure to go up," Marcus grinned. "What if . . ."

"There is no *what if*. It's a kiss."

"There are kisses and then there are kisses. Sometimes . . ."

"Not this time. I know all about kisses. Jackie Bristol told me about kissing when I was six years old. He was ten and he knew *everything*. He liked to play doctor. He learned all that stuff by watching his older sister and her boyfriend."

She was *that* close to him. She could see a faint freckle on the bridge of his nose. She just knew he thought she was all talk and no action. Well, she'd show him and Keith, too. A kiss was . . . it was . . . what it was was . . .

It wasn't one of those warm, fuzzy kisses and it wasn't one of those feathery light kind, either. This kiss was reckless and passionate. Her senses reeled and her body tingled from head to toe. Maybe it was all the wine she'd consumed. She decided she didn't care what the reason was as she pressed not only her lips, but her body, against his. He responded, his tongue spearing into her mouth. She tasted the wine on his tongue and lips, wondered if she tasted the same way to him. A slow moan began in her belly and rose up to her throat. It escaped the moment she pulled away. His name was on her lips, her eyes sleepy and yet restless. She wanted more. So much more.

This was where she was supposed to say, *Okay, I kept my promise, I kissed you like I said.* Now, she should get up and go to bed. But she didn't want to go to bed. Ever. She wanted . . . needed . . .

"I'm still wearing my socks," Marcus said. "Maybe you need to try again. Or, how about I try blowing your socks off?"

"Go for it," Mo said as she ran her tongue over her bruised and swollen lips.

He did all the things she'd done, and more. She felt his hands all over her body — soft, searching. Finding. Her own hands started a search of their own. She felt as warm and damp as he felt to her probing fingers. She continued to tingle with antici-pation. The heavy robe was suddenly open, the band of the underwear down around her waist, exposing her breasts. He was stroking one with the tip of his tongue. When the hard pink bud was in his mouth she thought she'd never felt such exquisite pleasure.

One minute she had clothes on and the next she was as naked as he was. She had a vague sense of ripping at his clothes as he did the same with hers. They were by the fire now, warm and sweaty.

She was on top of him with no memory of getting there. She slid over him, gasped at his hardness. Her dark hair fanned out like a waterfall. She bent her head and kissed him again. A sound of exquisite pleasure escaped her lips when he cupped both her breasts in his hands.

"Ride me," he said hoarsely. He bucked against her as she rode him, this wild stallion inside her. She milked his body, gave a mighty heave, and fell against him. It was a long time before either of them moved, and when they did, it was together. She wanted to look at him, wanted to say something. Instead, she nuzzled into the crook of his arm. The oversized robe covered them in a steamy warmth. Her hair felt as damp as his. She waited for him to say something, but he lay quietly, his hand caressing her shoulder beneath the robe. Why wasn't he saying something?

Her active imagination took over. One night stand. Girl lost in snowstorm. Man gives her shelter and food. Was this her payback? Would he respect her in the morning? Damn, it was already morning. What in the world possessed her to make love to this man? She was in love with Keith. *Was. Was* in love. At this precise moment she couldn't remember what Keith looked like. She'd cheated on Keith. But, had she really? *No,* her mind shrieked. She felt like crying, felt her shoulders start to shake. They calmed immediately as Marcus drew her closer.

"I . . . I never had a one night stand. I would hate . . . I don't want you to think . . . I don't hop in and out of bed . . . this was the first time in two years . . . I . . ."

"Shhh, it's okay. It was what it was — warm, wonderful, and meaningful. Neither one of us owes anything to the other. Sleep, Morgan," he whispered.

"You'll stay here, won't you?" she said sleepily. "I think I'd like to wake up next to you."

"I won't move. I'm going to sleep, too."

"Okay."

It was a lie, albeit a little one. As if he could sleep. Always the last one out of the gate, Bishop. She belongs to someone else, so don't get carried away. How right it all felt. How right it still felt. What had he just said to her? Oh yeah — *it was what it was.* Oh yeah, well, fuck you, Keith whatever-your-name-is. You don't deserve this girl. I hope your damn dick falls off. You weren't faithful to this girl. I know that as sure as I know the sun is going to rise in the morning. She knows it, too — she just won't admit it.

Marcus stared at the fire, his eyes full of pain and sadness. Tomorrow she'd be gone.

He'd never see her again. He'd go on with his life, with his therapy, his job, his next operation. It would be just him and Murphy.

It was four o'clock when Marcus motioned for the retriever to take his place under the robe. The dog would keep her warm while he showered and got ready for the day. He rolled over, grabbed the arm of the sofa and struggled to his feet. Pain ripped up and down his legs as he made his way to the bathroom with the aid of the two canes he kept under the seat cushions. This was his daily walk, the walk the therapists said was mandatory. Tears rolled down his cheeks as he gritted his teeth. Inside the shower, he lowered himself to the tile seat, turned on the water and let it beat at his legs and body. He stayed there until the water turned cool.

It took him twenty minutes to dress. He was stepping into his loafers when he heard the snowplow. He struggled, with his canes, out to the living room and his chair. His lips were white with the effort. It took every bit of fifteen minutes for the pain to subside. He bent over, picked up the coffeepot, and carried it to the kitchen where he rinsed it and made fresh coffee. While he waited for it to perk he stared out the window. Mr. Drizzoli and his two sons were maneuvering the plows so he could get his van out of the driveway. The younger boy was shoveling out his van. He turned on the outside lights, opened the door, and motioned to the youngster to come closer. He asked about road conditions, the road leading to the main house, and the weather in general. He explained about the Cherokee. The boy promised to speak with his father. They'd search it out and if it was driveable, they'd bring it to the cottage. "There's a five gallon tank of gas in the garage," Marcus said. From the leather pouch attached to his chair, he withdrew a square white envelope: Mr. Drizzoli's Christmas present. Cash.

"The phones are back on, Mr. Bishop," the boy volunteered.

Marcus felt his heart thump in his chest. He could unplug it. If he did that, he'd be no better than Keith what's-his-name. Then he thought about Morgan's anxious parents. Two cups of coffee on his little pull-out tray, Marcus maneuvered the chair into the living room. "Morgan, wake up. Wake her up, Murphy."

She looked so pretty, her hair tousled and curling about her face. He watched as she stretched luxuriously beneath his robe, watched the realization strike her that she was naked. He watched as she stared around her.

"Good morning. It will be daylight in a few

minutes. My road is being plowed as we speak and I'm told the phone is working. You might want to get up and call your parents. Your clothes are in the dryer. My maintenance man is checking on your Jeep. If it's driveable, he'll bring it here. If not, they'll tow it to a garage."

Mo wrapped the robe around her and got to her feet. Talk about the bum's rush. She swallowed hard. Well, what had she expected? One night stands usually ended like this. Why had she expected anything different? She needed to say something. "If you don't mind, I'll take a shower and get dressed. Is it all right if I use the phone in the bedroom?"

"Of course." He'd hoped against hope that she'd call from the living room so he could hear the conversation. He watched as she made her way to the laundry room, coffee cup in hand. Watched as she juggled cup, clothing, and the robe. Murphy sat back on his haunches and howled. Marcus felt the fine hairs on the back of his neck stand on end. Murphy hadn't howled like this since the day of Marcey's funeral. He had to know Morgan was going away. He felt like howling himself.

Marcus watched the clock, watched the progress of the men outside the window. Thirty minutes passed and then thirty-five and forty.

Murphy barked wildly when he saw Drizzoli come to what he thought was too close to his master's property.

Inside the bedroom, with the door closed, Morgan sat down, fully dressed, on the bed. She dialed her parents' number, nibbling on her thumbnail as she waited for the phone to be picked up. "Mom, it's me."

"Thank God. We were worried sick about you, honey. Good Lord, where are you?"

"Someplace in Cherry Hill. The Jeep gave out and I had to walk. You won't believe this, but a dog found me. I'll tell you all about it when I get home. My host tells me the roads are cleared and they're checking my car now. I should be ready to leave momentarily. Did you have a nice Christmas?" She wasn't going to ask about Keith. She wasn't going to ask because suddenly she no longer cared if he showed up in front of the tree or not.

"Yes and no. It wasn't the same without you. Dad and I had our eggnog. We sang 'Silent Night', off-key of course, and then we just sat and stared at the tree and worried about you. It was a terrible storm. I don't think I ever saw so much snow. Dad is whispering to me that he'll come and get you if the Jeep isn't working. How was your first Christmas away from home?"

"Actually, Mom, it was kind of nice. My host is a very nice man. He has this wonderful dog who found me. We had a turkey dinner that was pretty good. We even sang 'Jingle Bells'."

"Well, honey, we aren't going anywhere so call us either way. I'm so relieved that you're okay. We called the state troopers, the police, everyone we could think of."

"I'm sorry, Mom. I should have listened to you and stayed put until the snow let up. I was just so anxious to get home." Now, *now* she'll say if Keith was there.

"Keith was here. He came by around eleven. He said it took him seven hours to drive from Manhattan to his mother's. He was terribly upset that you weren't here. This is just my opinion, but I don't think he was upset that you were stuck in the snow — it was more that he was here and where were you? I'm sorry, Morgan, I am just never going to like that young man. That's all I'm going to say on the matter. Dad feels the same way. Drive carefully, honey. Call us, okay?"

"Okay, Mom."

Morgan had to use her left hand to pry her right hand off the phone. She felt sick to her stomach suddenly. She dropped her head into her hands. What she had wanted for two long years, what she'd hoped and prayed for, had happened. She thought about the old adage: Be careful what you wish for because you might just get it. Now, she didn't want what she had wished for.

It was light out now, the young sun creeping into the room. The silver-framed photograph twinkled as the sun hit it full force. Who was she? She should have asked Marcus. Did he still love the dark-haired woman? He must have loved her a lot to keep her things out in the open, a constant reminder.

She'd felt such strange things last night. Sex with Keith had never been like it was with Marcus. Still, there were other things that went into making a relationship work. Then there was Marcus in his wheelchair. It surprised her that the wheelchair didn't bother her. What did surprise her was what she was feeling. And now it was time to leave. How was she supposed to handle that?

Her heart thumped again when she saw a flash of red go by the bedroom window. Her Jeep. It was running. She stood up, saluted the room, turned, and left.

Good-byes are hard, she thought. Especially this one. She felt shy, schoolgirlish, when she said, "Thanks for everything. I mean to keep my promise and send Murphy some steaks. Would you mind giving me your address? If you're ever in Wilmington, stop . . . you know, stop and . . . we can have a . . . reunion . . . I'm not good at this."

"I'm not, either. Here's my card. My phone number is on it. Call me anytime if you . . . if you want to talk. I listen real good."

Mo handed over her own card. "Same goes for me."

"You just needed some antifreeze. We put five gallons of gas in the tank. Drive carefully. I'm going to worry so call me when you get home."

"I'll do that. Thanks again, Marcus. If you ever want a building or a bridge designed, I'm yours for free. I mean that."

"I know you do. I'll remember."

Mo cringed. How polite they were, how stiff and formal. She couldn't walk away like this. She leaned over, her eyes meeting his, and kissed him lightly on the lips. "I don't think I'll ever forget my visit." *Tell me now, before I leave, about the dark-haired, smiling woman in the picture. Tell me you want me to come back for a visit. Tell me not to go. I'll stay. I swear to God, I'll stay. I'll never think about Keith, never mention his name. Say something.*

"It was a nice Christmas. I enjoyed spending it with you. I know Murphy enjoyed having you here with us. Drive carefully, and remember to call when you get home."

His voice was flat, cool. Last night was just what he said; *it was what it was.* Nothing more. She felt like wailing her despair, but she damn well wasn't going to give him the satisfaction. "I will," Mo said cheerfully. She frolicked with Murphy for a few minutes, whispering in his ear. "You take care of him, you hear? I think he tends to be a little stubborn. I have my ribbon and I'll keep it safe, always. I'll send those steaks Fed Ex." Because her tears were blinding her, Mo turned and didn't look at Marcus again. A second later she was outside in the cold, bracing air.

The Cherokee was warm, purring like a kitten. She tapped the horn, two light taps, before she slipped the gear into four-wheel drive. She didn't look back.

It was an interlude.

One of those rare happenings that occur once in a lifetime.

A moment in time.

In a little more than twenty-four hours, she'd managed to fall in love with a man in a wheelchair — and his dog.

She cried because she didn't know what else to do.

Mo's homecoming was everything she had imagined it would be. Her parents hugged her. Her mother wiped at her tears with the hem of an apron that smelled of cinnamon and vanilla. Her father acted gruff, but she could see the moistness in his eyes.

"How about some breakfast, honey?"

"Bacon and eggs sounds real good. Make sure the . . ."

"The yolk is soft and the white has brown lace around the edges. Snap-in-two bacon, three pieces of toast for dunking, and a small glass of juice. I know, Morgan. Lord, I'm just so glad you're home safe and sound. Dad's going to carry in your bags. Why don't you run upstairs and take a nice hot bath and put on some clothes that don't look like they belong in a thrift store."

"Good idea, Mom."

In the privacy of her room, she looked at the phone that had, as a teenager, been her lifeline to the outside world. All she had to do was pick it up, and she'd hear Marcus's voice. Should she do it now or wait till after her bath when she was decked out in clean clothes and makeup? She decided to wait. Marcus didn't seem the type to sit by the phone and wait for a call from a woman.

The only word she could think of to describe her bath was *delicious*. The silky feel of the water was full of Wild Jasmine bath oil, her favorite scent in the whole world. As she relaxed in the steamy wetness, she forced herself to think about Keith. She knew without asking that her mother had called Keith's mother after the phone call. Right now, she was so happy to be safe, she would force herself to tolerate Keith. All those presents she'd wrapped so lovingly. All that money she'd spent. Well, she was taking it all back when she returned to Delaware.

Mo heard her father open the bedroom door, heard the sound of her suitcases being set down, heard the rustle of the shopping bags. The tenseness left her shoulders when the door closed softly. She was alone with her thoughts. She wished for a portable phone so she could call Marcus. The thought of talking to him while she was in the bathtub sent shivers up and down her spine.

A long time later, Mo climbed from the tub. She dressed, blow-dried her hair, and applied makeup, ever so sparingly, remembering that less is better. She pulled on a pair of Levis and a sweater that showed off her slim figure. She spritzed herself lightly with perfume, added pearl studs to her ears. She had to rummage in the drawer for thick wool socks. The closet yielded a pair of Nike Air sneakers she'd left behind on one of her visits.

In the kitchen her mother looked at her with dismay. "Is that what you're wearing?"

"Is something wrong with my sweater?"

"Well, no. I just thought . . . I assumed . . . you'd want to spiff up for . . . Keith. I imagine he'll be here pretty soon."

"Well, it better be pretty quick because I

have an errand to do when I finish this scrumptious breakfast. I guess you can tell him to wait or tell him to come back some other time. Let's open our presents after supper tonight. Can we pretend it's Christmas Eve?"

"That's what Dad said we should do."

"Then we'll do it. Listen, don't tell Keith. I want it to be just us."

"If that's what you want, honey. You be careful when you're out. Just because the roads are plowed, it doesn't mean there won't be accidents. The weatherman said the highways were still treacherous."

"I'll be careful. Can I get anything for you when I'm out?"

"We stocked up on everything before the snow came. We're okay. Bundle up — it's real cold."

Mo's first stop was the butcher on Main Street. She ordered twelve porterhouse steaks and asked to have them sent Federal Express. She paid with her credit card. Her next stop was the mall in Menlo Park where she went directly to Gloria Jean's Coffee Shop. She ordered twelve pounds of flavored coffees and a mug with a painted picture of a golden retriever on the side, asking to have her order shipped Federal Express and paying again with her credit card.

She spent the balance of the afternoon

browsing through Nordstrom's department store — it was so full of people she felt claustrophobic. Still, she didn't leave.

At four o'clock she retraced her steps, stopped by Gloria Jean's for a takeout coffee, and drank it sitting on a bench. She didn't want to go home. Didn't want to face Keith. What she wanted to do was call Marcus. *And that's exactly what I'm going to do. I'm tired of doing what other people want me to do. I want to call him and I'm going to call him.* She went in search of a phone the minute she finished her coffee.

Credit card in one hand, Marcus's business card in the other, Mo placed her call. A wave of dizziness washed over her the minute she heard his voice. "It's Morgan Ames, Marcus. I said I'd call you when I got home. Well, I'm home. Actually, I'm in a shopping mall. Ah . . . my mother sent me out to . . . to return some things . . . my dad was on the phone, I couldn't call earlier."

"I was worried when I didn't hear from you. It only takes a minute to make a phone call."

He was worried and he was chastising her. Well, she deserved it. She liked the part that he was worried. "What are you doing?" she blurted.

"I'm thinking about dinner. Leftovers or Spam. Something simple. I'm sort of watching a football game. I think Murphy misses you. I had to go looking for him twice. He was back in my room lying in the pillows where you slept."

"Ah, that's nice. I Federal Expressed his steaks. They should get there tomorrow. I tied the red ribbon on the post of my bed. I'm taking it back to Wilmington with me. Will you tell him that?" Damn, how stupid could one person be?

"I'll tell him. How were the roads?"

"Bad, but driveable. My dad taught me to drive defensively. It paid off." This had to be the most inane conversation she'd ever had in her life. Why was her heart beating so fast? "Marcus, this is none of my business. I meant to ask you yesterday, but I forgot. Who is that lovely woman in the photograph in your room? If it's something you don't care to talk about, it's okay with me. It was just that she sort of looked like me a little. I was curious." She was babbling again.

"Her name was Marcey. She died in the accident I was in. I was wearing my seat-belt, she wasn't. I'd rather not talk about it. You're right, though — you do resemble her a little. Murph picked up on that right away. He pulled the towel off your head and kind of sniffed your hair. He wanted me to . . . to see the resemblance, I guess. He took her death real hard."

She was sorry she'd asked. "I'm sorry. I didn't mean to . . . I'm so sorry." She was going to cry now, any second. "I have to go now. Thank you again. Take care of yourself." The tears fell then, and she made no move to stop them. She was like a robot as she walked to the exit and the parking lot. Don't think about the phone call. Don't think about Marcus and his dog. Think about tomorrow when you're going to leave here. Shift into neutral.

She saw his car and winced. Only a teenager would drive a canary yellow Camaro. She swerved into the driveway. Here it was, the day she'd dreamed of for two long years.

"I'm home!"

"Look who's here, Mo," her mother said. That said, she tactfully withdrew, her father following close behind.

"Keith, it's nice to see you," Mo said stiffly. Who was this person standing in front of her, wearing sunglasses and a houndstooth cap? He reeked of Polo.

"I was here — where were you? I thought we had a date in front of your Christmas tree on Christmas Eve. Your parents were so worried. You look different, Mo," he said, trying to take her into his arms. She deftly sidestepped him and sat down.

"I didn't think you'd show," she said flatly.

"Why would you think a thing like that?"

He seemed genuinely puzzled at her question.

"Better yet," Mo said, ignoring his question, "what have you been doing these past two years? I need to know, Keith?"

His face took on a wary expression. "A little of this, a little of that. Work, eat, sleep, play a little. Probably the same things you did. I thought about you a lot. Often. Every day."

"But you never called. You never wrote."

"That was part of the deal. Marriage is a big commitment. People need to be sure before they take that step. I don't believe in divorce."

How virtuous his voice sounded. She watched, fascinated, as he fished around in his pockets until he found what he was looking for. He held the small box with a tiny red bow on it in the palm of his hand. "I'm sure now. I know you wanted to get engaged two years ago. I wasn't ready. I'm ready now." He held the box toward her, smiling broadly.

He got his teeth capped, Mo thought in amazement. She made no move to reach for the silver box.

"Aren't you excited? Don't you want to open it?"

"No."

"No *what?*"

"No, I'm not excited; no, I don't want the

box. No, I don't want to get engaged and no, I don't want to get married. To you."

"Huh?" He seemed genuinely perplexed.

"What part of *no* didn't you understand?"

"But . . ."

"But *what,* Keith?"

"I thought . . . we agreed . . . it was a break for both of us. Why are you spoiling things like this? You always have such a negative attitude, Mo. What are you saying here?"

"I'm saying I had two long years to think about us. You and me. Until just a few days ago I thought . . . it would work out. Now, I know it won't. I'm not the same person and you certainly aren't the same person. Another thing, I wouldn't ride in that pimpmobile parked out front if you paid me. You smell like a pimp, too. I'm sorry. I'm grateful to you for this . . . whatever it was . . . hiatus. It was your idea, Keith. I want you to know, I was faithful to you." And she had been. She didn't make love with Marcus until Christmas Day, at which point she already knew it wasn't going to work out between her and Keith. "Look me in the eye, Keith, and tell me you were faithful to me. I knew it! You have a good life. Send me a Christmas card and I'll do the same."

"You're dumping me!" There was such outrage in Keith's voice, Mo burst out laughing.

"That's exactly what you did to me two years ago, but I was too dumb to see it. All those women you had, they wouldn't put up with your bullshit. That's why you're here now. No one else wanted you. I know you, Keith, better than I thought I did. I don't like the word *dump*. I'm breaking off our relationship because I don't love you anymore. Right now, for whatever it's worth, I wouldn't have time to work at a relationship anyway. I've decided to go into business for myself. Can we shake hands and promise to be friends?"

"Like hell! It took me seven goddamn hours to drive here from New York just so I could keep my promise. You weren't even here. At least I tried. I could have gone to Vail with my friends. You can take the responsibility for the termination of this relationship." He stomped from the room, the silver box secure in his pocket.

Mo sat down on the sofa. She felt lighter, buoyant somehow. "I feel, Mom, like someone just took fifty pounds off my shoulders. I wish I'd listened to you and Dad. You'd think at my age I'd have more sense. Did you see him? Is it me or was he always like that?"

"He was always like that, honey. I wasn't going to tell you, but under the circumstances, I think I will. I really don't think he would have come home this Christmas

403

except for one thing. His mother always gives him a handsome check early in the month. This year she wanted him home for the holidays so she said she wasn't giving it to him until Christmas morning. If he'd gotten it ahead of time I think he would have gone to Vail. We weren't eavesdropping — he said it loud enough so his voice carried to the kitchen. Don't feel bad, Mo."

"Mom, I don't. That dinner you're making smells soooo good. Let's eat, open our presents, thank God for our wonderful family, and go to bed."

"Sounds good to me."

"I'm leaving in the morning, Mom. I have some things I need to . . . take care of."

"I understand."

"Merry Christmas, Mom."

Mo set out the following morning with a full gas tank, an extra set of warm clothes on the front seat, a brand new flashlight with six new batteries, a real shovel, foot warmers, a basket lunch that would feed her for a week, two pairs of mittens, a pair of fleece-lined boots, and the firm resolve never to take a trip without preparing for it. In the cargo area there were five shopping bags of presents that she would be returning to Wanamaker's over the weekend.

She kissed and hugged her parents, accepted change from her father for the tolls, honked her horn, and was off. Her plan was to stop in Cherry Hill. Why, she didn't know. Probably to make a fool out of herself again. Just the thought of seeing Marcus and Murphy made her blood sing.

She had a speech all worked out in her head, words she'd probably never say. She'd say, *Hi, I was on my way home and thought I'd stop for coffee.* After all, she'd just sent a dozen different kinds. She could help cook a steak for Murphy. Maybe Marcus would kiss her hello. Maybe he'd ask her to stay.

It wasn't until she was almost to the Cherry Hill exit that she realized Marcus hadn't asked if Keith showed up. That had to mean he wasn't interested in her. *It was what it was.* She passed the exit sign with tears in her eyes.

She tormented herself all of January and February. She picked up the phone a thousand times, and always put it back down. Phones worked two ways. He could call her. All she'd gotten from him was a scrawled note thanking her for the coffee and steaks. He did say Murphy was burying the bones under the pillows and that he'd become a coffee addict. The last sentence was personal. *I hope your delayed Christmas was everything you wanted it to be.* A large scrawled "M." finished off the note.

She must have written five hundred letters in response to that little note. None of which she mailed.

She was in love. Really in love. For the first time in her life.

And there wasn't a damn thing she could do about it. Unless she wanted to make a fool of herself again, which she had no intention of doing.

She threw herself into all the details it took to open a new business. She had the storefront, she'd ordered the vertical blinds, helped her father lay the carpet and tile. Her father had made three easels and three desks, in case she wanted to expand and hire help. Her mother wallpapered the kitchen, scrubbed the ancient appliances, and decorated the bathroom while she went out on foot and solicited business. Her grand opening was scheduled for April first.

She had two new clients and the promise of two more. If she was lucky, she might be able to repay her father's loan in three years instead of five.

On the other side of the bridge, Marcus Bishop wheeled his chair out onto his patio, Murphy alongside him. On the pull-out tray were two beers and the portable phone. He was restless, irritable. In just two weeks he was heading back to the hospital. The door-die operation he'd been living for, yet dreading. There were no guarantees, but the surgeon had said he was confident he'd be walking in six months. With extensive, intensive therapy. Well, he could handle that. Pain was his middle name. Maybe then . . . maybe then, he'd get up the nerve to call Morgan Ames and . . . and chat. He wondered if he dared intrude on her life with Keith. Still, there was nothing wrong with calling her, chatting about Murphy. He'd be careful not to mention Christmas night and their love-making. "The best sex I ever had, Murph. You know me — too much too little too late or whatever that saying is. What's she see in that jerk? He is a jerk, she as much as said so. You're a good listener, Murph. Hell, let's call her and say . . . we'll say . . . what we'll do is . . . *hello* is good. Her birthday is coming up — so is mine. Maybe I should wait till then and send a card. Or, I could send flowers or a present. The thing is, I want to talk to her now. Here comes the mailman, Murph. Get the bag!"

Murphy ran to the doggie door and was back in a minute with a small burlap sack the mailman put the mail in. Murphy then dragged it to Marcus on the deck. He loved racing to the mailman, who always had dog biscuits as well as Mace in his pockets.

"Whoaoooo, would you look at this,

Murph? It's a letter or a card from you know who. Jesus, here I am thinking about her and suddenly I get mail from her. That must mean something. Here goes. Ah, she opened her own business. The big opening day is April first. No April Fool's joke, she says. She hopes I'm fine, hopes you're fine, and isn't this spring weather gorgeous? She has five clients now, but had to borrow money from her father. She's not holding her breath waiting for someone to ask her to design a bridge. If we're ever in Wilmington we should stop and see her new office. That's it, Murph. What I could do is send her a tree. Everyone has a tree when they open a new office. Maybe some yellow roses. It's ten o'clock in the morning. They can have the stuff there by eleven. I can call at twelve and talk to her. That's it, that's what we'll do." Murphy's tail swished back and forth in agreement.

Marcus ordered the ficus tree and a dozen yellow roses. He was assured delivery would be made by twelve-thirty. He passed the time by speaking with his office help, sipping coffee, and throwing a cut-off broom handle for Murphy to fetch. At precisely 12:30, his heart started to hammer in his chest.

"Morgan Ames. Can I help you?"

"Morgan, it's Marcus Bishop. I called to congratulate you. I got your card today."

"Oh, Marcus, how nice of you to call. The tree is just what this office needed and the flowers are beautiful. That was so kind of you. How are you? How's Murphy?"

"We're fine. You must be delirious with all that's happening. How did Keith react to you opening your own business? For some reason I thought . . . assumed . . . that opening the business wasn't something you were planning on doing right away. Summer . . . or did I misunderstand?"

"No, you didn't misunderstand. I talked it over with my father and he couldn't find any reason why I shouldn't go for it now. I couldn't have done it without my parents' help. As for Keith . . . it didn't work out. He did show up. It was my decision. He just . . . wasn't the person I thought he was. I don't know if you'll believe or even understand this, but all I felt was an overwhelming sense of relief."

"Really? If it's what you want, then I'm happy for you. You know what they say, if it's meant to be, it will be." He felt dizzy with her news.

"So, when do you think you can take a spin down here to see my new digs?"

"Soon. Do you serve refreshments?"

"I can and will. We have birthdays coming up. I'd be more than happy to take you out to dinner by way of celebration. If you have the time."

"I'll make the time. Let me clear my decks and get back to you. The only thing that will hinder me is my scheduled operation. There's every possibility it will be later this week."

"I'm not going anywhere, Marcus. Whenever is good for you will be good for me. I wish you the best. If there's anything I can do . . . now, that's foolish, isn't it? Like I can really do something. Sometimes I get carried away. I meant . . ."

"I know what you meant, Morgan, and I appreciate it. Murphy is . . . he misses you."

"I miss both of you. Thanks again for the tree and the flowers."

"Enjoy them. We'll talk again, Morgan."

The moment Marcus broke the connection his clenched fist shot in the air. "Yessss!" Murphy reacted to this strange display by leaping onto Marcus's lap. "She loves the tree and the flowers. She blew off what's-his-name. What that means to you and me, Murph, is maybe we still have a shot. If only this damn operation wasn't looming. I need to think, to plan. I'm gonna work this out. Maybe, just maybe we can turn things around. She invited me to dinner. Hell, she offered to pay for it. That has to mean something. I take it to mean she's interested. In *us*, because we're a package deal." The retriever squirmed and wiggled, his long tail lolling happily.

"I feel good, Murph. Real good."

Mo hung up the phone, her eyes starry. Sending the office announcement had been a good idea after all. She stared at the flowers and at the huge ficus tree sitting in the corner. They made all the difference in the world. He'd asked about Keith and she'd responded by telling him the truth. It had come out just right. She wished now that she had asked about the operation, asked why he was having it. Probably to alleviate the pain he always seemed to be in. At what point would referring to his condition, or his operation, be stepping over the line? She didn't know, didn't know anyone she could ask. Also, it was none of her business, just like Marcey wasn't any of her business. If he wanted her to know, if he wanted to talk about it, he would have said something, opened up the subject.

It didn't matter. He'd called and they sort of had a date planned. She was going to have to get a new outfit, get her hair and nails done. Ohhhhh, she was going to sleep so good tonight. Maybe she'd even dream about Marcus Bishop.

Her thoughts sustained her for the rest of the day and into the evening.

Two days later, Marcus Bishop grabbed the phone on the third ring. He announced

411

himself in a sleepy voice, then waited. He jerked upright a second later. "Jesus, Stewart, what time is it? Five o'clock! You want me there at eleven? Yeah, yeah, sure. I just have to make arrangements for Murphy. No, no, I won't eat or drink anything. Don't tell me not to worry, Stewart. I'm already sweating. I guess I'll see you later."

"C'mon, Murph, we're going to see your girlfriend. Morgan. We're going to see Morgan and ask her if she'll take care of you until I get on my feet or . . . we aren't going to think about . . . we're going to think positive. Get your leash, your brush, and all that other junk you take with you. Put it by the front door in the basket. Go on."

He whistled. He sang. He would have danced a jig if it was possible. He didn't bother with a shower — they did that for him at the hospital. He did shave, though. After all, he was going to see Morgan. She might even give him a good luck kiss. One of those blow-your-socks-off kisses.

At the front door he stared at the array Murphy had stacked up. The plastic laundry basket was filled to overflowing. Curiously, Marcus leaned over and poked among the contents. His leash, his brush, his bag of vitamins, his three favorite toys, his blanket, his pillow, one of his old slippers and one of Marcey's that he liked to sleep with, the mesh bag that contained his shampoo and flea powder.

"She's probably going to give us the boot when she sees all of this. You sure you want to take all this stuff?" Murphy backed up, barking the three short sounds that Marcus took for affirmation. He barked again and again, backing up, running forward, a sign that Marcus was supposed to follow him. In the laundry room, Murphy pawed the dryer door. Marcus opened it and watched as the dog dragged out the large yellow towel and took it to the front door.

"I'll be damned. Okay, just add it to the pile. I'm sure it will clinch the deal."

Ten minutes later they were barreling down I-95. Forty minutes after that, with barely any traffic on the highway, Marcus located the apartment complex where Morgan lived. He used up another ten minutes finding the entrance to her building. Thank God for the handicapped ramp and door. Inside the lobby, his eyes scanned the row of mailboxes and buzzers. He pressed down on the button and held his finger steady. When he heard her voice through the speaker he grinned.

"I'm in your lobby and I need you to come down. Now! Don't worry about fixing up. Remember, I've seen you at your worst."

"What's wrong?" she said, stepping from the elevator.

"Nothing. Everything. Can you keep Murphy for me? My surgeon called me an hour ago and he wants to do the operation this afternoon. The man scheduled for today came down with the flu. I have all Murphy's gear. I don't know what else to do. Can you do it?"

"Of course. Is this his stuff?"

"Believe it or not, he packed himself. He couldn't wait to get here. I can't thank you enough. The guy that usually keeps him is off in Peru on a job. I wouldn't dream of putting him in a kennel. I'd cancel my operation first."

"It's not a problem. Good luck. Is there anything else I can do?"

"Say a prayer. Well, thanks again. He likes real food. When you go through his stuff you'll see he didn't pack any."

"Okay."

"What do you call that thing you're wearing?" Marcus asked curiously.

"It's my bathrobe. It used to be my grandfather's. It's old, soft as silk. It's like an old friend. But better yet, it's warm. These are slippers on my feet even though they look like fur muffs. Again, they keep my feet warm. These things in my hair are curlers. It's who I am," Mo said huffily.

"I wasn't complaining. I was just curious. I bet you're a knockout when you're wearing makeup. Do you wear makeup?"

Mo's insecurities took over. She must look

like she just got off the boat. She could feel a flush working its way up to her neck and face. She didn't mean to say it, didn't think she'd said it until she saw the look on Marcus's face. "Why, did Marcey wear lots of makeup? Well, I'm sorry to disappoint you, but I wear very little. I can't afford the pricey stuff she used. What you see is what you get. In other words, take it or leave it and don't ever again compare me to your wife or your girlfriend." She turned on her heel, the laundry basket in her arms, Murphy behind her.

"Hold on! What wife? What girlfriend? What pricey makeup are you talking about? Marcey was my twin sister. I thought I told you that."

"No, you didn't tell me that," Mo called over her shoulder. Her back to him, she grinned from ear to ear. Ahhh, life was lookin' good. "Good luck," she said, as the elevator door swished shut.

In her apartment with the door closed and bolted, Mo sat down on the living room floor with the big, silky dog. "Let's see what we have here," she said, checking the laundry basket. "Hmmm, I see your grooming is going to take a lot of time. I need to tell you that we have a slight problem. Actually, it's a large, as in *very large,* problem. No pets are allowed in this apartment complex. Oh, you brought the yellow towel. That was sweet, Murphy," she said, hugging the retriever. "I hung the red ribbon on my bed." She was talking to this dog like he was a person and was going to respond any minute. "It's not just a little problem, it's a big problem. I guess we sleep at the office. I can buy a sleeping bag and bring your gear there. There's a kitchen and a bathroom. Maybe my dad can come down and rig up a shower. Then again, maybe not. I can always come back to the apartment and shower. We can cook in the office or we can eat out. I missed you. I think about you and Marcus a lot. I thought I would never hear from him again. I thought he was married. Can you beat that?

"Okay, I'm going to take my shower, make some coffee, and then we'll head to my new office. I'm sure it's nothing like Marcus's office and I know he takes you there with him. It's a me office, if you know what I mean. It's so good to have someone to talk to. I wish you could talk back."

Mo marched into the kitchen to look in the refrigerator. Leftover Chinese that should have been thrown out a week ago, leftover Italian that should have been thrown out two weeks ago, and last night's pepper steak that she'd cooked herself. She warmed it in the microwave and set it down for Murphy, who lapped it up within seconds. "Guess that will hold you till this evening."

Dressed in a professional, spring-like suit, Mo gathered her briefcase and all the stuff she carried home each evening into a plastic shopping bag. Murphy's leash and his toys went into a second bag. At the last moment she rummaged in the cabinet for a water bowl. "Guess we need to take your bed and blanket, too." Two trips later, the only thing left to do was call her mother.

"Mo, what's wrong? Why are you calling this early in the morning?"

"Mom, I need your help. If Dad isn't swamped, do you think you guys could come down here?" She related the events of the past hours. "I can't live in the office — health codes and all that. I need you to find me an apartment that will take a dog. I know this sounds stupid, but is it possible, do you think, to find a house that will double as an office? If I have to suck up the money I put into the storefront, I will. I might be able to sublease it, but I don't have the time to look around. I have so much work, Mom. All of a sudden it happened. It almost seems like the day the sign went up, everybody who's ever thought about hiring an architect chose me. I'm not complaining. Can you help me?"

"Of course. Dad's at loose ends this week. It's that retirement thing. He doesn't want to travel, he doesn't want to garden, he doesn't know what he wants. Just last night he was talking about taking a Julia Child cooking course. We'll get ready and leave within the hour." Her voice dropped to a whisper. "You should see the sparkle in his eyes — he's ready now. We'll see you in a bit."

Once they reached the office, Murphy settled in within seconds. A square patch of sun under the front window became his. His red ball, a rubber cat with a hoarse squeak, and his latex candy cane were next to him. He nibbled on a soup bone that was almost as big as his head.

Mo worked steadily without a break until her parents walked through the door at ten minutes past noon. Murphy eyed them warily until he saw Mo's enthusiastic greeting, at which point he joined in, licking her mother's outstretched hand and offering his paw to her father.

"Now, that's what I call a real gentleman. I feel a lot better about you being here alone now that you have this dog," her father said.

"It's just temporary, Dad. Marcus will take him back as soon as . . . well, I don't know exactly. Dad, I am so swamped. I'm also having a problem with this . . . take a look, give me your honest opinion. The client is coming in at four and I'm befuddled. The heating system doesn't work the way he wants it installed. I have to cut out walls, move windows — and he won't want to pay for the changes."

"In a minute. Your mother and I decided that I will stay here and help you. She's going out with a realtor at twelve-thirty. We called from the car phone and set it all up. We were specific with your requirements so she won't be taking your mother around to things that aren't appropriate. Knowing your mother, I'm confident she'll have the perfect location by five o'clock this evening. Why don't you and your mother visit for a few minutes while I take a look at these blueprints?"

"I think you should hire him, Mo," her mother stage-whispered. "He'd probably work for nothing. A couple of days a week would be great. I could stay down here with him and cook for you, walk your dog. We'd be more than glad to do it, Mo, if you think it would work and we wouldn't be infringing on your privacy."

"I'd love it, Mom. Murphy isn't my dog. I wish he was. He saved my life. What can I say?"

"You can tell me about Marcus Bishop. The real skinny, and don't tell me there isn't a skinny to tell. I see that sparkle in your eyes and it isn't coming from this dog."

"Later, okay? I think your real estate person is here. Go get 'em, Mom. Remember, I need a place as soon as possible.

Otherwise I sleep here in the office in a sleeping bag. If I break my lease by having a pet, I don't get my security deposit back and it was a hefty one. If you can find something for me it will work out perfectly since my current lease is up the first of May. I'm all paid up. I appreciate it, Mom."

"That's what parents are for, sweetie. See you. John . . . did you hear me?"

"Hmmmnn."

Mo winked at her mother.

Father and daughter worked steadily, stopping just long enough to walk Murphy and eat a small pizza they had delivered. When Mo's client walked through the door at four o'clock, Mo introduced her father as her associate, John Ames.

"Now, Mr. Caruthers, this is what Morgan and I came up with. You get everything you want with the heating system. See this wall? What we did was . . ."

Knowing her client was in good hands, Mo retired to the kitchen to make coffee. She added some cookies to a colorful tray at the last moment. When she entered the office, tray in hand, her father was shaking hands and smiling. "Mr. Caruthers liked your idea. He gets what he wants plus the atrium. He's willing to absorb the extra three hundred."

"I'm going to be relocating sometime in the next few weeks, Mr. Caruthers. Since

I've taken on an associate, I need more room. I'll notify you of my new address and phone number. If you happen to know anyone who would be interested in a sublease, call me."

Caruthers was gone less than five minutes when Helen Ames bustled through the door, the realtor in tow. "I found it! The perfect place! An insurance agent who had his office in his home is renting it. It's empty. You can move in tonight or tomorrow. The utilities are on, and he pays for them. It was part of the deal. It's wonderful, Mo — there's even a fenced yard for Murphy. I took the liberty of okaying your move. Miss Oliver has a client who does odd jobs and has his own truck. He's moving your furniture as we speak. All we have to do is pack up your personal belongings and Dad and I can do that with your help. You can be settled by tonight. The house is in move-in condition. That's a term real estate people use," she said knowledgeably. "Miss Oliver has agreed to see if she can sublease this place. Tomorrow, her man will move the office. At the most, Mo, you'll lose half a day's work. With Dad helping you, you'll get caught up in no time. There's a really nice garden on the side of the house and a magnificent wisteria bush you're going to love. Plus twelve tomato plants. The insurance man who owns the house is just glad that someone like us is renting. It's a three-year lease with an option to buy. His wife's mother lives in Florida and she wants to be near her since she's in failing health. I just love it when things work out for all parties involved. He didn't have one bit of a problem with the dog after I told him Murphy's story."

Everything worked out just the way her mother said it would.

The April showers gave way to May flowers. June sailed in with warm temperatures and bright sunshine. The only flaw in Mo's life was the lack of communication where Marcus was concerned.

Shortly after the Fourth of July, Mo piled Murphy into the Cherokee on a bright sunshiny Sunday and headed for Cherry Hill. "Something's wrong — I just feel it," she muttered to the dog all the way up the New Jersey Turnpike.

Murphy was ecstatic when the Jeep came to a stop outside his old home. He raced around the side of the house, barking and growling, before he slithered through his doggie door. On the other side, he continued to bark and then he howled. With all the doors locked, Mo had no choice but to go in the same way she'd gone through on Christmas Eve.

Inside, things were neat and tidy, but

there was a thick layer of dust over everything. Obviously Marcus had not been here for a very long time.

"I don't even know what hospital he went to. Where is he, Murphy? He wouldn't give you up, even to me. I know he wouldn't." She wondered if she had the right to go through Marcus's desk. Out of concern. She sat down and thought about her birthday. She'd been so certain that he'd send a card, one of those silly cards that left the real meaning up in the air, but her birthday had gone by without any kind of acknowledgment from him.

"Maybe he did give you up, Murphy. I guess he isn't interested in me." She choked back a sob as she buried her head in the retriever's silky fur. "Okay, come on, time to leave. I know you want to stay and wait, but we can't. We'll come back again. We'll come back as often as we have to. That's a promise, Murphy."

On the way back to her house, Mo passed her old office and was surprised to see that it had been turned into a Korean vegetable stand. She'd known Miss Oliver had subleased it with the rent going directly to the management company, but that was all she knew.

"Life goes on, Murphy. What's that old saying, time waits for no man? Something like that anyway."

Summer moved into autumn and before Mo knew it, her parents had sold their house and rented a condo on the outskirts of Wilmington. Her father worked full-time in her office while her mother joined every woman's group in the state of Delaware. It was the best of all solutions.

Thanksgiving was spent in her parents' condo with her mother doing all the cooking. The day was uneventful, with both Mo and her father falling asleep in the living room after dinner. Later, when she was attaching Murphy's leash, her mother said, quite forcefully, "You two need to get some help in that office. I'm appointing myself your new secretary and first thing Monday morning you're going to start accepting applications for associates. It's almost Christmas and none of us has done any shopping. It's the most wonderful time of the year and last year convinced us that . . . time is precious. We all need to enjoy life more. Dad and I are going to take a trip the day after Christmas. We're going to drive to Florida. I don't want to hear a word, John. And you, Mo, when was the last time you had a vacation? You can't even remember. Well, we're closing your office on the twentieth of December and we aren't re-opening until January second. That's the final word. If your clients object, let them go somewhere else."

"Okay, Mom," Mo said meekly.

"As usual, you're right, Helen," John said just as meekly.

"I knew you two would see it my way. We're going to take up golf when we get to Florida."

"Helen, for God's sake. I hate golf. I refuse to hit a silly little ball with a stick and there's no way I'm going to wear plaid pants and one of those damn hats with a pom-pom on it."

"We'll see," Helen sniffed.

"On that thought, I'll leave you."

At home, curled up in bed with Murphy alongside her, Mo turned on the television that would eventually lull her to sleep. She felt wired up, antsy for some reason. Here it was, almost Christmas, and Marcus Bishop was still absent from her life. She thought about the many times she'd called Bishop Engineering, only to be told Mr. Bishop was out of town and couldn't be reached. "The hell with you, Mr. Marcus Bishop. You gotta be a real low-life to stick me with your dog and then forget about him. What kind of man does that make you? What was all that talk about loving him? He misses you." Damn, she was losing it. She had to stop talking to herself or she was going to go over the edge.

Sensing her mood, Murphy snuggled

closer. He licked at her cheeks, pawed her chest. "Forget what I just said, Murphy. Marcus loves you — I know he does. He didn't forget you, either. I think, and this is just my own opinion, but I think something went wrong with his operation and he's recovering somewhere. I think he was just saying words when he said he was used to the chair and it didn't bother him. It does. What if they ended up cutting off his legs? Oh, God," she wailed. Murphy growled, the hair on the back of his head standing on end. "Ignore that, too, Murphy. No such thing happened. I'd feel something like that."

She slept because she was weary and because when she cried she found it difficult to keep her eyes open.

"What are you going to do, honey?" Helen Ames asked as Mo closed the door to the office.

"I'm going upstairs to the kitchen and make a chocolate cake. Mom, it's December twentieth. Five days till Christmas. Listen, I think you and Dad made the right decision to leave for Florida tomorrow. You both deserve sunshine for the holidays. Murphy and I will be fine. I might even take him to Cherry Hill so he can be home for Christmas. I feel like I should do that for him. Who knows, you guys might love Florida and want to retire there. There are worse things, Mom. Whatever you do, don't make Dad wear those plaid pants. Promise me?"

"I promise. Tell me again, Mo, that you don't mind spending Christmas alone with the dog."

"Mom, I really and truly don't mind. We've all been like accidents waiting to happen. This is a good chance for me to laze around and do nothing. You know I was never big on New Year's. Go, Mom. Call me when you get there and if I'm not home, leave a message. Drive carefully, stop often."

"Good night, Mo."

"Have a good trip, Mom."

On the morning of the twenty-third of December, Mo woke early, let Murphy out, made herself some bacon and eggs, and wolfed it all down. During the night she'd had a dream that she'd gone to Cherry Hill, bought a Christmas tree, decorated it, cooked a big dinner for her and Murphy, and . . . then she'd awakened. Well, she was going to live the dream.

"Wanna go home, big guy? Get your stuff together. We're gonna get a tree, and do the whole nine yards. Tomorrow it will be a full year since I met you. We need to celebrate."

A little after the noon hour, Mo found herself dragging a Douglas fir onto Marcus's back patio. As before, she crawled through the doggie door after the dog and walked through the kitchen to the patio door. It took her another hour to locate the box of Christmas decorations. With the fireplaces going, the cottage warmed almost immediately.

The wreath with the giant red bow went on the front door. Back inside, she added the lights to the tree and put all the colorful decorations on the branches. On her hands and knees, she pushed the tree stand gently until she had it perfectly arranged in the corner. It was heavenly, she thought sadly as she placed the colorful poinsettias around the hearth. The only thing missing was Marcus.

Mo spent the rest of the day cleaning and polishing. When she finished her chores, she baked a cake and prepared a quick poor man's stew with hamburger meat.

Mo slept on the couch because she couldn't bring herself to sleep in Marcus's bed.

Christmas Eve dawned, gray and overcast. It felt like snow, but the weatherman said there would be no white Christmas this year.

Dressed in blue jeans, sneakers, and a warm flannel shirt, Mo started the preparations for Christmas Eve dinner. The house was redolent with the smell of frying onions, the scent of the tree, and the gingerbread cookies baking in the oven. She felt almost light-headed when she looked at the tree with the pile of presents underneath, presents her mother had warned her not to open, presents for Murphy, and a present for Marcus. She would leave it behind when they left after New Year's.

At one o'clock, Mo slid the turkey into the oven. Her plum pudding, made from scratch, was cooling on the counter. The sweet potatoes and marshmallows sat alongside the pudding. A shaker of sesame seeds and the broccoli were ready to be cooked when the turkey came out of the oven. She took one last look around the kitchen, and at the table she'd set for one, before she retired to the living room to watch television.

Murphy leaped from the couch, the hair on his back stiff. He growled and started to pace the room, racing back and forth. Alarmed, Mo got off the couch to look out the window. There was nothing to see but the barren trees around the house. She switched on more lights, even those on the tree. As a precaution against what, she didn't know. She locked all the doors and windows. Murphy continued to growl and pace. Then the low, deep growls were replaced with high-pitched whines, but he made no move to go out his doggie door. Mo closed the drapes and turned the floodlights on outside. She could feel herself start to tense up. Should she call the police? What would she say? My dog's acting strange? Damn.

Murphy's cries and whines were so eerie she started to come unglued. Perhaps he wasn't one of those dogs that were trained to protect owner, hearth, and home. Since she'd had him he'd never been put to the test. To her, he was just a big animal who loved unconditionally.

In a moment of blind panic she rushed around the small cottage checking the inside dead bolts. The doors were stout, solid. She didn't feel one bit better.

The racket outside was worse and it all seemed to be coming from the kitchen area. She armed herself with a carving knife in one hand and a cast iron skillet in the other. Murphy continued to pace and whine. She eyed the doggie door warily, knowing the retriever was itching to use it, but he'd understood her iron command of *No*.

She waited.

When she saw the doorknob turn, she wondered if she would have time to run out the front door and into her Cherokee. She was afraid to chance it, afraid Murphy would bolt once he was outside.

She froze when she saw the thick vinyl strips move on the doggie door. Murphy saw it, too, and let out an ear-piercing howl. Mo sidestepped to the left of the opening, skillet held at shoulder height, the carving knife in much the same position.

She saw his head and part of one shoulder. "Marcus! What are you doing coming in Murphy's door?" Her shoulders sagged with relief.

"All the goddamn doors are locked and bolted. I'm stuck. What the hell are you doing here in my house? With my dog yet."

"I brought him home for Christmas. He missed you. I thought . . . you could have called, Marcus, or sent a card. I swear to God, I thought you died on the operating table and no one at your company wanted to tell me. One lousy card, Marcus. I had to move out of my apartment because they don't allow animals. I gave up my office. For your dog. Well, here he is. I'm leaving and guess what — I don't give one little shit if you're stuck in that door or not. You damn well took almost a year out of my life. That's not fair and it's not right. You have no excuse and even if you do, I don't want to hear it."

"Open the goddamn door! Now!"

"Up yours, Marcus Bishop!"

"Listen, we're two reasonably intelligent adults. Let's discuss this rationally. There's an answer for everything."

"Have a Merry Christmas. Dinner is in the

oven. Your tree is in the living room, all decorated, and there's a wreath on the front door. Your dog is right here. I guess that about covers it."

"You can't leave me stuck like this."

"You wanna bet? Toy with *my* affections, will you? Not likely. Stick *me* with your dog! You're a bigger jerk than Keith ever was. And I fell for your line of bullshit! I guess I'm the stupid one."

"Morgannnn!"

Mo slammed her way through the house to the front door. Murphy howled. She stooped down. "I'm sorry. You belong with him. I do love you — you're a wonderful companion and friend. I won't ever forget how you saved my life. From time to time I'll send you some steaks. You take care of that . . . that big boob, you hear?" She hugged the dog so hard he barked.

She was struggling with the garage door when she felt herself being pulled backward. To her left she heard Murphy bark ominously.

"You're going to listen to me whether you like it or not. Look at me when I talk to you," Marcus Bishop said as he whirled her around.

Her anger and hostility dropped away. "Marcus, you're on your feet! You can walk! That's wonderful!" The anger came back as swiftly as it had disappeared. "It still doesn't excuse your silence for nine whole months."

"Look, I sent cards and flowers. I wrote you letters. How in the damn hell was I supposed to know you moved?"

"You didn't even tell me what hospital you were going to. I tried calling till I was blue in the face. Your office wouldn't tell me anything. Furthermore, the post office, for a dollar, will tell you what my new address is. Did you ever think of that?"

"No. I thought you . . . well, what I thought was . . . you absconded with my dog. I lost the card you gave me. I got discouraged when I heard you moved. I'm sorry. I'm willing to take all the blame. I had this grand dream that I was going to walk into your parents' house on Christmas Eve and stand by your tree with you. My operation wasn't the walk in the park the surgeon more or less promised. I had to have a second one. The therapy was so intensive it blew my mind. I'm not whining here, I'm trying to explain. That's all I have to say. If you want to keep Murphy, it's okay. I had no idea . . . he loves you. Hell, *I* love you."

"You do?"

"Damn straight I do. You're all I thought about during my recovery. It was what kept me going. I even went by that Korean grocery store today and guess what? Take a look at this!" he held out a stack of cards and envelopes. "It seems they can't read

English. They were waiting for you to come and pick up the mail. They said they liked the flowers I sent from time to time."

"Really, Marcus!" She reached out to accept the stack of mail. "How'd you get out of that doggie door?" she asked suspiciously.

Marcus snorted. "Murphy pushed me out. Can we go into the house now and talk like two civilized people who love each other?"

"I didn't say I loved you."

"Say it!" he roared.

"Okay, okay, I love you."

"What else?"

"I believe you and I love your dog, too."

"Are we going to live happily ever after even if I'm rich and handsome?"

"Oh, yes, but that doesn't matter. I loved you when you were in the wheelchair. How are all your . . . parts?"

"Let's find out."

Murphy nudged both of them as he herded them toward the front door.

"I'm going to carry you over the threshold."

"Oh, Marcus, really!"

"Sometimes you simply talk too much." He kissed her as he'd never kissed her before.

"I like that. Do it again, and again, and again."

He did.

My True Love

Jo Goodman

San Francisco, 1875

Raleigh Montgomery didn't know why he was surprised. Even from her sickbed his grandmother was trying to foist her wishes on everyone from the cook to the city council. Perhaps the surprising thing was that he had avoided this particular trap until now.

"Are you listening to me, Raleigh?" There was an edge of impatience in Millicent Montgomery's tone. Her grandson was staring at her politely but with a certain blankness in his expression that warned her his interest had already wandered. He was masterful at keeping his thoughts to himself but Millicent recognized the signs of his quiet rebellion. "It's no good thinking you'll get out of it," she said firmly. "I'm quite set on the idea."

Sitting at her bedside, Raleigh stretched his long legs in front of him and leaned back in the cream brocade wing chair. He rubbed his knee absently. Outside the skies were overcast and the first fat droplets of rain splashed against the window. The pain would ease now that the clouds had opened up.

"Is your leg bothering you?"

He realized he was massaging it and withdrew his hand, laying it on the curved arm of the chair. "A little," he said. Nine months ago he had been trapped by fallen timbers and rock when the entrance to the No. 12 silver mine collapsed. It had taken a dozen men ten hours to dig him out. He had survived because of the stone pocket that had formed around his head, which had given him air and protected his skull. He never lost consciousness. He had had an eternity to contemplate his own death, or life without the use of one of his legs. Awareness had been a mixed blessing. The pain in his crushed leg had been excruciating and there had been moments when he would have welcomed death.

But, Raleigh Montgomery reflected, he had inherited a stubborn, willful streak from his grandmother. The same refusal to give up or give in that kept Millicent Scofield Montgomery going at eighty, saw Raleigh through at thirty-three. It was probably his own brush with death that had prompted his grandmother to make this latest outrageous demand. Knowing Millicent as he did, she had been planning it since he returned from the Nevada mine, waiting for just the right moment to spring it on him. Now that he was walking again, she no doubt thought he was fit enough for other, more intimate, activity. Raleigh had no intention of explaining to his grandmother that from his experience being bedridden had never been a deterrent. If she had realized that she would have begun to apply pressure months ago.

"Have you been doing your exercises?" Millicent asked, her clear blue eyes focused sharply on her grandson's face. She would know if he lied to her.

"Religiously until this morning," he said gravely. His gray eyes concealed his amusement but there was a faint, ironic smile lifting one corner of his mouth. "An audience with you has upset the schedule, I'm afraid."

"Don't be impertinent," she said sternly. "It isn't as if I commanded your presence here."

He laughed softly, rose stiffly to his feet, and laid a kiss on his grandmother's cool cheek. "That's exactly what you did, Grandmother, so it's no good denying it." Raleigh settled back into his chair. His grandmother was flustered for a moment before she busied herself by shifting the pillows at the small of her back and rearranging the blankets that covered her legs. He didn't miss her pleasure at his spontaneous display of affection. "And here I am," he said.

"Ever the dutiful grandson, prepared to do your bidding in an effort to remain in your good graces." He paused a beat, then added dryly, "And in your will."

"You *are* impertinent."

"Yes, ma'am." He watched her struggle to keep her smile in check. "You're looking remarkably well, however," he said. "I don't expect to hear that I've come into the family fortune anytime soon." His grandmother made an effort to affect frailty. Her slender shoulders fell forward and she lowered her chin a few notches. When she smoothed the blankets this time, her hands shook ever so slightly. "It's no good, Grandmother," he said calmly. "I've talked to your doctor. He assures me you're in fine health."

"I have pneumonia."

"You have a cold."

"That's hardly fine health," she pointed out. "It could become pneumonia."

"It *could* become pneumexico, but I don't think we should worry about it. Dr. Harvey says you're going to outlive us all." He smiled faintly as she sniffed her disapproval. Nevertheless he saw her lift her shoulders and chin and resume her regal posture. He could almost make out her silent plotting. "And you can't let Dr. Harvey go because I pay his bill," Raleigh said.

"That's why he tells you I'm fiddle-fit," she

440

said tartly. "I'll be seven days dead and stiff in this bed before he'll admit it to you. He knows a golden goose when he sees one."

"So do I, Grandmother." He rose to his feet again but this time he reached for his ebony walking cane so he could remain standing. "That's why I'm not going to let anything happen to you."

"Then you'll do as I've asked," she said confidently. "I assure you, my good health rests entirely in your hands."

"Tomorrow is Thanksgiving," he told her. "I can hardly present you with a great-grandchild by Christmas. At least not one of my own making. It will take at least nine months, you know." Millicent's mouth puckered with censure. Raleigh was uncertain if it was his plain speaking or the inevitable delay to her plans which prompted her reaction. "I trust your fragile constitution can survive that long," he said dryly.

"I'm sure I would feel better if you had a young lady's hand by then," she said, her tone a trifle wistful. She watched her grandson's handsomely sculpted features take on a certain rigidity. His eyes were as gray and cool as the overcast skies and his right hand rested with white-knuckled intensity on the knob of his cane. "I don't want a bastard," she told him. "If that's how you thought to honor my request then put it out of your mind. It is an unsatisfactory solution and will certainly put me in my grave. I raised you better than that and I deserve more regard and respect. Besides, not all women are like Catherine Hale. It's high time you stopped mourning a woman who isn't even dead."

Raleigh's eyes narrowed fractionally. A muscle worked in his lean cheek but he accepted the putdown without comment. "Good day, Grandmother," he said quietly.

Watching her grandson's uneven gait as he crossed the wide expanse of her bedroom, Millicent felt some regret for her words. She shouldn't have mentioned Catherine Hale. Raleigh had been desperately in love with her but she had been more interested in finance than fidelity. Millicent never knew if Raleigh understood the key role she had played in making certain he discovered his fiancée's liaison with his best friend. It had been ten years ago and they had never discussed it in all that time. Until a few minutes ago, Millicent had never even mentioned Catherine's name. But she had never forgotten her. Raleigh had made that impossible. His discovery, the betrayal by both a lover and a friend, had raised Raleigh's guard. On occasion he dropped it for her but she had never seen him drop it for anyone else.

His remoteness had served him well in

business. The reserve, the distancing, had kept competitors guessing at his strategy. He had negotiated land contracts with the government for western rail lines. The interest was low and the profits enormous. The completion of the transcontinental rail six years earlier had raised Raleigh's own stock with his investors and board. He had backed the Central Pacific and the deal had quadrupled his worth. The family fortune was in mining but Raleigh didn't see it as the Montgomery future. There was no way to know how long the earth would give up its bounty of gold in California or silver in Nevada. Whole towns had already gone bust.

Perhaps it had been Catherine Hale who had taught Raleigh not to put all his eggs in one basket. In business and in pleasure, Raleigh Montgomery cultivated a variety of interests.

From belowstairs Millicent heard the front door close. She hoped her grandson wasn't so angry that he would foolishly attempt to walk the distance from Nob Hill to the financial quarter. Sighing, she leaned back against the scrolled walnut headboard. The smooth crown of her hair was even whiter against the dark wood. Her hands were folded in her lap and she stared at the portrait on the far wall, her eyes pensive. Unchanged by the passage of time, her beloved son and daughter-in-law seemed to return her gaze. She wished they were with her now; they would have known how to handle their son. Instead, they reminded her of the unexpected and tragic turns life could take.

Millicent's resolve hardened. Twenty years ago she had lost her husband in a riding accident; her son, seven years later at Bull Run. An earthquake fire took the life of her daughter-in-law and the part of her grandson that hadn't been claimed by Catherine Hale, Millicent had almost lost to a mine collapse. She could not watch the family die in her own lifetime. Raleigh had a duty to do by his grandfather and his parents, and yes, by her as well. She could only hope that he would come to see it that way.

Linden Street let the curtain fall back in place as soon as she saw Raleigh step out of his carriage. She knew the instant she saw his face that his leg would not support him. She had even opened her mouth to call a warning but realized that she would never be heard. Running from her bedroom, which had the front street vantage point, Linden called out to the servants to attend her outside.

It had been raining intermittently throughout the day. The lull was appreciated now as the housekeeper, two maids, the butler, and a cook's helper all followed Linden onto the wet pavement. The carriage driver had already climbed down from his perch and was assisting Raleigh to a sitting position. Careless of her gown, Linden knelt beside him and ran her hands along the length of his injured leg.

"Get the hell away from me," he snapped. Pain made his voice tight. Embarrassment made him swear. He actually pushed Linden's hands away when she didn't comply immediately. Out of the corner of his eye he saw her lean back suddenly, her face flushed, her expression stricken. Still, she managed a dignified response. Raleigh Montgomery couldn't imagine a situation where she might have offered less.

"Mr. Simmons, Mr. Fine, help Mr. Montgomery to his feet," she said with quiet authority. She stood and backed away as the driver and the butler hunkered beside their fallen employer. "Support him under the arms. You may have to carry him. Kwei Po, take Mr. Montgomery's cane. He won't be able to use it."

As the cook's young helper moved eagerly to obey, Raleigh was fighting with Simmons and Fine. "I will *not* be carried," he fairly growled.

"Molly, Hsia To, please bring Mr. Montgomery's chair." The maids hurried off, disposed to do Linden's bidding if only to remove themselves from their employer's hard and angry stare.

"I don't need the damn chair," he said. He didn't call to the maids who were already out of earshot. His protest was addressed to Linden, who was fast becoming the focus of all his terrible fury.

"Mrs. Adams," Linden said to the housekeeper, "if you'd be so kind as to see that a bath is drawn for Mr. Montgomery and that his bed is turned back, I would appreciate it."

"Of course," the housekeeper said. "I'll see to everything. He'll take the evening meal in his room, then."

Linden nodded.

"I'm not dead," Raleigh said sharply as he was ignored by both women. "I'm not even an invalid. I'll take dinner in the dining room." He tried to move away from the support on either side of him and felt his injured leg give out immediately. If not for the redoubled efforts of Simmons and Fine, he would have kissed the pavement a second time.

Mrs. Adams's look was straightforward and knowing. When her employer of a dozen years could stand on his own feet again she'd take her orders from him. In the meantime, she was quite willing to let Linden Street have her way. "I'll see to everything," she told Linden. "You'll want warm towels and liniment."

"And bath salts," Linden replied. "Thank you, Mrs. Adams."

"Traitor," Raleigh said under his breath. If the housekeeper heard, she ignored him. Kwei Po was running up the walk to help the maids with the wheeled chair. They brought it down the granite steps, then let Kwei Po roll it along the sidewalk.

Linden waited patiently while Raleigh held his ground when the chair was placed behind him. Simmons and Fine weren't going to force him into it and neither was she. But in this particular battle of wills, she was confident of who would be standing in the end. She merely regarded him solemnly with a level stare while his frosty gray eyes chilled her.

White lines of tension and pain creased the corners of Raleigh Montgomery's mouth. "You work for me," he said tightly.

"Yes, sir. This is what you've hired me to do."

"Then I'm letting you go."

"Very well," she said calmly. "I'll collect my things now." Linden turned to go.

"Damn you, Miss Street." He sank in the chair and let Mr. Simmons begin to push him. A raindrop splashed the back of his hand. The chair picked up speed as the butler tried to beat the rain. The driver helped Simmons lift the chair up the steps and wheel it in the house. Kwei Po followed, stepping lively and tapping the cane that was only a few inches shorter than he was.

Raleigh had to stare at Linden's stiff, narrow back as they followed her up the expansive main staircase to the second floor. He noticed she had a tiny waist and her hips rolled ever so slightly as she took each step. One of her hands glided delicately along the banister but he knew the lightness of her touch was an illusion. Her long, lean fingers had the same steely strength as her spine.

Linden opened the door to Raleigh's bed-chamber. "Help him with his clothes, Mr. Simmons. I need to get my apron." Her gray day dress was already stained with water so a little more shouldn't have mattered. In truth, it didn't. Linden needed a moment alone to collect herself before she bearded the lion in his den.

The water was hot, the salts soothing as Raleigh leaned back in the tub. As relaxed as he was, he was alert to the sounds Linden made while moving about in the adjoining room. She had a soft tread, a silent and graceful step that he admired all the more in his current state of awkward-ness. "What are you doing in there?" he called brusquely.

Positioning the rack, she wanted to say. *Affixing the thumbscrews.* "Warming a pan for your bed," she said without inflection.

"Well, don't make me shout at you. Come here."

Linden steeled herself, first drawing in a calming breath, then letting it out slowly. Her reflection was captured in the full-length mirror on the other side of the room. She saw that she was worrying her lower lip. She released it and laid the warming pan aside. Her hands smoothed the crisply starched material of her apron. She began rolling up the sleeves of her gown as she walked into the adjoining dressing room.

Butter wouldn't melt in her mouth, Raleigh thought, as Linden approached his bath. She was incapable of warmth and, with the exception of a brief lapse in front of the others earlier, she was almost incapable of being ruffled. He recalled the stain of pink across her cheeks. Until then he hadn't thought he could rile her.

He didn't raise his head when she approached. His gray eyes were hooded as she folded a towel several times, laid it down beside the tub, then knelt on it. She might have been praying, with the bath as an altar. Raleigh's lip curled slightly. He harbored no illusions that she worshiped him. It was more likely he was the sacrifice.

Long, dark lashes shaded her eyes as she

reached across the copper tub for a wash-cloth. Raleigh didn't have to see them to know the pale violet color of her irises would darken slightly as she bent to her task. Her slender hands opened the cloth and she dipped it in the water. Tendons stood out sharply on the backs of her hands as she wrung it out. It was not the first time Raleigh had noticed the combination of beauty and strength.

Thick ebony hair framed an oval face. The features were evenly placed, given to a serenity of expression that was calming to others. The brows were dark, lightly feath-ered and perfectly arched over wide-set eyes. Her complexion was smooth and un-lined. It had the vigor and health of youth, though she was closer to thirty than not. Her mouth was perhaps the only feature not suited to her face, for it was too wide and the lower lip a shade too full to meet the strict discipline of fashionable beauty.

She bent forward over the tub. There were beads of perspiration at the hollow of her throat. A few loose strands of hair clung damply to her long neck.

"Can you raise your leg?" she asked.

Her question was posed quietly and fol-lowed by a silence that Raleigh had come to expect of her. She was always patient in waiting for a reply. With some effort, includ-ing the assistance of both his hands and the buoyancy of the water, he raised his injured leg just enough to hook his heel on the edge of the tub. Water dripped over the side and splashed the hardwood floor and Linden's crisp apron.

She placed her hands on his damp leg, one over the knee and the other on his ankle. There were jagged scars on the shin and calf where splinters of wood from the falling timber had gouged him. The bones of his leg had knit better than anyone, save for Raleigh Montgomery himself, had hoped for. His knee was still stiff and his ankle weak but because of Linden's prodding and manipulation, combined with Raleigh's own efforts, the muscles of his leg hadn't atrophied. The limb was straighter and firmer than the doctors had predicted would be the case at the onset of treatment.

"How far did you walk today?" she asked. Her hands moved firmly along his shin and calf. The damp hair on his legs was crisp under her touch. She ignored the surface texture and probed deeper, feeling for the hard muscles beneath the skin, inspecting for the damage that had been done to tendon, joint, and sinew. Linden kept her eyes on the injured leg. Bath salts had clouded the water but if her gaze strayed she knew what she would see. The sight of a naked man didn't embarrass her but she would be hard pressed not to let the comments that would surely follow get under her skin. "How far?" she asked again.

Raleigh permitted himself a small, satisfied smile. He had already answered her question, but she hadn't heard. Linden Street wasn't as self-composed as she appeared. "From Grandmother's halfway to the office," he repeated.

Which meant he had taken Powell Street. The steep hill was hardly suited for walking in any circumstances. He had deliberately tested the limits of his endurance. Millicent Montgomery had warned Linden that her grandson would be a challenging patient. Thus far, *challenging* hardly described Linden's experience. "Only halfway?" she asked, gracing him with a swift, sidelong glance. "That isn't like you."

Raleigh winced as her fingers kneaded with more pressure than he thought was strictly necessary. Tight knots of muscles began to work loose under her touch and he wondered if he was flattering himself by assuming she was angry. "The damn leg buckled under me when I stepped off the curb."

"Then you were lucky," she said, "because if you had somehow managed to force yourself there, you could have done irreparable damage to your knee." She rubbed her palms together hard and swiftly, allowing friction to heat her skin. She laid them over his knee.

Heat suffused Raleigh's flesh, traveled up his thigh, and radiated across the flat expanse of his belly. His shoulders stiffened slightly and his fingers tightened on the rim of the tub. He pulled himself upright and hunched forward. "That's enough," he said grimly. His groin was throbbing.

"But I —"

"That's enough." His voice was gritty this time, terse and husky. He looked pointedly at the hands which were still lying over his knee. They were lifted quickly, as if the heat had suddenly been turned on her. He dropped the leg back into the water. "I'll want to soak a little longer. I'll call you when I need you."

Nodding, Linden got to her feet and left. She busied herself in the bedroom, folding the towels that Mrs. Adams brought and warming the sheets of Raleigh's bed with the long-handled pan. At Raleigh's brusque order, her heartbeat had quickened and it was refusing to slow. A glance in the mirror assured Linden that none of the disconcerting turmoil she felt inside showed on her face.

She sat on the edge of a maroon-and-cream-striped wing chair, perched as calmly as a bird. Although she was as familiar with this room as she was with her own, she enjoyed looking around. The room bore her employer's masculine stamp. His hairbrush and comb sat neatly on a black lacquered tray on the highboy, a lather brush and a shaving cup beside it. This morning's edition of the *Gazette* was lying unopened on the darkly stained oak bedside table. Raleigh's gold pocket watch and chain rested on the table on the opposite side of the four poster. The spindles of the poster bed were carved without excessive scrollwork or ornamentation. The headboard was a smooth arch with no embellishments across its panel.

The windows were large and when the maroon drapes were drawn back there was a lovely view of the garden and pond behind the mansion. French doors opened onto a balcony with a heavy stone balustrade. When it was warmer, Linden had wheeled Raleigh onto the balcony to take advantage of the fresh air and sunshine. Sometimes she exercised his leg out there. More often she dragged the small writing desk out and left him alone to do work that he insisted could not wait.

Linden rose from the chair and poked at the fire. She added a log and moved the stack of towels closer to the heat. Her eyes studied the photographs on the mantel. Among them was a sepia-toned daguerreotype of Raleigh's grandfather. He was posing with four other miners, all of them wearing loose flannel shirts, dungarees, wide-brimmed, shapeless hats, and carrying flashing pans or picks. She had no difficulty recognizing Millicent's husband, although she had never asked to have him pointed out. Raleigh Montgomery shared many of the handsome features of his grandfather.

Linden's attention was pulled away by the sound of splashing in the other room. He had said he would call her, but, of course, he hadn't. Without announcing herself, she reentered and was just in time to slip her shoulders under Raleigh's arm. In another moment he would have collapsed heavily into the water or stumbled out of the tub altogether. In either event he would have risked further injury.

Water dripped freely from his arms and chest and the curling tips of his dark hair. Linden thrust her hip against the smoothly naked curve of his to support his weight. He was a splendidly beautiful man but he was also a damnably stubborn one. "Don't move," she said. "I need to get my balance." *And my breath.* Only to herself could she admit that it wasn't exertion that put a catch in her ability to breathe.

Raleigh felt one of her arms slide across his back and curve around his waist. He had absolutely no dignity left, he thought. At his grandmother's insistence, Linden Street had arrived at his home three days after he returned from the Nevada mine. For the better part of nine months she had been resolutely stripping away his armor of arrogance and masculine pride.

Early in their acquaintance, when the shattering pain had receded to the point where he could acknowledge other aches, Raleigh had mistaken Linden's lack of embarrassment regarding her intimate care of him for experience of another sort. He had propositioned her rather crudely. She had set him straight. They had never mentioned it again but it was always there between them.

"Let me lower you back into the tub and ring for Mr. Simmons," Linden said.

Raleigh shook his head. He didn't want to wait and his conceit had been compromised again. "Just help me out." He distributed his weight between her and his good leg and managed to drag the injured one out of the tub, step lightly, and follow it with the other.

Linden's fingers clutched the sleeve of his robe, which was hanging on the open door of his armoire, and yanked. It slipped off the hook and she thrust it into his hand. "Put this on."

Standing on one leg, Raleigh shrugged into his hunter green dressing gown and belted the sash. Linden waited patiently, prepared for the weight of him when he slipped his arm around her shoulder again. She was a slight thing, he realized. He had always known it but then in situations like this, when he was next to her, it struck him with some surprise to have it confirmed afresh.

In spite of the differences in their height and weight — he had seven inches and eighty pounds on her — she held him so solidly he had no fear of falling or even stumbling. She guided him to the bed and didn't release him completely until he was sitting. The pillows were plumped behind his back as he scooted toward the head-board and leaned against it. Linden's fingers curled around the hem of his dressing gown and drew it modestly over his thighs. He smiled to himself as she turned away to get the towels warming near the fire. Her figure was trim and her skirts swayed around the length of her long legs. In profile, with the exception of the high curve of her full breasts, she was reed slender. He watched her pick up the towels and raise them to her chest almost defensively. The gesture piqued his interest.

Linden's step faltered as she turned toward the bed. Raleigh was looking at her with that remote expression that revealed nothing about his thoughts. She only knew that the outcome did not usually bear well for her. When she reached the bed she pressed a warm towel into his hand. "For your hair," she said.

Raleigh took it and ran it briskly through his hair. Linden was already raising his leg and placing towels beneath it. The movement made him grimace but he held back the groan. From the pocket of her apron she retrieved a brown bottle of liniment and uncorked it. She poured some of the clear liquid into her palm, put the bottle aside, then began massaging his leg. She began at a point just above his knee and worked her way down slowly. He watched her hands dissolve the tension in his muscles and let himself appreciate the penetration of heat into his joints.

"Why aren't you married?" he asked suddenly.

Linden's hands didn't stop moving. It surprised her because she was certain her heart skipped. She didn't look at him, but concentrated on her work instead. "I think that's a private matter," she said.

"Humor me."

There were times when that's all Linden felt she did. "I don't think —"

"Has anyone ever asked you?"

She raised her head and looked at him frankly, her darkening violet eyes level with his. "Yes," she said simply.

"And you said no."

"I said yes." She bent her head again and

returned to massaging his leg. She rubbed the length of his calf, toning the muscles between her palms. "My father became ill a few months before the wedding. I spent a lot of time with him, caring for him. I couldn't make plans . . . I was tired . . . and worried." She shook her head faintly and her long lashes lowered another fraction. "After a while I just wasn't interested in marriage any longer. I suppose the same thing happened to Edward." She sighed. "Our engagement ended by mutual agreement."

"How long ago?"

"Seven years."

She would have been about twenty-two, he thought. And twenty-six when her father died. Alexander Street had been Millicent's personal physician until he had taken ill. The wasting disease that had sapped the strength from his limbs, and eventually taken his life, was also the source of Linden's knowledge and her particular strength. Since her father's death she had found herself employable as a companion and caretaker for patients with similar crippling illnesses or disabilities.

"Do you have regrets about Edward?"

She shook her head.

"About not marrying?" This time there was an infinitesimal pause before she made her denial. Raleigh was thoughtful. "My grandmother's got it in her head that I should have heirs to the Montgomery fortunes."

"Doesn't she realize how hard you've been trying?"

Raleigh blinked, not quite believing what he'd heard. "How's that again?"

"My room is only down the hall," she said. "And it overlooks the street. I know about the women who come up here at night . . . the ones your friend Chapman procures for you." She added more liniment to her hands and worked it into Raleigh's leg. "You may have already begotten an heir or two to the Montgomery dynasty. Perhaps your grandmother will be satisfied with that."

"I see we're speaking very plainly this evening," he said dryly. "Since that's the case, let me say that my grandmother has already stated quite firmly that she's not accepting bastards. Fortunately for me, I haven't any to present to her."

Linden wondered why this particular news should give her any relief, yet she acknowledged it was precisely what she felt. Suspecting what Raleigh might make of that, she was careful to school her features and keep her head lowered. She wiped her hands on one of the towels, then wrapped his leg in it. "Is this why she wanted to see you today?" she asked. "To tell you?"

"Yes."

It explained his ill-conceived attempt to walk to the financial district. Linden understood that Raleigh Montgomery didn't brook interference in his life, even from his beloved grandmother.

"I've been thinking about what she wants," he said when Linden didn't respond in any way.

"Oh." She wondered who it would be. The parade of women to his room weren't all whores. There had been one young woman in particular, a cousin, she thought, of Chapman's, who had a fair smile and bright laughter. She had worn a daffodil yellow satin ballgown and carried a parasol the color of sunshine. She would be a good match for Raleigh Montgomery — perhaps a trifle silly, even a little vain — but she would look lovely on his arm and they would turn heads when they went to the theater. And they would have beautiful children.

He could have any woman he wanted — and frequently did. Linden had always known that and she had held herself from him when she had been given the chance to be one of them.

He was an improbably handsome man, with his clear gray eyes and glossy black hair. He had strong, aristocratic features that gave his face clean, linear definition. His nose had an arrogant line to it, his mouth was firm. The cheeks were lean, the bones high and masculine. His body was lean and hard, muscular even now because of the exercising he did each day with her. He had been used to riding and hunting and walking and the inactivity brought on by his accident chafed at him.

Linden was thoroughly familiar with the breadth of his shoulders, the tapering waist, the faint hollows on either side of his buttocks. She had massaged his thighs and arms, and when he had been nearly insensible with the pain of his injury, she had laid his head in her lap and kneaded his neck and scalp. His body became sleek and shiny with the oils she worked into his skin; the muscles held their tone and suppleness.

During the time he had been completely bedridden — his injured leg splinted, raised by pulleys, and stretched by weights — it was Linden who had bathed him. It hadn't been her idea, but his. A test of sorts to measure her mettle or run her off. Under the watchful, even cynical, eye of Raleigh Montgomery, she hadn't flinched; over time she became more familiar with the planes and angles of his body than any of the women who graced his bed, perhaps even more familiar than Raleigh was himself. He had two small dimples at the base of his spine and a tiny, star-shaped scar on the right side of his flat abdomen where he'd fallen on some jagged rocks as a youth.

She was almost as familiar with his moods as she was with his body, and contrary to her stoic expression, she was indifferent to neither. He despised his helplessness and she was an easy target for his anger. Linden was confronted by cold civility, bitter invective, or silence. He baited her with his cool gray eyes, watching her so closely that when she retired to her room she still felt the force of his stare. On better days he coaxed her with smiles and sweet talk. Depending on what he wanted on a particular day, he might also offer her money.

He was a man used to having what he wanted, not because he was spoiled, but because he was used to being able to get it for himself. If he wanted to go out to dinner, it didn't matter if the weather was inclement. If he wanted to work at his office, he didn't care that the previous evening's pain had caused him to toss and turn all night and that it would be visited upon him again. That Linden was able to respond to the spirit, if not the letter, of his demands did not appease him greatly. She had food from some of San Francisco's finest restaurants delivered to his room. She arranged for his assistants to bring work to him from the office and every day young Kwei Po ran to the financial district and dutifully recorded the figures of the stock exchange. When he complained the room was too hot, she opened the French doors to let in the breeze. When it was too cold she laid a fire. And, on one memorable occasion, she had cheerfully done both, confounding him again with her unflappable demeanor.

She did not feel quite so tranquil now, sensing his eyes on her. His gaze was watchful and curious, as if she weren't a person at all but something to study under a magnifying glass.

Raleigh ran his fingers through his dark hair, lifting the damp ends away from the collar of his dressing gown. He rubbed the back of his neck with the towel, then returned it to Linden. He noticed she balled it up and her fingers worked convulsively around it, flexing and relaxing. Her violet eyes were calm, her features perfectly placid. "Grandmother would like to see me engaged by Christmas," he said. "It would be a nice present for her."

"Perhaps you should consider a bonnet or a shawl," she said. "Those are also nice presents."

Her dry, quiet humor was unexpected. Raleigh wanted to put a finger under her chin, raise her face, and see if she was smiling. "Is that what you'd like for Christmas?"

"Me?" Her voice rose slightly with the single word. Discomfort claimed the pit of her stomach. "No," she said finally, quietly. "I'm afraid I can't be satisfied with less than a partridge in a pear tree."

"Just the partridge?" he asked, wondering at her sudden seriousness.

Linden forced a carelessness she didn't feel. "*In* a pear tree," she reminded him, then shrugged. "It could mean everything or nothing." She saw him frown but she didn't explain herself.

Linden folded the towel with painstaking precision and slipped off the edge of the bed, almost jumping free when she felt Raleigh's fingers slide around her wrist. His fingers were lean and strong and the grip was just tight enough to force a struggle if she tried to remove it. She had touched him hundreds, thousands of times. She had supported, cradled, and held him. She had run her fingers through his hair, along his spine, and down the backs of his thighs. She had done all of that to him, yet Raleigh Montgomery had rarely attempted to touch her.

Linden looked down at the hand closed over her skin. His clasp was like a ring of fire. She was trembling. "Yes, Mr. Montgomery?"

Raleigh's fingers opened and he watched Linden take her hand back, massaging the fragile bones of her wrist as if they'd been bruised. He knew his grip hadn't been hard or hurtful. His eyes narrowed slightly and his look became more considering. "I was thinking you might agree to be my fiancée, Miss Street."

She looked at him now, her composure shattered. Her violet eyes had widened and her lips were slightly parted. Her complexion was pale as salt and the last breath she had drawn was trapped at the back of her throat. "Whatever made you think I might agree to that?"

"It would make my grandmother happy."

Linden felt her heart being squeezed. "I like your grandmother very much," she said quietly. "She never forgot my father. When he could no longer attend to his patients, she supported us both so I could care for him. Mrs. Montgomery is largely responsible for me being able to work after the death of my father, but I don't know that I could —"

Raleigh cut her off. "She's dying," he told her. "There wouldn't have to be a marriage. Only an engagement."

Linden clutched the towel in her hands. She dropped back slowly onto the edge of the bed. "Millicent is dying?" Her vision blurred a little and she blinked back tears before they spiked her dark lashes. It wasn't possible, she thought. Not Millicent.

Even at eighty she was the most energetic, lively, spirited woman Linden knew. She turned to Raleigh suddenly. "What does she need? Is there something I can —" She stopped because he was simply regarding her expressionlessly, his eyes frank. He had already told her what his grandmother needed and what she could do to help. "It wouldn't be real?"

"The engagement would be very real," he said. "There would simply be no marriage."

He meant they would end it after his grandmother was dead. It was calculating and a little ghoulish. Gooseflesh rose on her arms and she rubbed them absently. "I don't know," she said uneasily. "Isn't there someone else you can ask?"

Raleigh had been prepared for that question. "There's no one else my grandmother would accept as easily as you. Except for Chapman, you've been my steadiest companion. For the last nine months you've practically lived in my pockets — when I had pockets." He ignored her sharp look and went on calmly, making his points seem reasonable and logical. "My grandmother's known you for years and she admires your steadiness and loyalty. She's remarked on your sensibility and reserve. She thinks you have character, intelligence, and good sense and I'm inclined to agree with her."

"Thank you," she said softly. "I think."

"But Millicent has her peculiar notions, and at her age she's entitled to them. I wouldn't put it past her to suppose it would be highly romantic if we had fallen in love during my convalescence."

"Which we both know is absurd," she said quickly.

"Absurd," he agreed. "But you can see how she might take it into her head."

Linden nodded slowly. "So she wouldn't find the announcement odd."

His smile was faint. "Not odd at all. Especially if we were to warm her further to the idea. Say, if you were to join me for Thanksgiving dinner in her home tomorrow?"

So it was that Linden found herself sharing the large dining room table with Millicent and Raleigh Montgomery and nine others from Millicent's cadre of friends. Cornucopia overflowing with hothouse flowers decorated the table in three distinct and fragrant arrangements. The meal was served in waves by amiable, competent maids wearing severely cut black dresses with wide, white pilgrim collars, starched aprons, and stiff bonnets. Young Kwei Po, on loan to his grandmother from Raleigh, was incongruously dressed in Indian garb, much to Raleigh's horror. Throughout the meal, each time one of the maids clunked around the table in her heavy buckled shoes while serving courses of clam soup and fore-quarter lamb with mint sauce, Linden caught Raleigh regarding his grandmother with an expression that could most kindly be described as consternation.

"It was a great success," Millicent announced later when only Raleigh and Linden remained. She had had coffee brought up to the second floor sitting room and shared it with Linden while Raleigh sipped cognac. Sitting back on the chaise longue, she adjusted the shawl over her legs. The evening was cool and the warmth from the fire did not reach her as she might have liked. "Though I wish I had realized about the shoes. All that noise. Clunking here. Clopping there. Such a racket."

Raleigh, who had been about to raise the snifter of cognac to his lips, paused and said softly, "I know it made *me* long for another war cry from Kwei Po. What were you thinking, teaching him that? I'm sure half of Nob Hill thought itself under attack. And the boy's Chinese, Grandmother. I don't think he has a drop of Indian blood in him."

Millicent ignored him and addressed Linden. "He's much too serious, don't you agree?" she asked. "What is the fun of a holiday if one can't celebrate it with a bit of panache? Although it's not quite Raleigh's style, is it? I'm afraid he wouldn't know a flamboyant gesture if it presented itself as a gift." Out of the corner of her eye she saw her grandson poke at the fire to make it give up a little more heat. She smiled. He was a dutiful boy in his own way, she thought sweetly. He had noticed that she was chilled and had responded. Millicent felt she could count on her grandson. Which made her wonder about Linden Street. "But then you're not precisely bursting with good humor yourself, are you, dear?"

"I enjoyed myself very much this evening," Linden said gravely.

"Stuff!" Millicent said heartily. She could inject enough feeling into that single word to give it all the force and flavor of a sailor's saltiest phrasing. "Raleigh got you here under false pretenses, I'll wager." She saw Linden start, her violet eyes flickering. "He didn't tell you about my other guests, did he?"

Linden recovered herself. For a moment she had thought Millicent was going to say something else, some comment about her health. "No, he didn't mention it."

"Well, that was very bad of him, but I suppose he didn't think you'd come and I very much wanted you to be here. You keep entirely too much to yourself."

Raleigh interjected smoothly, "I think Linden will be getting out more, Grandmother. Now that I'm able to get out myself more often, I've pressed her into accompanying me occasionally."

"Why, that's wonderful," Millicent said. "She deserves a little entertainment for having to put up with you all these months." She saw that Linden was going to politely object to this pronouncement and she raised her hand. "Oh, don't bother, dear. He's a wretch. I told you that when I asked you to take him on as a patient. I confess myself pleased that you're still on speaking terms. I fully expected that someday you'd march into my home and demand that we put him down like a horse with a broken leg."

Raleigh almost choked on his liquor. "Well, thank you for that, Grandmother. Lucky for me, Linden is more patient with an injured animal than you are." He left his place by the fire and sat beside Linden on the small sofa. He noticed her flinch slightly at his nearness and it surprised him. She had never done so before and he could only imagine that it was their changing circumstances, or rather the pretense of them, that had brought it about. It would never do. "Perhaps you'd like Linden to visit you?" he asked.

"Oh, I'd like that," Linden said immediately. "It would give me the greatest pleas—"

"Stuff!" Millicent said again. "You don't need to spend time with me. Where's the pleasure in that?" She caught the brief exchange between Raleigh and Linden and Millicent nodded sagely. "Oh, I see. Raleigh's told you I'm not feeling quite the thing, I suppose. I might have known you'd offer your services. I wondered why you were looking at me so closely all through dinner. Did you think I might keel over?" She waved one hand dismissively. "I have Dr. Harvey to order me around. He's not as good as your father was, of course, but he's competent. Raleigh pays for his time so I couldn't get rid of him even if he weren't." She sipped her coffee, then set the cup firmly in the saucer and put it aside. "Enough about the state of my health, or ill health, as the case may be. How is my grandson? He doesn't tell me anything important. I can see for myself that he was walking better yesterday than he is today."

Linden told Millicent that Raleigh had taken too much on himself. She finished her coffee while the man who employed her, the man who commanded hundreds of others in mining and railroading and financial matters, listened solemnly while he was lectured by his grandmother.

472

"It would be less painful if she'd just box my ears and be done with it," he said later.

"You enjoyed it," Linden disagreed softly. "I watched you."

They were riding home in the open carriage. Perched beside the driver, Kwei Po was still wearing his headband and feather, a souvenir from Millicent for services rendered. Linden sat beside Raleigh on the thickly padded leather seat. The night was clear and chilled and as they rode along, icy fingers of air worked under their woolen capes and the heavy rug that covered their legs. Linden's soft calfskin gloves were inadequate and when she rubbed her hands together to keep warm, Raleigh took them between his. Linden's bones were narrow and fine and he held her hands as carefully as he would have held china.

In spite of his gentleness he felt her shrink from his touch. "You're going to have to get used to that," he said. Moonshine limned her delicate profile in cool blue and silver light. "My grandmother will think it strange if my fiancée is repelled by my touch."

"I'm not repelled," she said hastily. "I'm . . ."

"Yes?"

Confused, she wanted to say. And a little frightened. Not of him, but of herself. "I'm not used to it," she finished lamely. "I shall try harder. I wouldn't want to upset your grandmother."

She was not looking at him so she didn't see Raleigh's rather grim smile. "No," he said. "We wouldn't want that."

Over the next three weeks Linden did try harder. It was difficult, pretending in public to be falling in love, then pretending in private that the public face was a lie. She wasn't prepared for the attention she received when she was escorted by Raleigh Montgomery. He took her to the theater, the opera, and let her lose five hundred dollars, then win it back, in one of the city's most opulent and exclusive gaming halls. She attended church with Millicent and Raleigh on three successive Sundays and had dinner with them afterward. Still later she and Raleigh were driven to Point Lobos, where their carriage could make a circuitous route in the moonlight.

She complained that it was too much, that she didn't need to be seen everywhere with him. After all, weren't they simply doing this to convince his grandmother? He countered that his grandmother would expect him to court his prospective fiancée and she wouldn't be taken in by a shabby, hastily announced engagement. It was groundwork that needed to be laid.

Linden told herself she gave in because

Raleigh Montgomery was convincing and insistent. She didn't like to think that she might be swayed by the novelty of wearing so many beautiful gowns or gaining the front entrance to social circles that would have been closed to her before. It also didn't bear scrutinizing that she welcomed the pleasure of his company.

It was at the Chamberlains' annual Christmas ball that she was forced to re-evaluate all her motives — and his. She shouldn't have been so naive, she realized later. What was it she had overheard? Oh, yes. *"She's no green girl. Or did you think that's the bloom of youth on her cheeks?"* That was one of the kinder things she had been privy to when two young women — still in *their* first flowering — hadn't realized they weren't alone in the guest bedchamber.

Linden didn't know if she resented them for speaking their minds or for speaking them unwittingly in front of her. *"That's a harlot's red rouge putting color in her face."* Linden had been incapable of moving from her stool in the adjoining dressing room. She had gone there to repair a hem that had been torn by an enthusiastic but incautious partner. *"She lives with him, you know. They used to say she only took care of him, but I think this proves she's been Raleigh's mistress all along."* This was followed by a spurt of bright laughter and Linden pricked her finger with the needle as she recognized the voice. It was Chapman's cousin, she of the daffodil gown and sunshine parasol. *"Everyone's been forced to accept her. I mean, who wants to risk alienating Raleigh Montgomery or his grandmother? Mrs. Chamberlain was scandalized, my mother said, but her hands were tied. She had to include Linden with her invitation to Raleigh. Her poor husband is invested heavily in Montgomery holdings."* Closing her eyes, Linden raised her injured finger to her lips and sucked gently.

When they were gone she repaired her gown and returned downstairs. Long swags of pine decorated with lace and strings of pink glass beads bordered the ballroom. Swan ice sculptures floated in a fountain of raspberry punch. The spray bobbled the frozen lily pads and full blooming ice flowers on the current. Pots of pink and cream poinsettias with light-green-veined leaves were set out in tiers three deep along the stage where the string orchestra played.

Prior to the repair that took her out of the ballroom, Linden would have said the gathering glittered. On her return she wondered why she had ever thought it. Raleigh stood when Linden reappeared on the threshold of the room and bent his head solicitously as she approached.

"You're all of a piece again?" he asked politely.

She was shattered but they were thinking of different things. "The dress is repaired," she told him. She forced a carelessness into her voice that did not quite suit her.

Raleigh smiled but it did not reach his eyes. He regarded her closely. Her violet gaze had drifted away from him and was following the lilting progress of a pair of dancers on the floor. He recognized his friend Chapman and the cousin Chapman had ill-advisedly thought might be interesting to him. The last vestige of Raleigh's smile faded and a small crease appeared between his dark brows. Although Linden had never lacked for partners, Raleigh himself had not asked her to dance, nor anyone else. He had no desire to look clumsy in front of her, but now, watching Chapman and his cousin, he thought he saw a wretched melancholy about Linden that made him screw his courage to the sticking place.

"Would you take this dance with me?" he asked somewhat diffidently.

She turned to him, surprised. It occurred to her to remind him of his leg. He had been standing a great deal throughout the evening and was leaning heavily on the ebony handle now. Yet Linden heard something in his voice that kept her silent on that count. Raleigh Montgomery was not so certain of himself or her answer this time and it was important to him. The expression in his beautiful gray eyes was unreadable now as he guarded himself against disappointment. "I'd like to dance with you," she said and raised her hand for him to take.

Raleigh knew she offered her hand as much for support as for escort. It was done with such graceful ease that no one but the two of them were aware of it. He gave his cane to a friend to hold and led Linden onto the floor.

"You're looking very thoughtful," he said, as they were immediately drawn into a series of sweeping turns in time to the music. "Are you concerned I'll embarrass you?"

Her head jerked up. "No!"

Her denial was so immediate and heartfelt that he had to believe her. "I'm sorry," he said. "I'm being selfish, thinking only of me."

"You're a very good dancer," she said dutifully.

Raleigh smiled faintly. "Liar."

"No, it's true." He was graceful and so much at his ease on the floor that his limp was hardly noticeable. Had he had a better partner, she thought unhappily, there would be no sign at all. She was the one who was stiff and unyielding. She could feel a hundred pairs of eyes on her and now she knew the thoughts behind them. *She's his mistress, you know. What can we do? She's on Raleigh's arm. We have to accept her.* Linden lowered her eyes and stared at Raleigh's cunningly tied neck cloth. She blinked once against her tears.

"Linden?"

She could not look at him. "Please," she said softly. "I'd like to go."

Raleigh did not hesitate. "Of course." In the course of the dance he drew her to the entrance of the ballroom and motioned to his friend to bring the cane. He called upon his friendship to press Rand into making their thanks and farewells to the Chamberlains. "Linden's not feeling well," he explained to a concerned but agreeable Rand.

In the carriage Raleigh tried to draw her out but she was having none of it. Except for an apology, she was silent. He escorted her to the door to her suite and laid his hand on the leaded glass knob, effectively trapping her for a moment. Simmons had helped her out of her coat belowstairs and her gown shimmered with iridescent shades of emerald and deep marine blue. "Have I done something to offend, Linden?" he asked quietly.

She drew in a shallow breath and shook her head.

"Look at me," he commanded, his solemn

tone brooking no argument. Her features were very still but her eyes glittered with unshed tears. "Has it all become too much?" he asked. They were a week shy of Christmas Day and the announcement of their engagement. He braced himself to ask the next question. "Do you want to back out?"

She had known it was coming and had been preparing herself. Here was her chance to give up the pretense — and the pleasure of his company. She could remove her name from the gossip mill and retire quietly into another position where no one would know what had come before. It would have to happen eventually. The engagement was never meant to be permanent. Now, given the opportunity to cut it short — really, to call it off before it had truly begun — Linden discovered she couldn't do it. "No," she said with sober calm and infinite gravity. "No, I don't want to back out."

Raleigh hesitated, his eyes searching hers. Except for a brief flash of defiance, the violet gaze she returned was maddeningly without any hint of expression. "Very well," he said after a moment. "Good night, Linden."

For three weeks Raleigh had been cautious about touching her, recognizing the need to ease into anything but the most casual contact. Now he bent his head slowly, giving her time to move her head to one side. He would have settled for kissing Linden on the cheek. He would have been disappointed, but he would have accepted it. As he drew closer he realized he was not going to be disappointed. Linden was offering her mouth.

The kiss was gentle and brief. His lips were cool and dry. Her mouth parted slightly beneath his and for just an instant the pressure increased. He straightened, watching her. Her long lashes fluttered, then opened. A diamond teardrop sparkled and pink color lightly stained her cheeks. He raised one hand and brushed the clean line of her jaw with his knuckles. A strand of her dark hair had come loose from its anchoring pins and he lifted it, feeling the silky texture between his fingertips, then tucked it behind her ear.

"Good night," he said again. He made a slight bow and left.

Linden slipped inside her room. She could still taste him on her mouth and she raised her fingers to her lips as if she could preserve the imprint. They had never discussed kissing. She supposed that he felt the time had come to broach it. Millicent would expect some modest display of affection between them at the time of their announcement. She wondered if the kiss had met his expectations or if she had disappointed him. The contact had been so brief. She would have liked him to linger. Unbidden, the silly, trilling voices from the party came back to her. *She's been living with him since the accident. Of course she's his mistress.*

No, Linden thought, but she wanted to be.

She pressed her fingers to her lips harder, not to hold the passing shape of his kiss, but to force back a sob. She swallowed hard and began to undress. One of the maids came to help but Linden dismissed her. After all, she was an employee and used to fending for herself. Since she had begun to be Raleigh's public companion there had been an inevitable chasm developing between her and the house staff. Even Kwei Po, with whom she had enjoyed an easy camaraderie, had begun to treat her with more deference than her position strictly warranted. He could only have taken his cue from the others. Linden felt more isolated and alone than she had at any time since her father's death.

Self-pity did not sit well on her shoulders and Linden shrugged it off as she slipped into her plain gray day dress. She pinned an apron to her bodice and tied the ribbons at her back. Her elegantly arranged hair was inharmonious with her serviceable gown. Linden removed the beaded adornments and unwound the coil. She brushed it out hard, then braided it, trapping the blue-black luster in a thick plait.

She knocked softly on Raleigh's door. On the chance that he was already sleeping, she let herself in quietly when there was no response. He was not already in bed. His clothes were tossed haphazardly over the back of the wing chair. From the adjoining room she heard a small splash and knew that she was right to suspect his leg was bothering him more than he had wanted to let on. In concession to his pain, he had asked for a hot bath to be drawn. The bed had already been turned down and now Linden laid out two towels from the stack Mrs. Adams made certain was available. She removed the brown bottle of liniment from her apron pocket and set it on the bedside table.

Raleigh was leaning back in the tub, a folded towel behind his head. His eyes were closed. There was the faint suggestion of pain at the corners of his mouth. When he moved, water lapped gently at the crisp, dark hair on his chest. Steam made his skin glisten. Linden entered silently and knelt beside him.

The sweet scent of pine teased his senses. At first he thought it was a residual fragrance from the Chamberlains' ballroom — then he felt a ripple in the water around him and realized it was Linden's hair that had captured nature's heady perfume. He opened his eyes. She was reaching for a washcloth and he put one hand over hers, stopping her. "What are you doing here?"

She frowned. The question surprised her. She was still his caretaker, responsible for his recovery. Weeks of playacting for Millicent hadn't changed that. She had continued to help him exercise his leg in the predawn hours before he went to his Union Square offices, and she had carefully gauged his ability to accept the slew of invitations that had accompanied the festive frenzy of Christmas. Most evenings she massaged his leg after he had prepared for bed. Tonight did not strike her as different from any of the nights that had come before it. She did not understand his question.

"I've come to see to your leg," she said. She attempted to reach for it under the water but his hand still held her back.

"No," he said. "Not tonight." He didn't let her go until he saw acceptance in her expression. "Get my robe," he said.

"But you haven't soaked long enough."

The bath that Simmons had drawn for him was totally ineffective. Raleigh knew he needed ice water for this ache. "Get my robe," he repeated tersely.

Linden blinked at his tone but she passed it to him. He stared at her a moment longer and she realized he was waiting for her to go. She got to her feet and took her leave. She didn't go far. Linden was waiting for him when he entered his bedroom a few minutes later. He seemed surprised that she was still there. She held up the bottle of liniment.

Short of picking her up and carrying her out of the room, Raleigh didn't know how to dislodge her. She had that patient, militant look in her eyes, the one that said she held the high ground and could wait forever. Raleigh acknowledged with painful honesty that if he were going to carry Linden anywhere it would be to his bed. The irony of it was that she was waiting for him there, sitting on the edge, composed yet somehow expectant.

Raleigh was aware of her eyes on his hip and injured leg and, unassisted by his cane, he strove to make crossing the room appear as easy as possible. He sat down on the bed. The pillows were already plumped, the towels were in place. He stretched out and rested the crown of his dark head against the headboard. Even though he was anticipating her touch, he was not completely prepared for the way it raised prickles of heat on every part of his body. He thought he would come out of his skin.

"You're doing better than I would have thought," she said, rubbing the oil into his flesh. "It won't be much longer before you won't be needing my services."

"You said you didn't want to back out."

Still bent to her task, her thumbs running along the length of his shin. Linden shook her head. "I wasn't thinking about the engagement," she said. "Of course I'll stay as long as it's necessary." She felt an ache at the back of her throat as she thought of it ending only when Millicent was gone. It was all too bittersweet. "I was referring to your leg. I'll have to make plans for myself. Another engagement of sorts, I suppose, with another patient who needs me."

He didn't like the sound of that. It was something he hadn't thought of when he walked across the room. Had he suspected the direction of her thoughts he would have emphasized the limp. "That won't be necessary," he said.

She smiled at the way he dismissed her concerns as if they were of no account. She couldn't be angry with him. He simply didn't understand. "I have to have work," she explained. Beneath her fingers she could feel tension in the line of his leg. She kneaded with more deliberation and pushed forward on his toes to stretch the muscles. "I have to earn my living and somewhere in the city is someone who needs me as much as you did."

"I'll hire you," he said. His tone was harsh

and meant to convey that the subject was closed.

Frowning, her fingers slowing, Linden looked at him. The severe set of his mouth wasn't the result of pain, but anger. "I don't think I understand," she said with deliberate calm. "What is it that I would do for you?"

"Play the role of my fiancée," he said. "In just a week it will be a fact. I'd pay you what you're earning now and you would be given a larger allowance for clothes and jewelry. If you decided it wasn't seemly to remain here I'd set you up in a house in some other part of town — overlooking the bay, if you think you'd like that." He had added the last because he thought it would cheer her. He was aware that the longer he talked, the more disappointed, even bitterly resigned, her expression had become. "Linden? What is it? What are you thinking?"

Shrugging, Linden applied herself to her task again. She cried out when her wrists were taken and she was hauled up the bed toward him. She tried to push away but she was grappled and kept at the level of his hips, her legs not quite able to touch the floor and find purchase. Her position, with her legs folded partially under her and her gown tangled around them, was uncomfortably off-balance and she had to rely on Raleigh to support her upright. "Please," she said breathlessly. "You're hurting me."

He knew he wasn't. She had said it automatically because she was helpless and frightened and thought it would make him release her. She was appealing to his better instincts, not understanding the baser ones guiding him now. "What were you thinking?" he asked again. "What did you hear me say?"

She didn't recognize the voice that replied yet she knew it was her own. Desperation had made it a touch shrill, hurt had made it halting. "You were talking about making it fact instead of fiction," she said. "Confirming what they all think anyway. Chapman. His cousin. The Chamberlains. Probably even Millicent. You haven't thought this through very well. Your grandmother may not approve of you marrying your mistress. Indeed, the news of this engagement may send her straight to her grave."

The lines of Raleigh's face were strained with tension. He gave her wrists a little shake, hard enough this time to press a bruise into the soft underside of her skin and cause her slender body to shudder in reaction. "*Who* says?" he demanded. "What are you talking about?"

Linden caught her breath. His grip was like a vise now. "I think they all do," she said frankly. "I overheard Chapman's cousin talking to one of her friends."

Raleigh remembered seeing Emily leave the ballroom shortly after Linden had gone to make repairs to her gown. "That twit," he said, partly in astonishment that Linden would pay any attention to her, partly in disgust that the issue had been raised at all. "I'll have Chapman speak to her. She has no business —"

"No." Linden cut him off and gave her head a quick, violent shake. Her heavy, glossy braid fell forward over her shoulder. "It will only make matters worse."

Raleigh saw that it could. Emily was a spoiled brat and a woman scorned. "All right," he said heavily. He loosened his grip on her wrists but when she would have withdrawn her hands he resisted and massaged her skin instead. He could already make out the faint bluish marks that had pressed into her tender and delicate flesh. "But I'll still speak to Chapman. He knows the truth. There are ways to quiet Emily without taking a direct approach."

She would have to be satisfied with that, Linden thought. Raleigh wasn't asking permission. "You can't blame her for thinking it," Linden said. "It's a natural assumption, one that I should have foreseen myself. After all, you did proposition me once."

"And you politely declined." Actually she had delivered her refusal in very plain, cutting language, practically unmanning him with her sharp and biting lecture.

Linden's cheeks pinkened. "I should have boxed your ears," she said.

He glanced at her, surprised at the faint, playful smile on her lips. He grinned in return. "It would have hurt less," he agreed. "Still, Emily has no right to say what she's thinking. If everyone did that it would mean the collapse of civilization as we know it." He thought he could tease another smile out of her but the moment had passed. She was staring at the play of his fingers over her wrists. He was no longer massaging her skin. He was stroking it. He had no idea how it had come to pass but recognizing it now did not put a stop to it. His thumb lightly brushed back and forth across the delicate blue-veined webbing on the underside of each wrist.

"Linden?" He willed her to look at him. She didn't, but this time she spoke.

"I think I was so upset because in my heart of hearts it's what I'd been thinking. Emily only gave voice to thoughts I had buried. You spoke them again when you made your offer about the wages and the gowns and the house. There's part of me that wants to accept." She drew in her lower lip for a moment, worrying it, then she went on hurriedly, softly. "If it's what everyone believes and if it's what I want, then where is the harm?" She raised her face and felt his cool, fathomless gray eyes on her. "That is," she added, "if I'm still interesting to you."

"Still?" *Always,* was more descriptive of the way he felt.

For the first time in her life, Linden's patience deserted her. Afraid it would be something sensible, or worse, a denial of his desire, she could not wait to hear what he had to say. She leaned toward him a fraction and the lack of balance in her posture did the rest. She fell into him and was caught in his arms.

Raleigh let her momentum carry her and rolled Linden onto her back, following her with his body. His good leg trapped both of hers but she wasn't struggling to be free of the embrace. "Are you certain?" he asked, searching her face. The centers of her violet eyes widened and darkened and it was all the answer he needed. Taking her face in his hands, Raleigh lowered his head and slanted his mouth across hers.

Her breath was warm. Her lips hinted at the flavor of ripe raspberries. He tasted the corners of her mouth, ran his tongue along the line of her lips, savoring her sweet and innocent offering. His fingers drifted across her cheek, then her neck. He worked loose the plait of her hair and threaded his fingers into the ebony thickness of it. The

texture of it was like gossamer, hardly sub-
stantial against his skin.

His kiss deepened and he drew out her
breath and shared it as if it were so precious it was meant to be rationed. He felt
her return the pressure and engage the
teasing forays of his tongue as he ran it
along the edge of her teeth. He felt her arms
slip around his back. Her touch was tentative at first, light and uncertain. Her hands
alighted on his shoulders with the skittish-
ness of a hummingbird. They rested there,
withdrew, then rested again. Finally her
fingers pressed into his flesh, his satin
dressing gown a smooth barrier to their
naked touch.

She knew almost every inch of him inti-
mately, but this was different. There was
another purpose to her touch now. She was
no longer trying to relieve pain, but induce
pleasure. Linden didn't know anything
about it.

Her shyness intrigued Raleigh and moved
him. It reminded him of the rare flower he
had in his hands. "It's all right," he said
softly. "Let me teach you."

Linden hardly knew what he meant but
she gathered her courage and risked discovery. Raleigh sat up swiftly, turned back
the bedside lamp so the flame was merely
a flicker, and lay down beside her again.
"You wouldn't make me turn it all the way

back, would you?" he asked. The word *yes* hovered on her lips but her head was shaking *no*. He smiled and touched the tip of his nose to hers, then he kissed her again, long and deeply. "That's what I thought," he whispered against her lips.

He removed the pins from her apron and turned just enough to release the ribbons. He drew up the hem of her gown, removed her shoes and stockings, then left the hem where it was. His palm curved along her calf from her slim ankle to the sensitive backs of her knees. His thumb passed over the small bones of her feet and she retracted her leg as the sensation tickled her. He laughed and captured her ankle and pulled her toward him. The hem of her gown rose higher. Her petticoat was as crisp and white as the sheet beneath her. His hands slid under the small of her back and he raised her to a sitting position. Her body was lifted languorously so that it was bent in an exquisitely graceful curve. Her back was arched, her breasts thrust forward, the smooth line of her neck exposed. He laid his lips on the hollow of her throat and suckled gently. Her heartbeat vibrated against his mouth and he could hear her breathing catch for a moment.

His fingers twisted the cloth-covered buttons that held her bodice closed. He kissed her skin each time a new area was revealed.

She sat very still for him, patient as he knew she could be, while he slipped her gown over her head, then removed her shift and camisole. She was not wearing a corset but she had had one on earlier and the faint pink markings of the stays were still visible on her tender skin. He touched one with his index finger just below the curve of her breast.

She was lovely with her slender body and full breasts. Taking his fill, his gray eyes darkened to pewter. Her rosy nipples peaked under his gaze, just as if he had touched them. Her hands came forward shyly, not to cover herself, but to loosen the belt of his dressing gown. He shrugged out of it and let it fall over the edge of the bed to join her discarded clothes.

Raleigh waited. The shadows in the dimly lighted room were insufficient to hide the evidence of his desire. For the first time his need was fully revealed to her and he didn't know what to expect. He needn't have worried. The color in her cheeks wasn't embarrassment and the expression in her eyes wasn't fear. Her flush was full arousal and that frank look was flattering.

He laid her back, his body flush to hers. He covered her with the heat and weight of his body. Her arms stole around his back and her hands trailed the length of his spine and his mouth closed over her breast.

He drew on her skin lightly, laving the tip with the rough, damp edge of his tongue. He could almost feel the spark of heat just below the surface of her skin. Her breast swelled and her abdomen retracted as his hand slipped between them.

Linden's fingers threaded into his hair. Her nails lightly scraped the back of his neck and followed the curve of his ear. He was stroking her skin from breast to hip, tracing the turn of her waist and the roundness of her thighs. She felt as if she was learning the shape and texture of her own flesh for the first time. It was natural for her body to turn into the one that was more familiar to her. His.

She was defined by the hard planes and angles of his form, her curves fitted flesh to his flesh. Her legs were trim and light against the taut length of his. Even his injured leg, which he favored ever so slightly, was stronger than hers. Her skin was smooth and pale next to his but when his face was close to hers their hair mingled and it was impossible to tell one from the other. It seemed to Linden that she was meant to cradle this man's body. Months of supporting and lifting and shouldering had finally brought her to this. And love. For Linden it had been about love for a very long time.

He came into her as carefully as he could.

She was not so innocent that she didn't expect the pain. He paused and held himself still while he waited for her body to accommodate his entry. Her skin was glowing, her eyes were bright. He kissed her for a long time and when he felt her entire body respond to the foreplay of his mouth and tongue he taught her to move with him.

Not understanding what could be waiting for her, Linden would have settled for his pleasure. Raleigh was wiser than that. He made her give up the secrets of her body, finding the most sensitive places and filling them with the sweetest caresses.

It was not so different the second time he turned to her that night, except that she was hungrier, more demanding, perhaps even a bit selfish to experience the reawakening of pleasure. The kisses were harder now, more urgent. Their bodies were resilient, not fragile, and they could touch each other freely. She trembled. There was less control rather than more. Her skin was warm, her mouth hot. She relearned his body with her lips and made him shudder. Anticipation made her hold her breath and the thrust of his body drove it out again.

"Say my name," he said softly. "You never say my name."

She was a silent lover, afraid the wrong words would tumble past her lips. But this she could give him. She turned her head so her mouth was near his ear. "Raleigh," she whispered. She stroked the back of his head. "Raleigh." She heard her own name then and it had never sounded sweeter or more reverent. She felt adored.

Excitement carried the night and it was almost dawn when they fell asleep in each other's arms.

Raleigh was the first to wake. A glance at the clock warned him he was already late rising and he remembered there was important business to attend to at the office. Still, he stretched leisurely and turned slowly on his side. Linden's naked shoulder was presented to him in all its smooth wonder. There was important business to attend to in his bed, too, he thought. He bent his head and kissed the curve of her white shoulder. She smiled sleepily but didn't stir. He liked that. Seeing her replete in the aftermath of loving and still in his bed stirred something in him even if she didn't move.

Her dark hair, lustrous against her pale skin, was spread across her back. He gathered it in one hand, made a fist around the black silk, and moved it aside to reveal all of her. His fingers trailed down the length of her spine. The sheet was folded at the rounded edge of her buttocks. Out of the corner of his eye he saw her lashes flutter.

He raised his cupped hand and gave her a light slap on the bottom. She started, not because it hurt, but because the hollow sound of it was like a clap of thunder in the quiet room.

"Slug-a-bed," he said. "You can't sleep if I have to get up."

The lamp had long since burned itself out. It didn't matter now because there was plenty of misty, gray morning light coming around the edges of the closed drapes. She had meant to rise before him. He had experience waking up beside someone in his bed; she had none.

As if he could read her mind, Raleigh said, "This is new for me, too. I've always chased the others out." He watched her wrestle with the double-edge sword. She didn't like being reminded of the others, but by the same token she was glad to be different from them.

Linden sat up slowly, drawing the sheet to her breasts and covering her legs modestly. Raleigh woke her more thoroughly with a kiss that lingered in her blood long after he had left the bed. She turned, drew her legs up, rested her shoulder against the headboard, and listened to him moving around in the adjoining room, washing, shaving, dressing. She was still abed when he reentered the room.

She flushed to the roots of her hair when

he said, "I was only teasing about you being a slug-a-bed. You can wait there all day if you like. In fact, I think I prefer it."

She was not so sufficiently in his thrall that she couldn't muster the spirit to throw a pillow in his direction. He caught it easily and his smile was wicked as he approached the bed. Linden held up her hands and arms to protect her head and the sheet dropped to the level of her waist. When the pillow did not come crashing over her she risked a glance at Raleigh through splayed fingers. He was staring appreciatively at her breasts. There was nothing the least remote about his gray glance.

"Very nice," he said.

Linden hurriedly raised the sheet so that he was only getting half an eyeful. She managed to sound disapproving and look pleased at the same time.

Raleigh's smile deepened at the contradiction. He let the pillow fall harmlessly to the bed, bent toward her, and kissed her full on the mouth when she raised her face. He would have liked to have stayed but he had a business to run and she had to return to her room before her position with his staff was thoroughly compromised. That's not what he wanted for her. His plans were decidedly different and they always had been.

He glanced at the clock again and saw he

was already late for his first meeting. He sat on the edge of the bed for a moment and took Linden's hand. His smile was gone now and his expression was earnest. "Listen to me, Linden," he began. "There's something I need to tell you, something I think will make you happy." Raleigh felt her expectant expression and he drew hope from it. "My grandmother's not dying," he told her. "At least no more than any of us is dying, which is to say her doctor expects her to see out the turn of the century with bells on." He squeezed her hand. "We'll talk about it tonight. Wear that lovely lilac gown you have. I'm taking you to the Cliff House this evening." He kissed her cheek this time, oblivious to the fact that it was cool to the touch and not offered to him. Though Raleigh felt he could walk to work on a cushion of air, he nevertheless picked up his cane. At the doorway he paused once to look at Linden over his shoulder, toss her a smile, and swing the cane jauntily.

His astonishment was quite real that evening when he was informed by a dour and disapproving housekeeper that Linden Street had packed her bags and fled.

"My dear," Millicent said helplessly. "My poor, poor dear. You have to quit crying sometime. You're breaking *my* heart." She took the sodden handkerchief Linden was clutching in her hand and replaced it with a fresh one. When Millicent's housekeeper entered the bedroom to take the breakfast tray, Millicent waved her away impatiently. Linden's copious tears were not responding to entreaties or reason. Millicent Montgomery was very much afraid she was going to have to slap the girl.

It did not come to that. Millicent let silence do her work for her and eventually the eerie echo of Linden's own sobs seemed to help her gain control. By Millicent's estimation it had been just minutes short of an hour since Linden had been shown to her bedroom and she had been tearful for most of that time. Millicent still hadn't been able to divine the details but her faculties were not so dulled by her earlier-than-usual rising or her age that she couldn't make out Raleigh's fine hand in the mess.

"You shall have to tell me eventually, dear," she said, putting enough starch in her voice to prevent another bout of tears. "But first you must wash your face. There's a girl. Go on with you. The water's fresh in the pitcher and there are cloths under the stand." She watched with some satisfaction as Linden obeyed. "No, no, no. You must pat your face dry, not rub it as if it were a floor. My face would look like a corduroy road by now if I had rubbed it like that." Millicent was quite proud of her skin, which was still amazingly taut over the fine bones of her face. She pointed to the lines fanning out from her eyes. "I earned every one of these creases with good honest emotion and by appreciating the vagaries of life. I'd have more, but I try not to let everything bother me. And staying out of the sun helps, of course."

This last had the desired effect of raising Linden's watery smile. "Good," Millicent said approvingly. "It's a beginning. Now, come sit by me on the bed and tell me what's happened. There will be no more crying because I can't understand you."

The story came out haltingly at first but Millicent proved to be a good listener and refrained from interrupting at any point during Linden's discourse. She had plenty to say at the end, however.

"Ring for tea, Linden," she said briskly. "That won't come amiss. Now that you've stopped weeping, it's safe to fill you up again. And if you haven't had breakfast, ask Mrs. Bristol to bring it here. Poached eggs, I think. They would suit you nicely . . . and some toast with a spot of marmalade. You don't want anything too heavy. Your father taught me that." She added the last when Linden looked as if she were preparing to object. It was a sly way of eliciting Linden's cooperation, but Millicent had not learned how to manage influence without first learning how to manage opportunity. She took advantage of whatever was available to her. In this case, evoking the memory of Linden's dear, departed father was a perfectly acceptable tactic.

While breakfast was being prepared, Millicent attended to her own toilette. She very purposely dismissed her maid and allowed Linden to act as one. What was more, she gave over the chore as if she were conferring great privilege. By the time Linden had brushed out Millicent's thick, silvery hair and assisted her in dressing, breakfast had arrived and nerves had come a long way toward being calmed.

Millicent recounted the story in her own words while she watched Linden eat. Occasionally, when Linden paused too long between bites, Millicent directed her back to the task with an imperious waggle of her index finger. "As I understand it, my grandson — with whom I may finally have a serious parting of the ways — has compromised your virginity through trickery. Specifically he has made spurious claims about the state of my health, to wit, that I was set to kick the bucket."

"I don't think he mentioned that it would be soon," Linden said in fairness to Raleigh.

"Perhaps not, but he allowed you to assume the time was closer than not." She waved her hand airily. "It's an old trick, dear, and it's the kind of bait that's caught more experienced fish than you."

"You mean he's done this before?"

Millicent cleared her throat. "I mean nothing of the sort," she said with some asperity. "I was speaking in generalities then, not specifics. Letting other people assume what they will is something I taught Raleigh. It can serve one well in business but not so wisely in love."

Linden choked on her toast. "There's been no mention of *love*," she fairly gasped.

"Of course not. That would have made everything too simple. Now, drink some tea, wash down that toast, and let me finish. You've come here today because Raleigh's admitted that I'm not ready to turn up my toes and you've realized it was all a ruse to get you into his bed. Is that the gist of it?"

Linden nodded, swallowing hard.

"It's no use flushing. Thanks to my grandson, you're not a great green girl any longer."

Linden's mouth sagged a little at this observation and she stammered something unintelligible which Millicent ignored.

"Very well," Millicent said. "You must stay here. Have you brought your bags? Yes? Good. That showed some foresight on your part. Raleigh will come here this evening when he realizes you're gone, but I don't think you should see him just yet."

"I don't want to see him again — ever."

"Stuff! You love him, don't you?" Millicent was so certain of the truth that a reply one way or the other did not interest her. She went on with her planning. "I'll talk to him myself and let him know that you're quite safe. That will be a concern. Then he'll have to sort this out himself. Frankly, I'm ashamed the boy is so dense."

The *boy* arrived that evening, and even to his loving grandmother's eyes he looked a decade older than his thirty-three years. She ordered Scotch for him in the library and when it arrived she didn't raise an eyebrow as he helped himself to the tumbler *and* the crystal decanter. When the maid was gone she looked at him sharply. "Are you going to drink yourself insensible?"

"I may." He lowered himself onto the wide arm of a chair and stretched his injured leg out in front of him. His handsome face was graven with lines at the corners of his mouth and eyes. A muscle worked in his lean cheek and there was a new crease between his dark brows. "You're telling me she's here but that I can't see her. Frankly, Grandmother, I may drink until *that* seems perfectly sensible."

Millicent sat regally in a slate-blue wing chair. Her mouth was set firmly and her

505

eyes were clear and grave. She had steeled herself not to feel pity for her grandson although clearly he was suffering. "I believe I said that it wasn't a good idea to see her. She doesn't want to see you."

"Then how am I supposed to explain?" He rolled the tumbler between his palms but what he felt like doing was banging his cane against the floor. "She has to listen to me."

"Linden doesn't have to do anything of the sort, Raleigh. Where has listening to you got her thus far? She accepted your lies and was promptly relieved of her virginity."

"That's too much, Grandmother," Raleigh said firmly. The look he gave her was hard and unyielding. "Even for you."

Chastened, Millicent fell silent.

Raleigh sighed and put his unfinished drink on a nearby table. "I got the idea from you," he told her. "That's not an excuse and I'm not blaming you. If anyone's to be blamed, it's me for thinking one of your schemes had merit." The uneven, self-deprecating smile he flashed in his grandmother's direction took some of the sting from his words. "I thought Linden would do for you what she wouldn't do for me." He saw one of Millicent's silver brows arch skeptically. "I didn't expect her to fall in bed with me, Grandmother. I was hoping she'd fall in love. I want her to be my wife, not my mistress."

Millicent sniffed. "Well, you've gone about the thing rather badly. Telling the girl I was at death's door to gain her cooperation — well, you can see that she feels ill-used." She made no comment that she remembered trying to manipulate Raleigh in the same way. "All that squiring her around the town. What was that in aid of?"

"I wanted to spend time with her," he explained patiently. "Linden wouldn't have had anything to do with me outside of caring for my leg."

Millicent made a thorough, relatively unbiased, assessment of her grandson's features. "What's wrong with you?" she demanded imperiously. "Hasn't the girl got eyes in her head? You're a fine figure of a man and rich to boot."

Her fierce defense raised a small smile. "Linden doesn't trust me," he admitted after a moment. "I'm afraid I behaved rather badly in the beginning."

Millicent held up one hand. "I don't want to know the details."

"I wasn't going to tell you." His grip tightened on the knob of his cane. "Suffice it to say, Grandmother, that I haven't thought about Catherine Hale in quite some time." He pulled himself up and went to Millicent's side. He bent and kissed her on the forehead. "I think we both know that when you sent Linden Street to my home you were hoping she'd heal more than my gimpy leg."

Millicent made a show of blustering then she abandoned it. "Well," she said heartily, "if my work isn't going to go to waste then you have to do something. Words won't work, my boy. Not now. I'm afraid you must attempt a grander gesture. Panache is required in this situation."

Raleigh considered that. Now that he knew Linden was safe he could think more clearly. He wondered what he knew about panache. As Millicent pointed out to Linden at Thanksgiving, he wouldn't know a flamboyant gesture if it presented itself as a gift. How was he supposed to prove to Linden that he loved her? What proof could there —

Millicent recognized the change in her grandson immediately. Lines of tension simply vanished from his face and his gray eyes lightened and took on a distant, thoughtful expression. There was a softening to his mouth and a quirky grin that was so youthful it made her heart ache. "Where are you going?" she demanded as he headed toward the door. He didn't respond and she didn't press. Apparently he was a man on a mission.

Tears came to Millicent's eyes as she

watched him go. Surely that was a spring in his step.

Christmas morning dawned clear and bright . . . and with a racket that had Linden rushing down the hall to Millicent's room. At one point the house actually shook.

Bleary-eyed but amazingly spry, Millicent met Linden at the door. "Is it a quake?" she asked. She fastened the belt of her robe as she looked up and down the hall. One picture along the corridor was askew. Everything else appeared to be intact.

"I don't know what it was," Linden said. Even as she spoke there was the distinctive roll of thunder belowstairs. "What on earth?"

"I think we'd better go down, dear." Linden, she noticed, was dressed better for disaster than she was. The deep green gown and scarlet grosgrain ribbon brought to mind the colors of the holiday. "Lord," Millicent exclaimed, "It's Christmas. Get my slippers, Linden. The gold ones, please. If we have to flee for our lives then I want to look festive."

Linden gaped at her. Millicent was perfectly serious. Rather than argue and possibly risk both their lives, Linden dutifully ran for the slippers. There was more commotion downstairs, the sound of shouting,

horribly shrill screams, and even more improbably, high-pitched laughter. So much
was going on that for the first time in a
week, Raleigh Montgomery was not at the
forefront of her thoughts.

Linden led Millicent down the front staircase, holding the older woman's arm on one
side while Millicent held the banister on the
other. Halfway to their destination they
were greeted by Millicent's distressed
housekeeper. The woman's thin face was
ruddy, the gray threads in her hair were
more starkly apparent, and she was actually wringing her hands. Clearly she was
within moment of becoming unraveled.

"I didn't know what to say to him," she
began hurriedly. "You know how he is when
he's got a thing on his mind. Just like you.
I told him to put them all in the library but
there's simply not enough room. I realized
that after the young ladies arrived and
everyone here knows there's more to come.
I can't think that we can accommodate it
all." At the end her voice was barely audible
because she hadn't drawn a breath. She
drew one now, a deep one, and began again
before Millicent or Linden could interject a
question or comment. "So I've shooed them
all out into the backyard. The house shook,
I can tell you, with all that stomping and
leaping and twirling around." Somewhere
from the vicinity of the kitchen a loud,

raucous cackle split the air. The house-keeper threw up her hands. "That's it! That's what I'm trying to tell you. He's gone completely insane, surpassed even the most outrageous thing you've ever staged." She pointed to Linden accusingly. "Pardon me for speaking frankly, but it's because of you. We've all seen you moping about this past week and we've put our own construction on it. And now . . . and *now* we have this!"

Surprised by the housekeeper's outburst, Linden looked to Millicent for her defense.

There was no rescue. Millicent simply nodded, her temperament serene. "Mrs. Bristol's right, dear. You *have* moped. And my staff's not foolish. They know Raleigh's to blame." She turned to Mrs. Bristol. "I assume my grandson is the 'he' to whom you have referred."

"No one else," she said tersely. Another cry from the kitchen captured her attention. "You'll have to come now. I'm taking a broom to the last of them this very minute." She marched off militantly to get her weapon.

Linden's violet eyes were apprehensive. Her hand tightened on Millicent's arm. "Raleigh's here," she whispered.

"It seems that way," Millicent agreed calmly. "Perhaps he's brought you a Christmas present. This is the day for it after all."

She gave Linden a little nudge. "Go on, dear. See what he's done to make Mrs. Bristol throw him outside." Linden was already off on a run and Millicent was forced to call after her, "And be gracious, child! He's tried so hard!"

Millicent lowered herself to sit on one of the steps. She'd let them have this moment to themselves, she thought. It was her gift.

Linden came to a complete halt on the lip of the stone portico. Her stop was so sudden, her surprise so swift and complete that her entire body vibrated for a moment like a plucked string. She caught her breath, raising one hand to her heart to contain the slamming beat, and stared open-mouthed at the circus Millicent Montgomery's backyard had become.

Dozens of people were running around the magnificent garden. Their costumes were varied. Some wore silvery white wigs of courtiers and satin breeches, others were looking self-important in regimental uniforms better suited to revolutionary times. The women were either dressed like princesses with wide panniers under their skirts, or common servants with white aprons and little mob caps. A menagerie of animals, mostly birds of one kind or another, were scurrying along the flagstone paths trying to avoid being herded back toward the house. A swan preened grandly in the marble fountain and a fat little colly bird perched on the head of one of the spouting cherubs. It flew off when Kwei Po, dressed in white satin and gold braided livery, attempted to net it. The bird left a bit of its business behind on the cherub's sculpted curls.

"Bad bird!" Kwei Po scolded, swinging his net. "Can't get it, Mr. Raleigh!" But he was off to try again, his sloe eyes bright with the excitement of the chase.

The spectacle of it all had held Linden's attention so fully that she didn't notice Raleigh until now. He was sitting just below her, on the edge of one of the stone steps, his elbows on his knees, his head in his hands, looking rather disgusted, and more than a little dejected. She went to sit beside him. Without a word she slipped her arm through his. "Thank you," she said softly. There were tears of gratitude in her eyes.

Just then one of the young men leaped across a hedgerow to tackle a honking, bad-tempered goose and collided head over bucket with one of the dairy maids. The crying that ensued was every bit as piercing as the goose's squawking.

Linden's smile was watery as she laid her head on Raleigh's shoulder. "It's all quite beautiful," she told him.

"I'm surprised you know what it is," he

said, still unhappy with the result of his efforts. With a sweep of his hand he indicated the rowdy, clamoring melange in front of them. Kwei Po had just netted the bird but had plunged into the fountain in the process. "It was supposed to be a more solemn presentation. At least it was supposed to be orchestrated with more *panache.*"

His disappointment actually touched Linden deeply. That he had wanted it to be perfect for her was very special. "It has plenty of panache," she assured him gently. "Have you been planning it long?"

"Since you left me." He turned to her and searched her face. There was a hint of a rueful, abashed smile on his lips. "Grandmother suggested a flamboyant gesture." He shrugged a bit diffidently, his gray eyes uncertain. "This is what I came up with. I wasn't certain if you'd understand."

Linden's hand rose to his face and she touched his cheek, memorizing the features that were so infinitely dear to her. "I understand, Raleigh, but I wonder if you do." She looked out in the yard again, her fingers dropping away from his face to lie gently on his knee. "Twelve drummers drumming."

"When they collect their instruments," he said, sighing. The percussion section was currently surrounding two swans and a lady. It was difficult to know who was the target of their attention.

"I count eleven pipers and ten lords." She cast him a sideways glance. "I see you commandeered Kwei Po's services again."

He nodded. "He wanted to wear a feather. It took an amazing amount of explaining. I still don't think he's got the gist of it."

Linden pointed to where Kwei Po was shaking off water and still grappling with his catch. "No, but he's got his bird and plenty of feathers if he wants them." She felt Raleigh squeeze her hand. "And there are nine ladies and I assume those others are milking maids." That would explain the eight goats that were contentedly munching on Millicent's greenery. Raleigh must not have been able to get milk cows and decided on goats instead. She liked his flexibility. "Seven swans," she said. "All of them nearly captured. And six geese." She paused, her eyes darting around, then continued. "Four colly birds. Three French hens. And them." Linden pointed to the two caged turtledoves which Raleigh had placed on the stone balustrade. They were being eyed hungrily by Millicent's golden tabby who had come to the celebration uninvited.

"You've found most everything," she said. "And in so little time. It takes my breath away."

He shrugged, hesitating a moment. Then he said quietly, "There's something else. It could mean everything or nothing." It was a phrase she had used once with him. "I got it in case you didn't care about the flamboyant gesture."

Linden's smile faltered at the intensity of his searching eyes. In the background the cacophony of singing and chirping and honking faded. "There was only one thing I wanted," she said softly. "All this —"

Raleigh raised one finger to her lips and stopped her. He gestured to Kwei Po. The boy understood the command. He let his hard-won prize fly away and ran around the corner of the mansion. In less than a minute he reappeared, hugging a heavy burlap bundle to his chest.

It was only when he laid it at Linden's feet that she saw the small sapling rising out from the neck of the sack. It was a pear tree. "Oh, Raleigh," she said softly. Her blurred vision made Raleigh's sleight-of-hand appear more adept than it really was. He cupped his hand and seemed to draw out a large egg from the branches of the slender young tree. He placed it carefully in Linden's open palms.

The egg was warm and Linden held it carefully. "Open it," she heard him say. She looked at him oddly, not certain she'd heard correctly. Past the shimmering tears that shielded her violet eyes she could see he was smiling. "Open it," he said again.

516

A few tears fell and her vision was restored. She could see now that the egg wasn't real. "It's porcelain," she said.

"Partridge is hard to find, even for me. Go on, open it."

Her fingers found the delicate silver clasp and twisted. The hinged top of the egg opened easily. On a bed of bright yellow velvet rested five gold rings.

"I didn't know your size," he said, watching her closely. Did she understand? "I think one of them will fit."

She raised her face and looked at him, comprehension slowly brightening her beautiful eyes. "It was never about the gifts," she whispered, going into his arms. His embrace was solid and secure and he held her as if he never planned to let her go. "It was about you. You mean everything to me." Then her mouth was covered by his and they kissed long and deeply and shared a single thought: *My true love.*